THE OLD MAN DOWN THE ROAD

THE OLD MAN DOWN THE ROAD

Ken Hall Jr.

AuthorHouse™
1663 Liberty Drive
Bloomington, IN 47403
www.authorhouse.com
Phone: 1-800-839-8640

First published by AuthorHouse 08/30/2011

ISBN: 978-1-4567-6756-3 (sc)
ISBN: 978-1-4567-6755-6 (hc)
ISBN: 978-1-4567-6754-9 (ebk)

Library of Congress Control Number: 2011906954

Printed in the United States of America

This book is printed on acid-free paper.

Acknowledgment

I owe a very heartfelt thanks to the many people who helped make this book possible, and if I fail to name you here, please accept my apologies with the feeble but truthful excuse that I can be a bit scatterbrained and disorganized. What can I say–my mind wanders.

First, thanks to Beth Mitchell, who edited the story and had the unenviable task of helping me organize what was sometimes a clutter of rambling thoughts into more coherent and simplified themes, as well as correcting what must have looked at times like the punctuation of a sixth-grader. Thanks also to Shawnassey Howell for your encouragement and advice in the early stages of this project, and to A&A Graf-X for your help with the cover design. Thanks to the good people at AuthorHouse for making the publishing process as painless as possible, and to the many people who somehow managed to slog through five-hundred-plus loose pages of copy paper, offering positive feedback and encouragement to move forward toward publication. I owe all of you guys big time!

And finally I want to thank God for waiting patiently while I slowly figured out that, what for so long seemed to be a curse, might actually be a blessing.

Author's Note

Once upon a time there really was a Logtown, Mississippi. It did indeed spring up during the timber boom in south Mississippi and, along with a few other riverfront communities, chugged along pretty good for a while as home to several saw mills, and therefore quite a few jobs. Eventually the chugging little town began to slow down, then it began to sputter and wheeze. I guess you could say it was put out of its misery when the United States government bought up what was left of the small town, along with vast surrounding acreage, when they decided to build the rocket test facility now known as the John C. Stennis Space Center–this would have been around 1962. Now, along with several other small communities, all that is left of Logtown lies somewhere in the vast wilderness, known as the "Buffer Zone", that surrounds the test site.

The Logtown of my story has a happier future. In fact, its name and approximate location are the only things it has in common with the real place. The history, founder, geography, county, etc. are all products of my ridiculously busy imagination.

It should also be noted that, although I've seen signs directing me to the town of Tunica while traveling in north Mississippi, I've never actually been there, and all descriptions of that place are, like those of the city of Logtown, purely fictional. I kept it pretty simple, though, so hopefully nobody will be offended.

In the book Fletch, by Gregory Mcdonald, one of the characters tells Fletch he would have made a good actor. Fletch replies to the effect that he's just a liar with a good memory, to which the other character responds, "That's what an actor is." I've often wondered if maybe a writer is just a liar with a good imagination . . .

Ken Hall, Jr.

Dedication

For my wonderful wife Karen who, throughout this entire project, never doubted me.

And for my awesome son Matthew, who is still young enough to understand: the magic might be real . . .

INTRODUCTIONS

"But there is nothing covered up that will not be revealed, and hidden that will not be known."

Luke 12, verse 2

1

Jim Hanes wasn't just a grumpy old man. He was *the* grumpy old man, a total and complete embodiment of the archetype if ever there was one. He stood about six and a half feet tall, weighed about 145 pounds, and had the sickly, pale complexion of a toad's underbelly. His thin hair was long and greasy; mostly gray but with a few surviving streaks of black. And of course he had a beard, a nasty, scraggly thing that hung all the way down to his hollow chest. The beard mostly hid the creased skin that was stretched tightly around his narrow face, but couldn't hide his sharp, protruding cheekbones. His bushy eyebrows grew low over wild, deep-set, dark circled eyes, and his ears could boast of hair that was almost as bushy as his eyebrows, but for the fact that it was lost amid the nasty, greasy stuff growing out of his face and scalp. His six remaining teeth were yellow and brown and half rotten. His breath stank, his hair stank, and his clothes stank. This wasn't just a "been workin'-and-sweatin'-in-the-hot-sun-all-day" stink. It was a deep-down, ground-in, un-holy and rancid foulness that emanated from his filthy, crusted body like heat roiling off asphalt on a hot summer day. Each night he went to sleep smelling that way, and each morning he got up smelling that way. He did bathe, occasionally (if you can call lying in a tub of tepid water once every two weeks or so bathing; there was no soap or scrubbing involved), but even he didn't refer to it as bathing. He called it soaking; as in *yeah, I tied on a big 'un last night; I need a soak.*

Unfortunately (and not so much for him as for the rest of the city of Logtown, Mississippi, where he lived), his personality was as unattractive as his appearance. He was grumpy, selfish, and hateful. He was ornery and spiteful, low-down and dirty. Jim Hanes was a sorry and no-count good-for-nuthin'; not worth killin', as they say.

Jim lived alone in a trailer that sat by itself near the back of a square, unkempt lot just inside the city limits of Logtown. He rarely ventured out of his trailer. In fact, if not for his need for food and (especially) drink, Jim would likely never have been seen by human eyes. As it was, the only eyes that saw him (it was not at all considered a privilege) were those belonging to the employees and customers of Dee Dee's Quick Stop and Liquor Store, where Jim shopped once a week for food, and at least twice a week for drink. There may have been a time when Dee Dee Johnson, owner of this small establishment, tried to converse with old man Hanes. If so, she had long since given it up, as had any employees or customers who happened to be in her store at the same time as Jim. Usually, anyone caught in the store with him cursed his or her luck and tried to get the "heck out of Dodge." Some people would actually keep driving past the small store if they saw his car in the gravel parking lot. It was hard to miss: an old, gray, rusty Ford that left billowing clouds of blue smoke in its wake. People sometimes joke about cars that "burn more oil than gas" . . . well, Jim's car really did. The good news was that the trail of smoke usually led directly from his trailer to the store, then back again, and the smoke usually hung around longer than he did. If you *were* unfortunate enough to be caught in the store with Jim, it was best to keep your head down and your mouth closed. Many an unfortunate cash-register clerk (Dee Dee usually hired high-schoolers part-time) had made the mistake of trying to be helpful, and most (be they boys or girls) ended up in tears. Mrs. Johnson had come close to banning Jim from her store several times, but he was a frequent, and more importantly, cash-paying customer. She eventually just made him a part of her training program: NOT speaking to Mr. Hanes was as heavily emphasized as having all of the money in your cash register accounted for.

Jim's trailer was a sight to behold. It must have been at least a quarter-century old, and looked like it had been neglected for twenty-four of those years. It was more like a big, mildewy box with windows; only two of which didn't have at least one crack, and all of which had been covered with tin foil (some speculated that the foil served as insulation, others that it served to keep out mind rays from alien spacecraft or perhaps an overly-intrusive government). There were patches of moss growing from the trailer's top and mold growing from its bottom. The moss and mold appeared to be racing each other toward the center of the trailer, perhaps trying to give it a more *natural* look. The body of the trailer was supported by cinderblocks, but had long since begun to sag in the middle, almost to the point that it appeared to be made of rubber. To many, this seemed to be the only reasonable explanation for the fact that had not yet broken into two equally pathetic eyesores.

The lot upon which Jim's "home sweet home" sat was about three acres. It was all brush, weeds, and (with the exception of one medium-sized pine that stood off to the right of the trailer) pathetically scraggly trees that bore few leaves on writhing, skeletal limbs that seemed to be reaching upward to the heavens, pleading for the mercy of a quick death. In one corner behind the trailer, there was a mountain of cans, bottles, and other non-biodegradables that seemed to either have been built or grown around the old, rusting shell of a washing machine. The washing machine must have belonged to a prior owner; the clothes worn by Mr. Hanes did not appear to have ever been April Fresh.

Once, when Jim had been at his less-than-humble abode for only a few years, some well meaning (and obviously very optimistic) Mormons dropped by to discuss the future of his eternal soul. Mr. Hanes answered the door dressed in only his underwear, which looked like it had been purchased around the time that his two visitors were born. The stretched elastic barely had enough strength to keep the yellow, stained undergarment from slipping down to his ankles. In Jim's left hand was a bottle and in his right was an old but still fully functional shotgun. As one of the young men stared open-mouthed, the other began to stammer an introduction that got as far as " . . . uh . . . good afternoon . . . uh . . . sir . . . we . . .". Jim then let loose with a marathon of words, many of which neither of the poor fellows had ever heard before. The one who had remained silent promptly wet his pants. As soon as Jim took one step forward, they both turned, half fell down the unsteady cinderblocks that served as steps up to the front door, and began running. As soon as Jim fired his shotgun in the air (probably just to punctuate the string of nearly indecipherable obscenities he had just screamed), they decided to leave the bikes that were parked just outside the gate and make their getaway on foot. Taking the time to get on the bikes might make them better targets.

The city police paid Mr. Hanes a visit later that afternoon. He wasn't arrested (he hadn't actually shot *at* the two young men, and nobody had been hurt), but his shotgun was taken. Surprisingly, Jim offered little protest. This made the police officers a little suspicious; Jim was notorious for his abrasive, uncooperative manner (and for good reason, as he had proved earlier that very day). But they decided to let it go. They simply wanted to get out of the foul-smelling trailer more than they wanted to arrest an old drunk who, for the most part, kept to himself. And anyway, as one of the officers (a veteran of the Logtown Police Department who had been born, raised, and would soon retire in this city) had later joked, Jim Hanes had only done something he, the officer, had secretly wanted to do for a long time. It was, perhaps, not a very professional thing to say, but it earned a hearty round of laughter regardless. The responding officers *did* give Jim a stern warning and advised him to put up "no trespassing" signs if he was really that averse to visitors. Then they left, taking the bikes of the two young Mormons (who had converted to Methodist by the following Sunday) with them. And so the years passed. The trailer grew nastier, the lot more overgrown, and as far as the police and townsfolk knew, Mr. Hanes had no more visitors.

Jim Hanes had become more of a fixture than a legend long before the first week of August, 1999, when Jacob Hunter and his family came to town. This was Jacob's first move, and although he was nervous that the word "home" would now mean a place he'd never even heard of until two months before, he was also excited. Jacob was twelve; old enough to realize the friendships he'd be losing because of the move, but not quite old enough to be paranoid about making new friends. He was still at that wonderful, almost magical age where friendships weren't something that had to be worked at and cultivated. They instead seemed almost to form on their own between him and those with whom he had things in common. At that age, friendships seem to be made of something simpler but much stronger than the friendships forged later in life: they are bonds that seem to define right and wrong, rather than the other way around.

Jacob's family (there were only three of them: Mom, Dad and Jacob) was moving south from Tunica, a small city just south of the Mississippi/Tennessee border. Tunica was also about thirty minutes south of Memphis, where his father had worked for a Memphis newspaper. His father would now work for *The Logtown News,* a small newspaper for a small town, writing about mostly unimportant local events. According to Jacob's father, this was a strategic move that would allow more time for his hobby and pet project: writing fiction. Mr. Hunter was an avid reader, and a fairly imaginative writer. His biggest problem was that he had trouble finishing projects that he started. The reason for this, he claimed, was his unrelenting schedule in Memphis, a problem he felt confident had been left behind when he accepted his new position in Logtown.

The move itself had taken three days. The first day had been spent loading furniture and boxes that had been packed over a two-week period (mostly by Jacob's mother and father, who didn't quite trust the organizational skills of a twelve-year-old) into the rented moving van. Most of the second day was spent driving. Although the drive would ordinarily have taken six hours, Jacob's father refused to go the speed limit in what was obviously the largest vehicle he had ever driven, plus they had to stop for lunch and bathroom breaks. As a result, what should have been a six-hour trip ended up taking more than eight hours. Jacob and his mother were following the moving van in the family car, and Jacob spent most of the time reading comic books, playing with his Gameboy, and finally wondering how they could possibly be in the same state after such a long drive.

They finally arrived at their new home around six o'clock that evening. This gave the family a chance to do a quick walk-through (it being early August, the hot summer days were still stretching out past eight-thirty) and then begin the task of unloading the van. Jacob wanted to get a quick look at his new neighborhood, but his parents insisted that he help. Because many of the boxes were too large for him or his mother to lift by themselves, they took turns holding the door open while the other helped his dad bring a load in, then closing it as quickly as possible before the mosquitoes could follow them in. The sun eventually began to set, and still the small family worked, all of them drenched in sweat. By nine o'clock, the van was finally unloaded. Mrs. Hunter suggested that they eat, then unpack only what they needed for the night. Jacob's father took a few moments to study her face – it was half-past weary and quickly approaching exhausted. He decided not to argue. Instead, he went to the car, opened the trunk, and got out a medium-sized ice chest that had been packed the night before. When he returned he found his wife and son flopped down onto the floor in front of the fireplace in the den, one of the few spaces in the house where there weren't boxes and furniture stacked haphazardly about; it was the only spot large enough for the three of them to sit together like a small tribe, cross-legged and in a small circle, to finally eat supper.

As Mrs. Hunter began to unload sandwiches and drinks from the ice chest, her husband began to talk enthusiastically about what had become his favorite topics: his new job and new boss.

"Y'all are really going to like Jerry MacDonald. He's a super-nice guy. He was born and raised here, you know."

"We know," Jacob and his mother answered together, rolling their eyes at each other.

"Anyway, it was good of him to insist I take the rest of the week to get the house in order, then start fresh on Monday."

"We know that, too," Jacob intoned while his mother's weary eyes beheld the massive clutter around them. Her face seemed to say *wow, two whole extra days. Maybe we can re-paint the house and build on a few additions while we're at it*. Jacob's father ignored the look and continued talking.

"I figure we can be unpacked and maybe even finished arranging furniture by Friday." Mr. Hunter spoke optimistically, but his wife didn't seem too impressed.

"By the way, Jacob, we're having supper with Mr. MacDonald's family Friday night."

Jacob looked up from his paper plate. "Please say that by *we* you mean you and Mom!"

"Nope," his father answered, "By *we* I mean *us*, as in all three of us. And you know the drill. I expect you to act like a civilized human being from a civilized family."

Jacob feigned a weak British accent.

"Really, Father, I'm *surprised* at you. I am actually quite looking forward to it, quite so, indeed! I say, I *do* hope they'll be serving tea and crumpets afterward. Jolly good, jolly good indeed!"

"I'm serious, Jacob," said his father. "If not for us, then for Jerry's daughter. I forget her name, but she's about your age." Mr. Hunter put on an extra cheesy grin and arched his eyebrows.

Jacob rolled his eyes again but said nothing. He had been to dinner with his parent's friends and co-workers before. It was usually nothing to get excited about – two or three hours of being extra polite, eating food that could not possibly have been prepared with a twelve-year-old boy in mind, and listening to grown-ups talk endlessly about grown-up things. Anytime it seemed that the talk might get interesting, they remembered children were present and changed the subject. *Little pitchers with big ears* always seemed to rule the day.

After he finished eating, Jacob took a quick bath, put on a pair of pajama bottoms and a t-shirt, brushed his teeth, and finally set about the task of clearing a space on the floor of his new bedroom. He would sleep in his sleeping bag tonight; his mattress, box springs and bed frame were leaning against one of the bedroom walls, still unassembled. He slid and stacked boxes for ten minutes and had soon constructed what vaguely resembled a small, rudimentary fort. His sleeping bag went in the center of the small, cardboard box garrison. As he lay down, his mom came into the room to say goodnight while his dad, down the hall in what would be his parent's room, struggled loudly, trying to inflate an air mattress: Jacob's parents' mattress and box springs had been unwisely stacked against a wall in the den and could only be reached by re-arranging several chairs, the sofa, and a bookshelf. She looked at her son nestled cozily in the center of his hastily built fortress and smiled.

"I'm proud of you, sweetheart," she said. "I know it's not easy moving to a new place, but you've had a great attitude so far. Good-night." She leaned over and kissed him on his ear.

"Good-night, Mom."

She walked out, pulling the door almost closed behind her.

Actually, Jacob was pretty excited. While his parents had done their quick walk-through inside the house earlier that evening, he had conducted his own inspection outside. The fenced backyard was large and, with the exception of a small tool shed in the far left corner, empty. He had poked around the empty yard for a while, then checked inside the shed. It was also empty except for a rusty pair of pruning shears, a rake with a broken wooden handle, and a small coil of nylon rope. He then went to look over the fence and saw that his yard backed up to a heavily wooded area. A trail was running along the outside of the fence, and directly behind Jacob's new house it was adjoined to another trail, which cut straight into the woods. Both trails were definitely wide enough and smooth enough for a bicycle, and both the trails and the woods seemed to demand exploration. He already knew how he planned to spend the day tomorrow. With the exception of Friday night's dinner at the home of his father's new boss, everything seemed fine and dandy to Jacob.

He gradually fell asleep to the sounds of his father wrestling with the air mattress.

2

The next morning, after a quick breakfast that his father had picked up from Hardee's, Jacob headed out with the promise that he would be back by noon for lunch. Then it would be time to help unpack his bedroom. He had to ride his bike down the street a short distance before he found a place where he could enter the woods without cutting through someone's yard (something he wouldn't feel comfortable doing for another week or so.) Not far down the street from his house there were several adjacent, vacant lots. Although they needed mowing, they were not overgrown with shrubs and briars, just a few small trees, and Jacob had no difficulty riding his bike through the tall grass. There, at the back of the lot, was what he had hoped to find: his trail. It appeared to run parallel to all of all the lots on his street. He rode his bike onto the trail, turning left, back toward his house. When he reached his own backyard, Jacob turned right onto the trail he had seen the evening before and plunged straight into the woods.

Despite the early hour, Jacob was already sweating in the hot, humid August-in-South-Mississippi air, but like most boys his age, he didn't seem to notice (the only time that sweating in the hot sun seems to bother boys that age is when they are being forced to work; then it's simply unbearable). The trail rolled along in one general direction, weaving gently from side to side between thickets of brush and around trees, and soon the ground began a gradual slope downward. After a few minutes, Jacob came suddenly to a fork in the trail. To the left, it seemed more worn and used; to the right it was narrow and overgrown. Feeling adventurous in this strange new territory, Jacob turned right. After only a minute or so, the trail became almost non-existent, and began a slow curve to the left. Small tree limbs and shrubs began to slap at his face as he bent lower over his handlebars, trying to duck beneath the overhang. He had just decided to turn around and try the other direction when he noticed, maybe twenty feet ahead and to the left, a small chain-link fence. What was left of the trail seemed to dead-end at the fence. Jacob hopped off his bike and walked carefully, almost wading through the undergrowth to the fence. Before him was an old, nasty looking trailer sitting in a litter-filled yard. He listened for any sounds: voices, a TV or radio, but heard nothing. He took a few steps to his left, along the fence, until he drew even with the trailer's back door. He stood on his toes, straining to see inside the trailer through one of the dirty windows, but they all seemed to be covered with tin foil. The only exception was the small window in the back door, where thick, dirty drapes hung loosely, denying the entry of sunshine nearly as effectively as the foil. Nestled in the fence corner to his right was a huge pile of cans and bottles around a big, rusty piece of machinery that he couldn't make out. He wondered if anyone could possibly be living in such a filthy, run-down place. Jacob listened carefully, straining his ears for any evidence of occupancy and hearing nothing but complete silence. From where he stood, he couldn't tell if there was a car parked in front of the trailer. *It's got to be abandoned*, he thought. Of course, an abandoned trailer sitting in an unkempt, filthy, littered lot demanded exploration. He had just reached out and begun to climb the fence when . . .

"Dude . . . what are you doing?"

Jacob jumped back from the fence and spun around, gawking. A boy, who appeared to be about the same age as Jacob, was standing before him. He was maybe a half-inch taller than Jacob, with sandy-blonde hair and a good-natured face that was quickly morphing from a friendly smile to a full-fledged grin (possibly at the startled expression on Jacob's face – a gape-mouthed, wide-eyed stare). Jacob wasn't as surprised by the boy's sudden appearance as he was by the fact that he hadn't heard him coming. There were still no sounds coming from the trailer, but Jacob hadn't heard a thing.

"You were about to climb that fence and trespass on someone's private property, weren't you?"

Jacob didn't know how to respond – the boy's tone was almost identical to the type of accusatory sound you'd get from a stern teacher who'd caught a kid in the act of breaking some rule or other, but his face still had that silly grin on it. Jacob finally responded as if it *was* a teacher addressing him.

"Well, I guess . . . I mean . . . I didn't know if . . ." . . .

"Relax, dude, I'm not a cop. And anyway, I'm always down for a little fence-climbin' and trespassin'. But not here." His smile suddenly vanished, replaced by a look of utmost seriousness. "That, my friend, is the home of Mr. Jim Hanes. Mr. Hanes does not look kindly upon trespassers, especially kids. In fact, Mr. Hanes doesn't look kindly on much of anything. Mr. Hanes is a bit of a . . . um, how should I put this? Oh yes, a psycho-nutjob!"

His grin returned for a moment, then vanished again as he looked over Jacob's shoulder at the trailer.

"C'mon, let's get outta here," he said. "Hanes might hear us and charge out with a rocket-launcher or somethin'. I was on my way to the Ice House to meet some guys, anyway. You can come, if you want."

Jacob took a last, nervous look over his shoulder, then followed as the boy led the way back to the spot where he'd left his bike.

"So . . . you got a name?" The boy asked.

"Huh? Oh . . . Jacob. Hunter. I, uh, just moved here."

"Yeah, I saw y'all unloading the truck yesterday. I'm David, by the way. I live down the street from you. It's a red brick two-story just around that big curve."

Jacob, who hadn't noticed (and therefore wouldn't recognize) any of the houses in the subdivision besides his own, nodded as if he knew exactly which house the boy was referring to.

"So what's the Ice House?" he asked as both boys ducked and weaved under and around the branches and shrubs along the way.

"It's where we hang out," David answered. "Kind of like a clubhouse. I was on my way there when I saw you headed for the trails from the street. You better be glad I decided to follow you – if Hanes had caught you in his yard . . . *we may never have found the body*!" David had uttered those last seven words in a deep, hoarse whisper while contorting his face into a preposterous version of an evil glare.

Jacob burst out laughing, but still found himself looking over his shoulder again, this time to make sure that this mysterious mad-man wasn't following, wearing a psychotic grin and armed with a gun or machete, but he and his companion seemed to be alone. When they reached their bikes, Jacob was pleased to see that David's was almost identical to his own. Only the colors were different; David's was yellow and red, Jacob's was black and silver.

They quickly rode back down the trail and soon passed the fork Jacob had come upon a few minutes earlier, where the trail immediately became smooth and wide again. Eventually the trail forked again, and they turned right. The woods quickly got thicker, but the trail stayed wide and clear. In a few places it was muddy and once they crossed a small creek, though in the dry August heat it was little more than a collection of puddles. In these places, old two-by-fours and small strips of plywood had been laid down as makeshift bridges.

Soon, Jacob could hear voices. The trail veered left, then dead-ended in a small clearing. Off to the left of the clearing, resting beside a huge old oak tree, was what looked like the back of an old refrigerator truck. The outside was spotted with patches of rust, as was the back door, which was wedged open with a piece of wood stuck between the door and the trailer above one of the hinges. Jacob immediately knew that he was looking at the Ice House, and decided it was one of the coolest things he had ever seen. Three boys, who also looked like they were about the same age as Jacob, were standing around just outside the door of the trailer and talking. They immediately grew quiet and turned to stare at him as he and David parked their bikes between the large oak and the old trailer.

"Who's your new buddy, David?" one of the boys finally drawled. He was about an inch shorter than Jacob, but at least ten pounds heavier. Nor were those ten pounds fat: he appeared to be almost muscular for his age, and his age that seemed greater than that of the other boys. He had a fair complexion, but his hair was coal-black. It was his eyes, however, that caught Jacob's attention. They were ice-blue, almost gray, bright and alive. And they laughed. But it wasn't a happy, joyful kind of laugh. It was a mocking laugh, a scornful laugh. They were the kind of eyes that said *I'm not laughing with you, I'm laughing* at *you.*

"This is Jacob. He just moved here."

"Where'd ya move from, Jacob?" the boy asked, his eyes sparkling.

"Tunica," said Jacob.

"Tuna-what?" asked the boy. His eyes had apparently found a new target for their laughter: Jacob.

"TU-NI-CA," Jacob replied. He knew already that he did not like this boy. Not even a little.

David took a step forward and began pointing as he named names.

"This is Greg, Stevie, and Jared."

Greg looked pretty much like an average eleven or twelve year old boy. His only distinguishing feature was a head full of tight curls that desperately needed to be cut. Stevie, on the other hand, was an interesting study. He was a good two and a half inches shorter than Jacob. He probably weighed twenty pounds less, as well, but not because he was skinny. He was just very small. His eyes flicked back and forth between Jacob and the boy with ice-blue eyes. As the saying goes, there are leaders and there are followers. There is also a third group, a sub-group of followers—those who live only to impress the leaders, usually by feeding the leader's ego. If the leader laughs, they laugh. If the leader is mad, they are mad. And may God have mercy on anyone who even *appears* to be taking their place at the leader's side. They will cut anyone's throat (figuratively speaking, *most* of the time) without even wincing. And yes, there are children who can execute the duties of this office just as efficiently as adults. There are several terms, most of them rather colorful, that accurately describe a member of this sub-group; flunky was the word that came to Jacob's mind. He had Stevie pegged as Jared's flunky pretty quick. And odds were that Stevie would always be *someone's* flunky, throughout his entire flunky life. Jared, of course, was Mr. Laughing Eyes. Those eyes had not left Jacob from the moment he and David had ridden into the clearing.

"Well, Jacob, we're all just real pleased to meet you," said Jared. His smile seemed sincere, but Jacob was sure that it wasn't because he was pleased to meet a new kid. Most likely he was pleased at the idea of meeting a new target. "How'd you like a peek in the Ice House?"

"Sure," Jacob replied, not wanting to sound too eager, trying to sound . . . well, cool. "I can't stay too long, though. I'm supposed to be back home by noon to help my folks unpack and stuff."

"Well, we won't keep you long. I'd hate to hear that you got spanked or had to sit in time-out." Jared's mouth was still smiling (just a little), along with his eyes, (which smiled a lot). *Laughing at you, not with you* both his eyes and mouth said. Greg made a small noise that may have been a chuckle, but Stevie actually *giggled.* It wasn't girly, but it *was* a giggle. It was clear that Stevie wouldn't decide if he liked the new boy until Jared had made up his mind for him. Much to Jacob's relief, David acted as if he hadn't heard Jared. He decided to do the same.

Jared turned and led the way into the Ice House, followed by Stevie, Greg, David, and finally Jacob. The light was pretty dim at the back, but close to the entrance it was very well lit by the sunlight shining in through the open door. The air inside the trailer felt stale and damp but cool; the heat outside had not yet penetrated the insulated walls. Jacob looked around at the inside of what he hoped would soon be *his* clubhouse, too. It was about five feet wide and ten deep. Against the far wall stood a small folding card table surrounded on three sides by three old lawn chairs. On the table was a battery-powered lantern and what looked like a stack of comic books and magazines. On the wall behind him was a poster of a racecar and its driver. On the wall in front of him was a centerfold pin-up. Jacob tried hard not to stare at the pin-up. He didn't want the others, especially Jared, thinking that he had never seen one before. He had, in fact, seen only two pictures of naked women before. Both times he had felt a twinge in his conscience, but at his age a twinge wasn't quite enough to hinder a boy's natural curiosity.

"So, whatcha think?" asked Jared. "You have anything like this back in Tuna-ca?"

"No," answered Jacob, pulling his eyes away from the pin-up. "I had a friend who had a treehouse that his father built in the backyard. We used to camp out there sometimes. But it wasn't this cool. This is awesome!"

That earned another smirk from Jared.

"We camp out here sometimes," said David, "but we have to sleep outside. There's not enough room in here."

"What house did you move into?" asked Greg. It was the first sound out of his mouth since his brief chuckle at Jared's spank/sit-in-time-out comment.

"The Pearson's old house," David answered for Jacob, who didn't know who the prior owners were any more than he knew who founded the city of Logtown.

"Crazy Mary," said Jared with a grin. Even his grin didn't look happy. It was just another *laugh at*.

"What?" asked Jacob.

"Mary Pearson," said David. "She was the Pearson's daughter. She was in high school. Kind of a weirdo."

"She was crazy," insisted Jared with authority. "Mike went to school with her . . ."

"Mike is Jared's older brother," explained David.

" . . . and he said she's crazy. She dressed like a freak; she never talked to anybody. Mike said she was always readin' books about witchcraft and magic and stuff like that. I bet she did drugs."

I bet your mom did drugs thought Jacob. *That would explain a lot.*

"Anyway, she finally went mental," Jared concluded, still wearing that amused grin. "Her folks had to move up-state to put her in Whitfield with all the other psycho freaks. She'll probably end up like Hanes, livin' in a piece of junk trailer, drinkin' and stinkin' and all that."

"That's where I found Jacob; at Hanes's backyard," said David.

This time, Jared actually laughed. "Why didn't you knock on the front door and introduce yerself?" he asked. Another chuckle from Greg, another giggle from Stevie. Even David smiled, making Jacob feel obligated to smile, too. It occurred to him that if anyone was keeping score, Jared was now up: two – zilch.

"Is he really like, you know . . . *insane*?" Jacob asked. He was determined to keep the conversation focused on something besides THE NEW KID.

"My mom says he's as crazy as a run-over dog," said Greg with a grin. Jacob, who'd never heard that figure of speech before, laughed along with the other boys for a few moments; an excited, nervous laugh. The idea of a psychopath living freely among the other townsfolk seemed both exciting and a little frightening; it was almost exactly the type of thing a boy his age hopes to discover on his first day in a new place.

"So how does he get to keep living there by himself if he's insane? Why isn't he locked up or somethin'?"

"I guess 'cause he never hurts anyone," said David. "He just stays in his trailer all the time."

"I heard he murdered some people in another city and came here to hide from the cops," said Stevie in a serious and authoritative voice.

"No way! What city?" Jacob asked, more excited than ever.

"*I don't know.*" Stevie replied, as if this were the most ignorant question he had ever heard. "What, you think I'm lyin'?"

This response caught Jacob completely by surprise. Stevie had sounded more defensive than sarcastic, and Jacob wondered if he would have spoken at all if Jared weren't here. He looked uncertainly at David, who rolled his eyes.

Jared, still smiling with both his eyes and mouth, abruptly turned toward the table, grabbed a magazine, and flopped down in one of the chairs. After casting a glare meant to wither Jacob, Stevie did the same. Jacob relaxed a little, hoping that the interrogation of the new boy was finally over. It wasn't, but it definitely lost that "inquisitional" feel after Jared and Stevie dropped out of the questioning. Jacob remained standing with David and Greg by the door of the trailer as they asked him a few questions about Tunica (where it was, what it was like), and they soon lapsed into the kind of talk important to boys that age: sports, TV shows, video games, girls, and even school. Jared and Stevie did not participate in the conversation. They only looked up from their magazines occasionally – the former offering a sneer from time to time, the latter offering a glare.

Eventually, Jacob looked at his watch. It was eleven-thirty, late enough for him to have an excuse to leave. He shot a last, quick look at the pin-up, then said "Hey, I gotta go; Mom and Dad are probably waiting on me." He looked at David. "I guess I'll see you around."

David nodded and said, "Yeah, I'll come by your house later, maybe tomorrow."

Jacob walked out, hopped on his bike, and began to ride back up the trail. Over his shoulder, he heard Jared shout, "Can you find your way back, or do you need someone to hold your hand?" This was followed by another Stevie giggle. Again, Jacob pretended that he hadn't heard.

Lunch that day was the same as supper the night before: sandwiches that had been made and packed in an ice chest before the family had left Tunica. Jacob ate in silence, thinking alternately about the Ice House and Jared as his mother and father laid out strategies for the unpacking of the remaining boxes and the moving of furniture. It was soon very clear that it would be done Mom's way, and eventually Jacob's father turned to him.

"Well, how was your exploring expedition? Find anything interesting?"

"Yeah, it was pretty cool," Jacob answered. "There's a bunch of trails and they go pretty deep in the woods. And I met a couple of guys."

"Wow, new friends already!" said his mom.

"Well, do they have names?" Dad asked.

"Yes."

"And these names would be . . . ?"

"David, Greg, Stevie, and Jared."

"Do they have last names?" asked his mom.

"Probably."

"Well, what are they?"

"I don't know! I didn't say 'Hey, guys, I need your last names so my mom can check you out with the FBI and make sure you're okay."

"Jacob, don't get smart." His father had a stern look on his face. Jacob's parents were pretty laid back about most things, but they didn't put up with anything that they felt was disrespectful.

"Yes, sir." Jacob hoped this simple, respectful answer would satisfy his parents. It seemed to.

"So, where did you meet these boys?" Dad had taken charge of the questions again.

"In the woods. They have a clearing where they go camping sometimes." Jacob knew better than to mention the clubhouse made of an old refrigerator trailer to his mom. She, like most mothers in the world, suffered from what Jacob and his friends in Tunica had called "chronic mom syndrome." Telling her about the Ice House would almost be the equivalent of telling her that they had played with loaded guns in the middle of the highway while wearing plastic bags on their heads.

"Do they seem like nice boys?" asked his mom.

Jacob wanted desperately to roll his eyes, but managed not to.

"Yep. One of them, David, lives right down the road."

"Well, make sure they're good kids before you get too buddy-buddy with them."

Must . . . roll . . . eyes. Must . . . roll . . . eyes Jacob's subconscious seemed to scream.

"I will," he answered. "By the way, Dad, where is Whitfield?"

"What, the mental hospital?" his father asked.

"Yeah."

"It's up around Jackson. I can't remember if it's actually *in* Jackson. Why?"

"One of the guys I met said the girl that used to live here got put in Whitfield. That's why the family had to move."

Mr. Hunter started laughing. "The Pearson's daughter? No, she went to Georgia with the rest of the family. Her dad got a promotion or something. I think he's working in Atlanta."

"Are you sure?"

"I'm positive. I actually met her the second time we looked at the house. She dressed a little odd and seemed kind of shy, but I'm sure she wasn't *crazy*. I think whoever told you that was just pulling your leg, buddy."

Jacob seemed satisfied. He finished eating, and spent most of the rest of the day unpacking boxes in his room, putting away clothes and toys, hanging up posters, and hooking up his thirteen inch TV and Nintendo 64 system, a gift from the previous Christmas. After he finished, he rode around his neighborhood on his bike for a little while. He saw what he assumed was David's house, but not David. That evening he ate his first real meal in several days: his mom had gone grocery shopping that afternoon. Then he took a bath and was in bed by ten. His dreams, forgotten the next morning, were mostly about the Ice House and Crazy Mary.

3

After breakfast Friday morning, Jacob made a break-through discovery: the cable had been turned on!! He was allowed to watch television for about an hour and a half before he was put to work. The morning's project was to arrange the furniture in the den. Because of the location of the cable outlet, the positioning of the entertainment system – a behemoth fixture that housed the family's TV, VCR, and stereo system, as well as an assortment of pictures and books – was pre-ordained. It had been put there as soon as it was taken off the moving van, and Mr. Hunter had hooked up the electronic components the night before (under the direction and careful supervision of his son). This left a sofa, three chairs, two end tables, a floor lamp, a coffee table and an oriental-style rug to be reckoned with. Jacob hoped to be finished and outside within the hour, but his mother soon dashed that hope into itty-bitty pieces. They ended up trying four different arrangements of the furniture. After each re-positioning, Jacob and his father would collapse – Jacob into a chair and his father on the couch. His mother would then stalk about the room, studying the furniture from every possible vantage point with narrow, scrutinizing eyes. She finally selected option number two, and Jacob wondered why they had tried the last two positions if she had already found one she liked. His father wondered the same thing, but both had the good sense to keep these thoughts to themselves.

It was lunchtime when the den project was finally completed. The family had just sat down to leftovers from the night before when the doorbell rang. Mr. Hunter got up to answer the door, grumbling all the way

"Every time I sit down to do something . . ."

Jacob heard the door open and his father ask, "Can I help you?"

"Is Jacob home?"

It was David, his new friend from the day before. Jacob hopped up from the table and trotted to the front door while his father explained that they were just sitting down to lunch.

"Hey David!" he called out. "Dad, this is David, one of the guys I met yesterday. Can he eat with us?"

Before his father could reply, David informed them that he had already eaten lunch.

"Well, can he wait in my room while we eat?" Jacob asked, without missing a beat.

"Sure," Mr. Hunter replied. He turned to David, "Jacob shouldn't be too long. By the way, David, do you have a last name?"

"Yes, sir. Phillips."

"Pleased to meet you, Mr. Phillips." He held out his hand, which David shook with a grin. "C'mon, Jacob. The sooner you finish, the sooner you can take off."

Jacob led the way to his bedroom and gave David a quick run-down on stuff he could do while the Hunter family partook of its daily bread. He took special pride in pointing out his Nintendo system and his selection of eleven game cartridges to choose from. He then ran back to the table and began to shovel food into his mouth at such a rate that he almost gagged twice. He was cautioned to slow down at least three times, then firmly *instructed* to by his father. Even so, he finished his meal in under five minutes, then shocked both parents by turning down dessert. He was hoping to escape safely without any further questioning (he thought of it as an interrogation, perhaps a little less intense but probably even more intimately probing than what he'd been subjected to the day before) of his new friend. His mother, as usual, quickly brought him back to Earth. It sometimes seemed to Jacob that her primary maternal instincts included keeping the house clean, cooking, and embarrassing him. They had almost made it to the door that led from the laundry room to the garage when . . .

"Boys, can you step in here for a minute?"

"Aw, man," Jacob muttered, then turned to and David said, "Time to share your life story. Hopefully it's short, without too many dark secrets."

David smiled as they turned and headed back to the kitchen. "Well, I used to sell drugs and worked as a male prostitute for a while, but I'll skip all that and stick with the boring stuff."

It went better than Jacob thought it would. His mom started out with the basics: where do you live, how old are you, what grade will you be in this year? It turned out that David had just turned twelve in July, and would be starting sixth grade with Jacob in about three more weeks. Mrs. Hunter then turned the question knob up a notch.

"What do your parents do?"

"My mom teaches third grade at the school, and my father owns a print-shop here in town. He worked for a bigger one in Biloxi, but we moved here when I was about five and he opened his own."

"Do you have any brothers or sisters?"

"I have an older sister who will start eighth grade this year and a five-year-old brother. He's okay in small doses." This earned a laugh from the interrogator.

"Where do you go to church?"

Jacob's eyes bugged in his head, and he wanted to scream, but David handled the question as smoothly as a politician listing his qualifications for office in a TV commercial.

"We've gone to First Baptist since we moved here. My dad's a deacon there, and they've got a lot of stuff for kids to do. They're taking us to Ship Island in two weeks, kind of a 'before school starts back' deal. Maybe you guys can visit."

At last Jacob's mother seemed satisfied. She got David's home phone number, then released the them with, "You boys be careful."

As they rode their bikes down the street toward David's house, Jacob apologized for the intimate Q&A ("all that was missing was a lie detector and a two-way mirror," he grumped), then congratulated his friend on an impressive performance.

"Nuthin' to it," David replied with a sly grin. "If you tell them more than they ask, they run out of questions faster. And lots of 'sirs' and 'ma'ams' don't hurt either."

They spent an hour at David's house, throwing a football and comparing notes on the things there were to do in Logtown and Tunica. David seemed impressed by Jacob's descriptions of Memphis and especially Graceland, although neither boy was familiar with any Elvis songs besides *You Ain't Nuthin' But a Hound Dog*, which they had recently heard in a movie. They eventually gave up throwing the football around when David's five-year-old brother Dillon came outside and began pestering them. It began as "Can I play? Pleeeeeze? Why not? I'm tellin' mom," and matured into his doing poor impersonations of his favorite cartoon characters, over and over and over. David finally threw his football at the little brat and called him an ignorant little baby as he and Jacob left the back yard. As they rode away on their bikes, they could hear Dillon screaming at the top of his lungs: "Pooh-pooh heads! Pooh-pooh heads!!" over and over. They both laughed all the way down the street.

It turned out that the empty lots Jacob had used to access the trails behind his house the day before were the primary passage used by the neighborhood kids. He and David quickly cut through the tall grass and weeds onto the trails. Jacob assumed they were headed for the Ice House, but after turning left at the first fork in the path (turning right would have taken them back to Jim Hanes trailer), David kept going straight, passing the curve to the right at the second fork that would take them to the clubhouse.

"You got any money?" he called back over his shoulder.

"Yeah, a couple of dollars. Why?"

"Let's go to Dee Dee's and get something to drink."

"What's Dee Dee's?"

"It's a quick stop about a half mile from the entrance to our subdivision. This trail comes out almost right across the street from it," David shouted without turning his head.

The path went on smoothly for a while. Unlike the trail leading to the Ice House, there were no puddles or creeks, thus no make-shift bridges, and the boys could ride faster. Soon, however, small dirt mounds appeared, lying right across the path. They looked like oversized speed bumps made of dirt, and David jumped them on his bike with great flourish.

"This is part of our racecourse," David hollered between jumps. "Jared and his big-brother built most of it."

After about three minutes of hard riding, David began to slow down. The woods ended abruptly. There was a fifteen-foot stretch of grass, then the road. Jacob could see Dee Dee's as soon as he had cleared the woods. It was, as David had said, right across the street, but the "street" turned out to be Old Highway 43. To his right, the highway curved to the right around a bend, so he couldn't see very far. To his left, it stretched out straight and level. If not for the woods, he could probably have seen the entrance to his new neighborhood, despite the half-mile distance.

"You have to watch for gravel and logging trucks," David explained. "They come tearing around that curve all the time, but you can usually hear them coming. A kid got clobbered by one a few years ago, 'bout two miles or so further down the road, close to the interstate. My mom wouldn't let me leave the subdivision for about a year after that."

"Did you know him?" Jacob asked as they crossed.

"Nah, he was older than me; in junior high, I think."

They parked their bikes outside and walked into the cool air-conditioned store, a cowbell hanging on the door announcing their arrival with a dull *clunk*. David led the way to a display shelf covered with magazines. Soon he was deep in a racecar magazine, while Jacob flipped through one featuring motorcycles. The attention of both boys was evenly distributed between the cars and motorcycles in the photographs and the bikini-clad models posing alongside some of the vehicles. Jacob, carefully studying a blonde scantily clad in a florescent pink number that only barely managed to conceal the absolute essentials, hardly noticed the sound of the cowbell as another customer entered the store, but David looked up.

"Oh, geez," he hissed. "It's him, it's Hanes. Don't look . . . wait . . . wait . . . okay, just peek."

Jacob looked up. The man his friend had identified as Jim Hanes had walked directly to the counter, where the tobacco products and hard liquor were kept. He was wearing a dirty, scraggly cap pulled down over his dirty, scraggly hair, a t-shirt that was no longer white, dirty jeans, and an old pair of work boots. The t-shirt hung loose around his neck and had holes at both armpits. The jeans were missing one back pocket and the other hung halfway off, flapping as he walked. There were also holes in both knees and the jeans were frayed at the bottom. Jacob wasn't sure how they stayed on: the pitiful-looking man appeared to have no stomach, waist, or rump. His dirty boots were untied, and the frayed laces were dragging on the floor, trailing almost six inches behind the boots.

By the time he reached her, the young clerk had already brought a bottle of Jim's drink of choice and put it on the counter. Jacob couldn't see what kind it was, but the bottle looked more like a jug; it even had a handle. She rang up his purchase on the small register, but didn't tell him how much money was owed. Instead, she simply held out her hand without speaking as he gave her a small wad of cash; she then handed him his change and the transaction was complete. She didn't even smooth out the bills he had given her until he was out of the building.

Jacob had stared unabashedly during the entire, brief event without even realizing it. As Jim stalked toward the door in long, even strides, he suddenly turned his head towards Jacob, looking right into the young boy's eyes with a black glare. Jacob felt his friend's elbow in his ribs and quickly dropped his eyes to the motorcycle magazine he still held. There was another dull *clunk* from the cowbell, and Jim was gone.

"Dude, are you crazy, why were you staring? Don't ever *stare* at him!" David almost sounded angry. "He's probably just looking for a reason to attack someone, especially a kid. He hates kids!"

After seeing the man in person and having received that black glare, Jacob had no doubt that his friend spoke the truth.

"C'mon, let's go," said David, apparently sufficiently disturbed by Jacob's indiscretion that he was no longer interested in hanging out in the store.

They replaced the magazines on the rack and went to the coolers built into the back wall of the store. Jacob grabbed a Coke, David a root beer. As they approached the counter, Jacob realized he could still smell the old man. It wasn't just old sweat, either. It was more like a public restroom at a truck stop – one that had never been cleaned.

"Aw man, we could probably follow him back to his place in the dark, just from the smell."

"Or we could just follow the trail of smoke his junky old car leaves," David answered.

They paid the clerk (who wore the expression of someone who had just survived a car wreck without a scratch: "Did that really just happen? . . . am I still alive? . . . I *am*, I'm alive!") for their drinks and left. As they rode their bikes across the gravel parking lot, David pointed to the big curve in the highway, which was now to their left.

"That's where Hanes lives, just around the curve. His trailer is about a quarter mile down the road, on the right."

They crossed the highway and were soon headed back up the path. This time, when they reached the trail leading to the Ice House, they took it. When they got to the clearing it was empty, and the door to the trailer was closed. David hopped off his bike and pulled on the door's latching handle. Yanking the door open, he stuck the homemade wedge in the crack above the bottom hinge. They stepped in together, sat on a two of the old lawn chairs, and took a couple of long pulls at their drinks. Jacob studied the pin-up on the wall.

"You know, I'd really like to meet her."

"I used to date her," said David with a straight face "but I broke up with her when I found out what she did for a living."

The two boys looked at each other, then exploded in laughter. The insulated walls of the Ice House absorbed most of it, the rest escaped out the door and into the woods. It took about three minutes to finally quit; as soon as one would stop, the other would start again. When he finally caught his breath, Jacob got up out of his chair and walked to the door.

"Where's the rest of the guys?" he asked.

"Greg said his folks were going to spend the weekend at his grandmother's house. She lives on the coast, close to Mobile. I don't know where Jared is, but Stevie is probably there too, with his nose stuck up Jared's behind."

They laughed again, and Jacob was glad to hear his suspicions about Stevie confirmed. He looked back at David.

"What's Jared's story? I don't think he likes me too much."

David stopped smiling and actually looked kind of thoughtful.

"Jared's okay, he just likes everyone to think he's tough; you know, like he's our leader or somthin'. And he's had it kinda rough lately. His dad left about a year and a half ago. I'm not sure if his folks are *divorced* or not, but his dad moved out. He lives down in Gulfport now with Jared's brother, Mike. Jared and his mom had to move into a trailer park after that. Also, he'll be in sixth grade with us next year. He should be starting junior high, but he flunked out last year. I think he'll probably be the only thirteen-year-old in our class."

Jacob actually began to feel a little sorry for Jared, but not enough to allow himself to forget those laughing eyes and trust the boy the way David seemed to. Something about those cold, grayish eyes wouldn't let him.

"Yeah, he's kind of pushy, and he talks a lot of trash," David continued "but he's alright. He's a whole lot better than Stevie. You can't believe *anything* that little bird-turd says."

Jacob agreed completely with David's assessment of Stevie. As it had the day before, the talk eventually moved on to other points of interest that are pretty much universal for pre-adolescent boys. Around four o'clock, they finally left. David secured the door of the trailer, and they rode their bikes back toward their subdivision, still talking and laughing. They agreed to meet at the Ice House early the following afternoon; both would spend the first half of the day doing Saturday morning chores.

4

The Hunter family arrived at the MacDonald household around six-thirty. The house was located in an older but still very nice part of the small city that had earned its name during the timber boom of the late 1800s and the early 1900s. Logtown had actually flourished during this period. The city was founded by a northerner named James Stockton, who had purchased vast realms of southwestern Mississippi forestland at the turn of the century. In those days, the timber companies knew nothing about replanting and conservation and cut through the woodlands unmercifully. What had begun as a settlement grew quickly, and its benefactor, Mr. Stockton, added character to his fledgling city. He built a library, a small hospital, and even a theater, all bearing his name. He became all but royalty, and most of the residents of the town (with the exception of a few farmers) worked for him. At one point, his employees were actually partially paid in vouchers, which could be redeemed at the food and clothing stores owned by the Stockton family.

But even as the city grew, the woodlands were shrinking. Before the Great Depression had even taken hold of the rest of the country, the timber well was beginning to run dry. The Stockton family eventually moved on, leaving the city with only a few streets and buildings bearing the family name to remember them by. Some locals tried to keep the sawmill and a few other timber-related businesses going, but it was the tung-oil industry that kept the dwindling city of Logtown alive. What had once been forest-land was transformed into white-flowering orchards of tung trees. These trees bore a fruit that produced an oil used to make paint and varnish. The small city was kept afloat, but the glory days had left it, following in the footsteps of its founder. And by the end of the 1960s, the quaint southern town was facing another crisis: new synthetic paints and other such scientific breakthroughs were making the tung-oil industry obsolete. Then, on August 17 and 18 of 1969, the entire region of south Mississippi was ravaged by the unprecedented fury of Hurricane Camille. Entire cities and industries were devastated, along with thousands of acres of tung trees that had once lined the highways and back roads of southwestern Mississippi. It was as if God Himself had decided that it was time for this small community to either sputter and die or move firmly and resolutely into a new era. Again, residents of the small town felt the panic of possible doom creeping over the horizon.

Then, in the mid-seventies, a near miracle occurred. People from nearby larger cities, many from across the state line in Louisiana, finally discovered the small, quaint city of Logtown and its surrounding wilderness. To people from these other cities, especially New Orleans, the costs of living and of owning property there were almost too good to be true. Acreage could be purchased for less than the cost of a small lot in the big city. They began to move, slowly at first, eventually almost in droves. Some took jobs or opened businesses in Logtown, opting to leave their old, hustle-bustle city life behind; others kept their jobs in New Orleans or whatever other larger city they had moved from, and became commuters. The cost of a forty-five minute drive to New Orleans or the Gulf Coast was easily outweighed by the decrease in other living expenses. And while the locals were a bit wary at first, there could be no denying that this growing number of transplants kept their city alive. Twenty-five years later, only the old-timers remembered "the way things used to be."

Jerry MacDonald opened the front door before Mr. Hunter even had a chance to knock. Jacob's first impression was that with a little more age, a little more weight and a long, white beard, Mr. MacDonald might make a pretty good Santa Claus at the local mall when Christmastime rolled around. He certainly seemed jolly enough. He *was* overweight, but not quite fat. Gray was creeping up the sides of what had once probably been a jet-black head of hair. And though his cheeks weren't quite rosy, his face was round and seemed very friendly.

He stood in the doorway and regarded the Hunter family through his big, round glasses with a warm smile on his face. The smells of dinner drifted out from the house and past Mr. MacDonald, and Jacob smiled. One of these smells was fried chicken. Maybe he'd get to eat something decent after all.

"Alex and Sharon!" Mr. MacDonald exclaimed. "It's great to see you again."

He looked down at Jacob, smiling.

"And you must be Jacob! I'm very pleased to meet you, young man." He took Jacob's hand and shook it vigorously. Jacob was unpleasantly surprised by how sweaty the man's hand was, but didn't want to embarrass his parents by pulling away. So he endured the hearty handshake with a feigned smile on his face. Finally, the man released him.

"A fine young man," Mr. MacDonald was still smiling as he looked back up at Jacob's parents. "That's a real fine young man you got there. Well, please, come in, come on in," and he led the family into the house. As soon as his host's back was turned, Jacob wiped his hands on his jeans.

The house was a beautiful Victorian of the type seen in many old southern towns. The family followed their host through a large entrance hall into the living room. It was at least twice the size of the den at Jacob's house, and was all wood floors, oriental rugs, and antique furniture. To his left, a staircase ran alongside the wall to the second floor. The entire place seemed like a mansion to Jacob. He had been in two mansions before: Graceland (he'd been there twice, in fact), former home of who his parents had enthusiastically described to him as the King of Rock & Roll, Elvis Presley; and the Biltmore Estate, into which Jacob supposed most of the subdivision he now lived in would fit. Both places were now actually museums, complete with roped-off rooms and tour guides. This house, though nowhere nearly as large and grand as the two actual mansions he'd visited, also reminded him of a museum (only without the roped-off areas and tour guides).

On a couch in the living room sat the two MacDonald children, looking very bored and rather put-out, as if they frequently had dinner with many of the families of business associates of their father (which they did). Behind them, a smartly dressed woman had entered the room through a long hallway that led off from the right side of the room. She was smiling as she wiped her wet hands on a dishtowel. Mr. MacDonald began pointing and naming names.

"Okay, this is my daughter Melissa, my son Eddie, and my beautiful wife, Ruth." Then to his family, "This is Alex and Sharon Hunter, and their son Jacob."

Mrs. MacDonald quickly walked over and shook hands, telling the Hunters how excited she was to be meeting them, how happy she was that they were able to come to dinner, how she hoped they would become great friends, and so on and so forth. Jacob glanced over at Melissa, who still looked bored but was at least now talking to her brother. Jacob, remembering his father's sly words and cheesy grin when referring to Melissa, had asked David about the young girl while they were still at the Ice House earlier that afternoon. He had gotten the following response: "She's kind of a snot. Probably 'cause her family's rich. She is pretty good looking, though. Maturing into a fine young lady, if you know what I mean," he had concluded with a grin.

From his quick, discreet glance, Jacob saw that his friend was right: she was, in fact, maturing quite nicely. Based on the blouse she was wearing, Jacob assumed that she was aware and very proud of this fact. Eddie finally looked up and motioned for Jacob to join them on the couch, which he did, sitting next to the older boy.

"How ya doin', little man?" Eddie asked, making Jacob feel about three feet tall.

"Okay, I guess," he replied, searching his brain for small talk. "You guys have to do this a lot? Dinner with your dad's employees, I mean?"

"At least once a week. Employees, people from church, people from Rotary. Most don't bring their kids, though."

"Nice, Eddie!" chided Melissa, "Could you be a *little* more tacky?" Her tone suggested that she was more distressed about an impropriety than Jacob's feelings.

"Shut up! He knows what I meant." Eddie turned back to Jacob. "Sorry, guy, I guess I'm just uncivilized or something. A real barbarian. No offence." He was smiling now.

"No problem."

For the next ten minutes, Jacob was treated to a hearty dose of Eddie's ego. Even when the older boy bothered to ask a question about Jacob or his family, the topic always ended up being about Eddie. Jacob soon learned that Eddie played football and baseball (he'd be in the "starting lineup" in both sports this year, the only sophomore to earn that honor); he was dating a cheerleader, was in the National Honor Society, and had even sung a solo in a church service earlier this very year. Jacob considered asking for his autograph but was afraid Eddie might think he was serious and actually give him one. Instead, he just tried to tune the older boy's voice out. He stole a quick peek at Melissa, and saw that she appeared to be doing the same thing. He almost jumped up and exclaimed *We thank thee, O Lord, in our hour of need* when Mrs. MacDonald finally announced that dinner was ready.

The group marched into the dining room, where Mrs. MacDonald pointed everyone to their pre-ordained seats around the large table. Dinner consisted of salad, fried chicken, mashed potatoes and gravy, cornbread, and some kind of pea casserole. Everything was homemade. Mr. MacDonald prayed eloquently, asking the Lord to bless the food, the family and their new friends, the church, the city, the great State of Mississippi, and the country. It was a prayer easily worthy of a ceremony much greater than Friday night supper, and Jacob began to fear it would never end. But eventually it did, and they dug in.

Eddie ate like he was at a fast food restaurant with the football team, which seemed to disturb his younger sister more than his parents. Jacob, who was seated next to Melissa, ate carefully, wiping his mouth frequently. He tried to strike up a conversation with her, and soon discovered that she would be starting junior high this year, was a cheerleader, took dance lessons, and wasn't very interested in talking to him. He returned his full attention to the food on his plate, adopting a "hey, sweetheart, I'm not real interested in you either" attitude. He hoped she'd notice.

After dinner, the group relocated to a covered patio behind the house for desert: ice-cream and peach cobbler. The grownups drank coffee and continued their conversation, which had begun with talk of the newspaper business, but quickly branched out, spanning everything from the church that the MacDonald family attended (First Baptist, of course) to local politics, and finally, back to the newspaper business. Jacob sat by himself in a wicker chair, eating his dessert, thinking about the Ice House, and occasionally stealing quick glances at Melissa, who was eating her own dessert on a porch swing that hung on the far side of the patio. Eddie was nowhere to be seen. Mr. MacDonald was still talking about the newspaper, recounting the story of an employee that he had to "let go" recently. It appeared that it was *his* position Mr. Hunter was filling.

" . . . poor fellow was obviously an alcoholic. I tried to help, even offered him time off to try and get it together, you know, rehab or something. He refused, and I simply could not allow him to stay on. When he bothered to show up, his work was shoddy at best. So . . ." He let that last word hang in the air, everyone knowing the inevitable result.

It was probably the discussion of an alcoholic that brought the subject into his mind, and before he even knew that he was going to speak, Jacob blurted out "Who's Jim Hanes?"

Mr. MacDonald looked at him with an odd expression, as if he were surprised not by the question, but by it being asked so soon by a newcomer to the area. It reminded Jacob of the look his father had worn three years ago when Jacob had broached the topic of sex (he had heard three or four different versions of what was involved, and wanted his father to set the record straight). Mr. MacDonald discussed Hanes much more comfortably and smoothly than Jacob's father had discussed the other topic.

"Where'd you hear about Jim Hanes?" he asked.

"Some guys I met told me about him."

"What did they tell you?"

"That he was crazy."

Mr. MacDonald regarded Jacob for a moment, and Jacob noticed that his face was no longer very jolly.

"Well, son, they got it about half right. Jim Hanes *is* crazy, and he's also a drunk. He lives in a trashy trailer where he does nuthin' but sit around all day, drinkin'. He don't work, don't go anywhere or do *anything* to speak of; just sits in his trailer drinkin' and rottin' away while his trailer rots around him." Jacob idly wondered why Jim was a *drunk*, while the former employee of the newspaper had been an *alcoholic*.

"Where does this man live?" asked Mrs. Hunter, sounding a bit concerned.

"Just inside the city limits, 'bout a mile and a half west of *The Pines*."

"Is this someone we need to worry about, Jerry?" Now Jacob's father had taken an interest.

"Nah. He took a shot at some young boys one time. They were Jehovah's Witnesses or somethin'. They just went up, a-knockin' on his door like he'd invited them or something. He ran 'em off, cussin' and shootin' a gun in the air. I heard one of the boys peed in his britches." He actually started chuckling at that, and his wife gave him a light slap on the forearm, reminding him how to behave in front of guests.

"He *shot* at them?' asked Mrs. Hunter in disbelief. "Gee, isn't that what dangerous *means*?"

Mr. MacDonald smiled gently. "You needn't worry about him, he's more pathetic than dangerous. Everyone just leaves him alone, and he leaves them alone. It's all he seems to want. I just wish he'd clean up that rat-hole. It's a shame for folks gettin' off the interstate to have to see that kind of trash on the way into town."

Jacob suddenly had another thought. "If he doesn't work, how does he live? You know, pay for things?"

Mr. MacDonald just shrugged. "He's probably on the dole. You know, welfare. Our tax dollars at work." He shook his head, clearly disgusted at the idea that his tax dollars supported the likes of Jim Hanes.

"How can he buy booze with welfare vouchers? He must do odd jobs or something," suggested Mr. Hunter.

"I'm telling you, that man don't do nuthin', least of all work. Maybe he has some under-the-table type deal with someone, you know: cash money for vouchers."

"I think it's sad," Mrs. MacDonald finally offered, in a tone that was an odd blend of sympathy and condemnation. Maybe she thought it was sad that the good townsfolk had to put up with such riff-raff.

The adult's conversation moved on to other things, leaving Jacob to continue thinking about Jim Hanes on his own. He wasn't about to mention his encounter with Hanes at the quick stop that afternoon, any more than he had mentioned a clubhouse built inside a refrigerator trailer. Jacob seldom actually *lied* to his parents, but like most kids, especially boys, he was a firm believer in *what they don't know won't hurt them*. This motto could be more accurately interpreted *what they don't know won't hurt ME*. He had no doubt that any True Confessions about seeing Jim at the quick stop would result in severe restrictions, chiefly where and when he could ride his bike. That would mean kissing the trails and the Ice House farewell, something he had no intention of doing. So he sat quietly, thinking of how Jim Hanes had looked him right in the eyes, holding them with his piercing glare until David's elbow to the ribs had broken the spell. It hadn't been a friendly look, and it was hard *not* to believe all of the stories he'd heard about Jim Hanes, including Stevie's theory about Jim being a murderer from another town. It hadn't been a friendly look at all.

Around nine-thirty, The Hunters finally said goodnight and took their leave. Jacob was relieved that the visit had finally ended. Melissa had vanished at least thirty minutes before, leaving the porch swing to Jacob without so much as a word. It seemed David's description of her personality was as accurate as his description of her physique. But that was okay with Jacob. He told himself that he had bigger fish to fry.

5

Jacob woke to silence the next morning. He rolled lazily over to look at the clock sitting on the table beside his bed. 6:45. His folks rarely got up before 7:30 on Saturday mornings, and they usually had to *make* him get up. He lay back on his pillow, staring at the ceiling fan as it whirled slowly about and letting his mind wander aimlessly. He thought about Melissa, her snotty attitude, and, of course, the way she'd looked in that blouse last night. He thought about her brother Eddie and the way he could talk about himself for hours on end. He thought about Jared, with his ice-blue eyes, and remembered what David had told him, about his father and mother, and flunking out of school, and having to move into a trailer. It suddenly occurred to Jacob what David had probably been trying to say: Jared was likely more insecure here in the town where he had grown up than Jacob was in a town he had lived in for barely three days. He rolled over again, this time facing the window. The pale morning light was peeking through the blinds his father had hung just yesterday. And suddenly, for the first time, Jacob was homesick.

He missed his old bedroom in Tunica. He missed Kevin, who had been his best friend since third grade. He missed Mr. Stevenson, who had been his baseball and soccer coach. He missed the Ridgeview Cinema, where just this summer, he and Kevin had finally managed to sneak into an 'R' rated movie. He missed Jacky's Grill, where his father took him at least once a week for burgers. But mostly, he just missed the feeling that he was where he *belonged*, the feeling that he and Kevin could ride off on their bikes and have untold adventures filled with excitement and danger, knowing all the while that he would return home safely in the evening, unscathed, just in time for supper. His new home certainly seemed to offer danger and adventure, but not the safety and security he had known before. He craved the adventure, but needed that security.

Around 7:45, Mr. Hunter, wearing nothing but a pair of sweat pants, came shuffling down the hallway and into the den, where Jacob was slouched on the sofa with his feet propped on the coffee table, watching television. He peered through bleary eyes at his son. The way he was walking made Jacob think of a zombie in a horror movie he had recently seen. A newly re-animated corpse, stiffly staggering along in search of human flesh.

"Mornin', Jacob. Get your feet off the table."

Nope, not a zombie, just his dad. He kept shuffling right along, past Jacob and into the kitchen where he began work on the morning's pot of coffee, leaving his son to wonder: if his father *was* a zombie, would he ask Jacob to take his feet off of the coffee table before he attacked? About five minutes later, his mother came down the hall, doing the same barefoot zombie-shuffle.

"Good morning, sweetheart. Get your feet off the table."

The family was soon seated around the table, eating apple and cinnamon muffins Jacob's mom had baked. As he had every morning since the family had arrived in Logtown, Mr. Hunter began laying out what he had taken to calling the 'plan of action' for the day. Jacob didn't say much, though he was pleased to learn that his only chores for the day would be to mow the yard (which was smaller than the yard they'd had in Tunica) and then help his father organize the tool shed behind the house. He felt confident that he would be finished by lunchtime, and could spend the rest of the day hanging out with David. After devouring three muffins and a full glass of chocolate milk, he got up from the table and strolled down the hall to his bedroom, where he donned his usual attire for summer yard work: a pair of cut-off shorts, an old Atlanta Braves t-shirt, a Nike baseball cap (turned around backwards on his head) and a pair of flip-flops. He also grabbed his Walkman and a cassette tape containing dubs of his favorite songs from his favorite CD's (he'd been pestering his folks for a Discman for the past year, but so far it was a no-go).

He ended up having to wait twenty extra minutes before starting while his dad drove to Dee Dee's to fill up the gas can. Then the entire Hunter clan marched outside to begin their assigned yard duties: his mother in the front yard tending the flowerbed, his father operating the weed-eater/sidewalk edger, and of course, Jacob on the mower. He and his father had the yard (front, back and sides) looking neat and trim in just forty-five minutes, then moved on to the more daunting task of getting the tool shed in order. There turned out to be more involved in this task than Jacob had originally hoped.

First, his father cautiously went in armed with a can of wasp spray. There were two occupied nests on opposite sides outside of the shed, under the overhang of the neatly shingled roof, but none inside. Jacob was mortified that he had walked directly beneath one of them without noticing on the family's first evening in town.

Once the two outside nests had been thoroughly doused, both he and his father took a few moments of perverse pleasure to watch the wasps struggle fruitlessly on the ground, unable to fly or crawl but trying desperately to do both before finally succumbing to the poison. Once certain that the wasps were dead, they proceeded to sweep the dusty floors and the cobweb-ridden corners and ceiling of the small shed. They threw out the shears and broken rake, hung a tool-rail on one of the walls, and finally began filling up the shed with the lawn-care equipment they had brought from Tunica. Jacob didn't mind the work. In fact, he almost enjoyed it. Just as he had in Tunica, his father eventually began rambling, telling Jacob stories about some of the things he and his friends had gotten into when he was a kid. His father was a great storyteller, and seemed to enjoy telling the stories as much as Jacob enjoyed listening to them. These tales were never recited in his wife's presence, and they always ended with *you probably shouldn't tell your mom that I told you that one*. Jacob never did.

By the time he and his father finished the shed, the homesick feeling Jacob had experienced earlier that morning was gone. He was still with his family and they were still doing the kind of things they had always done together. After a typical Saturday sandwich/chips/Kool-Aid lunch, he put on another set of clothes, these classified by his mother as "play clothes." This meant that they were not quite grungy enough to be work clothes, but were no longer fit for public viewing except on playgrounds, backyards, or in the woods. He then grabbed a phonebook and flipped to the letter "P." The name Phillips took up half a page, but only one showed an address on Pine Crest, which was the main street running through *The Pines* subdivision. He dialed the number and waited. It was answered after just one ring.

"Hello?" said a man's voice.

"Uh, hello, Mr. Phillips? This is Jacob Hunter. Can I talk to David?"

"Sure, hold on a sec."

Jacob heard the sound of the phone being set down. He then listened with amusement to the following, half-muted exchange.

David's father: "David!! Telephone!!"

David: "Yeah, I got it."

Dillon: "Who is it? Can I talk? Why not?? Pleeeze??"

David: "Would you please just shut up and get away from me, ya dingleberry?"

Dillon: "I'm tellin' Mom! Mooooommy!!"

Finally, the phone was picked up and Jacob was spoken to.

"Hello?"

"Hey, it's Jacob. You free yet?"

"Yep, just finished lunch. You?"

"Yeah, me too. You wanna do something?"

"Sure, but not over here. Dillon's been a real booger-head all day. Hey, you think your folks would let me move in with you guys?"

Jacob laughed. "Not if you use words like booger-head, you booger-head!"

More laughter. "I'll be over in a little while."

Jacob was grinning as he hung up the phone.

They spent an hour or so in Jacob's bedroom, playing Nintendo while Jacob recounted his Friday evening with the MacDonald clan. David seemed to get a kick out of Jacob's description of Eddie, who he didn't know very well. After a while, David suggested they go out and "hit the trails." They could go by the Ice House and hang out, or he could show Jacob the rest of the racecourse that they had ridden past the day before. Jacob agreed. They stopped in the kitchen for a drink on the way out. Mrs. Hunter was in the kitchen, putting shelf paper in the cabinets. On the way out the door, Jacob told her that they were going bike riding and that he would be back before supper. She almost managed to tell them to be careful before they were gone.

"Let's swing by the Ice House first before we hit the track," David suggested. "Jared and Stevie might be there." Jacob wasn't thrilled at the idea of either boy joining them in whatever activities he and David might pursue, but he said nothing. David must have seen a look on his face, though, because he added "If they hear us out on the track, they're gonna come over anyway. By the way, I bet I can beat you there." And he sped away. Jacob cursed silently and sped after David, but he didn't have a chance. His friend obviously knew every bump, curve and dip that the trails had to offer. He nearly caught up as he watched his friend's movements on the bike ahead of him, imitating them in order to take the trail as smoothly as David. They finally broke into the clearing where the trailer sat, both boys locking their brakes and skidding to a stop, laughing as the dust and pine needles flew.

"You sorry cheater," Jacob grinned. "Give me some warning next time."

"I'll give you a head start next time," David replied with a smirk, "but I hope you don't cry when I beat you, anyway. I just couldn't stand to see you cry."

"I'll take both of you on the race-course, and I really don't give a rip if you both weep in shame after I thoroughly humiliate you."

Something inside of Jacob, right around his midsection, seemed to groan as he looked up to see Jared standing in the door of the Ice House. Just as they had the day before, his face smiled a little and his eyes laughed a lot.

"David and Tuna-ca. How *are* you guys today?"

"What's up, Jared," David said as he parked his bike.

"Hey" was all that Jacob could bring himself to say as he followed David.

As they stepped into the trailer, Jacob saw Stevie sitting in a chair by the table, looking at one of the comic books. He looked up as they entered, but said nothing. As he took a seat in one of the lawn chairs, Jacob's eyes once again fell on the woman pictured on the pin-up. She smiled seductively at him. Jared followed his gaze and saw the object of his attention.

"What's up, Tuna-ca? Never seen a bare-naked woman before?"

Jacob was embarrassed, and became defensive.

"My name is *Jacob*, and yes, I've seen a naked woman before."

"Yeah," David said suddenly. "He was hangin' out with a naked chick when I got to his house a while ago, and no, it wasn't his mom."

Everyone laughed, and Jacob was grateful that his friend had come to his rescue.

"Oh. Well, I'm really sorry 'bout that, Jacob," said Jared. "And I'll be sure to call you Jacob from now on, Jacob. And I'm sure you've seen many, *many* naked women in your time, Jacob." His eyes told Jacob just how sorry he was even more than his words. Not even a little.

"By the way," said David, changing topics smoothly, "Jacob got to see Hanes live and in the flesh yesterday. We were at the quick-stop when he came in to re-stock his supply of fire-water."

"Well, Jacob, did you say hello? Did you shake his hand? Did you tell him 'pleased to meet you, ya crazy old drunk lunatic'?" asked Jared. He didn't have to sneer when he said this. His eyes did it for him. Stevie giggled, his own eyes shining with pleasure and admiration for Jared's wit.

"Of course we did," said David, again answering for Jacob. "And he said hello back, said it was great to see us, and invited us back to his place for tea and crumpets. It was a splendid evening, I have to tell you."

All of them, including Jared, had another good laugh at that.

"Oh yeah, by the way," Jacob added suddenly, "I heard that he may be running some kinda scam; trading food-stamps for cash to buy booze and stuff."

Although he didn't want to admit it, Jacob hoped that his breaking news might even be enough to impress Jared. One look at the boy's face informed him that this was wishful thinking.

"Where'd you hear that?"

Before he even had time to consider, Jacob heard himself answer "Joe." It was an old joke, but apparently one Jared didn't know.

"Joe who?" asked Jared, right on cue, and Jacob's heart thrilled with the knowledge that he was about to score one on Mr. Laughing Eyes.

"Jo Mama!" Jacob's grin threatened to split his head and, had he known it, was every bit as cheesy as the one his father had worn three nights ago when informing his son that Mr. MacDonald had a daughter.

Stevie started giggling timidly, but David exploded with laughter, kicking back in his chair. He kicked back too far, and fell with a crash against the wall of the trailer, ending up in a tangled heap with the chair. At this point Stevie's giggle kicked into high gear and became a kind gasping shriek: "Eeeeeeee hee-hee-hee, eeeeeeee hee-hee-hee." He began rocking back and forth, holding his stomach with one hand, pointing at David with the other, and trying desperately to catch his breath.

As if a switch had been flicked, that ever-present laughter vanished from Jared's eyes.

"What did you just say, jerk?"

Stevie immediately turned off his psychotic giggle and looked up expectantly.

"Lighten up, Jared," said David, struggling to untangle himself from the chair as he continued to laugh. "He was just messin' around."

But Jared wasn't lightening up. His eyes had become two ice-blue stones: cold, glittering jewels in his pale, emotionless face. He stood up, slowly and deliberately, and took a step in Jacob's direction. Jacob jumped up, knocking his own chair over, and braced himself. David, one foot still caught in the straps of his lawn chair, staggered between them. It was actually a fairly amusing sight to see – David dragging his chair across the floor with one foot, trying to keep both his balance and dignity while at the same time trying to diplomatically prevent what would probably be a one-sided fight. Amusing or not, nobody was laughing.

"Come on, Jared, relax. Back off."

Jared didn't back off, nor did he proceed. He stood perfectly still and tense, those cold eyes boring into Jacob with animosity. Even the air inside the old trailer seemed rigid and alive, as if it wanted something to happen, anything that would relieve the pent-up pressure that surrounded them.

"Come on, Jared," David repeated. "Look at me. *Jared! Look at me!"*

Jared finally looked.

"He don't know, man," David lied. "He wouldn't have said that if he knew. He's okay, man, he was just messin' around."

Then Jacob suddenly remembered what David had told him Friday – especially the part about Jared's father leaving him and his mother and how they'd had to move into a trailer – and realized that was probably why Jared was so angry at such a goofy little joke. He also picked up on the cue that he was not supposed to know about Jared's situation. Feeling like maybe he *was*, in fact, a jerk, Jacob stepped up next to David.

"I didn't mean to make you mad, man," he said quietly. "I didn't mean anything by it; I was just . . . you know . . . messin' around."

Jared stared hard for a long moment, then gave a quick, indifferent nod and finally sat back down. He said nothing, but his expression relaxed a bit.

David finally yanked his foot loose from the straps of his overturned lawn chair and set it back up, and they were all seated once more. The inside of the trailer echoed with silence for an endless few seconds before David finally spoke.

"Anyway, Hanes isn't on welfare."

"How do you know?" Jacob asked.

"We *all* know," said Stevie. "David's aunt is a mail carrier."

"So?"

David looked over at him. "So, welfare checks come from the government. All Hanes ever gets is junk mail. Well, he gets a letter or something every month or so from New York. I guess it's a letter, it's a big envelope."

"Who's it from?"

"I dunno. Aunt Doreen was tellin' my mom about it once, and she said there's never a 'return to' name, just a P.O. box number, in New York."

"It's probably porno mags," said Jared, finally coming back to life as he hitched his thumb toward the pin-up. "Even Hanes has to get satisfaction once in a while."

They all laughed, but Jacob felt like it was a tentative laugh. The atmosphere still felt tense, and Jared still hadn't looked at him since they'd sat back down. All was quiet for a moment as Jared and Stevie seemed to return to their magazines and David retied the laces on the shoe that had caught in the straps of his chair. Then, so suddenly that it made everyone in the trailer jump, Jared stood up.

"Tell ya what, since Jacob here's already met Hanes, maybe he's ready for the rites of passage. What do you boys think?"

Stevie looked up with a nasty little smile as David glanced at his friend. He was also smiling, and though it wasn't nasty like Stevie's, it was tainted with just a touch of amused excitement. Jacob had never seen David smile that way, and looked around the trailer with some suspicion.

"What exactly are the rites of passage?" he asked, trying to hide his nervousness.

"You're about to find out, if you think you can handle it" Jared answered, vaguely daring Jacob to accept and refuse at the same time. "Come on."

"It's okay, I did it," David quietly reassured him as they filed out of the trailer. "Even Greg did it."

Jacob wasn't very sure that David's words of consolation were making him feel any better about the 'rites of passage', whatever it was. He had caught a look in Jared's eyes on the way out of the trailer. They no longer seemed angry, but they were laughing at him again, and harder than ever.

The boys rode their bikes up the trail away from the Ice House in a single file line: Jared first, followed by David, then Jacob. Stevie brought up the rear, as if to guard against the possibility that Jacob may try to break away from the group in a desperate rush, or more likely, casually and quietly slip into the woods or onto the trail that would lead him safely back home. When Jared reached the main path and turned left, Jacob suddenly knew exactly where they were headed, and did indeed entertain the idea of slipping away as quickly as he could. There was no way Stevie could stop him, but there was also no doubt that the little creep would immediately raise the alarm. In his heart, though, Jacob knew that he wouldn't try to make a break for it. There were two reasons: pride and trust.

While Jacob had done his share of foolish things, both in the name of fun and to demonstrate his bravery, he wasn't one of those boys that would do just about anything for attention. He had known a boy like that in Tunica named Brian Stockstill. Like Stevie, Brian was a physically small boy. Unlike Stevie, he tried to make up for what was (in his own mind, at least) a shortcoming not by trying to get under the wing of a bigger, tougher kid, but by taking every single dare ever placed before him. It didn't matter how crazy or dangerous: in fact, the crazier and more dangerous, the better. Half the time, Brian would come up with the dare himself. And he held undisputed records in Tunica, not only for some of the wildest stunts attempted, but also for the most visits to the local emergency room. Jacob had actually witnessed some of these legendary stunts firsthand, but most he had only heard about. Those that he had heard about included scaling a water tower and spray painting his initials at the top (a common stunt for teenagers; Brian had been ten years old at the time), rolling the principal's house with toilet paper, and mooning the crowd while perched upon the Boy Scout's float in a Christmas parade (which not only ended his Boy Scout career, but any chances of his ever participating in *any* parade ever again, unless it be Mardi Gras down 'yonder in New Orleans). Both of the two dares that Jacob actually witnessed had ended in injuries.

Once, when the boys had been riding across town to the theater to catch a Saturday matinee, they had to stop at a railroad track and wait on a passing freight train. On a dare, Brian had *hopped on* the moving train. Granted, the train had been stopped to switch cars at a small train yard just outside of town, and had only just started moving again, but it was quickly gaining momentum. Brian hopped right onto a ladder on the side of a boxcar and rode that sucker for over half a mile. At first, Jacob and his friends rode on their bikes alongside the train, laughing and pointing and saying things like "Have a nice trip to Memphis, you idiot." Soon, they were saying things like "Okay, Brian you better get off" and "C'mon, stupid, bail off that thing." Brian just kept on grinning and shouting obscenities back at them, holding onto the ladder with one hand and waving and making offensive gestures at them with the other. When the train had accelerated to the point that the boys on bikes could no longer keep up, he finally jumped. He tried to land like a professional stuntman would, rolling into the fall with his arms pulled up to his chest. But he wasn't a stuntman, trained and wearing pads for protection, he was just an eleven-year-old boy that desperately craved attention. He limped away from the tracks with a sprained ankle and some pretty nasty cuts and bruises from landing amidst the rocks piled alongside the railroad tracks. He was out of commission for less than two weeks. He was hurt much worse performing his next stunt, and it wasn't even a dare. It had been his own idea.

Jacob and Kevin had been riding their bikes in the woods and come across Brian and some other boys just as they finished construction of a ramp. It had been built on one side of what everyone called a drainage ditch, but it was really more like a drainage canal, which could be followed upstream to a larger, concrete canal that ran throughout the west side of "downtown" Tunica, often through huge culverts under the streets (yes, Brian had explored each and every one of these thoroughly). The cement ended within the city limits, but the canal continued for nearly a mile, growing narrower and shallower until it finally joined with a small creek outside of town. At the place where Brian had constructed his two-by-four and plywood ramp, the "ditch" was still almost ten feet across. Jacob had to give the boy credit; he came within about one and a half feet of clearing the ditch. When he saw that he *wasn't* going to clear the opposite side, Brian bailed off the bike and tried to land on his feet. Jacob watched in frightened fascination as Brian flew through the air, arms and legs flailing like a muppet. He struck the edge of the canal just below his right hip and seemed to almost bounce into a cartwheel as his bike hit the side of the canal with a heavy thud and fell down into the muddy water. Brian came out of the semi-cartwheel by landing flat on his back with a hearty *whoof*, sliding about five feet, and finally coming to rest in a very ungraceful heap.

Jumping off the bike when he did was probably the smartest thing Brian had done in several weeks. Without a doubt, doing so had saved him from serious injury to a part of his anatomy that, as any guy will tell you, is most sensitive to even the slightest hint of injury. Unfortunately, he *didn't* manage to avoid injury to his right arm (broken), three ribs (fractured), his head (mild concussion and a wicked scratch under his right eye), and right leg (a piece of broken limb about as big around as a pencil and almost as long stuck in and broke off, protruding like the shaft of an arrow). The other boys stayed behind with Brian while Jacob and Kevin raced on their bikes to the nearest house to get help. And according to the boys who had stayed behind, Brian had sat there, broken and bleeding and pale, laughing about the whole thing and explaining what had gone wrong.

"Next time," he had told them, "I'll make it with five feet to spare."

Jacob, like most of his friends, got a kick out of Brian at first, but eventually began to avoid him when possible. It seemed that none of the dares and stunts were ever enough to satisfy the boy, and Jacob figured it was just a matter of time before Brian ended up killing either himself or some innocent bystander. Also, he was quickly becoming a form of entertainment for older, junior-high aged kids who, always looking for laughs, spent afternoons and weekends thinking up dares, all of which Brian would happily perform. He seemed to bask in their laughter as if it were applause. Jacob and his friends doubted that Brian would manage to live through high school, especially after the boy grew old enough to drive a car.

Now, as he followed Jared and Co. down the trail, passing the turn-off that led safely back to his new home, following instead the narrow, overgrown trail leading to home of one Jim Hanes, resident drunk and rumored mad-man of the city of Logtown, Jacob's pride made him want to be accepted into this circle of boys, but it was his trust in his new friend David that allowed him to cling to the hope, deep in his heart, that whatever the 'rites of passage' were, they wouldn't be too dangerous. After all, David had done it and survived. Furthermore, David had already shown a willingness to stick up for Jacob, risking a fight with Jared not even thirty minutes ago. Surely he wouldn't turn right around and put Jacob at any serious risk.

Even so, Jacob had one of those feelings in the pit of his stomach: a dull, nervous ache that was growing by the second. He knew the feeling well; it usually arrived just before something long anticipated finally occurred (this once included Christmas mornings until some little jerk kid broke the truth about Santa Claus to him when he was in first grade; now it occurred when he did things like trying to sneak into an R-rated movie for the first time). The feeling also manifested itself anytime he got into trouble and was awaiting sentencing, which was usually carried out by his father.

When the overhang was low enough that the boys had to duck, they got off of their bikes and started walking. Jared turned and warned the others to be quiet with the universal finger-to-the-mouth sign. It was unnecessary. The minute that the trailer had come into view, they all slipped smoothly into 'young boys that are up to something' mode, a natural talent that usually stays with boys into their late teen years.

They moved slowly and quietly, right up to the chain link fence surrounding Mr. Hanes lot. Then they turned left, and Jacob saw that the trail didn't end right at the fence as he originally thought. Instead, it continued alongside the fence to their left, all the way to the corner, where he assumed it continued to follow the fence, possibly right up to the front of the lot. The four boys crept along the small path, turning right at the fence corner then quietly moved forward until they were even with what would be the front, right side corner of the trailer, if faced from the highway. The shrubs and overgrowth on both sides of the fence had kept them sheltered from view, and a medium-sized pine tree stood about three feet from the fence inside the yard, directly between them and the trailer. At this point they stopped and hunkered down in a small circle. By now, Jacob could feel his heartbeat not only in his chest, but pulsing behind his eyes and ears as well. The pit in his stomach had advanced to the point of being only a few notches shy of diarrhea, and it required concentrated effort to keep the nervous, twitchy tremble in his legs from shaking his entire body.

"Okay, Tuna-ca," whispered Jared, "The moment of truth has arrived. All you gotta do is walk up and knock on the front door, then haul tail back to your bike before Jim comes after you."

Jacob's trust in David was quickly evaporating. What the heck *this*? For the first time in his life, he experienced Total Recall; it seemed to Jacob that he could actually hear Mr. MacDonald's voice in his ears, talking in an amused way about the time Mr. Hanes had come out with a gun when some "young boys had come a-knockin' at his door." What had seemed a funny story just last night now made Jacob's heart quake. But as he looked from one face to the next, all eyes were on him. And, much to his surprise, he couldn't bring himself to refuse. Not just yet.

"Won't he see me coming?" He almost began the question with *what if*, but instinctively knew how whiney phrasing the question that way would sound. There were explicit words reserved by boys for other boys who phrased questions that way. Jared probably knew them all and wouldn't hesitate to use the worst of them.

David answered. "Naw, man, he's got tinfoil in all of his windows. And he's old as the hills. By the time he gets up and makes it to the door, we'll be history. Hey, he might even be sittin' on the pot with his pants around his ankles. The best part is listenin' to him cuss and holler. When I did it, I swear we could still hear him all the way back at the Ice House." David was grinning now, and Jacob felt a little better. He remembered noticing the foil-covered windows on his prior visit.

"That one was the best, man," Jared agreed with a smile, then turned to Jacob. "Tell you what, I'll come part of the way with you."

This offer came as a complete surprise to Jacob. It seemed to surprise the other boys as well. David looked a little suspicious, and Stevie started to complain.

"Everyone else had to go alone. Why does he get to . . . ?"

Jared cut him off. "Because Jacob's new here. I'm only going halfway, just past the tree. He'll still have to do the rest by himself."

The fact that Jared was not only offering to do something nice but also calling him by his name (instead of 'Tuna-ca') made Jacob feel a little uncomfortable, but he decided to hope that it meant Jared might actually be considering accepting the new boy into the group. Jacob had not yet learned to listen to (much less seriously consider) gut instincts, at least as they applied to scenarios bigger than the instincts that assist young boys learning to ride bikes or catch a football or make up extravagant stories to explain why they did something they weren't supposed to (or didn't do something that they *were* supposed to). One of his father's favorite nuggets of wisdom was "If something seems too good to be true, it probably is." Most young boys have to learn this lesson the hard way. Most don't have to learn it more than once. Jacob certainly wouldn't. He would remember this lesson, and everything that came after, for the rest of his life.

"You ready, Jacob?" Jared asked, staring hard at the new boy. Jacob could no longer tell if his eyes were laughing or not, and this caused another thick surge of discomfort. Was it Jared's sudden and unexpected friendliness and support that was making him feel so uncomfortable, or just the task, the dare, the test that had been laid out before him? He didn't know, and there was no time now to consider. He took a deep breath.

"Let's do it!"

He started to climb the fence, but before he could get a good grip and hoist himself up, Jared grabbed his arm and pointed down. Jacob looked and saw that the chain-link fence had been cut away from the fence post closest to where they were huddled. The fence itself hadn't been stretched or twisted away from the post, and because it was almost directly behind the pine tree, he figured that Hanes had never even noticed. From the look of the place, he probably wouldn't have cared if he *did* notice.

Jared grabbed the bottom corner of the fence where it hung loosely next to the post and gently pulled back, just enough for Jacob to slip through on his hands and knees. Once through, Jacob stood behind the pine tree and waited until Jared made it through and slid up beside him. The older boy leaned in close and whispered into Jacob's ear.

"Alright, Jacob, you're on. Go for it!"

Jacob stepped from behind the tree and began to walk briskly toward the door. He began taking in quick, short breaths, his heart was racing, and his fingertips began to tingle. It seemed to him that, other than the sounds of his feet hitting the ground, the entire world had gone deathly quiet. Each step he took resounded in a dull *thud,* which was quickly swallowed up in the heavy, silent air.

Halfway there.

A strange sensation had begun to envelope Jacob. He felt that maybe this wasn't really happening to *him*: he was watching it happen to someone else, but not in the sense of watching a movie or television. It felt more like when he was caught up in a good book and visualizing in his mind a scene described in colorful, lively words. He was aware that he was walking quickly and his mind was racing, and yet the time seemed to crawl. He could now clearly see the windows on either side of the door. As David had promised, they were covered with tinfoil.

Ten more steps.

Now he could hear cars and trucks passing on the highway behind him and, although the sound seemed somehow distant and unimportant, somewhere in the back of his mind a new but urgent worry began to blossom: what if one of the people passing by saw him? Surely everyone in the city knew exactly who lived in this ramshackle old trailer, and would also know that a twelve-year-old boy had no business in this yard, approaching said trailer at a suspicious speed and from a suspicious angle: from the side rather than the front. But as the trailer grew nearer, these vague thoughts were not so much suppressed as buried by a more immediate threat: on a dare, Jacob was about to play a prank, albeit a small one, on a man who was, according to everyone Jacob had spoken with, an psychotic drunkard.

I've lost my mind! he thought. *This is completely stupid, please don't let him catch me, what am I* doing? His footsteps almost faltered at this point, but all eyes were on him and he knew there could be no turning back.

He refocused himself to the task at hand. Jacob began to look harder at the fixture before him. He could see the buckling, cracked and mildewy front door clearly now. There were three steps made of cinderblocks under the front door. They looked sturdy enough. The blazing sun was reflecting brightly from the tinfoil-covered windows on either side of the door, and Jacob had a strange sensation that the sun was shining on him from two directions at once; glaring in his eyes while it baked the back of his neck.

Five more steps.

Almost there, almost there, can't turn back now, almost there, gotta do it, just do it *and then run! Run* fast! *I mean MOVE YOUR TAIL, almost there*. He wasn't aware, but his mouth was forming the words as he thought them.

Out of the corner of his right eye, Jacob could suddenly see Jared, who had stepped out from behind the pine tree and begun walking quickly toward Jacob and the trailer. *What's he doing? Is he afraid I'll chicken out?* Jacob thought, even as he put one foot on the first step.

He heard David call out in a hoarse whisper "Jared, *NO!*"

Jacob caught another motion out of the corner of his eye, heard something whiz by him, and the window to the right of the front door suddenly *popped* loudly. The sound reminded Jacob of the noise made when a rock had hit the windshield of his father's car some years back.

His second foot never touched the cinderblock steps. He turned in time to see Jared clear the fence in one graceful leap. He also saw that the other boys were already gone. Even as Jacob began to run, too afraid to even curse Jared just yet, he heard the door opening behind him and realized he would never get past the fence without being seen. He swung around the pine tree and crouched down, holding his breath and trying to make himself thinner.

Jim Hanes came out screaming. "WHAT IN THE EVERLASTING HELL . . . !" was as far as he got before his voice was cut short by a sudden *thud*. And then Jacob heard only silence. He waited for what seemed like an eternity, now silently but enthusiastically cursing Jared while wondering what in the world had happened; why wasn't Hanes screaming anymore? His heart ached to make a dash for the fence, but he didn't dare. He couldn't bring himself to even try. After two agonizing minutes, he finally peered cautiously around the tree; half fearing that Jim Hanes would suddenly loom up in front of him with a snarl and a shotgun. Instead, he saw nothing but an old, frail-looking man lying motionless on the ground. His first thought was that he could easily turn, jump the fence, and get right the heck out of there. Then he looked harder at the old man, who didn't appear to be breathing.

Oh, no, Jacob thought, *oh no, please, no, no . . . what if he's dead?* He looked harder, straining his eyes in a vain attempt to detect even a little movement, but saw none.

"Jacob!"

He had barely heard the whisper, but it made him jump all the same. He turned and saw David crouched down and half hidden by some brush on the other side of the fence.

"Come on!" David was whispering behind clenched teeth. "Let's get outta here!"

Jacob held up one hand to say *hold on a minute* then looked back at Hanes. He still didn't appear to have moved. His legs were spread apart slightly, and both arms were underneath his motionless body. His face was turned away from Jacob.

Jacob's mind began to race. Whether Jim Hanes was hurt or dead, he knew he couldn't just leave the man lying on the ground that way. For one thing, he knew it would be *wrong*. A quick risk assessment made the concept of right and wrong a little vague in Jacob's mind, and he had, of course done plenty of things that he knew to be wrong in the past, sometimes suffering the consequences, sometimes getting away with it. But to just leave a emaciated old man lying in the dirt, probably hurt and possibly even dead when he himself had been at least partially responsible for the situation was *really* wrong, a much *bigger* wrong than anything he'd even considered in the past. It was the kind of *wrong* he sometimes heard his father speak angrily about while reading the newspaper or watching the news. The kind of *wrong* that helped make the world a bad place. It was a kind of *wrong* that Jacob could never imagine his father ever perpetrating or condoning.

The second reason was more of a self-preservation instinct. It came naturally and with very little analytical thought: it was very possible, he realized, that someone in one of the passing cars *had* seen him walking up to the trailer, and he could get blamed for whatever had happened. Whether Jim Hanes had tripped, had a heart attack, or simply fallen in a drunken stupor might not matter – Jacob might still be blamed. This possibility caused an immediate intensifying of the sick sensation in his stomach. What would happen if he *did* get blamed? Would he be arrested? Would there be a trial? What about jail; would he be sent off to one of those juvenile jails filled with the hardest and toughest pre-adolescent and teenaged boys society had to offer? His mind raced with the possibilities, and in a millisecond it had painted a horrible and detailed picture, based mostly on rumors he'd heard over the span of his short life.

He imagined being unable to see his parents except on weekends or maybe even just once a month and on holidays. The visits would take place under the watchful eyes of guards armed with machine guns and stationed in towers built in the four corners of a barren yard enclosed by a twenty-foot high stone wall topped with gleaming coils of razor wire. He and his family would sit at a small, concrete picnic table, cracked and chipped and scrawled with vulgarities and obscene pictures: the artwork of other residents of the prison. They'd eat food brought by his parents, food that had been prepared the night before by his mother (her eyes filled with tears as she wondered where she and her husband had gone wrong; how could their sweet young Jacob be in jail for *murder?*) The food eaten by the small family as they huddled together would, of course, be a feast compared to the food served at this place. This fact that would be glaringly obvious as the older, tougher guys would stroll about with their hands in their pockets and cigarettes hanging from their lips, slowly circling his family at a safe but closing distance, eyeing the food on the table like vultures. Then, after his parents were gone, some of these guys would corner him someplace dark when there weren't any guards watching, and tell him how delicious the food had looked, and how it might be a good idea for him to share, or things could get mighty tough for him, here on the *inside*. He saw each these images, almost *studied* them, distinctly and clearly as they sped before his eyes and through his mind at breakneck speed.

Could that really happen? Could all of that really happen just because he had been stupid enough to take a dare, a stupid, harmless little dare – just because he'd been stupid enough to trust Jared?

Jared! His mind almost spat the name. *That complete and total* jerk!! *How could he* do *this*? *I hate that little jerk*! *Hate him*!! And he truly did hate the boy with all his heart for a few fruitless moments more before finally accepting that he could hate Jared all he wanted later, for the rest of his life if necessary, but right now he had to do something, and fast.

He quickly formulated a plan: he would get as close as he dared to the prone body, then call out. If the man didn't respond, he'd try gently throwing something at the body. If he still didn't get a response, Jacob would ride his bike to Dee Dee's and say he'd been exploring the trails and had come upon an old man lying in front of a trailer down the road – the man wasn't moving, someone better get help. Then he'd try to slip away on his bike, ride straight home, and never set foot out of his house again. Jacob also figured that if Hanes *did* respond, he could outrace the old man to the fence, get to his bike and be zipping down the trails before Hanes could even get close. After all, Hanes had just taken a bad fall, didn't appear to be in great shape, and on top of everything, he was old. Even in the event that this second scenario was the one that played out, Jacob still planned to scoot home just as fast as his bike would take him, and never set foot out of his house again.

He turned to David and whispered, "Wait here; I'll be right back."

David looked at him as if he had gone mad, but said nothing.

Jacob then turned back and cautiously began to retrace his footsteps toward both the trailer and the man lying prone on the ground before him. He stopped when he got within fifteen feet of the body.

"Hey mister, are you okay?" His voice sounded hoarse and weak. The body didn't move. Jacob wasn't sure if the man couldn't respond, or just hadn't heard him. He had barely heard himself, but it was the best he could do. His throat felt dry and half closed.

Jacob took five more steps. He looked carefully at the body, searching for any sign of life but seeing none. Jim was wearing nothing but a pair of jeans, the same pair he had been wearing at the quick stop the day before. No shirt, no shoes or socks. Jacob could see the flesh of the man's back clearly as it stretched tightly across his shoulder blades and the knobs of his spine. The skin certainly appeared to have the hue of a dead man, but Jacob supposed that might be the man's natural complexion.

"Mister?" he called out again. No response. Jacob felt a lump in his throat, and that queasy, sick sensation in his stomach was back with a vengeance. *He IS dead!* Jacob thought, *God, please don't let this be happening, please don't let him be dead! PLEASE!!* Fighting against that rising sick feeling in his stomach, he stepped up to the body, then bent over to touch the shoulder.

Instantly, the old man rolled over, grabbed Jacob's right arm with fingers that felt as cold and hard as steel, and flipped him over onto the ground. Jacob landed on his back with a heavy thud and felt all of the air rush out of his lungs in a great *whoosh* as dust flew in thick, billowing clouds all around him. He tried to catch his breath, but couldn't, and in an instant, Jim Hanes was on top of him, holding the blade of a steak knife to his throat with his right hand while his bony left forearm pressed against Jacob's chest. Jacob was stunned and helpless. How could someone so old, so thin, so *frail looking* be so fast, so *strong*? Jacob tried to go limp, but his body kept jerking as his lungs struggled desperately to refill with air. Jim lowered his face to within inches of Jacob's, his grizzled beard resting on Jacob's chest and his greasy hair hanging down in clumps on either side of his old, bony face. The long, lank hair was almost touching Jacob's face: it blocked his peripheral vision so that all he could see at that moment was the twisted, wretched face of Jim Hanes looming before him, completely filling his sight. The old man's lip curled up slightly in a snarl, and he was breathing heavily. Jacob could smell the rottenness of his breath, mingled with a strong scent of alcohol; he could smell the greasiness of Jim's hair; he could smell sweat that was weeks old rising from Jim's skin. The odors mingled with each other, blending into one tremendous and nauseating stench. But there was something more, something behind the smell of old sweat and rotten teeth and foul breath. It was a deeper smell, a more powerful smell; the stench of what lay underneath the crusty, foul body that hovered above Jacob. It was the smell of hopelessness, bitterness, rage, and despair. And that stench *was* the complete, rancid foulness that *was* Jim Hanes.

"You little bastard," Jim growled, spraying Jacob's face with spit. "I ought to kill you right now." The fact that Jim was no longer screaming terrified Jacob even more. He lay there, gasping and looking into Jim's dark, wild, bloodshot eyes, unable even to cry. He could see with great clarity, as he looked into those eyes, that it wasn't just a threat. Jim Hanes was actually considering cutting

Jacob's throat. The irony that only seconds before he had been praying for Jim to be alive never occurred to Jacob.

"Please," he finally whimpered, still trying to catch his breath. "Please, don't. I only wanted to help. I was only trying to help."

It sounded so lame coming out of his mouth. After all, wasn't he at least partially responsible for what had happened? Still, Jacob couldn't think of anything else to say. He was desperately hoping for mercy from a man who looked as if he had none to give. What he got was a complete shock.

What little color it held instantly drained from Jim's face, and his mouth dropped open. It was as if he had been stunned by a sharp blow to the head, and was waiting for his senses to return. He seemed to be staring *through* Jacob now; staring with glazed eyes at something that wasn't there, and his breath came in short, shallow gasps. A string of spit crawled out of his open mouth, drifted all the way down to Jacob's left cheek, then (much to Jacob's horror and disgust, though he was too terrified to do anything about it) crept along slowly, all the way down to his ear. And it never broke! It just hung there, stretching from Jim's bottom lip to Jacob's left cheek and finally his ear, swaying and trembling with each breath the old man took.

Jim's mouth continued to hang open, and Jacob could still smell the reeking breath, thick with decay and old food and alcohol, heavier than ever. Worse still, he could now see the half rotten teeth: yellow, gray and brown nubs sticking up at odd angles from gums splotched with white patches. Jacob had finally managed to catch his breath, but the smell was making him sick to the point he almost gagged. He waited another agonizingly long twenty seconds, then tried again.

"Please."

Jim started slightly, as if wakened from a dream. He looked into Jacob's eyes, his own still dazed but slowly coming back into focus. He finally pulled the knife away from Jacob's throat, then stood and slowly backed away until he reached the cinder block steps in front of the trailer. He sat down roughly on the second step, as if still dazed, but he never took his eyes off of Jacob. The glare that he usually wore was finally fighting its way back through the confusion, though it now lacked the hard, brutal power that Jacob had seen before.

"Get your scrawny little tail outta my yard, boy," he finally whispered in a hoarse and unsteady voice, "right now."

Jacob got slowly to his feet, then walked to the fence without looking back. He climbed it quickly, about ten feet away from where he and Jared had slipped under it before, then walked back up the path, the same way he and the other boys had come. He passed David, still huddled in the brush, without even looking at him. There was a strange buzzing sound in his ears, and it was growing, filling the inside of his head and drowning out all other sounds. A cold sweat broke out on his forehead; droplets began trickling down to his face as he marched along on feet he could no longer feel. He was more than halfway back to where they had left the bikes when David finally caught up with him and grabbed him by the arm.

"Hey man, are you okay?"

Jacob turned and looked blankly at his friend, who seemed somehow vague and distant, even though he was standing right in front of him. It hit him hard in a sudden rush. He groaned, and then spoke weakly but urgently.

"Oh geez, man, I think I'm gonna . . ."

He turned, dropped to his hands and knees and began to vomit violently. His stomach was quickly emptied, but he continued to heave for almost two minutes, until his back ached and his eyes began to stream with tears. It eventually subsided, and he finally caught his breath, sucking in long, deep gulps of air, still hunched over on all fours. He stared through blurry, watery eyes at the surprisingly large puddle that had once been his lunch (*a pretty good lunch, too*, he thought absently), lying before him. He was almost amused at how bright and clear the colors and textures were, and for some reason decided it looked like a (purple, thanks to the Kool-aid) western omelet. That strange observation was all he could think about for almost ten full seconds, then it was gone. He spit a few times in a vain attempt to get the bitter taste out of his mouth, and wiped his runny nose on the sleeve of his t-shirt. Then he finally sat back and looked up at the sky through the thick overhang of the trees beside the path. He had been trembling, but it was beginning to subside, and taking those slow, deep breaths seemed to help.

"Hey . . . are you okay, man?"

Jacob turned and looked at David's concerned face, unaware that he was now as pale and pasty-looking as Jim Hanes had been just minutes before.

"Yeah, I think so," he replied weakly, climbing slowly to his feet. David put his arm around his friend's shoulder and said, "Let's get outta here."

They walked slowly alongside their bikes, and neither boy spoke. The world as they had always known it seemed finally to be returning: birds singing and flying in the trees, a squirrel chattering somewhere in the underbrush, cars speeding along the highway beyond the woods, someone's lawnmower humming in the distance. Both boys felt as though these familiar sounds had vanished for a while, disappearing completely from this part of the world, and it was greatly reassuring to hear them again. When they reached the point where the trail branched left, back to the neighborhood, David suggested that maybe Jacob should head back home and offered to accompany him. Jacob refused.

"Not yet," he said. "My folks will be able to tell something happened."

Suddenly, he sat down right in the middle of the path. David stared for a moment, then sat down beside him. Jacob looked at his friend with an expression of lost innocence, the face of a twelve-year-old boy who had just discovered that he was *not* immune from cruelty, danger or even death at the hands of another person. And all for no reason other than a boy had decided that he didn't like the new kid. His anger and hatred of Jared was temporarily gone, replaced with sadness and confusion.

"Why did he do that?" he finally asked. He might have been talking to David, himself, or even God, and he really wasn't expecting an answer.

David's feelings of shock were already beginning to fade, probably because he'd been watching the drama play out instead of participating. The look of concern on his face was quickly replaced by rage.

"Because he's a piece of trash, man, a total jerk, that's why! I don't care *what's* going on with his family anymore; that was a sorry thing to do. I can't *believe* he did that! I *swear* next time I see him I'm gonna kick his tail!" David stood up, and for a second Jacob thought he was about to go after Jared on the spot, but David only paced back and forth, swearing out plans of vengeance against a newly declared enemy.

Part of Jacob's mind seemed to cry out, *yes, my friend, what an excellent idea! Let the beatings begin, and let them begin now!* But the rest of his mind knew he couldn't let that happen. He didn't want everyone in town (himself included) thinking that he had to have someone else fight for him. That was a reputation he could do without. Besides, it would likely only make his situation with Jared worse.

"No!" he said firmly, his mind made up. "I can handle it." He got slowly to his feet, and took another deep breath. David looked surprised.

"You bein' serious?"

"Yeah, I'm . . . yes," Jacob replied, and at that moment he really believed it. The shock and sadness were already vanishing from his eyes, forced out by his new resolve. Then he looked at his friend and almost smiled.

"Thanks for not running off, man."

David almost smiled back.

"Sure," he said, shrugging, and left it at that. Anything more would border on cheesy, maybe even sissy, and would break any number of those unwritten rules that the male species, man or boy, lives by. Sometimes a look, a slap on the back, or even a crude joke is all the comfort they need. Whatever had just passed between those two boys, looking at each other and wearing half-smiles on that hot Saturday afternoon, certainly seemed to be enough.

They ended up going to Dee Dee's. Jacob still wasn't ready to go home yet, and they both agreed that the Ice House should be avoided until things had time to cool off. They both bought a couple of cold drinks, and Jacob also got a pack of peanut-butter crackers. By this time his stomach had been empty for nearly thirty minutes, and he was starting to feel hungry again.

On the south side of the quick stop was a carport-like awning that sheltered a padlocked icebox and a couple of old, wooden picnic tables. On Saturday mornings, this spot was populated by local good ol' boys not quite ready to head home after an early morning on the river, swapping jokes and telling stories about "the ones that got away." By lunchtime, most were back home, mowing their yards or tinkering with cars and trucks under the blazing sun, a task made slightly more bearable by the six-pack resting in a cooler nearby. Jacob and David had the south side of Dee Dee's to themselves this afternoon.

They sat and drank their drinks and talked for nearly an hour. They plotted several revenge scenarios involving the downfall of Jared. And they compared notes with amazing objectivity on what really *had* been a potential life-or-death situation for Jacob. Any customers coming in or out of the quick stop and passing the boys would never have guessed at the danger one of them had faced just an hour earlier that evening.

Finally, around five o'clock, they decided it was time to head back. Jacob was a little worried about seeing Jared on the return trip, but with the exception of a few squirrels, they had the trails to themselves and were soon back safely in *The Pines*. They both stopped in front of the Hunters' new house to say their goodbyes, and Jacob told David that he'd probably see him in church tomorrow: the fact that the MacDonalds went to First Baptist of Logtown seemed to have convinced his parents that it was probably where they should worship.

"Cool," said David. "I guess I'll see you then."

He started to ride off, then stopped and looked back at Jacob with a twinkle in his eye.

"You know, you're the only person I've ever heard of to have a run-in with Jim Hanes. And you came out of it okay." David started to grin. "You're gonna be a *legend*!" Then he rode away.

Jacob waved, then turned and walked his bike up the driveway, thinking about what David had just said. From what he had heard about Hanes during his first few days in Logtown, he thought that David might be – almost definitely was – right about the legend thing. But he wasn't as sure about the coming out of it okay part. He knew that he had somehow changed. Something *inside* of him just felt . . . different. He didn't know what it was, or even exactly *how* it felt different. He tried to dismiss the odd sensation, telling himself that it was just some kind of delayed shock that hadn't yet worn off.

As he had expected, Jacob's mother took one look at his clothes and wanted to know exactly what happened. He told her he'd wrecked his bike on one of the trails, but he and the bike were both alright. She gave him a quick inspection anyway and discovered that his left elbow was pretty scraped up. Jacob was surprised; he hadn't even noticed. Her inspection was followed by a story, one he'd heard from her many times before, about a boy she had known when she was a kid. He'd had an accident and hit his head *just the right way*, ending up in a coma and eventually dying. Jacob had never found out exactly what hitting one's head *just the right way* meant and was a little suspicious of the story, anyway. His mom had a horror story, always involving someone she'd known as a child and always involving that person hitting his head or twisting his arm or just plain falling down *just the right way*, for every activity Jacob ever participated in (with the possible exception of Sunday school).

He surprised his parents by jumping right into the bathtub, then lying down on his bed until suppertime. After supper, he lat back down in his bed, reading a book until he finally fell asleep with the lights on. At some point, his parents peeked in on him, then tucked him in and turned out his bedroom light. And at some later point, Jacob had a dream. For the rest of his life, it would always be The Dream.

AWAKENINGS

"Dream manfully and nobly, and thy dreams shall be prophets"

Edward Bulwer Lytton

6

Jacob was not what you'd call a heavy dreamer. It was possible that he dreamed every night, the way some people do, but if so he seldom remembered. When he *did* remember having a dream, he was only able to recall vague images or snatches – what he called *the highlights* of his dreams. He would sometimes mull over the few images he could recall while eating breakfast, and sometimes he'd tell his friends at school about the more humorous or ridiculous of these nocturnal adventures. But never before had there been a dream like the one he experienced on that hot Saturday night in early August, his fourth night in the city of Logtown, Mississippi.

He is walking on the path into the woods behind his house. He has no idea how he has gotten there or even why he would be out for a stroll in the middle of the night, but he doesn't bother to question the scenario; he never even considers it. His mind is operating in that dream mentality, where logic takes a break and everything seems to make perfect sense. It doesn't matter that he is walking down the path dressed only in the t-shirt and pajama bottoms he'd worn to bed (glancing down, he notices he isn't even wearing shoes or socks), walking all alone through the dark woods in the middle of the night. For night it is, and it must be very late because there are almost none of the sounds that Jacob usually hears, even after dark. There are no dogs barking in the distance. No cars or trucks speeding up and down the highway. He can't hear the harmonious, almost soothing hum of crickets and other nighttime insects singing their nightly songs. The only sound Jacob is immediately aware of as he continues his steady stroll down the path is the soft whisper of the wind in the treetops. Yes, it is obviously very late night, and it would be very dark but for the reddish glow that dimly lights the woods around him. He looks up into the whispering treetops, where the eerie light seems brighter against the pale fog that hangs low in the sky. Or maybe it is smoke, for now he is beginning to smell a vague scent of burning wood.

Are the woods burning? Jacob wonders. He pauses and looks around, peering into the silent, brooding darkness that surrounds the trees on either side of the path for a few moments and decides they are not. He suddenly understands that it is a house or building burning, but not the woods. He never even questions it; he just knows it.

Now he turns to look in the direction from which he has come and suddenly realizes that he cannot see his house. It isn't that he has walked too far away to see it in the dim red light. The house is simply gone. All the houses are gone. Where they should stand stretches an empty field, dotted with an occasional pine or sweetgum tree. The field is overgrown, and the tall grass seems to sway and dance in the red light. The scene strikes Jacob as beautiful in a way that he'll never be able to describe, and something about it reminds him of a Halloween song he learned in kindergarten. He stands watching for several moments, entranced by what he is seeing and not caring one bit that his house is no longer there. Because he knows that it isn't supposed to be there right now, anyway. He also knows that he is supposed to be walking down that path and deeper into the woods: so that's exactly what he does, turning his back to the empty field and plunging deeper into the woods.

As he continues to walk along the path, further and further into the woods and that hypnotizing red light, which seems to grow a little brighter with each step, the wind begins to blow around him in gusts. It is a chill wind, rattling through the trees and scattering leaves all around him. He stops and looks down at his t-shirt, pajama bottoms and bare feet. He should be shivering in this cold wind, but isn't. And once again, he doesn't care: everyday, logical ideas (such as being barefoot and alone in the dark woods at night in cold weather isn't a particularly comfortable situation) just don't seem to carry much weight in this place. Another strong breeze ruffles his hair, and he turns his face toward it, breathing deeply. It feels like the fresh, cool winds of Autumn, and when mingled with the smoke in the air, it reminds him again of that Halloween song he had learned. He can't remember the lyrics, but the tune is now playing merrily in his head, and it occurs to Jacob that the tune fits perfectly with the scene that he is now a part of.

Maybe it is Halloween, he thinks. That's why the grass in the field is dancing a Halloween dance. The thought makes perfect sense to him, and it somehow makes him feel happy. He smiles as he begins walking down the path once more, ever toward the red glow and deeper into the growing haze of smoke.

Soon, he is able to see flames through the trees. How they dance under the heavy sky! And yes, it is a house burning; he can see parts of its hulking mass through the trees. He continues to walk, quickly now, drawn irresistibly by the sight. It is a large house, large and beautiful. Even with flames pouring out of the windows and smoke billowing out from a collapsed portion of the roof, it is beautiful. Jacob is reminded of the Biltmore Mansion, which he and his family had visited while vacationing in the Smoky Mountains two years before. This house is nowhere near as large, but has been built in the same grand style. And somehow, the red glow of the flames make it seem more majestic; a great and noble giant dying a great and noble death.

Jacob steps from the edge of the woods into a huge clearing and can now see the house in its entirety. And suddenly, he isn't alone. Standing not three feet to his left is a boy. Jacob knows he is there before he sees him; he can feel the boy's presence. And now Jacob finally begins to feel a bit uneasy. He understands that he is supposed to turn and face that boy, but that sudden uneasiness is growing quickly, and he doesn't want to. It isn't that he's afraid of the boy; he just doesn't want to look at him. But he also knows that this is something he has to do, and he almost feels a sense of urgency about it. So he looks, not turning slowly, but quickly, as if trying to get it over with.

The boy seems to be about the same age as Jacob, though he is several inches taller and rail-thin. He is dressed in a style of clothes that is strange but vaguely familiar to Jacob. He has seen clothes like this before, but only in movies. What comes to his mind is a movie he once saw about a group of young men who attended a private school nestled in some beautiful, faraway countryside. The school itself had looked more like an old English manor, and the boys had spoken with strange accents. They had laughed, played, and studied together, very much like Jacob and his friends had always done. He had enjoyed the movie, and had almost been brought to tears when those boys had faced the untimely death of one of their own, because he'd felt an intangible bond with them, despite the fact that the public school he had attended in Tunica, Mississippi was a far cry from that private school setting somewhere in New England.

And now Jacob can feel some sort of bond, albeit reluctant, with this boy who stands silently at his side, watching that magnificent house (which also reminded him somehow of that movie, of that old, magnificent school) burn away.

The boy only stands there, quietly watching the house burn and wearing an indescribable look of sorrow on his face. There are no tears in the boy's eyes; they are dry . . . and they are empty. It seems to Jacob that maybe those eyes have already given up all that they have to give, and they are now – just empty, empty of everything but sorrow and regret. The boy finally turns his pale, gaunt face toward Jacob and by desperate force of will, pulls Jacob's eyes to his own. Jacob wants desperately not to look into those eyes, so vacant, but simply has no choice. And as he looks, the boy speaks to him in a hollow voice that seems to come from far away. But the words he speaks are very clear, and they fill Jacob's ears and mind, drowning out the sounds of the burning house; the words almost echo despite the fact that they are spoken in little more than a whisper.

"I only wanted to help. I was only trying to help."

Jacob is suddenly terrified. He wants to turn away from the boy, but can't turn away any more than he can run away. His feet and legs have no strength, and so there he stands, staring into eyes that he somehow knows, though he can't imagine how or why. And still the boy stares at Jacob, the red light glowing and dancing on his pale skin, his eyes filled with that unspeakable grief. And finally, Jacob begins to weep, for no reason he can think of other than for this strange boy's sorrow. He suddenly feels the boy's aching emptiness just as surely as he had felt that cold (and now somehow sad) autumn wind rustling the fallen leaves around his feet as he walked the trail through the woods. It is the sorrow of a great loss, the greatest of losses. It speaks of hollow voids, of an emptiness that will never again be filled. Things once dearly loved that are now gone forever. And above all, it speaks of utter hopelessness.

The boy watches as Jacob stands crying, but doesn't speak again. He watches with sadness, for although it is his sorrow that makes Jacob weep, there will be no comfort for his soul. He has wept until his own eyes have nothing more to give, and now he weeps with Jacob's eyes. Finally he turns back to the burning house, which is blazing brighter than ever. And when his eyes leave Jacob's, the spell is broken. The great sorrow Jacob had felt, the anguish that seemed to fill his heart until it would burst, now quickly fades until it seems only a distant memory. But it is now Jacob's memory, and will remain in the deepest part of his heart for the rest of his days. He now follows the boy's gaze to the house, which has become an inferno. It roars like some great beast come to life from a child's storybook, devouring everything it touches, and Jacob can feel its heat burning away the cool, brisk air around him. He turns back to ask the boy what was happening, what they are watching, but the boy is no longer with him. He is once again standing alone before an unleashed fury of blazing fire.

Now Jacob can hear other voices. They are too far away for him to understand what was being said; the roar of the fire is drowning out all other sounds. Jacob strains his ears, listening carefully to the sounds of those voices, and decides that they are coming from the far side of the house, to his right. He begins to walk slowly toward the sound, drawn by the same vague need that had forced him to look into the eyes of that strange, sad boy. This urgency somehow overpowers his fear, fear that continues to grow despite the disappearance of the strange, ghostly boy.

As he walks, the voice (there now appears to be only one person speaking) grows louder in a strangely disproportionate way, after only ten steps, Jacob can hear the words clearly, as though he were standing right next to whomever was speaking them. Only, the words aren't spoken, they are screamed.

After another ten steps, Jacob can finally see two people in the distance. One is an older man who appears to be going stark-raving mad. He paces in a crazy, unsteady circle; now grabbing at unseen things in the air, now slapping at those same things, now pulling at his hair. And throughout this odd and frightening display, a young boy grovels at his feet, actually grabbing at them whenever they pass within grabbing distance. The man finally stops in front of the boy long enough to lean over into the child's face and scream through snarling, bared teeth. And he curses the boy, curses him with words and a fury that make Jacob tremble. He curses the boy's very soul, swearing that he will one day see it in hell.

The boy, who had been on his knees, now curls himself into a kind a fetal ball, his face down on his knees and his hands pulled tightly over the back of his head. He begins to rock back and forth in that odd position, wailing. "I was only trying to help!! Please, Father, please!! I'm sorry, I'm so sorry, please, I'm sorry!" He reaches again for the man's shoes, which are quickly jerked away, leaving him to grovel once more on the ground.

Suddenly, Jacob hears other voices in the distance. They are coming from the opposite direction, the other side of the house. It seems as though the townsfolk have finally been roused and are now quickly and noisily heading toward the blazing house, picking up others along the way with cries of Fire! They won't need to get very close before realizing that the cause is already lost, and there is little for anyone to do but watch it light up the sky.

The minute that he hears those voices, the man grabs his son by the arm and yanks him up so hard that just watching it makes Jacob wince. The boy's feet actually leave the ground for a moment. Although he hears every word uttered, Jacob still isn't close enough to make out either face very well. But he understands that he is looking at the boy who had been standing beside him only moments before. Even before the boy had voiced his cries for mercy and forgiveness, Jacob had known. It is also at this moment that Jacob understands that what he is watching is really happening. The house was really burning, the townsfolk are really coming, and the boy's half-crazed father is really on the verge of killing his own son. Jacob isn't as sure that the boy had been real when he had stood at his side a few moments before, speaking in that distant, ghostly voice. This thought makes Jacob shudder.

The man jerks the boy again, right up to his face, and in the growing firelight, Jacob can suddenly see both faces quite clearly. The man wears an expression of such rage and hate that Jacob again fears for the other boy's life. His eyes dance with madness, his jaws clench, and his lips stretch across his face, baring his teeth like a snarling, rabid dog. The red glow that hangs in the air makes it seem all the more hideous, and even from this great distance, the look on the man's face is terrifying to Jacob. It is a look he can't imagine ever seeing on his own father's face, even in his worst nightmare.

"You will speak of this to no one, not ever, do you understand me? If you ever speak of it, I swear to the Almighty that you will regret it, boy. I swear you will regret it forever!!"

The man then turns his face away from the boy and stands, tall and motionless, as if gathering himself. He takes a few deep breaths, then nods, as if agreeing that he is finally in control. He looks back down at the boy, and though the blind fury seems to have subsided, he makes no attempt to mask the contempt in his eyes. He seizes the boy's arm once again and, dragging the whimpering child along behind him, stalks quickly around the far side of the burning house and toward the sounds of the gathering crowd. The two are quickly gone from sight.

Jacob decides he had seen enough and now wants nothing than to be back at home, safely in bed. He turns and begins to walk quickly along the line of trees, his eyes darting from the crackling flames of the burning house to the woods as he searches for the path that will lead him home. He finally reaches the spot where he had stepped out of the woods, and freezes. The path is gone! His heart skips a beat, kind of falls down into his stomach, then finally jumps back up into his chest where it belongs, now beating madly. He stands with his back to the roaring flames and looks wildly up and down the line of trees, wondering if he has somehow missed the trail that will (he prays) take him safely back to where he had come from. The fire burns as brightly as ever, and Jacob can clearly see the line where the yard meets the woods. He sees where the trail should be, but isn't.

"Jacob," calls a woman's voice from behind him. A chill runs up his spine and down his arms, causing every hair to stand on end. He feels as if his skin is actually shrinking; pulling tight against the

muscle and bone of his small body. And once again, Jacob finds himself turning against his will. Don't, don't, don't! his mind seems to scream, but his body won't obey. His throat has become as dry as sandpaper and his heart is going like a jackhammer.

It almost stops, though, when he sees who had spoken to him. Standing maybe twenty feet away, directly between him and the raging fire, is a young woman in a black dress. As with the boy and his father, she wears a style of clothes he has only seen in the movies. Her hair is shoulder-length, but as she stands between him and the glare of the burning house, Jacob can't see her face.

A sudden, horrible thought comes unbidden into his head. It's Crazy Mary he thinks, she's here, it's her world; her crazy world and I'm seeing her crazy dreams. I'm here with her and now she'll make me crazy too, then she'll take my crazy mind and leave my body in the woods for the ants and flies and maggots. I'll never go home again!! The fear is like nothing he has experienced before, even when Jim Hanes had held a knife to his throat, breathing his foul breath in Jacob's face while threatening to kill him. It's worse because Jacob now understands that he is in a place where reality doesn't matter; he is in a place dreamed up by madmen, the place where Alice went after passing through the looking glass. And here, Crazy Mary is queen, ruler over all she surveys. His fear grows until he can no longer think or even breathe.

The young woman seems to sense his fear and speaks to him, softly . . . gently.

"Do not be afraid," she says. But though she speaks in soft, gentle tones, Jacob's fear grows deeper still. "Listen and remember." Then her voice begins to change; it becomes urgent, desperate. "Help him! He has suffered for so long! And it wasn't his fault, any of it. Help him. Help us."

She steps forward, raising an arm and pointing a crooked finger at Jacob. As soon as she takes that first step, he can see her face. Only it isn't a face. It is a skull, the color of a lifelong chain-smoker's nicotine-stained teeth; a few strips of dried flesh still clinging listlessly. It leers at him with a skull's perpetual grin and empty eye sockets between hanging locks of dank, dark hair. Its bottom jaw falls, causing the mouth to open horribly wide, as though it means to swallow him whole.

"HELP ME!" it shrieks at him. The voice is no longer soft and gentle or even urgent; it is enraged with death and hatred and madness.

Jacob turns and flees blindly into the woods. He trips over something unseen and falls, but is up again in an instant. He runs faster than he has ever run, and soon it seems to him that he is flying through the woods, dodging trees and branches at an impossible speed. But even as he runs he remembers with dread that his house is gone; all of the houses are gone and there will be no shelter, no one to hear his desperate cries for help that will ultimately become cries of pain and death. There is only an empty field with scattered trees and tall grass, blowing in that cool autumn breeze; dancing a Halloween dance in the dim, red glow of the burning house. But still he runs, he has to, the monstrous woman with a skull instead of a face is surely right behind him, gliding effortlessly through the trees, closing on him with every passing second, no matter how fast he runs. Soon she will have him.

Finally he sees a light ahead, gleaming weakly through the trees and the haze that surrounds him. He runs harder, noticing for the first time that he isn't tired at all. I can make it *he thinks with sudden joy.* I'm really going to make it*!! The light slowly grows closer, and he finally burst from the woods. It is his house!! It is here, right where it's supposed to be!! He jumps the fence effortlessly; he feels weightless, and seems to almost glide through the air. He runs to the back door, barely able to stop before slamming into it. He tries the knob, but it is locked! Of course it is locked! All the doors will be locked; it is, after all, the middle of the night. Doors have to be locked at night in order to keep out thieves and murderers and hideous women with grinning, faceless skulls.*

Jacob runs to the patio door, knowing it will also be locked, but trying it just the same. He isn't disappointed. Finally, not sure what he hopes to accomplish, he runs around to the side of the house and looks into his own bedroom window. Although they'd been closed when he had fallen asleep, the blinds are now raised and he sees into his bedroom. And there he is, lying on the bed, apparently sleeping peacefully without a care in the world.

Jacob begins beating on the window, screaming at himself to open the window, please! just wake up and open the window, please hurry. The Jacob lying in bed stirs a little; his face seems troubled.

And why not? He is, after all, having the worst nightmare of his life. Of course he looks disturbed! But still he won't wake up!! And now Jacob, screaming desperately and shrilly but still unable to wake the sleeping Jacob, realizes with sudden horror that he isn't sure which Jacob is real and which is part of the dream. He is stricken by the terrible idea that if the Jacob he sees through the window, sleeping and dreaming fitfully in the safety of the house; if that Jacob wakes up, then the Jacob through whose eyes he is now seeing is just part of the dream. If the boy he is watching through the window wakes up, Jacob will be stuck in this mad, twisted, upside-down, Crazy-Mary dreamworld forever!

Jacob steps back, away from the window. He can feel the confused, terrified sensation of panic grip his heart. It is the kind of desperate panic that gives birth to madness, and Jacob knows he will indeed go mad if he doesn't get out of this dream, this far away place. It turns out that the decision isn't his to make. As he steps back from the window (remembering even as he does so the skull-faced woman who'd chased him here), he suddenly feels hot, wet breath on the back of his neck and a cold, bony hand gripping his shoulder. With a loud, terrified gasp and violent start, Jacob is finally awake.

He lay motionless in the bed for some time, barely even allowing himself to breathe. He wanted more than anything to reach down and grab his bed-sheet (the ultimate protection from whatever prowled the nighttime), which was rumpled around his waist, and pull it up over his head, but he did not dare move, understanding that remaining motionless was the second most effective protection from said nighttime terrors.

Waking as he did with such a violent jolt back into reality had put Jacob's mind and body on full alert, reporting every sensation he felt with amazing clarity as he desperately tried to assure himself that everything was fine, he was safe, it had in fact just been a dream. The most vivid, intense, and somehow *real* dream he had ever experienced, but only a dream nonetheless. He listened carefully, but heard no sounds other than the soft hum of the air conditioner unit in the hallway.

Eventually, he opened his eyes and let them wander the room without actually moving his head even an inch. The soft glow from a nightlight in the hallway spilled into his room through the open door, illuminating his surroundings enough for him to see that he was the room's only occupant. He was just beginning to relax ever so slightly when his mind reported a sensation of discomfort in the region of his crotch. He shifted his body ever so slightly, and noted with dismay a warm, dampness in his underwear and pajama bottoms. He groaned softly.

Aw, I don't believe this! he thought. *I wet my pants! I actually wet my pants!* For a moment his terror did battle with humiliation; the idea that, at the age of twelve, he'd just wet his bed because of a bad dream. That thought, of all things, was what seemed to finally break the lingering spell of the nightmare. Jacob moved one arm slowly down to his waist to verify his almost unbearably humiliating suspicions. The area wasn't soaked, but was certainly very damp. His arm then crawled slowly upward to his t-shirt. It too was wet. Finally, he checked the hair on his head. Wet. It was with an enormous sense of relief that he realized that he was drenched with sweat. And this was something he could live (or better yet, sleep) with, for although he was now wide awake and had met with moderate success in convincing himself that it *had* been just a dream – *only a dream, a stupid dream; no matter how horrible, it was only a dream, not real* – he had no intention of getting out of bed before the sun was up and shining brightly into his room. The idea of lying in bed soaked with sweat was much more acceptable than lying in bed soaked with urine.

Jacob finally turned his head, just enough to see the clock on his bedside table. 3:05 a.m. glowed in faint, green numerals. He took a deep breath, gathering his nerve, then reached down, grabbed the bed sheet, pulled it up to his head, and rolled onto his side, all in one quick, fluid motion. He then lay still and quiet, staring at the clock and trying in vain not to think about the dream. At some point before sunrise, Jacob finally went back to sleep.

7

Sunday brought what was by far the most hectic morning that Jacob and his family had experienced since arriving in Logtown. Mrs. Hunter had everyone up and out of bed by seven-thirty. Soon they were all sitting around the table eating cereal, plus one leftover muffin each for Jacob and his father. Because the newspaper subscription wouldn't start until Tuesday, Mr. Hunter had nothing to read. He sat quietly, munching his breakfast and staring at the table. Because Jacob's mind was still preoccupied with his dream of the night before (which was not fading or becoming hazy – or ridiculous – in the least, the way his dreams usually did), he too sat quietly, munching *his* breakfast and staring at the table. Only Mrs. Hunter seemed to be in high spirits, eager to get her first real look at the people – those who attended church, anyway – who made up the community of which she was now a member. She had already selected the clothes Jacob would wear and laid them out on his bed. She had done the same for herself and Mr. Hunter (who wasn't bothered in the least that his wife selected what he'd wear; it was one less thing to worry about).

Jacob's mother eventually looked up from the breakfast bar she had been nibbling on and gave her son a long stare. He sensed it and looked up at her. The expression she wore reminded him of the one she usually reserved for those times when he was (justifiably) under suspicion for something or other.

"What!" he finally barked defensively. He was both tired and a little stressed, not only from his lack of sleep, but also his frustration at the lingering fear and confusion he felt from the dream. His voice had an edge on it that surprised him, but his parents didn't seem to notice.

"Nothing, you just look a little tired," his mother replied.

"I *am* tired. I think I'll go back to bed when I finish eating."

"Nice try," she smirked. "Really, though, you look a little pale. Do you feel okay?"

"Yeah, I guess I'm just a little tired from yesterday. It was a long day." All of which was perfectly true, even if it did barely even scrape the surface of the real reason Jacob was pale and tired-looking. For some reason, Jacob felt a great reluctance to tell his parents about the nightmare, and his mind quickly searched for something he could use to change the topic. On a sudden inspiration, Jacob looked over at his father with an eagerness that was only partially feigned.

"By the way, Dad, how 'bout my allowance?"

"Oh, yeah, he's fine. Nothing wrong with *that* boy," smiled Mr. Hunter. He turned toward his son. "I'll settle up with you after church. Good enough?"

Jacob nodded that it was as Mrs. Hunter glanced at the clock for the tenth time since they had sat down at the table.

"Get a move on, guys, we're gonna be late."

Jacob finished his cereal, then tilted up the bowl and sucked out the leftover milk with a loud *sluuurrp*. His mom hated when he did that, and made a dour face.

"Jacob, please don't do that anymore; it's rude and it's gross!"

"Sorry," Jacob replied with an only mildly repressed grin. He knew, of course, that it drove her crazy when he drained the bowl that way. Though he would never admit it, the reaction he got was the main reason he kept doing it.

By way of contrition, Jacob took his bowl to the kitchen sink and rinsed it out without having to be told. Then he went to the hall bathroom and turned on the shower. While the water was warming up, he went to his room, stripped to his underwear, grabbed a fresh pair from his dresser, and was back in the bathroom in under two minutes. Once in the shower, he stood motionless for some time, letting the warm water run over his body as he stared blankly at the wall. It took all of ten seconds for his mind to return to the dream and begin replaying it in terribly vivid detail, leaving Jacob to wonder what in the world it had actually been *about.*

In the past, the few fragmented dreams that Jacob had actually remembered almost always seemed absurd the next morning; even the nightmares seemed to quickly lose their power when the sun rose. Especially when he tried to describe them to someone; then even the worst of them seemed downright ridiculous. Last night's dream still seemed frightening even in broad daylight, even when he'd been sitting at the table with his parents.

And the *quality* of this dream had somehow been . . . well, *different*. It had (and still did) felt more *real*. At the dream's beginning, as he had walked through the woods, he had experienced the usual vague, surreal, and illogical quality of most dreams. But from the moment he'd stepped from the woods and into plain view of the burning house, he had felt that he was watching something that was really happening. And he could remember it, *all* of it, with better clarity even than the previous day's adventure with Jim Hanes. Every sight and every sound. The hopelessly sad boy who had stood next to him as the house burned; the boy's father, who had cursed his own son *to hell* before nearly yanking the terrified boy's arm out of its socket; and finally the young woman in the black dress, who had spoken to him so gently before he had seen that she had no face, only a rotting, leering skull.

"What kind of freaky, bizarre dream *was* that?" he asked aloud.

He remembered that his first impression had been that the mysterious young lady in the dream was Crazy Mary. His father had actually met Mary, and had assured Jacob that she wasn't crazy, but would he really have been able to tell? Maybe her parents drugged her whenever they were expecting company, in order to keep her from running naked through the house, or babbling at the walls, or even attacking the poor, unsuspecting visitors. Jacob suddenly wondered which of the bedrooms in the house had been Mary's. The house had three bedrooms, the master and two others. His parents slept in the master bedroom, of course. Jacob had gotten the bedroom at the end of the hall nearest the den. The last bedroom, between the hall bathroom and his parent's bedroom, had been designated as his father's office/library. A desk, two bookshelves, and at least six unpacked boxes containing a computer, printer, and countless books were all crammed haphazardly into the room, which was last on Mrs. Hunter's list of priorities for arranging and decorating.

It seemed logical to Jacob that the room where he slept was the same room where Mary had slept. After all, it was furthest from the master bedroom, thus farther from her parents – most kids, especially teenagers, would prefer such an arrangement. On the other hand, if she *was* a kook, maybe her folks wanted her as close as possible so that they could keep an eye on her. But Jacob had an uncomfortable feeling that Crazy Mary had once occupied *his* bedroom. There she had lain at night, muttering to herself; drawing bizarre, obscene pictures and writing poems that only she could understand in a secret notebook; frequently staring at the blank walls and seeing things invisible to everyone else; other times staring out the window and gibbering at the moon. And when she slept, she dreamed crazy dreams, just like the one he'd had last night.

There came a brisk knock at the bathroom door, startling Jacob enough to make him jump and gasp aloud. His thoughts were scattered by the quick and harsh return to reality.

"Let's get a move on, Jacob," his mother called for the umpteenth time. "We don't want to be late."

"ALRIGHT!!" he almost screamed back, embarrassed at himself for being so jumpy.

As usual, both Jacob and his father – after being rushed along by Mrs. Hunter – ended up ready to roll fifteen minutes before she was. Mr. Hunter passed the time by flipping the television between Fox News and The Weather Channel. Jacob passed the time by staring blankly at the TV, pondering his new Crazy Mary theory.

He finally looked over at his father.

"Hey Dad, which room was Mary's?"

"Who?" asked Mr. Hunter, his eyes glued to the television.

"You know, the girl that used to live here. Which room was hers?"

Mr. Hunter glanced at his son with a little smile and shrugged.

"I'm not sure. Why do you ask?"

"No reason, I was just wondering."

His father's face grew thoughtful, as if he were trying to recall something. Finally, he nodded, having made up his mind.

"I'm pretty sure her bedroom was the middle room, the one that'll be my office."

"Oh, okay," Jacob answered, trying not to sound too relieved.

"Yeah," Mr. Hunter continued, "your bedroom was the one she used for all that *other* stuff."

Jacob spun his head around so fast that it almost snapped off. He eyed his father suspiciously.

"What are you talking about? What *other stuff*?" he asked.

Mr. Hunter's face remained deadpan as he answered

"You know, all the *crazy* stuff. Satanic rituals, animal sacrifices, howling at the moon, and playing Alice Cooper records. The really *craaazy* stuff." Then he started laughing hysterically.

Jacob glared hot sparks at his father.

"You're weird!!" he muttered, then got up and stormed out of the den. Just as he reached the hallway, he turned and asked, "Alice Cooper . . . who's *she*?" His father laughed even harder.

The drive to church took only ten minutes. It was located in the same part of town as the MacDonald's house; it was, in fact, only a few blocks away. The church sat on the equivalent of two city blocks off of Howard Boulevard, which was the main street running through the "downtown" area. It was large for a place the size of Logtown, and was structured in the same style of most Southern Baptist churches that had been built in the early-to-mid-sixties; four columns in front, red brick, white steeple. Mr. MacDonald had bragged Friday night that the church had been established in the late 1800s and was one of the oldest in that part of the state. According to him, the sanctuary stood on the same site as the original wooden church, which had been torn down and replaced over a three year period around 1962. Besides the large sanctuary, the church also boasted a two-story educational building, which housed the recently renovated offices for the church staff, all of the Sunday school classrooms, and the fellowship hall. A newly constructed gym/ family center sat on what had been several vacant lots across a side street that ran along the west side of the church.

As agreed upon Friday night, the Hunters met the MacDonald family in front of the church office. Jerry once again greeted them warmly, and after a bit of small talk, told Jacob that Melissa would show him to his Sunday school room. Melissa gave him a plastic smile, and off they went. They hadn't taken five steps before Mrs. Hunter called out, "We'll meet you in the foyer before the service, Honey. Have fun!"

Jacob cringed. He glanced nervously at Melissa and tried an eye-roll, hoping to convey a *can you believe the things parents say* look. Melissa appeared indifferent, as though she hadn't heard a thing. In fact, she didn't seem to notice he was even there. He looked away from her with a slight shake of his head, and followed her lead without speaking. They walked into the educational building, turned right, climbed up some stairs, and turned right again, stepping into a long hallway.

"Melissa!" someone called from behind them. They both turned to see three girls approaching. All three looked like they were about Melissa's age and all were attractive. Melissa immediately stepped away from Jacob, and the girls formed a small circle in the middle of the hallway, chatting up a storm. Jacob at first felt a little awkward, and soon embarrassed, standing alone outside the little circle while Melissa ran her mouth and pretended he wasn't even there. He had just decided to sneak away and find his classroom by himself when he realized that one of the girls in the circle was staring at him.

"Who's this?" she asked, smiling a genuine smile at him.

Jacob smiled back, but before he could even open his mouth, Melissa was talking again.

"Oh, he's new. *My* father just hired *his* father. I'm supposed to show him to the sixth-grade classroom so he won't get lost." She turned to Jacob and said, "Let's go." Like he was in kindergarten.

Jacob felt the hot burn of humiliation starting in his ears and creeping quickly down into his cheeks. He was sure both would be glowing bright red soon. He tightened his mouth, glared at Melissa, then silently followed the procession of girls down the hallway. Each room they passed was already half full of kids, and the further down the hallway they went, the older the kids got. The small group finally stopped at a door on the left, almost at the end of the hallway. Jacob glanced in and saw David was already inside, sitting and talking to two or three other boys.

"Here you are, Jacob, sixth grade." Then, in a voice designed to sound like his mother's, "Have fun." She flashed another plastic smile.

David had been right, she *was* a snot, and Jacob didn't care if it was because her family was rich, or because she was attractive and knew it, or because she was now in junior high while he was still a lowly sixth-grader, a *whole year* behind. All he knew was that he felt humiliated and angry, and that he didn't like her at all. Unfortunately, he couldn't think of a single thing to say or do about it. A few choice vulgarities came to mind, but he wouldn't dare utter them in a church (for some reason it didn't seem that big a deal to him and his friends to utter them *outside* of church), especially on his first day in this particular one. So, his face still burning, he simply replied, "Thanks so much." He then flashed a smile almost as plastic as her own, and turned, walking quickly into his classroom.

David had saved a seat for him. He looked up and smiled when he saw Jacob approach, then nodded his head toward the empty chair. As Jacob sat down, David leaned over and whispered, "And here he is, folks, the man who survived hand-to-hand combat with the notorious Jim Hanes. The man . . . the legend. I give you . . . Jacob Hunter." He then mimicked the sound of a crowed roaring in applause.

Jacob couldn't help smiling, but the topic of Jim Hanes, forgotten in the wake of his nightmare, made him immediately and profoundly uncomfortable.

"Have you told anybody?" he asked.

"Not yet, but I can't hold it much longer."

"Well, *try* to hold it, alright? I don't want to get in trouble."

"There's no way, dude." David was still grinning. "Who's gonna tell? Not us. Not Jared or Stevie; Jared's the one who broke the window. And not Hanes. How would he explain pulling a knife on a twelve-year-old kid? Anyway, you gotta let me tell Greg when he gets back tonight, before Jared or Stevie can tell him some made-up, bull-crud version."

Jacob didn't even want to think of what Jared's version would sound like, so he agreed. He wanted to believe what David said about there being little or no chance of getting in trouble, so he dropped it.

David then turned and introduced him to the boys he had been talking to before Jacob's entrance. Each nodded in turn and said their version of *hello, pleased to meet you* – "Hey, what's up?"

Shortly, the class was called to order by a short, portly woman. Jacob studied her absently for a moment and decided that she was probably about the same age as his mother. She was a great deal rounder, however, with short, dark hair and glasses. Her face beamed like a ray of sunshine as she stood behind a small podium at the head of the classroom, reading off a few short announcements about upcoming activities. Then she asked David to introduce his friend, which he did while Jacob stared blankly at his hands.

"This is Jacob. He just moved here from Tunica."

Jacob had a sudden, horrible idea that David would proceed to tell of their adventures of the day before, embellishing the story until he had Jacob Hunter and Jim Hanes in an all-out duel including swords and martial arts: an epic battle between good and evil. But he didn't.

"Well, Jacob, we are very happy to have you with us this morning." The lady beamed brighter than ever. "My name is Mrs. Garner. Behind you are Mr. and Mrs. Kennedy. Mr. Kennedy will be your teacher."

Jacob turned to see the smiling couple. They appeared to be in their late fifties or early sixties. He smiled back, gave a quick, half-hearted wave, then turned back around. After a short prayer, they were dismissed into separate classes, the boys following Mr.

Kennedy into a smaller room across the hall. The girls stayed in the larger classroom.

Sunday school at his new church was pretty much the same as it had been in Tunica. The boys had to take turn reading select Bible passages that applied to the lesson of the day, then Mr. Kennedy would explain to them the meaning of what they had just read and how it applied to them as good young Christians in a world full of evil. He frequently asked questions in an attempt to get the young boys involved, but even with his friendly prompting, they seldom did. Each seemed to be waiting for another boy to speak, so ultimately – with the occasional exception of David – *nobody* spoke.

Because he was new, Jacob wasn't required to read aloud, and soon his mind drifted once again to the dream. Thinking about it helped pass the time some, but not a whole lot. Finally, at a quarter 'til eleven, the dismissal bell rang. After another short prayer, the boys were released. They filed noisily out of the classroom and followed the crowd downstairs and out of the building. As he and David walked along the breezeway leading to the sanctuary, Jacob caught sight of Melissa again. She was standing with a boy, talking and giggling at almost everything he said. The boy was tanned and trim; his short, sandy-blonde hair spiked with the tips bleached, his face firm and handsome (although Jacob thought that his forehead seemed disproportionately large). Jacob decided that he was looking at a budding football star and his cheerleader sweetheart; surely the titles of homecoming king and queen would one day be captioned beside a picture of the two. After a moment, the boy slipped his arm around her waist and they began to walk toward the sanctuary, she gliding and he strutting.

"Who's that guy with Melissa?" Jacob asked quickly.

David looked. "That's Danny Sweeny, her boyfriend. He's in eighth grade, thinks he's king-o'-the-world. He ought to be named Danny Weenie. Why?"

"Just wondering. You were right, she's pretty snotty."

"Did you say 'pretty snotty' or 'pretty and snotty'?" David asked with a grin.

Jacob smiled back. "Both, I guess."

David, still grinning, shook his head. "I wouldn't waste too much time worryin' about her."

The two boys made their way to the foyer in front of the sanctuary and quickly found Jacob's parents, who were chatting with Mr. and Mrs. MacDonald and being introduced to passing members of the congregation. After greeting his parents and shaking Mr. MacDonald's sweaty hand (again), Jacob asked if he could sit with David's family during the service. He was granted permission, under the condition that the boys behave appropriately. Both quickly assured Jacob's parents that they had nothing to worry about. *Of course* they'd behave! Jacob caught one of father's *I'm serious* looks as he turned to follow his friend into the sanctuary.

Mr. and Mrs. Phillips were sitting in their usual spot on their usual pew, with Dillon strategically placed between them. David's older sister was nowhere to be seen. Aside from pictures he'd seen in David's house, Jacob had no real proof that the girl even existed.

As soon as Jacob and David were seated, Dillon slipped into little brother mode. He first whined about wanting to sit by the two older boys, then whined about wanting to go sit with one of his preschool friend's family. Jacob couldn't imagine what it would be like to live with the little booger. Luckily, he only had to endure it for the first fifteen minutes of the service. Almost ten years before, the church had instituted a program called *children's church.* At a designated time of the service, all children between the ages of four and ten would congregate at the front of the sanctuary, then be marched off to the fellowship hall for age-oriented activities and Bible lessons. It had been a very successful program and was one of the few church activities that had the full support of the entire congregation. Most liked it because it taught the kids Bible lessons in a style structured for children; the rest liked it because it kept the whiney, crying brats out of the regular service.

Both Jacob and David pretty much ignored the sermon. Jacob was busy thinking about his dream, and David was busy daydreaming about a movie he'd watched the night before. They did manage to behave themselves, and only flirted with getting a case of the 'church-giggles' once.

Out of nowhere, David slipped Jacob a note he'd scribbled on the inside cover of his Sunday school lesson book. It read *we should invite Jim Hanes to church, he clearly needs to invite Jesus into his heart*. Jacob glanced at David, who had only the faintest traces of a smile on his lips. Jacob immediately broke eye contact, but it was too late. An image popped into his mind of Jim sitting on the front pew, dressed in his dingy t-shirt and torn jeans, and stinking to the heavens. He could see a semi-circle of empty seats around Jim as the other members of the church stared from a safe distance in horror and disgust, some holding their noses. He could see Jim raising his hands to the sky, his hairy armpits clearly visible through the holes in his t-shirt, crying out *Amen* and *Halleluiah* to accentuate every point made by the pastor. The image was just too vivid and too silly, and Jacob began to tremble with suppressed laughter. David began to do the same, and so it started – both boys trying valiantly to keep it under control, but as soon as one stopped, the other would start again. After thirty agonizing seconds, Mr. Phillips reached over and gave David a thump on the arm. He immediately grew still, and Jacob was on his own. He looked up from the floor and began to focus on the pastor and his sermon, which seemed to help, and soon he too got the giggle fit under control. After that, he didn't dare to even glance in David's direction until after the prayer of dismissal.

After Sunday dinner at the Shoney's breakfast bar, Jacob changed clothes and headed out the door. He had agreed to meet David on the path behind his house; then they would go to the Ice House together. David had assured him that Jared spent every Sunday (in fact, he usually visited for the entire weekend, though that had unfortunately not been the case this time) with his father in Gulfport. And if Jared wasn't there, Stevie would likely be absent as well.

When they arrived at the clearing where the trailer sat, both boys were sweating heavily. The sun was hidden behind dark clouds that slowly moved across the sky, and the air was heavy and thick with the promise of an approaching summer thunderstorm. They could hear the deep rumble of thunder in the distance, slowly getting closer. David yanked open the door, then jammed the wedge above the bottom hinge just as he had done before, and they stepped inside. Jacob was again surprised at how cool it was inside. It wasn't cold, and the air always seemed stale, but it rarely got really *hot* in the trailer. David walked to the table at the back of the trailer and began flipping through magazines and comic books until he found something he liked. Jacob slumped down into the chair beneath the pin-up, still wiping the sweat from his face with the sleeves of his t-shirt.

"Hey, man, you want one of these?" David called from the table.

"Nah."

David flopped down into the chair next to the table and began flipping pages while Jacob sat, feet propped in the chair across from him, listening to the sounds of thunder inching closer and trying to decide if he should tell David about the dream. He would have done so in an instant if he didn't believe it was real. But he *did* believe. He remembered every detail *much* too clearly: every sight, smell and sensation. He remembered too clearly the way it had all . . . *felt*. He had *felt* the cold wind on his face, just as he had later *felt* the heat from the fire. He had *smelled* the cool, fresh air of autumn, followed by the strong scent of smoke as the house had burned before him. His heart had ached, had actually *despaired* with the sorrow of that strange boy who had stood beside him, watching the house burn away. And throughout the entirety of this dream, this *experience*, he had felt the strange displacement of being not just in another place, far from home, but in another time, a place in the world that had long since passed and been forgotten.

He felt frustrated at his inability to describe that feeling, and the way it would sound if he tried. And he knew that if, before last night, someone had tried to convince him that something they had witnessed in a dream had really happened, he would have thought that they were just pulling his leg. If they persisted, he'd probably conclude that they were as nutty as Crazy Mary herself. This idea led to another unpleasant thought: had Crazy Mary ever believed *her* dreams were real, and tried to convince others that they were? *Probably so*, he thought dismally. But he still believed, in his heart, and he needed to have it confirmed; he needed to find out, somehow, if it had happened, when it had happened, and how it had happened. He finally decided to try to find out what he could without disclosing his motives.

"Hey, David?"

"Yo."

"Did there used to be a house somewhere back here in the woods?"

"What?"

"A house. In these woods."

David looked up from his magazine wearing a face that said he didn't know and didn't care.

"Not since I've been here. Why?"

"I mean a long time ago. A big house."

"How should I know?"

"I thought maybe you might have heard something or learned something about the town's history in school."

"Nope. Just some State and American history, and that was enough. Why?"

"Just wondering."

David was now staring. "You suddenly just wondered if maybe there was a big house in these woods a long time ago."

"Yeah," Jacob answered, very aware of how stupid it sounded.

"Why the heck would you just suddenly wonder something like that?"

"I dunno, I just did."

David looked at him suspiciously.

"Liar."

Jacob ignored his friend for a moment, knowing that this attempt to discreetly gather information had fallen flat, and wondering why he had thought it wouldn't. Was David really any more likely to know the history of Logtown than Jacob was of knowing the history of Tunica? Probably not. But what other options did he have, especially if he didn't want to discuss the dream? He considered the problem for a little while longer, then wondered aloud "Maybe I could find out something at the library." He turned back to David.

"Where's the library?"

"What's with you, man? Why are you suddenly worried about an old house in the woods? Who cares if there was?"

Jacob was getting irritated. He understood David's curiosity, but he was still reluctant to share the dream and was beginning to fear that there was no way around it.

"Yes, I'm suddenly worried about an old house in the woods! So what? Where's the stinkin' library?"

David was staring at him as if he'd gone mad, but answered calmly "It's in town, a little ways down from the church. Same street, in fact."

"Thank you!"

Both boys were quiet for a few minutes. Thunder rumbled in the air again, much closer. It sounded muted inside the trailer, but Jacob could feel the floor trembling. David stared a few moments longer, then returned to his magazine, shaking his head in bewilderment.

Jacob stared at his dirty shoes for a while, struggling between the urge to tell his dream and fear of the ridicule he'd likely have to endure if he confided his belief that what he had seen in the dream had really happened. He glanced over at his friend, who still appeared to be deep in the magazine propped on his lap. David had proved himself as a friend several times since they'd met. He had stood beside Jacob on two occasions: one that promised to result in a fight, another that promised much worse – he was the only boy that hadn't run off when Jim Hanes had come storming out of his trailer the day before. *Has it only been one day since that happened?* Jacob shook his head and took a deep breath. Yes, he believed David could be trusted, at least enough to not tell anyone about the dream if Jacob asked him not to. Anyway, he felt like he'd go nuts (assuming he wasn't already) if he didn't tell *someone*.

"I dreamed about it last night!" he suddenly blurted out.

David looked up from the magazine again.

"About what, Hanes?"

"No! The house!"

"You dreamed that there was a big house in the woods?"

"No, I dreamed that there *used* to be a *huge* house in the woods, and it burned down. I saw it burning in my dream."

"And, what, you think it really happened?"

"Maybe." The more he talked, the sillier it seemed.

"Hey, I dreamed about Miss March last night." David indicated the pin-up with a tilt of his head. "Maybe that'll really happen." He started grinning.

"I'm serious, man. I've never had a dream like that before. And there was a man, screaming at a boy. I think maybe the boy started the fire." Jacob had decided to leave out the part about the skull-faced woman and stick to the burning house. It wasn't that any part of the dream had seemed less real while it was actually happening, nor did any of it seem less real now. But he was painfully aware of how it would sound, and so he decided to stick with what seemed to be the focal point of the dream, which was also the part of the dream that felt he had witnessed, rather than been a part of. Anyway, talk of believing a house had burned sounded more reasonable than talk of being chased through the woods by a faceless woman.

David was now staring, and his grin had been replaced by a look of skepticism, as if trying to decide whether or not Jacob was just messing with him.

"And so . . . you really believe that it *really happened*?"

Jacob barely heard his friend. He was remembering that boy's sad face, seeing those sad eyes in his mind. Remembering in such detail brought the feelings back immediately; emotions that were still strong enough to actually make him grimace.

"He was so *sad*."

"Who was?" David looked confused again.

"The boy. He said something to me about trying to help. I don't know *what* he was trying to help, but that's what he said. And he was so *sad*. I could *feel* it."

"You could feel his pain?" David asked in his best Bill Clinton voice, which was actually pretty good.

"Knock it off, man! I told you, I'm serious!"

"Alright, alright." He studied Jacob's face for a few seconds. "So you were actually there and talked to the man and boy?"

"No, the boy talked to me. And I don't think that part was real. But then it was like he disappeared, but then I saw him again over by the house, with the man who was screaming at him. I think the man was his dad."

"And you think *that* part was real?"

"Maybe. I don't know. I just want to find out if there was really a house there and, if so, what happened to it."

"You know, I saw a show on the Sci-Fi Channel once about people who have psychic dreams about the future."

Jacob gave him a dirty look, and he put both hands up defensively.

"I'm serious, man, I'm not messin' with you. A lot of people really believe that stuff, there were scientists and everything."

Jacob looked at his friend for a moment, trying to read his face.

"Do *you* believe in that kind of stuff?"

David shrugged. "I don't know, maybe. Do you?"

Jacob shrugged. He thought about it for a minute, and decided he might be dangerously close to freaking out and scaring off the only friend he had in Logtown.

"Well, I don't think I'm psychic or anything; it was just a weird dream. I usually don't even remember my dreams."

"I always remember mine," said David, looking up sadly at Miss March and letting out an exaggerated sigh.

They both laughed, but the sound was lost in an enormous crash of thunder, which shook the entire trailer. The wind had begun to gust outside while the boys were talking. Jacob could see that the door of the trailer was being buffeted as the wind picked up, and was straining hard against the wedge David had jammed in it when they first arrived. And he suddenly noticed with some alarm that there was no handle or latch on the smooth inside surface of the door. If it were blown shut, they wouldn't be able to get out. He looked back at David, who was also watching as the wind pushed against the door and the side of the trailer. Leaves, pine needles and dust began to sail through the air.

"Hey man, are we safe in here? If that door shuts, we'll be stuck, won't we?"

David reached under the table, then produced a piece of rope from a box that Jacob had not noticed before. It was about eight feet long, and had small loops tied into each end.

"No worries, mate." He answered in his best Australian accent. His Bill Clinton was better, and he must have known it because his voice quickly returned to normal. "We keep this rope in our box 'o goodies for just such an emergency as this! Here, give me a hand."

He stepped past Jacob and out into the wind. Jacob followed quickly, mortified at the idea of being trapped in the trailer by himself. The wind quickly tousled his hair as it whipped by in cool blasts. He knew that the rain would start at any moment.

"Watch this," cried David. Standing on his toes, he put one loop over the top corner of the door. Jacob saw that some of the steel had been beaten inward, maybe with a hammer, so that it was not only bent, but almost formed a crude hook. David pulled the rope under the hooked corner of the door, then gave it a good tug.

"Okay, hold the rope right here," David motioned Jacob to where he was holding it. "Keep it tight."

Jacob grabbed the rope where David had shown him and held tight while David took the other end of the rope and slid the loop over a large stake set in the ground a few feet behind the door, next to the side of the trailer.

"Alright, you can let go!"

"What about our bikes?" Jacob asked.

"We can bring them inside with us; put 'em against the wall. There's plenty of room."

They grabbed the bikes just as the rain began to fall. It was only a sprinkle at first, but the drops were huge. One splattered against the side of Jacob's face, and it actually stung a little, as if he'd been slapped by a small, liquid hand. Just as they got the bikes inside the trailer, the sprinkle became a downpour. It beat loudly against the roof and side of the trailer as they slid the chairs to one side and parked the bikes against the wall. Then each boy grabbed a chair and sat by the door, looking out into the storm. A fine mist blew into the trailer from time to time, whenever the wind would gust, and it felt good on their warm faces. But those gusts were also trying hard to slam the trailer door shut. Jacob watched as the door strained against the rope and wedge.

"You sure that'll hold?" he asked loudly, trying to make himself heard over pounding of the rain on the trailer.

"Aw, yeah, I've been out here in worse storms than this. Me and Greg were out here once when a tornado hit a few miles down the road; the other side of the interstate."

Jacob looked at him doubtfully, but David kept talking and looking out into the blowing rain.

"We used to use the rope to keep the door open all the time, but it was a hassle, especially trying to rig it up when you came out here by yourself. So now, unless the wind is blowing really hard, we just give the door a wedgie."

Jacob was about to ask how old (meaning how strong) the rope was when there was a blinding flash of white, followed almost instantly by a deafening crash of thunder that shook the trailer violently.

Both boys jumped up and hollered in unison. They looked at each other, eyes bugging out of their heads, then laughed nervously.

"Geez," said Jacob, "the hair on my arm is standing straight up!!"

David informed him that more than just his own hair standing straight up.

"Why do you think I want to know something like that?" Jacob asked. "Just stay on your side of the trailer, okay?"

They were both still too shaken to laugh much, and then, as if by unspoken agreement, both boys quickly moved their chairs a little further back from the doorway before sitting back down. They watched the rain quietly for a few more minutes before Jacob finally spoke.

"So, do you have a library card?"

"'Fraid so. I had to get one last year for a school report. I've used it two whole times."

"Are you allowed to ride your bike into town?" Riding "into town" would mean almost two miles down the highway, something Jacob knew his own mother would frown upon.

"Nope, but I've done it a few times, anyway. Greg lives in town, on the road that runs behind the church."

"So, what are you doing tomorrow?"

"I dunno, but I won't be going to the library, and neither will you."

"Why not?"

"Library's closed on Mondays. I guess 'cause they're open Saturday, and they want a two-day weekend, just like everyone else."

"How about Tuesday?"

"Sure, but I don't want to spend the whole day there."

"We won't," Jacob assured him. "I just wanna see what I can find out. It shouldn't take too long."

"Is *your* mom gonna let *you* ride into town?" David asked.

"What she don't know won't hurt her."

David smiled and nodded. The Gospel According to Boys. They both looked outside again. The rain was beginning to slack off, and each time the thunder rolled, it sounded a little further away.

David looked back over at Jacob.

"We couldn't go tomorrow, anyway. I just remembered—Mom is taking me and Dillon shopping. Back-to-school clothes and stuff."

"Back-to-school for Dillon?"

"He starts pre-school this year. And you know, I'm really looking forward to spending tomorrow with the little pimple. I cherish those moments spent building a bond with my brother. It helps me to better appreciate what a crusty little nose hair he really is." Jacob snickered, but David's face was, as usual, completely serious. He had to be the most eloquent smart-aleck that Jacob had ever known.

"Anyway, it shouldn't take all day. What are *you* doing tomorrow?"

"I'll probably have to help my Mom around the house or something like that in the morning. Dad starts work tomorrow, so I'm sure she'll need my help with something. There's still a bunch of stuff we haven't unpacked yet."

"How 'bout if I give you a call when I get back home?"

"Cool," Jacob answered. He stared out into the diminishing rain for a few moments before speaking again.

"Do you think Jared will be out here tomorrow?" He didn't want to sound scared in front of David, but he couldn't keep the worry out of his voice.

"Probably so. He spends most of his time out here, in the Ice House or riding on the race-course."

"Do you think he'll want to fight me?"

David looked at his friend, studying his face as if to size him up.

"I don't know. But I'll back you up if he tries to. That was a sorry thing he did." David turned away, shaking his head. "I *still* can't believe he did that." There was a pause, as if David was uncomfortable asking his next question. "Are you that worried about him?" Meaning *Are you afraid?*

Jacob shrugged, but didn't speak. He *was* afraid of Jared, but wasn't sure why. Jacob, like most boys, got into at least a couple of shoving matches every year, but his only real fight had been almost two years before, when he was in fourth grade, and he remembered it well. It had been a Saturday afternoon, a few weeks before Thanksgiving, and he was stuck out in the front yard, raking leaves and pine straw. Two boys, Cliff and Chris, had come riding by on their bikes. Jacob and Cliff had never gotten along, but until that very moment, he had considered Chris a friend. This would be his first lesson on just how finicky school-aged friendships could be.

Cliff had had a serious weight problem all his short life, and by first grade he had decided, either consciously or unconsciously, to take some initiative by dealing out insults to others (usually those who were smaller, which included most of his classmates) before they could insult him, hopefully striking fear into their little hearts and keeping fat jokes to a minimum. Most of his classmates, Jacob included, loathed the boy and cursed him (behind his back) for his meanness more than fatness. It never occurred to them that maybe, when Cliff was alone in bed at night with no one else to draw attention to, he too cursed his fatness, and his loneliness, and sometimes cried himself to sleep.

Jacob had glanced up from his work when he heard the two boys approaching. He was surprised enough at seeing Chris's companion that he failed to wave; he just stood, staring uncertainly. The two boys stopped when they were level with Jacob. Then Cliff raised his arm, pointing a fat little finger at Jacob with a fat little grin on his face.

"Check out that little fag-o-la, will you? Didja ever see such a little homo?"

Chris laughed, and Jacob stood, his ears burning, without saying a word. Insults from Cliff had not come as a surprise, but the laughter from someone he thought of as a friend had hurt. Cliff, still grinning and pointing, began to taunt Jacob again, this time employing the ever-proven technique of "baby-talk", almost singing the words nursery-rhyme style.

"Uh-ooohhh, I tink I hurt his feelin's, I tink he's gonna cwy. I tink maybe he's gonna wet his widdle briiiit-ches. Well, I hope you don't want to kiss and make-up with me. Maybe you can find another fag to make you feel better."

Cliff's fleshy lips grinned even bigger, his hateful little eyes nearly disappearing into his fat face. Chris was laughing again, and Jacob's hurt was quickly replaced by anger, more at Chris's betrayal than Cliff's insults.

"Bug off, chunky. Nobody around here wants to look at your big ol' butt!"

Cliff seemed genuinely surprised that someone smaller than himself (the only type he picked on) had finally hurled an insult right back at him. His mouth formed an almost perfect circle in his fat face. Jacob laughed at the sight.

"Looks like *you're* the one who's gonna cry," he jeered. "Anyway, please take that chunkyrump somewhere else, you're blocking the road!"

Cliff was off his bike now, stalking into the yard, while Chris, no longer smiling, watched from the street with a look of abstract interest. Jacob was getting nervous now, but figured he could outrun Cliff if necessary.

"I thought you *liked* to look at my rump, you queer!! I thought you dreamed of getting your hands on it!!"

"No, but I've dreamed of *kicking* it a few times!!"

Cliff was now standing right in Jacob's face.

"TRY IT, YOU FAGGOT!!" he almost screamed. His voice sounded shrill, exaggerating his already thick Mississippi drawl so that the word became FAY-GIT. And suddenly he reached out with both hands and pushed Jacob.

Jacob had been expecting it and had tried to brace himself, but he still had to step back to keep from falling down. Then he pushed back as hard as he could, afraid it would be about as effective as pushing against a wall. To his surprise, Cliff fell. He had tried to brace his short, stocky legs, but Jacob had pushed against his shoulders, not his chest, and the weight that had plagued him all of his life was once again his enemy. He fell flat on his back. Jacob was so surprised at this turn of events that he just stood there, staring at Cliff and trying to decide if he should laugh, hurl another insult at the boy, or just turn and scoot back into the safety of his house. He looked up to make sure Chris wasn't going to jump in, but the other boy seemed contented to just sit on his bike and watch.

Jacob's attention returned to Cliff, who had rolled over and was crawling to his feet. He hoped the little skirmish was over now that Cliff saw he wasn't backing down. No such luck. As soon as he was back on his feet, Cliff charged with speed Jacob hadn't thought possible of someone burdened by so much weight. He tried to side-step, but Cliff's left shoulder caught him squarely in the stomach, and Jacob heard himself go *oof* as the air was forced from his lungs. Both boys went down, and Cliff was on top. Jacob tried to catch his breath without panicking in front of the enemy, but the enemy was now sitting astride Jacob, his weight bearing down and making it impossible to breathe, swinging his fists clumsily. Despite their relative positions, Jacob deflected the punches easily, and he finally got in a good hit himself, striking Cliff hard on the left corner of his mouth. It was immediately answered by Cliff, who landed a quick pop to Jacob's right cheek, just under the eye. It began to throb instantly.

"Hey, what are you boys doing? Get off of him!!"

Jacob turned and saw his father jogging out of the carport. Cliff was up in an instant, again surprising Jacob with his speed. He jumped on his bike, and both he and Chris were quickly lost from view.

Jacob managed to keep his father from calling the parents of either boy, assuring him that it hadn't been that big a deal, and neither boy had been hurt. He didn't have to say that getting the other boys in trouble wouldn't help at all; if anything, it might make things worse. His mother wanted to call anyway, but finally relented to his father, who Jacob suspected was actually proud of his son for standing up to the bigger boy, though he never came right out and said so. The following Monday, everyone at school knew about the fight, and although Cliff told everyone that Jacob had to have his daddy rescue him, he didn't mess with Jacob much anymore.

Jacob didn't much care for fighting, but like his father, he'd been proud that he had stood up to Cliff. And technically, Cliff *had* been bigger (or at least weighed more) than Jared. But it wasn't Jared's size that worried Jacob. It was his eyes – the look that he always seemed to have in his eyes. That look really *did* scare Jacob, it had from the moment he'd first met Jared. If people's eyes really *are* windows to their souls, then there was something bad wrong with that boy's soul.

Jacob also felt stupid for letting Jared set him up at Jim Hanes's trailer the day before; he knew that he should have suspected something. Cliff had been a stereotypical bully who picked on those he thought weaker than himself. But when Jacob looked into Jared's eyes, he saw something more than just bitterness. He saw a malicious and intense mind that would cause hurt to anyone by whom he felt threatened. He couldn't imagine why Jared might feel threatened by him, but he knew the boy hadn't liked him from the moment they met. His "Joe Mama" joke had solidified that dislike into hate, and Jacob assumed that was because Jared's father had abandoned both him and his mother. Jacob absently wondered why Jared bothered to visit his father, even one day a week. How could he still care about a man who had simply left his own family, whatever the reason may be? That was a question Jared had asked himself many times, and he could answer it no better than Jacob.

"Yo, Jacob, you still with me?"

Jacob turned to his friend and made a face. "Can't you see I'm meditating?"

"Yeah, that's what I thought. You looked even dumber than usual."

Jacob quit smiling.

"I don't know, I guess I'm a *little* bit worried. Something's wrong with that guy, and he's hated me from the first time he saw me."

"He's always been a little crazy, you know, but he never did anything like what he did yesterday." David looked a little sad. "Like I told you before, I think he acts like he does 'cause his dad ran off, and then his brother left to live with his dad. Jared absolutely *worships* Mike. But he never talks about it, any of it." He looked back at Jacob. "I dunno, maybe you better not come out here by yourself until we can talk to him."

"Yeah." Jacob didn't *want* to talk to Jared, in fact, he'd be happy if he never even *saw* the boy ever again. But he felt a little better knowing David didn't seem to be afraid. He looked outside and saw that the rain had stopped, but the sun was still hidden behind the clouds. He turned back to David.

"You wanna go to my house? We can play video games or throw the football or whatever."

"Sure." David jumped up from his chair. "But I can't stay too long. We got church tonight. Here, help me with the door real quick."

They quickly worked the rope loose, and David stuck it back in the box under the table. Then they rolled their bikes back out the door, and David pulled the wedge loose, allowing the door to swing closed by itself.

They rode back up the trails slowly, trying to avoid slinging mud, but by the time they reached Jacob's house, both boys had little splatters all over the backs of their shirts and legs. Mrs. Hunter refused to let them into the house in that condition. Instead, she sent them around to the back yard, where she brought them cold drinks and ice cream. They ate on the patio, then horsed around with the football for a while, throwing it back and forth. Eventually, Jacob's father came out, and the boys took turns running patterns and trying to block passes while Mr. Hunter played quarterback. All three of them had a blast, and for the first time all day, Jacob forgot completely about Mr. Hanes, Jared, and the dream.

David finally left around four o'clock, explaining that he had to get home in time to get cleaned up for the evening church service. He thanked Mr. Hunter for throwing the ball with them, told Jacob he'd call him sometime tomorrow afternoon, then hopped on his bike and disappeared down the street. Jacob and his father continued to throw the ball for a few more minutes until his mom stepped out with drink refills. Then he and both parents sat on the patio furniture, sipping drinks as his mother discussed plans for planting flowers and shrubbery around the patio and throughout the backyard. Apparently, Crazy Mary's folks hadn't planted enough greenery to satisfy Mrs. Hunter. Eventually, she looked over at Jacob and smiled.

"You and David are getting to be pretty good friends, I see."

Jacob looked at her and waited to see if she was going to follow her comment with any critical remarks. He didn't really expect her to, and she didn't. In Tunica, both his parents seemed to really like Kevin, and inviting him to do things with Jacob was often their idea. He hoped it would be the same with David.

"Yeah, he's pretty cool. Why? Do you guys like him okay?"

"He seems like a nice young man," his mother answered.

"Yeah, he's kind of charming," his father added, "in a vaguely Eddie Haskell-ish way."

Both his mother and father had a good laugh at that, and Jacob, as usual, had no idea what they were laughing at. So he rolled his eyes, shook his head, and finished off his drink.

When they finally decided to go back inside, Jacob was forced to strip to his underwear in the garage so as not to get the new house dirty. He did so quickly, hiding behind the car and praying that no one would see him. He then gathered his mud-splattered clothes and dashed into the house, straight to the bathroom. He took a quick bath, then spent the rest of the afternoon playing video games until suppertime. The Hunters had always had trouble making it to Sunday evening services at church, and tonight their excuse was that they were just too worn out from unpacking and decorating. Jacob didn't mind. He watched TV in his room until ten o'clock, when his father came in and announced that it was bedtime.

Once Jacob had brushed his teeth and hopped into the sack, Mr. Hunter came into the bedroom and informed him that he would be expected to help his mother around the house the following day. Jacob was tempted to groan, but instead simply offered the ever-popular *yes, sir.* His father seemed satisfied, told him goodnight, and turned out the light. As soon as the door was closed, Jacob slipped out of bed, turned on the closet light, and opened the closet door a few inches. He wasn't quite over the dream just yet. It would be a long time before he was over it. And even then, it would never be forgotten.

8

There were no dreams that night about burning houses, grief-stricken boys, or skull-faced women chasing him through the woods. If Jacob dreamed at all, he didn't remember it the next morning. He was awake by seven-thirty, and the first thing he noticed was that his closet light was no longer on. He supposed that one of his parents had noticed it at some point after he was asleep and turned it off, probably when they were going to bed. He was glad that he had fallen asleep before it was turned off for two reasons.

The first was that he didn't want to have to explain to either one of his parents why their son, who was only one year away from being a teenager, was sleeping with the closet light on. The second (and more significant) reason was that he would have lain in bed, wide awake, until he was sure that they were asleep, then gotten out of bed and turned it back on. He felt pretty sure that there was no way he could have fallen asleep without that extra light illuminating the dark corners of his room. The images of his dream were still much too fresh in his mind for him to be able to sleep in a room filled with dark shadows that might be concealing skull-faced women, Crazy Mary, or any other number of dream-induced creatures whose existence seemed laughable in broad daylight, but perfectly reasonable in the darkness of night. After all, nighttime was their time, and their mystery and power didn't die at sunrise.

Like vampires, they only *slept* during the day, gathering strength until the sun went down again. Then they could once again roam the earth unfettered, always crawling in the shadows; just behind the veil that separates their world from reality, a veil that becomes dangerously thin at night.

Like most people, Jacob could forget that world during the day, but the dream from the night before had plunged him deeper than ever before into that world; he felt as though he had passed *through* the veil and had seen what lived on the other side. It was a world where anything imagined could instantly be brought to life, and once endowed with life, it could not be controlled. And now, as he lay in bed thinking about it, with the morning sun filling his room with daylight (which was somehow the only kind of light that felt *real),* he believed as firmly as ever that what he had witnessed really had happened. All of it. Somewhere beyond those woods bordering his backyard, a house had once stood. It had been home to the young boy and his terrifying father. And it had burned. It had happened long ago, and had happened in *this* world, on *this* side of the veil; Jacob had simply been watching a re-play – his own private screening of some great moment in history.

The other part, when the boy and the skull-faced woman had spoken to him, also had really happened. But *that* part had happened in that strange world on the other side of the veil, the world he'd had to cross over into in order to watch the house burn. He *had* walked in that world, breathed that real and unreal air filled with real and unreal smells. And when that that woman, who had surely been death, had chased him through the woods and back to his house, he had seen through that dangerously thin veil from the inside. He had seen himself, sleeping and dreaming, and had somehow pushed through back into his world just as death had reached out and touched him.

Jacob shivered and suddenly felt very alone, despite the fact that he could hear both of his parents talking and banging around in the kitchen. He decided it was definitely time for some company, so he hopped out of bed and strolled quickly down the hall, through the den, and into the kitchen. He found his father sitting at the table, coffee cup in hand. Mr. Hunter looked bright and chipper, ready for his first day at work. He was dressed much more casually than he had dressed for his old job: a short-sleeved polo and khakis versus a button-down, tie and jacket. Jacob's mother was also armed with the first coffee of the day, but she did not seem quite as chipper. She wore a t-shirt and shorts. Jacob's father smiled at him as he walked into the kitchen.

"Mornin', ace. How ya feelin' today?" Mr. Hunter sounded as chipper as he looked.

"All right, I guess."

Jacob's mother looked over from where she stood by the refrigerator and smiled.

"Morning, honey. Do you want some waffles?" she asked.

"Sure."

She opened the freezer and got out two waffles for her son, then grabbed a bagel out of the refrigerator for herself. All three items went into a small toaster-oven sitting on the counter beside the microwave, and she set the timer. Then she picked up her cup of coffee and sat down beside him at the table.

Mr. Hunter glanced at a clock that had been hung the day before next to the door leading from the kitchen into the garage.

"Okay, I've got to run." He looked at Jacob. "Remember what I told you last night about helping your mother today."

"Yeah, yeah, yeah," Jacob muttered.

"Yeah, yeah, yeah – I meant it." He leaned over and gave his wife a quick peck on the cheek. "Y'all have a good day. I should be home by five-thirty or so." He grabbed a briefcase that contained nothing but a few pens and pencils, two yellow legal pads, and a micro-cassette recorder, then dashed out the door.

Monday turned out to be the most boring day that Jacob had experienced since arriving in Logtown. After breakfast, he got dressed and turned on the TV, but was only allowed thirty minutes of viewing before his mother put him to work. Her project for the day was the room that was to become Mr. Hunter's office/library.

Together, they unpacked the boxes containing the computer and printer. All of the necessary cables and wires had been jammed into a box with the printer, and once it was all unpacked, Mrs. Hunter just sat back and stared at it with a dazed, lost look in her eyes. Like many parents from their generation, the Hunters delegated most jobs involving the assembly and/or connection of VCRs, stereos, televisions, telephones and computers to their children. After all, Jacob, like most kids his age, had grown up with computers and video games; to him, they had always been a part of life. He took pride in the fact that, with what he considered only a limited knowledge (he wasn't, after all, a computer *dork*), he easily figured out problems that stumped both of his parents. He sometimes ridiculed his parents for their lack of understanding of any but the most basic of computer programs, but eagerly assisted in everything from installing and explaining new programs to advising them on upgrading their system (something that was not done nearly enough, at least in Jacob's opinion).

Truth be told, he *enjoyed* coming to his parent's rescue from time to time. Although it felt more like play than work to him, his parents seemed to think he was a genius after the completion of even the most rudimentary of tasks. It pleased him to hear the praises they heaped upon him after each success, but he was also amused by it. He was very aware of the fact that, compared to many of those computer geeks he had known in school, he really wasn't *that* terribly proficient; like most kids his age, he simply had a good working knowledge of the basics.

Jacob quickly went to work assembling the computer on his father's desk while his mother began unloading books and accessories from the remaining boxes. By the time she finished loading the bookshelf and setting up a lamp and telephone on a small table next to the bookshelf, he had the computer up and running. As usual, she professed amazement and admiration for his skills, but she was *not* impressed enough to give him the rest of the day off, even though he said "please" when he asked.

The next hour was spent unpacking yet more boxes, some filled with framed pictures, others filled with various knick-knacks. Mrs. Hunter arranged then rearranged these items on the desk and small table while Jacob watched and complained about how long it was taking.

The worst task by far was the hanging of pictures on the wall. Jacob's job was to hold the pictures in place, ducking his head down so as to not block his mother's view (he looked a little like a young Atlas, holding up a square, flat Earth) while she stood back and said things like "a little to the left" or "a little higher" or "wait, perfect, hold it RIGHT THERE!!" Then she would run up to mark the spot while he struggled, arms trembling, to keep the picture perfectly still. If any part of it moved even a fraction of an inch, she would insist on starting all over again. Mercifully, she decided that three pictures hanging in the office were enough; and that the room was pretty much finished. Then the boxes were broken down, the packing paper stuffed into trash bags, and it was all hauled to the garage, where it would stay until garbage day. By the time all of this was done, it was time for lunch.

After lunch, Mrs. Hunter released Jacob from work for the rest of the day, but asked him to stay around the house just in case she needed any more help. That was fine with him because he had nowhere to go anyway. He wasn't about to venture out to the Ice House unaccompanied by David. Chances were that Jared would be there, along with Stevie. As far as Jacob was concerned, he could go the rest of his life without ever seeing either of those boys again.

And yet, for reasons he couldn't explain, he wasn't quite ready to relinquish whatever rights he may have to the clubhouse.

Jacob ended up playing video games for almost two hours straight, watching TV for another hour and a half, then just kind of goofing around in the back yard by himself, all the while waiting for David to call and announce that he had finished bonding with his little brother and was ready to do something with someone his own age so that he could recover from the experience. The call didn't occur until around four forty-five, and by then it was too late for them to do anything. David said that he had tried to persuade his mom to let Jacob come over for supper, but she answered that she was too worn out from a day spent at the mall with her two boys to deal with any company; but maybe he could come over later in the week. They made plans for getting to and from the library undetected the following day, and after a little small talk, said goodbye.

Mr. Hunter was home by five-fifteen. He looked almost as chipper as he had when he had walked out the door earlier that morning, which surprised neither Jacob nor his mother. In Tunica, he had had to leave for work no later than six forty-five every morning in order to allow for Memphis traffic and parking, and seldom got back home before six-thirty each evening. That equaled almost twelve hours every day, plus he was required to work at least two weekends each month. Mr. MacDonald had assured Jacob's father that it would be unusual if he had to work more than four weekends in an entire year. *The Logtown News* was, after all, a small newspaper for a small town. The loaded Sunday edition wasn't as large as a regular edition of the newspaper Mr. Hunter had worked for in Memphis, and a regular edition of *The Logtown News* was only a little bigger than the Wal-Mart advertisement insert in the Sunday edition of that Memphis paper. Furthermore, the newspaper printed no editions on Mondays and Saturdays, apparently to make up for having such a large Sunday edition (which drained the little city dry of any news). Besides, in a place as small as Logtown one was just as likely to pick up any scoop in barber shops and diners as in the local paper.

Upon his arrival home, Mr. Hunter was given a tour of his newly organized office. He was duly impressed by the transformation of what had been, just that morning, nothing more than a room cluttered with boxes and furniture. It was now fully functional, and he commented more than once that he would be putting it to good use very soon.

Mr. Hunter quickly changed clothes and asked Jacob if he wanted to go outside and toss around the football some. Having been stuck in front of the TV for most of the afternoon, Jacob eagerly agreed. Unfortunately, after spending the day inside an air-conditioned office, Mr. Hunter only lasted thirty minutes in the heat. By then it was almost time for supper anyway.

After supper, Jacob and his father sat in front of the television watching one of the new James Bond movies on television (Mr. Hunter shaking his head from time to time, saying things like *gimme a break* while Jacob sat in rapt attention, occasionally gushing forth exclamations like *whoa, did you* see *that*?), while his mother tinkered around with small decorations throughout the house. When the movie was over, it was bath time then bedtime for Jacob.

After his parents said goodnight and closed his bedroom door, Jacob waited for a full five minutes, watching the glowing numerals of his bedside clock and listening for his parents. Then he quietly slipped from the bed, tiptoed to the closet, turned on the light, and opened the door a few inches. He then slipped back into bed without a sound, and tried to pull his mind away from the persistent memory of that dream (a task he found almost impossible while lying alone in bed, terribly aware of the darkness both outside and inside the house; darkness held at bay only by the narrow beam of light slipping through the small opening in his closet door) by planning his clandestine trip to the library tomorrow.

Barely ten minutes had passed before his bedroom door was opened and his father peeked in. Jacob was startled out of his thoughts by the sudden intrusion. He jumped and looked over at the door, then immediately wished he had pretended to be asleep. His father pushed opened the door a little further, and stepped into the room.

"What's goin' on, buddy? What's with the closet light?"

Jacob was embarrassed, but saw no way out.

"No big deal, I just had a bad dream the other night."

Mr. Hunter looked at his son carefully for a few moments, then asked, "Was it about that girl you asked me about the other day, the one who used to live here?"

"Yeah," Jacob answered immediately, surprising himself. He felt strangely reluctant to tell either parent about what he had really dreamed, but he wasn't sure if it was because he believed in the reality of the dream, or some other reason that he didn't understand – something about the fact that they were grown-ups. Anyway, a lie naming Crazy Mary as the subject of a nightmare seemed as plausible as any other, considering that he *had* asked his father about her a couple of times. Jacob then prepared himself for the inevitable; expecting to hear his father explain once again that the girl hadn't been crazy and besides, Jacob was getting too old to be sleeping with the lights on. Instead, Mr. Hunter just smiled gently at his son.

"Alright, we'll leave the lights on for a night or two. But let's not make a habit out of it, okay?"

"Okay. Thanks, Dad."

Mr. Hunter smiled again.

"See you in the morning, buddy." He stepped back out of the room, pulling the door closed behind him.

Jacob rolled over onto his back and stared up at the spinning ceiling fan, feeling both relieved and a little embarrassed. More than anything, he was thankful that his father had let him keep the light on without making a big deal about it. Sometimes, parents really *were* alright.

It didn't take long, however, for Jacob's thoughts to quickly return to his plans to visit the library the following day. He wondered if he would be able to find any books about the history of Logtown, and if he did, would they even contain any pictures of buildings and houses? His hope was that the house might at least be mentioned, because (1) it had to have been, by far, the largest and nicest house in the area and (2) it had burned to the ground. He closed his eyes and tried to picture how the house had looked before it had been completely engulfed in flames. Jacob suddenly realized he had only seen the back of the house in his dream, and may not even be able to recognize a picture of the front of the house. He quickly decided that was unlikely, however, considering how large and grand the house had been. How many houses like that could there have been in a town this small? Even the MacDonald's house, as nice and large as it was, didn't compare to the one he'd seen in his dream. And again, he would be working with the knowledge that it had apparently burned to the ground. He figured that he had enough information to help him decide if he had found the house he was looking for.

Jacob slowly drifted toward sleep as his mind filled with the image of the burning house. He had just slipped into that odd and almost magical state of mind – that place where one is not quite asleep, but standing at sleep's doorway and about to take the last step, the place where one's thoughts begin to take the form of images, sights, and sounds – when he had a very strange vision.

He was standing, just as he had in the dream, by the edge of the woods. The sight of the house burning before him was quite vivid, but lacked the feeling of reality he had experienced in the dream: there were no sounds and no smells. Once again, he sensed the presence of the strange, sad boy standing to his left. And, just as in the dream, he felt compelled, against his will, to look at the boy. Jacob turned.

Standing beside him, watching as the house burned to the ground, was the boy. But this time, he wasn't alone. Standing behind him, his arms wrapped protectively around the boy's shoulders, was Mr. Jim Hanes.

9

As they had agreed on the telephone the night before, Jacob and David met at nine o'clock in front of the vacant lot used to get to the trails behind the subdivision. Both boys had simply told their respective mothers that they were going bike riding on the trails. They figured making up some intricate story about how they were going to spend their morning would sound suspicious, so they kept it simple. This was a better idea than they knew: most boys between pre-adolescence and twenty-one have little more than short answers and sarcastic comments for their mothers (unless, of course, they want or need something). Jacob had nearly panicked when, upon informing her of his plans for the morning, his mother told him she would probably need his help at some point in the day, but he easily negotiated an agreement designating some work time after lunch.

"Are we gonna take the trails to the highway?" Jacob asked. He had decided the night before that he wanted to avoid any possibility of meeting Jared.

David considered for a moment, maybe thinking the same thing.

"Uh-uh," he finally answered. "That would add over a mile to the trip. Let's just stick to the roads."

The main street running through *The Pines* subdivision was shaped like a large horseshoe, with both ends adjoining Old Highway

43, which ran from the interstate into the Logtown city limits. The boys rode along the street leading to the subdivision entrance closest to town. They soon passed between two large, brick walls bordered with flowers and shrubs and emblazoned with *The Pines* in bold, flowing script. Then they quickly crossed the highway and turned left, toward town. There was a smooth path about ten feet off to the side of the road made by years of both children and adults walking and riding into town, sometimes on bicycles, sometimes on motorcycles or four-wheelers. It was nearly three feet wide, and the boys stuck to it, riding side by side at an easy pace, sometimes veering one way or the other to avoid the trash occasionally thrown out by some slob that apparently couldn't wait until a garbage can was handy.

About three times a year, the county road department would bring out tractors to mow the overgrown grass alongside the highways and country roads in order to make everything look neat and tidy. For some reason, they never bothered picking up the litter first, and the result was neatly mowed grass filled with chopped up garbage, which looked like oversized confetti that everyone driving along the roads would have to look at until the grass had grown out of control again. Then the tractors would be brought back out. The overall result was that the areas alongside the roads only looked nice for about two weeks at a time, after the grass had grown enough to cover the trash but before it had grown enough to need mowing again.

After five minutes of riding, both boys were once again drenched in sweat. David looked over at Jacob and smiled.

"I talked to Greg last night. Told him about what happened Saturday."

"What'd he say?"

"He thought I was making it up at first. I had to swear on everything but the Bible before he'd believe me. He was totally impressed with your adventure with Hanes; I think you may be his new hero."

Jacob couldn't help grinning. As horribly afraid as he had been at the time, the terror of the incident was beginning to fade some with the passage of time. But it hadn't faded *too* much: if he allowed himself to, he could all too easily recall the terror; he could still feel the knife at his throat and smell the awful odor of Jim Hanes in his nostrils.

"He was blown away by what Jared did," David continued, "but I don't think he ever really liked Jared that much, anyway. I think he's always been kind of afraid of him."

"Well, that's a surprise," Jacob replied. "Jared's only the biggest jerk I've ever met in my *life*!"

"Yeah, I'm starting to think maybe you're right." David shook his head as if he *still* couldn't believe what Jared had done. Jacob looked over and shook his own head. He didn't understand why it was so hard for David to believe what had seemed obvious to Jacob almost from the moment he laid eyes on Jared.

"So," David said, changing the subject as deftly and effortlessly as ever, "What exactly do you think we're gonna find at the library?"

"I think we should look for anything on the history of Logtown, mainly houses, people, and anything about any big . . . I don't know . . . tragedies, I guess, that might have happened."

David looked over with that faint, ever present sarcastic expression on his face. "How about books on interpreting dreams? Or maybe self-help for delusional goof-balls who thinks their dreams are real?"

"How about self-help for guys who think they're funny but really aren't?" Jacob shot back with a smile.

"How about that book *Born Stupid, The Life And Times of Jacob Hunter*?" David was just getting warmed up.

"How about *The Art and Science of Picking and Eating the Perfect Booger,* by David Phillips?" Jacob felt very proud of that one.

"How about *Secret Shame – My Love Affair With the Neighbor's Dog,* by Jacob Hunter?"

Both boys howled, and this exchange of creative and mildly insulting book titles went on for aother five minutes before it finally got old.

The remaining ten minutes before the boys finally reached the "downtown" area of Logtown passed quickly. David played tour guide for most of the way, pointing out what were, in his twelve-year-old mind, places of interest.

About half a mile into the city proper, the highway met Howard Boulevard. There was a traffic light at the intersection, and the boys had to wait a few moments before they could cross. Then they turned left, keeping to the sidewalk that ran parallel to the main street running through the city of Logtown. After a mile they passed First Baptist Church, on their left. They kept going for another quarter mile, passing the hospital, which was on their right. Just across Bullens Avenue, which intersected Howard Boulevard at the far side of the hospital, sat Stockton Memorial Library. To the library's right was Eastover Pharmacy, and a few blocks further down the street sat Logtown High School. The boys parked their bikes at a long bike-rack that ran along the wall of the library between two of its tall, narrow windows.

At David's suggestion, they first went into Eastover's for something to drink. The building was old, having been built in the late fifties, and the owner didn't seem to have felt the need for any renovations other than a coat of paint on the wall (applied nearly fifteen years before) and linoleum tile on the floor, but both were kept spotless. The smell that greeted the boys as they walked through the front door was that of musty age, which somehow Jacob's brain couldn't quite reconcile with the building's appearance of almost hospital-like sterility. The only new looking item in the store, a computer terminal sitting on the counter where prescriptions were dropped off, looked very out of place.

Jacob followed David to an old-fashioned drink cooler with a glass door, which stood next to the checkout counter. Both boys selected power drinks, and took them to the counter, where a fiftyish looking man sat on a stool, looking at the sports section of Sunday's *Logtown News*.

The gentleman behind the counter was Sidney Eastover, son of Ira Eastover, who was the founder and original pharmacist of Eastover Pharmacy. After finishing school, Sidney had returned home and helped his father run Logtown's oldest pharmacy for fifteen years, until a massive stroke claimed the elder Eastover early one morning over breakfast. Now Sidney was the sole owner and resident pharmacist. He was a friendly man, an active member (and deacon) in First Baptist Church of Logtown; a member in good standing at the local Rotary and Lion's Clubs, and very well-liked all over town. He was physically unremarkable: a little overweight with a slight paunch visible through the unbuttoned white pharmacist's coat he wore almost everywhere except church, and his hair was beginning to recede, pushing back almost half an inch from his forehead. Both his beard and the hair on his head was suspiciously dark brown, without a single fleck of gray (Sidney Eastover liked to think it was his little secret, but most people knew he colored his hair; the dark brown didn't look much more natural than the pink and blue hair sported by some of the elderly women around town).

Mr. Eastover looked up from the paper and smiled as the two boys plopped their drinks down beside the cash register.

"Mornin', David. What brings you to town so early?"

David smiled back just as sweetly as the pharmacist had smiled at him.

"Mornin', Mr. Eastover. We're headed to the library to look at some books."

Mr. Eastover seemed pleasantly surprised at that. His smile broadened as he rang up the boy's drinks with a newly installed bar-code scanner.

"Well that's real good t' hear," he replied, and his face showed that he meant it. "Most boys these days spend all their time parked in fronuva TV, watchin' trashy movies or playin' them crazy video games."

David slipped Jacob a quick look that clearly said he'd rather be doing one or both of those things right now. Then he looked back at Mr. Eastover.

"By the way, this is Jacob Hunter. His family just moved here last week."

Mr. Eastover stared at Jacob for a second, looking thoughtful as he muttered "Hunter . . . Hunter" to himself. Then he smiled again, bigger and broader than ever. Jacob was afraid that if the smile grew any more, it would swallow the man's entire head.

"Oh, yeah, Hunter. I met'cher parents in Sunday school, day b'fore yesterday. Seemed like real good folks. Moved down here from the north part of the state, didn'tcha?"

"Yes, sir. From Tunica," Jacob answered.

"Well Jacob, It's good to meetcha."

He offered his hand across the counter, and Jacob took it. He was relieved that it wasn't sweaty, like Mr. MacDonald's hand had been. Instead, it was bone dry and soft; it almost felt powdery. Mr. Eastover, still smiling, released Jacob's hand and said, "Okay, boys, you owe me two dollar 'n seventy-eight cent."

As the boys dug in their pockets and began pooling their resources, he continued talking.

"I'm glad to see you're fallin' in with the right sort of boys, Jacob. Mr. Phillips here is a fine young fella."

David looked up and smiled while Jacob wondered again about the way his new friend seemed to have with adults. Was it this mysterious charisma that his father had been referring to when he'd said *charming in an Eddie Haskell-ish kind of way*? And who the heck was *Eddie Haskell*, anyway?

The boys each placed one dollar and fifty cents on the counter. Mr. Eastover took two seventy-five, dug three pennies out of his own pocket, and told the boys they could fight over the remaining quarter. David promptly reached up, took the quarter, and handed it to Jacob, who took it while beginning to understand the answer to the question he'd just been pondering.

The two boys both thanked the friendly man, who thanked them back and told them to be careful riding their bikes in town. They walked out of the small building already taking long pulls at their drink bottles, and emptied them in under five minutes, sitting on the sidewalk with their backs to the library wall. Then they walked into the library, tossing the empty bottles into a large, blue-colored steel drum lined with a white garbage bag that sat beside the entrance.

Once inside, David took the lead. He walked straight to one of two small desks which sat side by side next to a counter where an elderly lady stood, eyeing the boys suspiciously while sorting books that had been dropped in the overnight slot beside the front door. David sat down at the first of the two desks, both of which housed computers that were used to look up books in the same way old card catalogues (something neither boy had even heard of) had once been used: by author, subject, or title. David moved the cursor to the heading "subject," but before he could double click, a suspicious, nasally voice asked, "Is there something I can help you boys with?"

The elderly lady was now standing directly behind the computers, looking down her narrow nose at the two boys. She wasn't exactly frowning, but her tight lips formed a straight, narrow line across her thin, wrinkled face. She looked every part the elderly librarian: graying hair pulled up in a bun; reading glasses (with the obligatory silver chain dangling from said glasses) perched on the end of that haughty, narrow nose; and a prudish, dark brown dress speckled with small, white flowers. David gave her one of his patented smiles that was reserved for adults.

"Mornin', Mrs. Elway."

Mrs. Elway didn't smile back, which surprised Jacob (who by now assumed every adult in town loved his friend and probably wanted to adopt him), but didn't seem to phase David.

"We're looking for books about the history of Logtown," he said.

Mrs. Elway wasn't as pleased as Mr. Eastover had been at the prospect of boys reading instead of wasting away in front of a television, but her face did relax a little, just enough for one or two wrinkles to disappear.

"We have two. Both are in the Historical Reference section. Follow me, please."

She turned and began walking at a brisk pace away from the two boys, who looked at each other, and trying not to snicker, followed. She walked directly to an aisle between two long bookshelves, which were designated "Historical Reference" by a small sign suspended from the ceiling by two wires. She moved briskly down the aisle, finally stopping just before its end, then turned to the shelf on her right and began studying the books as the two boys stood silently beside her. She quickly located both books and removed them from the shelf.

One had a black cover, the other pale green. Both looked pretty old, and very unread. Instead of handing either book to David, whose hand was outstretched, she turned and walked right past them, carrying the books before her with both hands and looking like a butler or maid about to serve dinner from a tray. David rolled his eyes as they turned to follow.

The librarian led them to one of four long reading tables, all of which were empty at nine-thirty in the morning. The table she selected was the one closest to the counter where she would be working, obviously so that she could keep an eye on the two hooligans, ready to expel them from the library should the need arise. She placed the two books side by side on the table and began speaking.

"This first book is entitled *The Glory Days of Logtown, A History*. The second is *Old Time Living in Stratford County*. Both were written by Dr. Joseph Lee, who lived and practiced medicine in

Logtown until his death, I believe in 1982. If you have any questions, let me know." Her face stated quite clearly that she hoped neither boy would have any questions, but Jacob quickly asked if the books had any pictures.

"I believe they both do," she replied, "but there are probably more in the first one, *Glory Days*. It focuses more on the founding and development of Logtown. Anything else?" She seemed to be daring either boy to waste any more of her time.

"No, ma'am," David answered. "Thanks for your help."

Mrs. Elway nodded curtly, then returned to the counter and appeared to return to work, occasionally looking up to make sure the boys weren't up to anything untoward. As soon as she was out of earshot, David started whispering, keeping his voice so low that Jacob could barely understand him.

"That's Mrs. Elway. She's been the head librarian around here like, forever, and she's a real biddy. Everybody calls her Mrs. Hellway or Smellway."

"Do they call her that to her face?" Jacob asked, imitating his friend's sarcastic manner.

"Nah, but I keep hoping someone will. I'd love to see her face if they did. She'd probably fall down and croak of a heart attack on the spot." David paused for a second, and when he resumed, his voice had changed from wary and sarcastic to wary and excited.

"But you should see her assistant, Mrs. Ladner. Oh, man! She's about twenty-eight or twenty-nine; long blonde hair; real tan skin."

David paused for a moment, biting his lower lip and contorting his face into an expression of agonized despair.

"I think . . . maybe, just maybe . . . I think . . . I . . . love her!!" Then her buried is face in his hands and pretended to cry.

Jacob started to laugh, but caught Mrs. Elway's frowning face. His eyes dropped, and he pretended to study the cover of the book before him until she turned back to her own work.

"Where is she?" Jacob whispered cautiously, scanning the empty library not quite eagerly but with more enthusiasm than he meant to show.

"She only works on afternoons and Saturdays. But she's married."

David shook his head sadly (as if, had she *not* been burdened by both marriage and those laws and social mores established to govern such behavior between adults and children, Mrs. Ladner would eagerly have pursued an intimate relationship with a charming twelve-year-old such as himself).

Jacob grabbed *A History* and began fanning through the pages with his thumb. In the center of the book were about fifteen pages worth of grainy black and white photographs. Some appeared to have been torn or water-damaged before being copied for the book, and all had descriptive captions running underneath.

He began looking at the pictures, studying each carefully and slowly before turning the page. The first four or five pictures were of loggers, most wearing overalls and wide-brimmed straw hats. Some pictures showed these roughnecks from an era long since passed sawing huge trees with long, double-handled saws, others showed them leading sturdy-looking horses and oxen as they pulled large bundles of logs held together by huge chains across the muddy ground. One showed a picture of a massive, old-fashioned sawmill built on the banks of a river; another showed a vast countryside, which Jacob assumed had once been forestlands, now a barren waste of blackened stumps and rotting limbs.

He turned to the next page and saw a picture of the original First Baptist Church. It looked like something out of a western: walls of whitewashed wooden planks, wooden shingles, and a small steeple pointing upwards toward heaven. The opposite page showed a small train depot with a steam engine. It was being loaded with logs that had been stripped of bark and sawed in half.

Jacob turned yet another page, and froze when his eyes fell on the picture. He felt his heart skip a beat, and a chill ran the length of his spine. He actually shuddered.

The picture was of a magnificent house. It rose three stories into the sky and was capped with four chimneys spaced evenly along the long, steep roof. A man, woman, and child stood in front of a massive front door of oak, but it was impossible to make out their faces. The picture was of the entire house and had by necessity been taken at a great distance. The small family looked quite tiny standing before it. The caption below the picture simply read *Stockton Estate*.

The opposite page contained a blowup of the threesome, obviously from the same picture. The blurry, emotionless faces stared out at Jacob, and he immediately recognized two of them.

The caption beneath the blowup read *James Stockton, founder of Logtown, with wife and son: Melinda and James II.*

Jacob reached over and gripped David's arm, his eyes never leaving the picture. David, who had been thumbing through pictures in *Old Time Living*, looked over.

"That's it!" Jacob's whisper was strained with fear and excitement as he pointed to the pictures with a trembling hand. "That's the house I saw burning! That's the man and boy I saw in the dream!"

After lunch, Jacob locked himself in his room and began reading *A History*.

David had used his library card to check out the book. Halfway to the door of the library, Jacob turned back and asked Mrs. Elway if she had a bag that the boys could put the book in. She gave him a rather strange look without answering – as though he had asked for her home phone number so he could call Friday night and ask her out on a date. He quickly explained that they were riding bikes and he didn't want the book to get dirty or sweaty.

Once again, something Jacob had thought might please the old bag (two twelve-year-old boys having the forethought to take measures that would protect library property) instead only seemed to irritate her further and her eyes and lips grew even narrower in unison. She dug around behind the counter and finally pulled out a plastic grocery bag, which she handed over while explaining to the two boys how they would be responsible for any damage done to the book while it was in their care. Jacob thanked her (for all the good it did) and the boys left.

Jacob spoke little on the ride back home, but David couldn't shut up. Seeing the pictures seemed to have made a true believer out of him. He no longer had any doubt that the house had once stood exactly where it had been in Jacob's dream, and that it had burned to the ground, just as Jacob had described. Now he pondered the possibilities of Jacob having psychic powers, asking more than once if he was sure he'd never had this type of experience before. He seemed disappointed by Jacob's assurance that he had not, but moved on to his next hypothesis without missing a beat – maybe the woods were haunted and Jacob had been visited by the spirit of someone who had died in the fire.

Jacob had more trouble dismissing this idea, and became a little uncomfortable. The skull-faced woman quickly came to mind. Jacob knew that, even in broad daylight, he would be able to see that leering face if closed his eyes. He could almost see it with his eyes wide open. He decided that he'd rather try to find out what had happened at that house, the Stockton Estate, on that cool autumn night instead of worrying about *why* he'd had the dream. Somewhere in the back of his mind was the uncomfortable idea that thinking about the dream too much could cause it to recur. So he simply told David that he didn't feel like talking about it, not right now, anyway.

David had seemed surprised, but had dropped the subject without protest, instead suggesting that they take the book straight to his house to find out what it might say about the house burning down. Jacob had quickly shot that idea down as well, saying that he wanted to look at it by himself first. David was again surprised, and this time a little irritated, so Jacob explained that he would need to be alone so that he could remember the dream in as much detail as possible, searching for anything that might yield clues to be found in the book. It was a load of garbage, and Jacob had thought it sounded pretty dopey as the words came out of his mouth, but David ate it up. He was probably still stuck on the idea that his new friend had powerful, newly discovered psychic abilities.

They had eventually made it back to David's house, both boys sweaty and tired. Jacob had turned down an offer to come in for a drink and maybe lunch, but had assured his friend he'd call that evening with any info he might pick up from the book.

Mrs. Hunter was hard at work in the backyard when Jacob got home, so he was able to quickly and quietly slip inside undetected, where he hid the book in his closet. Then he had gone outside, cheerfully offering to assist his mother, hoping it would earn him some time to read after lunch. Mrs. Hunter was too hot and too deep into the job of digging up the future site of her flowerbed to be overly suspicious, and quickly put him to work.

Now, with his door locked, lying on the floor with a pillow behind his head, and with his mother's assurance that he could have an hour or so before resuming work, Jacob began to read.

First, he skimmed through a short preface, learning little other than the fact that most of the information in the book was of the word-of-mouth variety, obtained through dozens of interviews with older people who had grown up in the Logtown area. Jacob flipped back to find the publication date: 1977. He assumed that meant most of the people interviewed in the book were probably now dead. He then flipped to the table of contents.

The first several chapters seemed to deal with life in early Logtown and the rise and fall of the logging industry. He skipped over these chapters, looking instead for any information about the Stockton family and their magnificent house. Chapter eight was entitled *How James Stockton Turned an Industry Into an Empire*. He flipped to chapter eight, and began to read.

According to the book, James Stockton had been a successful young businessman from a wealthy family in the Northeast part of the country. Ten plus years of growth in the timber industry of the South (cotton had gone from king to pauper after the Civil War) caught his eye, and he enthusiastically pitched the idea of an opportunity to expand the family holdings and business to his father. Edward Stockton, who had always admired his son's aggressive business attitude, gave James his blessing and a sizable chunk of the family fortune. And so, in 1901, twenty-five years old and armed with one part his own money and two parts family money, James Stockton moved south.

He stayed in New Orleans for a while, making deals and buying vast parcels of land and already existing timber companies. He bought almost all of Stratford County, Mississippi, plus sizeable parcels of land in Hancock, Pearl River, Lamar, Forrest, and Harrison

Counties. Stratford County was the only one of these that did not already have a sawmill, so he built one, one of the largest in the region. The site where it was built had originally been an Indian village on the eastern banks of the East Pearl River, although early settlers had already sort of elbowed their way in, and the Indians had moved on long before Stockton had even arrived in this part of the country. A settlement soon formed around the sawmill, but as most of this area was swampland that flooded badly at certain times of the year, James moved the settlement a few miles further east. According to the book, the community around this original settlement was now called Pine Bluff (at least by the locals; according to the post office, it was still part of Logtown). The relocated settlement eventually grew into a town, and the town into a city, which James Stockton proudly (if not too imaginatively) named Logtown. His venture quickly became a success, and by 1915, he had more than tripled the money that he had arrived with.

Although he had built a nice home in Logtown, Stockton still spent a lot of time in New Orleans, both for social and business purposes. One of the New Orleans businessmen he dealt with on a regular basis was Henry Brooks, another native of the Northeast whose family had moved to New Orleans in the mid 1880s. Mr. Brooks' father had founded a shipping company, and Henry, being every bit as aggressive as James, practically ran the entire operation at age forty-five. What began as a strictly business-type acquaintance when James commissioned Mr. Brooks' fleet of barges to ship timber up the Mississippi River and along the coastline to Gulfport and Mobile soon evolved into a genuine friendship.

In 1920, James Stockton married the only daughter of Henry Brooks, Miss Melinda Brooks. Despite the age difference (she was twenty, he was forty-four), Mr. Brooks fully supported the union, probably as a means to fortify his business dealings with Mr. Stockton even further. In 1921, James II was born. In 1925, the mansion, which would eventually be known as The Stockton Estate, was completed. The small family moved in, and for the next several years appeared to be quite content.

As the twenties rolled on, however, the timber industry had begun to suffer. Uncharacteristically, Mr. Stockton either didn't see it coming or was unconcerned, believing he could weather the storm. Things went from bad to worse as the Great Depression took hold of the entire country, and by this time Mr. Stockton couldn't sell any of his holdings; even if he could have found a buyer, selling at that time would have meant suffering an almost catastrophic loss. The rest of his family, still somewhat comfortably ensconced in the Northeast, had already circled the wagons, although they probably would have done what they could to help him had he asked. But that was something his pride would not allow him to do.

Then, in late October of 1933, Stockton Estate had burned to the ground. Mrs. Stockton had been killed in the fire, the cause of which was never determined, and James simply took his son and left. Most people assumed that he moved back to wherever he had come from. His company and most of his land were eventually sold, but all transactions were handled by brokers and through a law firm in New York City. The last sentence on the page read, "As far as anyone knows, a Stockton has not set foot in Logtown, Mississippi since."

Jacob turned the page, hoping for more information about the fire, but Dr. Lee apparently had nothing to add – the chapter he was reading simply ended with that final, evocative sentence. Feeling a little frustrated, he flipped back to the table of contents, carefully reading the titles of each chapter. There were twenty-one in all, but none seemed to offer any more information on the name Stockton.

He let out a disappointed sigh and started to close the book, but instead turned back to the picture section. He found the close-up of the small family standing in front of the enormous house, and began to study it carefully. Even now, with the sun shining brightly through his open blinds, seeing the faces of that man and boy made Jacob uneasy.

As was the case with most other old pictures Jacob had seen, none of the people in the picture smiled. Their blurry faces seemed impassive at best and full of foreboding at worst, as if each somehow knew of the terrible fate looming in their very near future. It occurred to Jacob that the picture must have been taken shortly before the fire. Both the man and the boy looked almost exactly as they had in his dream.

He flipped back to chapter eight with one hand while saving his place with the thumb of the other and began scanning pages, looking for the year in which James Stockton II was born. It didn't take long; all of the chapters in the book were pretty short. 1921. He then flipped back to the pictures, doing some quick math in his head as he studied those solemn faces. The boy had been twelve years old (*the same age as me*, Jacob marveled) when the house had burned, taking away forever both his mother and his home. He and his father had moved after the fire, back to the northeast part of the country, home to James Sr. but a place Jacob assumed James II had never been.

Jacob turned his attention to the young lady identified as Mrs. Stockton. She was dressed in dark, solemn colors that seemed to fit perfectly with the dark mood of the picture, with one exception. Something hung from a chain around her neck, reflecting sunlight in a hazy glow. It was maybe a cross, maybe a star; it was impossible to tell from the poor quality of the picture. Jacob then began to study her face carefully. From what he could see, she seemed to be very pretty, but as he looked closer it seemed to him that her face was sad, and again he wondered if somehow she had maybe known that her time remaining with her husband and son was almost gone. And then another thought, this one disturbing, occurred to him. Was this the young woman who had spoken to him in his dream, who had implored Jacob to help the young boy, then stepped forward toward him, revealing her yellow, leering skull of a face before chasing him through the woods, surely bent on one thing only: stealing away his life and his soul?

Jacob shuddered at the memory, but refused to close the book and shut away the pictures that brought his dream back so vividly.

His brain had slipped into overdrive, and it seemed to him that at least some of the pieces of that puzzling nightmare were beginning to fall into place. It was impossible to be sure, since the woman in his dream had had no face, but he decided that if anyone would be haunting the scene of the tragedy, it would be her, the only one who had perished in the fire. Jacob closed his eyes, forcing himself to remember the words she had spoken to him during that brief span of time when he had thought she was human.

Help him, she had said, *it wasn't his fault . . . Help us*. Then, as she had stepped forward, allowing him to see not who but *what* was speaking to him, she had said – no, he corrected himself, she had screamed – *Help me*.

Help him, help us, help me.

Him had surely meant the sad-eyed boy, but how could Jacob help someone who he didn't know, someone who, for all he knew, was now dead. And for that matter, since by *us* and *me* the speaker had been including herself, how was he supposed to help a young woman who, based on her physical appearance, was definitely no longer a part of the world of the living?

Jacob's mind shifted gears again and began to accelerate further as he thought about the man, who he now knew was James Stockton, screaming at his son. He had cursed the boy viciously. He had cursed his own son's soul to hell, while the boy had cried over and over that he was sorry.

Had the boy caused the fire? This idea seemed to make the most sense to Jacob. Why else would the boy be begging for his father's mercy, saying *I'm sorry* over and over? Why else would his father have been so angry? His wife, the boy's mother, had died in the fire that had destroyed the Stockton Estate.

Then why did the woman tell me that it wasn't his fault? Jacob wondered. And if it wasn't his fault, why was he sorry?

Then another image from his dream came to mind – when he had first come to the clearing at the edge of the woods and began watching the house burn. Jacob had somehow felt the presence of the boy, turned, and looked into the boy's hollow eyes. Those eyes had pierced Jacob's as the boy spoke: *I was only trying to help.*

Help what? Jacob wondered. He didn't know, nor did he understand the source of the overwhelming grief that he had felt immediately after the boy had spoken. He had only known, somehow, that it was the boy's grief that he had not just *felt*, but had nearly been overcome by.

Jacob closed his eyes, trying to focus all of his thoughts on the memory of the boys face. *It was his eyes*, Jacob realized. *I somehow* knew *his eyes. But how?* His train of thought was now speeding like a runaway down a different track, this one leading to a memory less than twenty-four hours old. The night before, as he had been drifting slowly toward sleep, his mind had begun to wander. It had naturally fixated on the dream from the night before, and as he had remembered watching the house burn, visualizing it so easily with a mind that was already half dreaming, he had turned to look at the boy standing beside him. But the boy hadn't been standing alone.

Instead, Jim Hanes stood behind him, arms resting protectively on the boy's shoulders, as together they watched the house burn.

Jacob's heart seemed to skip a beat. When it started again, it was going triple-time, as if trying to make up for the split second it had stopped. Jacob *had* seen those eyes before. Jim had had him pinned helplessly on the ground, glaring darkly and, it had seemed to Jacob, seriously contemplating murder. But as soon as Jacob had uttered the words *I was only trying to help* (the very words, he suddenly realized, that the boy had spoken in the dream), Jim Hanes's wild, glaring eyes had seemed to melt away. They had become stricken – eyes filled with shock, horror, and *sadness*. Jacob could see those eyes even now, and the sight was enough to make him shudder as violently as any memory of the dream had.

He looked at the picture for the twentieth time, thinking *what is this? What the heck is going on here?* The eyes in the picture were just fuzzy, gray and black circles, but all Jacob had to do was close his own eyes to see the boy's eyes as clearly as if he was there in the room, at that very moment, staring sadly at Jacob.

Is that possible? he wondered. *Could the boy and Jim . . .*

An abrupt knock at his bedroom door startled Jacob back to reality. He jumped to his feet with a stricken face and let out a strange yell that sounded sort of like "Gaaaah!!" His mother's voice came through the door.

"Jacob, c'mon, I'm going to need a little more help outside," she called. "Just forty-five minutes or so, then you can go play with your friends."

Feeling both relieved and angry upon hearing her voice, Jacob could only shake his head. "Go play with your friends," he muttered. He was almost thirteen! He didn't *play with his friends*! They *hung out*, and by golly, there was a difference! With his heart racing faster than ever, he slid the book under his bed and, with hands that were still shaking, opened the door. His mother's face showed surprise and a little concern when she looked at him.

"What's wrong?" she asked. "You look like you've seen a ghost."

I think I might have, he thought, but simply answered, "Nuthin's wrong, you just surprised me."

"You certainly seem jumpy. Is it because of your bad dream from the other night?"

For a second he was surprised, wondering how she could possibly know about his dream. Then he remembered speaking with his father the night before; not exactly *lying* but allowing his father to believe he had dreamed about Crazy Mary. Obviously, his father had mentioned it to his mother.

Aw, maaan! he thought to himself. He felt embarrassed and angry at the idea of his parents discussing the fact that their pre-adolescent son had to sleep with the light on because of a bad dream, and concluded, not for the first time, that parents simply could not be trusted; at least to keep secrets.

"I'm not jumpy!" Jacob snapped. "I just fell asleep, and it surprised me when you beat on the door like that!"

His mother was not impressed by his short temper.

"You can lose the attitude, Jacob" she replied. "I was only a little concerned, that's all."

Lose the attitude. Jacob hated that phrase as much as his parents seemed to love using it. He started to pop off, but held his tongue. Smarting off would only get him in trouble, and he needed as much freedom from the prying eyes of his parents as he could get if he hoped to pursue the Mystery of the Burning House.

"Sorry," he finally said.

Mrs. Hunter looked at him for a few moments with that odd parental blend of suspicion and concern.

"All right," she said after completing the look to her satisfaction. She turned and walked down the hall, Jacob a few steps behind.

"Like I said, I shouldn't need more than forty-five minutes of your precious time."

She ended up keeping him for just over an hour, but he hardly noticed. Instead, he worked like a little robot, following instructions that were barely heard but somehow still registered enough to command response as he made and discarded several plans to pursue his little mystery.

By the time he was dismissed, Jacob had come up with what he felt confident were two good, workable strategies. He would call David later that evening with Plan A. Plan B would be initiated that very afternoon, before he had a chance to lose his nerve. It was something that he would have to do alone, and even thinking about it in an abstract way was enough to make his heart quail. He could think of no other way to verify this particular suspicion, however, so he made up his mind to at least try.

Once back in the house, Jacob went straight to the washroom and began rummaging through the odds and ends that, only days before, he had helped stack on the shelves built into the back wall. It only took a few minutes for him to find what he was looking for – packing tape. His father had bought a box of five rolls just two weeks before, and there were still two full rolls left. He grabbed one, then stuck his head out of the door leading from the den to the patio where his mother was hunched over, planting some kind of flower in one of the holes Jacob had dug earlier.

"Hey Mom, I'm gonna ride my bike for a while."

"Okay," she replied without looking up. "Be careful, and be back by suppertime."

"Yes, ma'am."

He hopped on his bike and, wearing the roll of tape on his wrist like a bracelet, headed for the trails by the usual route. As he approached his own yard on the first path, the one that ran along each of the backyards on his street, he considered getting off of his bike and trying to walk it stealthily along the fence, so as to avoid drawing his mother's attention. He quickly discarded this idea, realizing that she would be suspicious if she caught him trying to sneak by. Anyway, she knew where the trails were, and probably expected to hear him ride by. So that's exactly what he did, albeit faster than usual.

He followed the trail into the woods and soon came to the first fork in the path. He glanced quickly toward the left, down the trail that led in the direction of the Ice House, wishing for a moment that he were heading that direction. But he wasn't. He took a deep breath, then turned right onto the smaller, overgrown path. Jacob rode his bike as quietly as he could in the direction of Jim Hanes's trailer.

10

Jacob soon stood at the fence behind the dilapidated trailer of Jim Hanes, forcing himself to take slow, deep breaths in an effort to calm himself. He turned, looking back down the trail to the place where he had left his bike. It was still visible from where he stood, but barely. He had left it at the same point on the weedy, overgrown path where he and the other three boys had left their bikes Saturday (*Has it only been three days*? he thought), and he had positioned it so that it faced away from the trailer, just in case a hasty getaway became necessary. Twice, on the short (but only if measured in terms of actual distance) walk from his bike to the fence, Jacob had turned and started to go back. But he didn't. This was the only way he could think of to either confirm or refute the strange notion that had popped into his mind during his after-lunch brainstorm.

And so now he stood at the fence, trying to calm himself; reviewing the plan and script he had formulated, and trying to re-assure himself that he wasn't about to do the second dumbest thing he had ever done in his twelve years – the dumbest had already been done last Saturday. He took one last, deep breath, so deep it hurt his lungs, then blew the air out through pursed lips.

"Lets do it," he said, not remembering that he had said the same thing to Jared right before they entered the yard three days ago.

He followed the same path the boys had used Saturday, walking to the fence corner on his left, then turning right and following the fence as it ran alongside the lot and toward the trailer, walking as quietly as he could and taking quick, shallow breaths.

Once, while looking at the trailer instead of his feet, he stepped on a small limb, which had snapped in half loudly enough, it seemed to him, to be heard back at the Ice House. He froze, hardly daring even to breath, for a full sixty seconds. But he heard no sounds except those coming from the nearby highway.

During that brief pause, it suddenly occurred to Jacob just how quiet it always was around the trailer. He heard no animals in the trees or under the brush, no dogs, squirrels, or even birds. There was no steady hum of an air conditioner, even of the inexpensive window-unit variety.

How could anyone live in this heat without an air conditioner? he wondered. He didn't mind the heat when he was outside playing, but that might have been because he knew he could always go inside to that sweet, machine-generated cold air whenever he was ready. This did not appear to be the case for Jim Hanes. Jacob made a face. *No wonder he stinks so bad.*

Jacob looked around nervously. The strange, thick silence was making him feel even more uncomfortable with what had seemed a pretty clever plan while he was still at home. How could it be so *quiet*, especially in the middle of the day? The sounds of the highway seemed not so much distant as muffled, as though there were a large, invisible concrete wall between the trailer and the highway. Even the sounds generated by the noisy logging and gravel trucks as they passed seemed barely able to penetrate it. Jacob was beginning to feel very alone and very small.

Forget this, buddy! a voice seemed to say inside his head. *Did you forget what that man almost did to you? Turn around and scoot your happy behind back down the trail, and don't look back*!!

Jacob turned and looked doubtfully at the path he'd just walked. Then he closed his eyes, forcing himself to again take slow, deep breaths. In his mind he saw the burning house. In his mind he saw the boy with the sad empty eyes. And in his mind, he saw the eyes of Jim Hanes.

"No!" he whispered. "I'm gonna do this! I'm gonna find out!"

He opened his eyes, turned, and continued walking along the faint path, still taking those slow, deep breaths. And it wasn't just foolish, blind courage that drove him on. Deep inside, beneath the loud voice of logic arguing against every step he took, Jacob somehow *knew* that Jim Hanes wouldn't hurt him. Something had happened last Saturday, when Jacob had uttered those words to Jim and the old man had stared at him with those stricken eyes. Jacob now felt as if he understood why Jim had reacted the way he did. In his heart, Jacob believed that Jim Hanes had once uttered those same words, *I was only trying to help*, to his own father.

When he drew level with the pine tree, to the spot where the fence had been pulled loose from its post, Jacob stopped. Despite his efforts to calm himself by taking deep breaths, his heart was racing and he was trembling badly. He still wore the roll of tape on his arm, afraid it would slip from his sweat-slicked hands if he tried to carry it.

C'mon, man, almost there.

He pushed the fence back from its post, slipped underneath, then quickly stepped up to the pine tree he and Jared had crouched behind Saturday, peeking around into the empty lot in front of the trailer. He could see Jim's rust-bucket car parked at an angle by the fence at the front of the lot. The coast was clear. Clear – and silent as a graveyard.

Alright, man, go! JUST GO!!

He took one last, deep breath, and set off across the seemingly vast span of open yard between the pine tree and the front of the trailer.

Jacob was surprised at the fact that, the closer he got to the trailer, the more confident he began to feel. There was no sense of disconnect, as if he was watching himself approach the trailer from outside his own body, a sensation which he had felt very strongly Saturday. Still, as he put that first foot on the first cinder-block step, he could feel his heart pounding not only in his chest, but in his temples as well.

He stepped up to the door and raised his arm, letting it hang in the air for a few seconds. Then, using the side of his fist, Jacob beat on the door four times. He then backed down off the steps and held his breath.

Nothing happened. Jacob stood perfectly still and listened for any sounds coming from inside the trailer. Given the silence that seemed to hang like a shroud around the filthy, overgrown lot, even a small noise should have been easily heard. In fact, he had expected to hear the heavy footsteps of Jim storming down the hallway of the trailer, probably accompanied by a heavy voice bellowing obscenities. The unanticipated silence fed his growing feeling of unease.

Jacob suddenly spun around so quickly that he almost lost his balance, certain that the skull-faced woman from his dreams was standing behind him with arms upraised, grinning that perpetual grin. He was alone, of course. Nothing there but weeds and litter and wild shrubs. Only, he didn't *feel* alone. There was a feeling of watchfulness in that dirty, silent lot. The longer he stood there, the more he could feel it. Was Jim watching him through some small peephole or opening in one of his foil-covered windows? Or was it someone else? Maybe some*thing* else? Jacob shuddered.

This is crazy, his brain told him. *I'll give you one more chance to knock. If he doesn't answer, we're history.*

"You got that right," Jacob muttered aloud. He stepped back up to the door, made a fist, and began to knock. He only managed one before the door was yanked open so suddenly that Jacob actually let out a quick yelp, the kind of noise a dog makes after getting smacked on the nose with a rolled up newspaper. He stumbled backwards, nearly falling from the steps. Before him stood an enraged Jim Hanes, eyes blazing.

He didn't appear to have changed clothes since Jacob last saw him, and as he looked down at the frightened boy, his face showed instant recognition. If he was surprised, it didn't register on his face.

His eyes were no longer blazing, but they still glared at Jacob as fiercely as ever. A foul smell that Jacob could almost see seemed to pour out through the open door: a sickening blend of the trailer and the man. Moldy mildew and garbage mixed with a greasy, sweaty stench that almost smelled like decay. Jim finally spoke, and the sound of his voice seemed a perfect match for his appearance; it was thick and gravelly.

"What do *you* want?"

Jacob opened his mouth, but nothing came out. While helping his mother he had, in his mind, prepared a short speech, including a heartfelt apology that he felt certain the old man would have to accept, but the speech seemed to have left him, along with any other coherent thought. They had grown wings, fluttered free of his mind, and sailed off into the wild blue yonder.

Jim continued to glare, but now his face seemed to reflect some type of amusement. It was akin to the amusement Jacob's own face had reflected while watching the wasps struggle on the ground after his father had given them a hearty dose of wasp-spray.

"Boy, either say what'cha gotta say, or get your scrawny behind outta my yard."

Jacob lowered his eyes, looking at the cinder-block steps instead of Jim. This seemed to help a little bit.

"I . . . uh, just . . . I just wanted to say I'm sorry. You know. For the other day." His voice sounded thin and weak.

"Well, that's just real big of you, son. I'm touched. Now get *outta* here." Jim was clearly unimpressed. He stepped back and began to close the door.

"Wait!" Jacob squeaked, stepping back up onto the cinderblocks. Jim paused, the door only half closed.

"What?" he barked. The old man just wanted to be left alone.

Jacob held up the roll of tape, as if doing so would explain everything. Jim seemed to be on the verge of losing what little temper he may have had.

"A roll of tape! So what? Is that supposed to be a gift?"

"No, sir, I wanted to . . . I was just going to, you know, try to fix the window. Tape it up."

"If I wanted it taped, I'd've taped it myself!" he shot back, starting to close the door again.

Jacob took another step up.

"Please, Mr. Hanes. I really want to."

Jim shook his head in disgust.

"You're a stubborn little cuss, aint'cha?"

He glared at Jacob, who wasn't sure just how to respond to such a question: neither *yes* nor *no* seemed appropriate.

After a few moments, Jim added, "Alright, fine. You wait right there." He turned and disappeared into the trailer, muttering something. All Jacob could make out was something that sounded like *pesky, stubborn little jerk*.

Jacob backed down the cinderblock steps and waited, wondering what Jim was doing. He found himself remembering, once again, one of the stories Mr. MacDonald had told Friday night, the one about Jim Hanes shooting at a couple of boys several years back. Uncertainty began to creep back into his mind.

He's getting a gun!

The thought seemed to be mocking Jacob for his stupidity.

He's grabbing a loaded gun that he keeps handy for idiots like you who come knocking on his door, and you're just standing here like a fool, holding a roll of tape and waiting. Congratulations, idiot! You deserve *to get shot for being so stupid!*

Jim suddenly reappeared, but he was armed only with an ancient roll of gray duct tape. He thrust it toward Jacob.

"If you're just all-fire-determined to tape the blasted window, at least use this. That stuff you got ain't worth a dern."

Jacob took the oblong shaped, half empty roll, looking at it uncertainly.

"But the packing tape's clear. It won't show up as much." He felt stupid pointing this out, but did it anyway.

Jim actually laughed, though it sounded more like a cough, and leaned forward. "Do I look like I care? Huh, do I? You can use the duct tape, or you can leave."

He reached back inside and pulled out an old, rickety-looking wooden chair. "Here, you can stand on this."

Jacob put his tape down on the steps and took the chair, placing it beneath the cracked window. He grabbed Jim's roll, then climbed carefully into the chair, which creaked and wobbled badly. He was glad Jim had thought of the chair; there was no way he could have reached the window without it. At the same time, he wasn't sure how long the rickety thing would hold him up.

The crack from the rock Jared had thrown looked like a starburst with a small hole at its center. Jacob used his fingernails to get a strip of tape started, pulling back about two inches, enough to cover the small hole. He tried to tear it loose, but only succeeded in wrinkling the tape. He looked nervously at Jim, who was leaning against the doorway with his arms crossed.

"Do you have any scissors? It won't tear."

"Use your teeth!" Jim shouted, and continued to glare.

Jacob looked down at the warped roll of tape. He could clearly see grit and fuzz stuck to its tacky sides. Ordinarily, he didn't much worry much about germs and getting dirty, but it now occurred to him that he was looking at grit and fuzzy things from inside Jim's smelly trailer. He didn't even want to *think* about what the grit and fuzz might be from. Instead, he braced himself, then bit down on the strip of tape he'd pulled loose, using his teeth to tear it loose.

He could immediately feel tiny, foreign objects floating and swimming around in his mouth, sticking to his tongue and the roof of his mouth, but refused to spit them out in front of Jim. The small strip went over the small hole, and Jacob gently pressed down, trying to smooth it. The cracked glass seemed to press inward, and one of the cracks spread an additional inch or two with a faint *pop*.

"Sweet mercy, boy, what're you *doing*? Give me that before you shatter the entire blasted window!"

Jim stepped down from the doorway and over to the chair, where he roughly pulled Jacob down and jerked the tape out of his hands. He pulled a long strip of tape and somehow tore it neatly from the roll with his few remaining teeth. He kicked the chair aside and, standing on his toes, stuck the tape to the window, running the full length of one particular crack and covering the small hole in the process. He tore four more long strips of tape in the same way, and covered the remaining cracks in under three minutes, while Jacob used the opportunity to spit whatever had come off of the tape out of his mouth. When Jim finished he stepped back as if to admire his handiwork.

"There! You happy now?"

Jacob glanced at the window, which now looked like it had a large, gray asterisk at its center.

"I guess." he answered.

"I'm glad t' hear it! 'Specially since I had to do all the work. Think you can leave now?" Jim glared harder than ever, daring Jacob to stay.

"I guess," he said again.

"Good! Consider yer debt paid, and don't come back!" Jim grabbed his chair and began to storm back up the steps.

Jacob turned as if to leave, then stopped. Nothing had gone according to plan, and if he left now, he'd be leaving without knowing any more than he had when he'd left his house. He looked back toward the trailer, where Jim was stepping through the doorway.

Jacob's mind raced wildly, desperately searching for a way to get an answer to the question he hadn't even asked.

So just ask the question and get it over with, stupid!

He turned back around and shouted, "Wait!"

Jim stopped, threw down the tape and chair, and turned slowly around. His glare was now tinged with frustration. Not once, in all the years he had lived in the trailer, had anyone been so determined to hang around and talk to him.

"What do you want, boy?" He almost sounded weary. "What else can you possibly want?"

Jacob was undaunted. If anything, Jim's weary expression encouraged him. It was easier to look at than the glare he usually wore.

"I was just wondering, um, how long you've lived here?"

"Long enough for little snot-crusted punks like you t' know they oughta leave me alone." Jim paused, then let out a sigh and continued. "I moved into this trailer, on this piece of ground, in this city and in this state, back in the mid-seventies. I can't even remember what year, okay? Is that good enough, are you finally satisfied?"

It was the longest sentence Jim had offered him so far, and was probably given for the sole purpose of getting the boy to leave him alone. But it still didn't tell Jacob what he wanted, so he pushed a little farther.

"No, I mean were you, like, born here? Did you live in Logtown when you were, you know, a little kid?"

For a few, brief moments, Jim's face only reflected shock and surprise at the question. It wasn't the same stunned, stricken look he'd had Saturday, but it *was* surprise, and laced with maybe a little uneasy suspicion. The look seemed to be asking *just what do you know and how do you know it?* It lasted for only a few seconds, then was quickly replaced by the standard Hanes Glare, plus a little extra.

"You know what, hot-shot? That ain't none of your business, is it? Not a bit! And I'll tell you somethin' else, I've had all the questions I'm gonna listen to! Now, you take your tape, and your big mouth, and your nosey questions, and get outta my yard, or I'm gonna finish what I started the other day!" He had stepped back out onto the cinder blocks, and was pointing a bony finger.

Jacob recognized that he had pushed his luck far enough, so he gave a quick nod and answered "Yes, sir. And thank you."

He turned and walked toward the fence, wondering why he had *thanked* Jim.

Probably for not killing me, he decided.

As he had done Saturday, Jacob climbed the fence instead of using the opening by the pine tree, and began walking the trail back to where he had left his bike. When he reached the point on the path that stood directly behind the trailer, the spot where he had first seen the trailer and met David, he stopped and looked back. The dingy curtain hanging in the small window of the back door was pulled back just a little. Through the opening, Jacob could see the curious eyes of Jim Hanes, watching him as he left.

He turned back around and kept walking, a smile growing on his face. Not only had he survived two encounters with the notorious Jim Hanes, he felt certain that he had found out exactly what he had come to find out. The look on Jim's face had told him that much.

The phone rang three times before David answered.

"Hey, man, what'd you find out?"

Jacob paused a moment.

"How'd you know it was me?" he finally asked.

"Caller I.D., ya dope! Who else from your house would be calling? So what'd you find out? Did the book say anything?"

Jacob *felt* a little like a dope. His family had caller I.D. in Tunica, mainly for the purpose of weeding out telemarketing calls from real calls, but his parents hadn't bothered with it at their new house. Jacob wasn't sure why; they had been getting calls from telemarketers at the new number from day one.

"Yeah, it talked a little about the fire, but not much. The man who lived there was James Stockton. He was kinda like the founder of Logtown or something. He was from a rich family up north, and he moved down here, bought a bunch of land for the timber, and got even richer. I don't remember his wife's name, but the boy, his son, was James II"

"This is just freakin' unbelievable!" David sounded as if he might be slobbering all over the phone in his excitement. "Was the house where you thought it was, in the woods? And did it say how the fire started?"

Jacob had felt relieved Sunday after finally telling his dream to someone; it was as if the burden hadn't exactly been removed, but *had* been lessened. And he was pleased that the person he told now believed it just as surely as if it were The Gospel, delivered directly from God via Jacob Hunter. At the same time, David's unrestrained enthusiasm was making Jacob a little nervous.

For now, Jacob still wanted it to be their little secret. At least until he could find out more, and, better yet, until he could understand what the woman in his dream had meant by *help him* and *help us.*

"Hey, you're not where anyone can hear, are ya?"

"Naw, Mom's out back with Dillon, watchin' him jump on the trampoline. So spill yer guts, man, answer the questions!"

"Well, first, it didn't say where the house was or how the fire started. But it *did* say that the man's wife died in the fire."

"No way! Oh, man!" He was quiet for the three seconds it took him to formulate a new theory.

"Hey, maybe you got some kind of E.S.P. message from the dead lady. Maybe she was murdered and wants you to expose whatever happened. Whoa!" He paused again, then added "This is straight outta the X-Files, man."

Jacob could almost see the grin that David was doubtlessly wearing. He might be smiling himself, had he not been the one who had lived through the dream. And that's exactly how he thought of it; he hadn't just dreamed it, he had *lived* it. It had been a terrifying experience. What's more, he didn't feel as if he'd just awakened from the dream, he felt as if he'd *survived* it.

Another reason he couldn't quite bring himself to smile was the fact that David's latest theory was uncomfortably close to his own. He still hadn't told David the part of the dream in which the skull-faced babe had spoken a few gentle words, then proceeded to chase him through the woods with the clear intent to kill. Nonetheless, they had both arrived at the same possible conclusion – James Stockton's deceased wife had somehow sent Jacob a message in his dream.

An even more accurate – and frightening – way to look at it might be that she'd actually visited Jacob by way of the dream. She'd come into his dream, live and in the flesh (so to speak), all the better to deliver her message with that personal touch . . .

David's voice broke into his thoughts.

"So, what're we gonna do now? What's next?"

Jacob had the answer to this question ready. It was plan A, conceived earlier that very afternoon while he had worked with his mother in the yard.

"The newspaper," he said. "That's where my dad works, remember? We can tell him that we're trying to find out about the fire. We'll say that you checked out the book, which is true, and told me about the fire, and we just were trying to find out more about it."

"Is he gonna believe that two kids are really that interested in the history of Logtown?" David sounded doubtful.

"Probably not, so we'll tell him it's for school, like a report or an essay or something."

"I'm not sure if you've noticed, Jacob, but school hasn't started yet."

"Thanks for pointing that out, toe-cheese. I figure we can say that we heard that we're gonna have to write the paper sometime later, after school starts, and wanted to get a head start. Besides, my dad'll probably be thrilled that we're studying the history of the place instead of watching TV."

"Yeah, watchin' trashy movies or playin' them crazy video games," David replied, sounding remarkably like Sidney Eastover, the pharmacist. Jacob was becoming impressed with his friend's ability to impersonate.

"When are you gonna ask him?" David asked, getting back on track.

"Tonight, probably while we're having dinner."

"Well, call me as soon as you get an answer."

"Don't worry, I will. Go find something else to worry about. Why don't you go outside and play with Dillon? You know: bonding, brotherly love, all that stuff."

"Why don't you sniff my pits, jerk-wad? I think I'll just send him to your house and let him bond with *you*. Y'all can watch Sesame Street and talk about how awesome Elmo is. Then you can pretend that you're Ernie and Bert! Bye."

"See ya." Jacob hung up the phone and went to his room to play one of them crazy video games, laughing to himself and wondering, w*hat would Mr. Eastover think?*

Although he was pretty sure he'd had his suspicions confirmed, and could therefore chalk it up as a success, Jacob's "Plan B" (the visit to Jim's trailer) had almost been a disaster. By extreme contrast, his "Plan A" went almost exactly as he had hoped. In fact, it probably wouldn't have gone much better if all three participants had been reading from a script.

About halfway through the evening meal, Jacob began to casually question his father about his new place of employment.

"Hey Dad, how old is *The Logtown News*?"

Mr. Hunter took a sip of iced tea to wash down a mouthful of food, then answered.

"You mean, how long has it been publishing papers?"

"Yes, sir. You know, how long has it been around?"

"I don't remember, exactly. Mr. MacDonald told me during my first job interview, and again during my *grand tour* Monday morning, but I don't remember, exactly."

He paused for a few moments, then said, "Sometime in the early nineteen-hundreds. Not long after Logtown was incorporated, I think."

"So," Jacob spoke as if he was reasoning this out on the spot, as if he had *not* already rehearsed each and every line three times in his head that afternoon, "the newspaper was definitely around in the late twenties and early thirties, right?"

"Oh, yeah. Absolutely."

"Do they still have copies of old newspapers from, you know, around that time?"

Mr. Hunter started to become a little bit suspicious right on cue.

"Why are you so interested in the newspaper all of the sudden?"

"Well, David heard from one of his friends, an older guy, that we're gonna have to write a report this year in school. You know, like an essay. And it's supposed to be about something historical in the state or this area. So anyway, he checked out a library book about the history of Logtown, and was reading about a guy named Stockton, the founder of Logtown. He was really rich, and had a huge house, practically a mansion, somewhere around town, but it burned down sometime around the early 1930s."

Jacob took a short pause, and was pleased to see that both parents were now listening intently.

"Anyway, the book doesn't go into much detail, and we thought maybe we could find some old newspaper articles about it."

Mr. Hunter nodded thoughtfully and approvingly, seemingly impressed with his son's taking the initiative and getting a head start on the fictional school project.

"Well, I'm sure they have all of the old papers, at least on micro-film. But how are you and David gonna be able to turn in the same report? I mean, how can you both write a report on the same thing?"

This was another anticipated question.

"We're not. David's writing about the history of Logtown, you know, the whole city. *I'm* gonna write about the man, James Stockton, and about the fire that burned down his house. The book made it sound like the fire was the reason he left Logtown. His wife died in it. The fire, I mean."

"That's terrible," said his mother, speaking for the first time since Jacob began questioning his father.

"So you're asking if you and David can come to the office and look at some of the old articles?" Mr. Hunter thought for a few seconds while Jacob held his breath. "I don't see why not. You and David could ride in with me, spend the morning doing your research, and I could bring you back on my lunch hour. Sure, that'll work. Of course, I'll have to clear it with Mr. MacDonald, but I doubt there'll be a problem. I'll ask him tomorrow." He nodded at Jacob, then stuffed his mouth with spaghetti.

"All *right*, coolio! Thanks." Jacob stuffed his own mouth, trying not to smile. He had hoped to be able to go tomorrow, but he'd also suspected that it was unlikely that they'd be able to on such short notice. Overall, his little scheme had gone exactly as planned.

After he finished supper and took a quick bath, Jacob grabbed the cordless phone and took it to his bedroom for some privacy. He dialed David's phone number, this time from memory. Once again, David answered.

He must really be pumped about all this, Jacob thought.

David didn't even bother with a *hello*.

"So what's the story, man. Are we on?"

"Probably so, but it won't be 'til Thursday. Dad's gotta clear it with his boss first. But he doesn't think it'll be a problem."

"Excellent!" This time David sounded (almost) like Keanu Reeves. "So, he bought the school-essay story?"

"Yep. Did you ever really doubt me?" Jacob pretended to chide his friend.

"'Course not." A brief pause, followed by, "Man, this is just awesome!"

Jacob grinned and figured that his friend was probably pacing the room or maybe even doing some sort of spastic celebratory dance in his excitement.

Jacob was excited, too, of course. But he was also afraid, and not just because of the revelation that a *dream*, something that was supposed to be a random, nocturnal exercise for his imagination; a fantasyland where his mind played while his body slept, was turning out to be some sort of link to the past; to a tragedy that had happened more than sixty-five years ago. He was afraid because of the revelation he'd had after reading about James Stockton and his wife and son, about the house and the fire.

What exactly was he going to *do* once he confirmed what he had never doubted: that he had witnessed, in his dream, an actual event? Something that had *really happened*, no matter how many years ago it may have been. What if he *was* getting some sort of message from beyond the grave? What was he supposed to do about it? That same question kept coming back – how was he supposed to *Help him/ Help us*?

This might be a fun little adventure for David, and Jacob had to admit that it was kind of exciting, but he was beginning to realize that his greatest hope *wasn't* to solve the mystery in order to right a wrong or even bring peace to some restless, tortured soul that might be crying from the grave for justice. What he really wanted was to prevent the dream from recurring.

Jacob was beginning to understand his biggest fear. If he did nothing; if he didn't at least *try* to figure it out; if he and David were unable to find the elusive pieces to this strange, time-spanning puzzle and somehow fit them together, he might be revisited by those visions, or worse yet, that ghastly, leering woman.

Every night, while the rest of the world slept, Jacob would lie in bed, awake and alone, with the stupid closet light on, haunted by the realization that if sleep came, he might be cast once again into the dream to watch the house burn; he'd be forced to look again look into those vacant eyes and feel that strange young (Jim) boy's universe of grief; he would, again and again, find himself fleeing through the woods in blind terror, that faceless woman just behind him, flitting in and out of the trees, her teeth clicking and chattering, her dark dress billowing in the wind. And Jacob was afraid that one night, he wouldn't escape those clutching hands.

He was grateful when David's voice broke in on this horrible image.

"So, what'cha got going on tomorrow?"

Jacob took a deep breath, shook his head, and tried to clear his throat; his mouth had gone dry as those images had passed before his open eyes.

"Probably the same as today," he finally answered. "Help Mom do some junk around here for part of the day, then . . . whatever."

"Same here. Want me to call around lunchtime? Maybe you can eat over here or something."

That sounded fine to Jacob.

"Sure."

"Excellent, dude!" David had become Keanu again. "Well my dad's giving me some really bizarre hand signals that I think means he needs the phone. I'll talk to you tomorrow."

"Later."

Jacob punched the off button on the phone and set it down. He thought briefly about pulling the book out from under the bed, but decided that looking at the faces in those pictures wasn't a good idea at night; it would be asking for trouble. So instead, he lay back on his bed, staring at the ceiling and trying unsuccessfully to think of anything besides the dream, the burning house, Jim Hanes, or James Stockton.

After a few minutes he gave up. He hopped off of the bed and strolled into the den, where he watched television until ten-thirty, when his folks ran him off to bed. He brushed his teeth quickly and finally crawled under the covers. The closet light stayed on all night.

11

They'll come tonight.

He sits, alone as always and enveloped in the warm, stale air. He looks around with dim, foggy eyes. He tries to remember exactly how long he *has* lived here, but decides that it doesn't really matter. He's lived in this place, or others just like it, for more years than he wants to remember.

And they always find me.

And that, he muses, is probably why he finally came home. Sometimes he tells himself that he came home to guard and preserve old secrets. Sometimes he tells himself he came home to somehow make things right. And he always hoped that when he came home, he'd somehow, finally, find peace. But if there really is peace for him somewhere in this world, it isn't here.

They always find me.

Now he thinks that maybe he came home to wait. Just to wait, that's all. Because if he waits long enough he will, eventually, die. And, oh, please God, he will finally find peace. He used to fear death; fear what surely awaited his soul when it was finally released from this old, rusty cage his body had become. Death, when all that he really is will finally escape what he has become. Death will find us all, he knows. It finds some sooner

my fault

and it finds others later.

But in the end it finds us all.

He no longer fears death; but neither does he seek it. He only waits for it, accepting that when his penance has been paid, death will finally come and release him. And will he be forgiven? Will they (finally) love him? Will they see and understand that although he dreads their visits, he knows and understands why they come to him?

Ghosts.

And now he almost laughs. But the sound won't quite come; it stops at his lips. Because he knows that there *are* ghosts, he's seen them all of his life. At first they seemed contented to just visit his dreams. That's where they were born, he thinks, and for many, many years, that's where they grew and swelled past the point of obscenity, until his dreams weren't big enough to hold them anymore. Now they wander freely, and they come to visit from time to time, always to remind him (as if he could forget). That's why he can't laugh. Because he believes, he *knows*, that there *really are ghosts*. Whether they are the walking, unquiet souls of those that once roamed the earth as flesh and blood or spirits we ourselves create – souls conjured up and given life by our memories of love and fear, he does not know. Nor does he care.

Dear Lord, I need a drink.

He gets up from the sofa where he has been sitting; a piece of furniture even older than the trailer. He's pretty sure it stinks, just like the rest of the place (and just like him), but he's surrounded himself with such foulness and bitterness for so long that he really doesn't notice. He stumbles on his bare feet to the kitchen, stepping around bottles, cans, garbage bags, and old rags that may have once been clothes. He is aware on some level that he can feel the grit and grime on the floor sticking to those bare, sweaty feet, but it has been long indeed since such things really registered in his mind.

When he reaches the counter of the trailer's small kitchen, he is surprised to see that his supply of drink is getting dangerously low. He'll have to make another run to the quick-stop tomorrow. He grabs a dirty glass out of the sink, rinses it out and wipes it on his jeans, then reaches for the jug. As he fills the glass, he notices rat pellets on the counter.

"Stinkin' rats," he mutters, brushing the pellets into the sink with a wide, sweeping motion of his free hand. He makes a mental note to also pick up some rat poison at the quick-stop as he puts the jug back in its place. He doesn't much care if rats live in the walls, but he will be damned if they're gonna come prancing through and crapping up the place where he keeps his food.

He wanders back to the sofa and sits down on a cushion so worn and used it might as well not even be there; he can feel each and every spring as they not-so-gently poke his backside. He takes a very long drink, then lays his head back, holding the glass with both hands between his knees, and stares at the water-stained, mildewy ceiling.

The boy knows.

He figures that was why the boy had come today, pretending to be sorry and wanting to fix the window that he broke. *That's* why the boy had asked the questions he'd asked. And now, as he leans back on his sofa, seeing the shapes of faces from long ago in those stains on the ceiling, he cannot imagine *how* the boy knows. How a little pre-pubescent *kid* had discovered what only one other person in the world knew about Jim Hanes. And that one other person, who lived a world away from Logtown, Mississippi, didn't care a whit what Jim called himself. That one other person knew Jim's secret only because it was his job to know, just as it was his job to keep quiet. Jim knew that mundane things like morals and ethics rarely held much sway over such men, but he also knew that they'd do just about anything if the price was right. As long as the money was there, the man would continue to do his job.

He brings the glass back to his mouth and finishes off the drink in one long swallow, hoping desperately for the mind-numbing effect that alcohol once gave him. But he knows better. It has been many long years since drinking had provided such an escape; for many years now he only noticed a difference in the way he felt when he *didn't* drink. And now, as he looks around his trailer, his prison, and sees the torn and threadbare carpet; the scuffed and broken faux wood paneling on the walls; the sagging junkyard fossils that pass as furniture, and countless years worth of garbage and refuse on the floors, he feels so *tired.* His eyes begin to burn with tears; the back of his throat hurts.

I'm just so tired, he thinks. *How long will I have to wait*? He leans back on the couch, barely noticing how the frame bites into his back. And as sleep finally begins to take him, he thinks incoherently *I am the trailer, and the trailer is me. We're rotting away together, and when it finally dies, so will I.*

Not long after he finally fell asleep, they came. With a vengeance, they came.

12

If Monday had been boring, then Wednesday was excruciating.

The Hunter family was pretty well settled into their new home, and the only unpacking and decorating left to do consisted of the small odds and ends that never seem to really get finished anyway. Mrs. Hunter intended to handle these little jobs herself, and that was just fine with Jacob.

The bad news was that he was now relegated to doing the same old piddly-squat type summer jobs he'd had to do before the family moved: sweeping the garage and driveway, dusting, Windexing the windows, vacuuming. These jobs were outside of his usual spectrum of responsibilities, which normally just included mowing, taking out the garbage, and cleaning his bedroom. Once school started, these new responsibilities would no longer be his (at least until the holidays and *next* summer).

The tasks themselves were easy and boring, and therein was the problem. They required no brainpower, and thus Jacob's mind was left to wander freely. After the extraordinary events of his first week in Logtown, his mind would only wander in one direction. Tuesday had been non-stop activity: the visit to the library; reading about the fire at the Stockton Estate; visiting Jim's trailer; and finally developing and enacting the scheme leading to a visit to the newspaper offices. Now there was nothing to do but these menial tasks that, for reasons

Jacob didn't understand, both parents felt confident would assist in building their son's character.

David called around 10:15 with the news that his mother had okayed Jacob having lunch with them ("breaking bread at the Phillips household" was how David had put it), and instructed him to try to be there around noontime.

And so the morning dragged on. Jacob swept and dusted, all the while wondering why he was doing so when they hadn't even been in the house long enough to allow any dust to accumulate.

Lunchtime at the Phillips house wasn't much better. There was still no sign of David's sister, but both boys got a hearty dose of Dillon. The little creep spent his entire time at the table playing with his food, making bizarre noises, and doing just about anything his four-year-old brain could think of to get the older boys' attention, or failing that, to annoy them as much as he possibly could (which was a quite lot).

Even retreating to the assumed safety of David's bedroom and locking the door didn't help. The wretched little monster simply lay down in the hallway, his face pressed to the narrow space between the bedroom door and the floor, where he began making more of those weird noises and calling both boys the worst names his four-year-old vocabulary would allow. Whenever he saw the shapes of David's feet approaching from under the door, he'd run down the hallway to where Mrs. Phillips sat on the sofa with a laptop computer perched upon her outstretched legs, hollering all the way that David was trying to hurt him.

After the third such incident, Mrs. Phillips finally banished Dillon to his own room and closed the door. This gave the two older boys little relief – first they had to listen to a wailing, heart-felt temper-tantrum. Finally, after five minutes or so, he became suspiciously quiet. There was a blissful lull that lasted for all of a minute, which must have been all the time required for the little schemer to come up with a new strategy to antagonize his older brother.

Dillon's and David's rooms were side by side, and the younger brother began to knock on the common wall. At first it was only one or two knocks at a time, followed by brief moments of silence in which he tried to gauge what the older boys' reaction would be. Soon the one or two knocks became a series of random but somehow almost intricate taps and thumps. The two boys finally gave up any hope of peace and left. On the way out the door, David swore to his friend that Dillon would eventually see justice in the form of a power-wedgy.

They rode aimlessly around the neighborhood for a while, not particularly excited about going to either boy's house. Somehow, being inside seemed to make the wait for Thursday, and its promise of a new and adventurous fact-finding mission at the newspaper office even more drawn-out and torturous. They finally parked their bikes beside one of the trees in the vacant lot down the street from

Jacob's house, sat in the tall grass, and talked awhile about what they hoped to find tomorrow.

It was soon clear to Jacob that it really didn't really matter what they found. David's mind was made up: the restless spirit of Mrs. Stockton had paid Jacob a visit in the form of a dream as part of her effort to have her mysterious, untimely death avenged. Furthermore, David seemed firm in his belief that a couple of twelve-year-olds doing such a thing was well within the parameters of reality. He was practically gushing with ideas of finding out not only *how* it happened, but *whodunnit* as well. The body would be located and consecrated with a proper Christian burial; the evildoer would be discovered and brought to justice; everybody would finally be at peace and live happily ever after. Easy as pie, pretty as a picture, and neatly wrapped up with a cheery, colorful bow on top.

Jacob was amazed at his friend's optimism, especially when he considered the fact that both boys would probably be laughing hysterically if told, just a week before, that they'd be passing their time the way they now were. But the most glaring roadblock Jacob saw (and he could see it quite clearly) was the fact that they *were* just a couple of twelve-year-olds, for Pete's sake! Hence the fearful question that had been echoing louder and louder in his mind for the past few days: *what am I supposed to do about it*? Even if every suspicion he had formed were to be confirmed, what was he *supposed to do*?

At some point, as he was musing and David was rambling, the idea that *maybe Jim Hanes knows what I should do* presented itself. It wasn't a *Eureka!* lightening-bolt type of revelation; it was instead as if the idea had kind of snuck in the back door, waited for an opportunity, and then just casually slipped in with the other thoughts as they mingled among themselves, too busy and important and impressed with themselves to notice the newcomer. And Jacob realized that the simple, quiet, unpretentious idea made more sense than all those other loud, strutting ideas put together. Jim Hanes, of all people in the whole world, *must* know what had really happened on that cold October night in Logtown, Mississippi, more than sixty years ago. And if he knew what had happened, then he might know what to do about it.

Jacob turned to David, finally ready to disclose his suspicion about Jim's true identity and was surprised to see that his friend was still talking. Jacob hadn't heard anything the boy had said for probably two minutes. He stared at David with a look of amused curiosity on his face.

David caught the look and stopped talking in mid-sentence. He stared back for a second or two, looking a little confused, then finally asked "What?" Before Jacob could answer, a vaguely familiar voice called out from the woods behind them.

"Hey, guys, wassuuup! What're y'all doin'?"

The two boys turned in unison and saw Greg. He was at the edge of the vacant lot, sitting on his bike and smiling.

"Don't tell him," Jacob whispered as he and David stood. It was unnecessary, and David gave him a curt, *no duh* type nod before calling out, "Duuuuude . . . wassup, diggity-dawg?"

"Nuthin' much," came the reply. Greg's face didn't reflect that he was the least bit suspicious about what the other two might have been discussing before his unannounced arrival, and Jacob felt confident (and relieved) that Greg hadn't overheard any of the conversation. He and David grabbed their bikes and pushed them through the tall grass to where Greg waited.

"Why're y'all just sitting around here?"

"Nuthin' much else to do," David answered. "Can't hang out at my place because Dillon's being his usual irritating self; can't go to Jacob's 'cause his mom might put us to work." This wasn't really true but David felt he should offer a reason that they weren't inside playing video games. "Don't really want to go to the Ice House because that greasy, rump-sniffin' loser Jared might be there."

"Let's go to Hanes's trailer," Greg suggested. "He and Jacob can face off in another death match; winner take all." He supplemented his feeble joke with an innocent, toothy grin.

David glanced at Jacob, wanting to see how he would react before responding. Jacob gave the other two boys a small, quick smile and shook his head. It was obvious that this hadn't been a malicious, Jared-esque kind of cut, just some good-natured (if a little weak) ribbing. David was relieved that Jacob had seen it for what it was.

"Sorry," he told Greg, "all future matches have been postponed until we have a chance to sell some tickets and get some endorsements. Plus I'd like to sell some 'Jacob' merchandise: t-shirts, hats, maybe underwear."

Jacob laughed even louder than the other two at this, all the time wondering *where does he come up with this stuff*? When the laughter died away, the three boys looked expectantly at each other. It was Greg who broke the easy, calm quiet.

"Well, if you're worried about the Ice House, that's where I just came from, and nobody's there."

David and Jacob looked at each other with identical expressions: *if it's okay with you, then it's okay with me*. Jacob gave a slight shrug and said, "Let's go." David flashed a smile, and as the three boys began riding down the trail, Jacob found himself wondering about that smile. It was hard to read, but had definitely reflected some sort of anticipation. He concluded that David was either looking forward to somehow reclaiming the Ice House, or looking forward to some sort of confrontation with Jared. As if, after such a confrontation, what had happened last Saturday could somehow be rectified.

Jacob was correct – those were the *exact* thoughts currently swarming around in David's mind. He was earnestly hoping for both of those things to happen. He felt he had as much a right to the Ice House as Jared, although, in truth, neither boy had a solid claim; the old refrigerator trailer had actually been discovered by a group of kids who had by this time already graduated high school, kids whose parents were among the first to move into *The Pines* when it was a new subdivision. Each new generation of boys who frequented the place considered it their own until they reached the age of fifteen or so, then found other, more mature (but only slightly so) things to do and drifted away, leaving the small clubhouse to the next group of boys.

David was well aware of this natural progression of events, and therefore believed he had at least as much a claim as Jared. According to the unwritten rules that governed life at the Ice House, he was correct. And that's why as he, Jacob, and Greg rode along the trails, David wore a smile of grim determination. After three long days of absence, he looked forward to sitting in *his* accustomed spot and looking at *his* magazines and comic books. And if a nasty confrontation with Jared was the price to be paid, so be it.

Jacob could almost read these thoughts on his friend's face as he stole quick glances from time to time. But he didn't share his friend's naïve, optimistic outlook. The crazy part was that Jacob didn't consider David to be naïve. The boy had a way not only with adults, but other kids as well; so far, Jacob hadn't met anyone who didn't like David. No, if anything, David was less naïve than any other twelve-year-old, or even fifteen-year-old that Jacob had met. The problem was that they weren't dealing with issues that twelve-year-olds usually dealt with; both the dream and the situation with Jared were well beyond the realm of what had been, until just a few days before, regular, day-to-day life for both.

Jacob felt as though this quest they had begun was kind of like wading through a swamp; a bog of thick, putrid water that was deep and growing deeper; just beneath the surface were leaches and snakes and maybe other things. Things that were bigger and slimier than leaches and snakes; things with mud-crusted scales and evil, slitted eyes; things with gaping jaws and fangs stained with the blood and flesh of other foolish children; naïve children, who thought they were equal to the challenge of trespassing in a forbidden world.

Jacob feared that he and David were already up to their waists in the foul smelling, bubbling sludge-water of the bog. Soon they'd be up to their necks, then over their heads. And still he was afraid to stop. His dream would drive him on; the feeling in his heart would drive him on. He could only keep wading, onward and outward, trying to keep his head above the surface; praying that his friend would do the same. Because he also felt that whatever was going to happen was going to happen no matter what; all he could do was fulfill his role and hope to make it through okay. It was bigger than a group of boys and their clubhouse, bigger than their petty fights and jealousies. What it *was* about still eluded Jacob, but he thought he was getting closer.

David, in his own small way, was pretty close to the mark as well. There *were* wrongs to be righted, and that week – that hot, humid, August-in-South-Mississippi week; the second-to-the-last *free* week before the boys would have to return to school – would see many debts paid.

13

Even as these thoughts and revelations were swirling around in Jacob's head (more in the shapes of feelings and emotions that his young mind was unable to organize into coherent thought, much less verbalize), he had vaguely been aware of the exchange of words going on between his two companions. They were discussing the upcoming church youth trip to Ship Island – who was going; who wasn't going; what they would do while they were there; what they had done the last time they went. He was hearing the sounds of their voices and even understanding the words, but was so caught up in his own thoughts that they could have been plotting his death and he would be none the wiser. It was vaguely akin to the sensation he felt whenever he fell into a light sleep in the back seat of the car during a long, nighttime drive; maybe on the way home after a weekend at his grandmother's house or after a University of Memphis football game. He seemed to hear every word his parents said up in the front seat, but he just didn't give a rip.

That was why it took him a few moments to realize that nobody was talking anymore. He looked up from where he'd been staring at the ever-moving path, just above his front tire, to see both boys looking at him, waiting for an answer.

"Huh?" he asked.

David shook his head in mock disgust. "Wake up, man. I said, are you going on the church trip to Ship Island?"

"Oh. Yeah, I guess. Where is Ship Island, anyway?"

"Out in the Gulf, maybe five, ten miles from Gulfport." David answered. "You have to ride out on a big boat. It takes about an hour, but it's worth it. The waves there are better than the ones at the regular beach, and there's a really old fort, built for one of the old wars, I think."

Jacob was beginning to get interested. He had no idea that there were islands in the Gulf, let alone one with a wartime fort on it. He had no idea what David had meant by *better waves than the regular beach*, not understanding that Ship Island was only one of the barrier islands off the coasts of the states that bordered the Gulf of Mexico. While these islands served to protect these states, at least to some decree, from the storm surge of hurricanes, they also effectively broke up the larger swells coming in from the Gulf of Mexico. This resulted in beaches with waves not much bigger than you'd find at a large lake.

Jacob was more intrigued by the fort than waves. "What war is the fort from?" he asked.

"I don't know, it's pretty old – made of stone and stuff – maybe the Civil War?" David looked over to Greg for some help but got only a shrug, which he in turn passed on to Jacob.

"Geez, that's pretty old." Jacob thought a second, then asked "What's its name?" Another factoid he'd learned from TV shows and movies was that forts always had a name.

David and Greg looked at each other with blank faces, and both offered him another shrug. Jacob offered his own little shrug back; it really didn't matter, he was sure that he would probably go. He had never been on a real island before.

"Is it very big?" he asked.

"The island or the fort?" David replied.

"Both."

"No and no. I mean, from the top of the fort, you can see the whole island, and the fort is only two or three stories high. It's hot as heck in the summertime, but it's still pretty awesome, you should go if you can."

"I probably will."

"I think maybe it's French!" Greg suddenly offered, and the other two boys looked at him with puzzled faces. "The fort; the name of the fort," he explained.

"Ze Forte' de yo Ma-Ma's booty." David suggested in a weak French accent, earning a few snickers from his fellow bike riders. Jacob was feeling pretty good again. All of the talk about the upcoming church trip had distracted him from his obsessive thoughts about the dream, the fire, the man, and the boy. It had been natural and spontaneous, leaving Jacob none the wiser that that these subjects suddenly weren't dominating his thoughts; he was, once again, just another boy talking to other boys about boy stuff.

"I've got a body-board," David began as the boys rounded the last curve in the trail before it emptied into the clearing where the Ice House sat. "I'll bring it, and we can take . . ."

Jacob, who was last in the precession, hadn't rounded that last curve yet, and therefore couldn't see whatever it was that made David stop in mid-sentence. He had just enough time to think *Take* what*? Five? A powder? A dump?* before he saw and understood.

Standing in front of the Ice House were Jared and an older boy, someone Jacob had never seen before. They stood side by side, arms crossed, legs spread slightly, and faces grim, looking a little like a couple of under-aged bouncers guarding an exclusive dance-club against unwanted patrons. At least, that was how they were trying to look. Behind them, Jacob could see Stevie smirking from the safety of the trailer.

David and Greg had slowed to a stop, and Jacob had to lean on his brakes pretty hard to keep from rear-ending them both. Even so, he nearly hit Greg's bike, and had to swerve to his right at the last second. His bike came to rest just behind and to the right of David's. Greg's bike had stopped just behind and to the left of David's, so that the three boys looked like they were in a kind of formation.

For a few seconds the two groups of boys just stared at each other without speaking. Stevie still wore that irritating smirk; Jared's face was impassive, but his eyes practically sparkled with icy laughter. The other boy, the older one, wore an expression that Jacob couldn't read.

Jacob turned his head slightly to look at his companions. Greg looked a little confused, but not really scared. David didn't really look scared, either, but was clearly suspicious. His face had lost its usual cheeriness, and his eyebrows were furrowed together. Jacob prayed that his face wasn't the only one showing fear. He didn't know that his expression was every bit as impassive as that of the older boy, the one he didn't recognize, as he looked into those hated, laughing, icy-cold and calculating eyes of Jared.

They were fixed squarely on Jacob, those eyes, boring into him with laughter and contempt. And he could read those eyes so easily; he looked and understood that this wasn't a chance meeting, a "hey, looky here, fancy meeting you guys, we had no idea y'all still hung around these-here-parts" kind of thing. They had waited, probably since this morning, for Jacob to show.

Only, that wasn't entirely accurate, either, was it? *No, it wasn't,* Jacob's heart told him. They had been waiting for him all *week*. They probably wouldn't have stayed all day, every day, but he knew, *he knew,* that they had been coming by here regularly every day since Monday, knowing that sooner or later he'd return, probably with David, and they'd be waiting. The likelihood of this scenario infuriated him. He felt that familiar burn, beginning in his ears and creeping down into his cheeks.

It was Jared. He hated Jacob now, *hated* him. Jacob knew it, just as he knew that the "Joe Mama" joke wasn't the only reason. The joke had been a mistake; Jacob had realized that almost as soon as the words had left his mouth. But he understood now that the joke had just been an excuse for Jared; even if "Joe Mama" had never been uttered, he would have found another reason to hate the *newboy*. Jacob understood this with an odd clarity, but he still didn't understand *why*!

And that was why his ears and cheeks burned with a hot rage that was beginning to bubble and froth inside of him, a rage that that made him clench and unclench his jaws, grip then release the handlebars of his bike with his hands; unaware he was even doing these things as he stared back into those gray, malicious, laughing eyes, wanting to scream *why? There's no reason for you to hate me, so WHY?*

It was David who finally broke the tense, uneasy silence.

"Hey, Mike," he said, giving Jacob the *name* of the older boy but leaving him to wonder still who exactly Mike *was*, and how David knew him, and if was good or bad that David knew him.

"Mike" gave a barely perceptible nod, just a slight tilt of his head in David's direction, and answered, "Hiya, David."

"So, what's up? You just visitin', or moving back, or what?" David was speaking in a perfectly calm voice, but it wasn't the friendly voice he used when speaking to Jacob or Greg; it wasn't the tone of someone who is glad to see the person he's speaking to. Jacob finally pulled his eyes away from Jared's unwavering, ice-blue, laughing stare to steal a quick glance at his friend, and saw that David's face was like granite. He didn't look angry, but he sure looked serious. Jacob had a sneaking suspicion that David not only knew who this boy Mike was, but also why he was here. Jacob had a sneaking suspicion that *he* knew why Mike was here, too.

"Naw, not movin' back, just visitin' my brother. School's about to start back up and I won't get to see him as much."

The bell finally went off in Jacob's head – Mike was Jared's older brother. The one who had helped build the race-course; the one who had told Jared that Crazy Mary *was* crazy, the one who now lived in Gulfport with their father; the one who, according to David, Jared *worshipped.* Jacob looked at Mike, who had now uncrossed his arms and stuck his hands deep into the pockets of his faded blue jeans.

The boy (he was seventeen, actually) stood just over six feet tall and was lean but not skinny. He had about three days worth of stubble on his face, which under different circumstances, Jacob might have admired. A NASCAR cap was pulled down low over his forehead, and David could see part of a tattoo peeking out from beneath the right sleeve of his t-shirt.

Mike pulled his right hand out of his pocket. It held a battered pack of cigarettes. He fished one out, stuck it between his lips, and lit it with a Bic lighter pulled from the other pocket. He took a long drag, then ever-so-casually blew the smoke out of his mouth and nose as he began talking again.

"Anyways, I thought I'd pay the Ice House a visit; see if you guys were takin' care of it. And I wanted to meet the new boy." As he spoke the words 'new boy', his eyes fell squarely on Jacob. Jacob, ears and cheeks still flushed and burning, struggled to keep his face impassive. Mike's eyes were brown, and lacked the cold intensity of Jared's, but they conveyed their own message quite clearly: *New boy has made me mad; he has done somethin' to insult my little brother, and I plan on makin' things right.* He lifted the cigarette to his mouth and took another hearty drag. This time he blew the smoke out of one corner of his tightly drawn lips, for maximum *I really* am *as bad as I look, so don't mess with me* effect.

"His name is Jacob. He just moved here last week." David, still speaking calmly, casually, paused a moment before adding "He's okay, Mike."

Another drag on the cigarette. Another cloud of smoke blown forcefully out of one side of Mike's mouth.

"Oh, he's okay, huh? That's funny, 'cause I heard he had some cute stuff to say about my mama."

A huge, jagged chunk of ice immediately formed in Jacob's stomach. It actually hurt enough that for a moment he thought he might double over with pain, maybe even poop in his pants, right in front of his friends and enemies alike. Was he about to have to face-off with a high school boy who wanted to settle a score that didn't even exist? He took a deep breath, held it for a second, then blew it out slowly through his pursed lips. If he'd been smoking, he would have looked a lot like the older boy, who had re-crossed his arms, standing before him. When his lungs were almost completely empty, he began to slowly re-fill them. As he did so, he became aware that David was speaking again. His voice was still calm, the same voice of reason he'd used with Jared a few days before, but it seemed to Jacob that its tone had gone up an octave. Now it was the voice of someone who understood that all the words in the world were useless, but had to be spoken anyway.

"He didn't say anything about your mama, Mike. It was just a misunderstanding."

He paused again, and Jacob assumed he was trying to figure out a way to explain the *Joe Mama* joke without making it sound even remotely insulting. Jacob felt pretty sure that, under the circumstances, there was no way to do so. He also knew that Mike would believe whatever story he'd been fed by his own brother over whatever story he'd be fed now.

God only knows what that *story sounded like*, Jacob thought to himself. And he was once again surprised at the rage boiling up inside of him, melting that chunk of ice in his stomach and burning his face and ears and his heart. The adrenaline seemed to shoot through his body in an instant; he felt his arms and legs, even his fingers twitch suddenly, tingling with the electricity of that rage. He decided that if he sat still for another second, he would either burst into flame or just dissolve into a puddle around his bike. He wasn't angry at being threatened, or at being lied about, or even being the target of a vicious prank that could have gotten him seriously hurt or even killed. He was enraged by a simple fact of life, a fact he'd discovered two years before, when Cliff and Chris had come upon him raking his yard and minding his own business – *there was no reason for it, ANY of it!!*

Jacob jumped off of his bike. He took a step forward, listening to his bike fall to the ground behind him. He felt his right arm raise, finger pointing, into the air. He opened his mouth, and listened as the words came pouring out.

"I didn't say nuthin' for him to get mad about, and he knows that but he *don't care*! David just explained it to you, and *you* don't care! Did he tell you what he did to *me* at Hanes's trailer? Did he tell you *THAT*?"

Jacob paused long enough to look from one brother to the other, and his question was answered without a word being spoken. If he'd been in a different frame of mind, he would have been horrified by the expressions those boys wore. Yes indeedy, Jared had told, and Mike had probably yukked it up pretty good before telling his little brother how proud he was, and how now he thought he'd like a turn with the little jerk who'd insulted their mama. In another frame of mind, Jacob might have thought, *oh, well, necessary or not, that just the way the world is: the sky is blue; gravity keeps us from floating off into that blue sky; water's wet; and necessary or not, guys like Mike and Jared can only keep* their *place in the world by keeping others down*. But he wasn't in another frame of mind, and the idea of those two, sitting side by side, sharing a smoke and having a good ol' knee slappin' laugh about what had happened to Jacob at Jim's trailer burned his heart even more.

Jacob took another step forward, finger still pointing, and felt his mouth open again, spewing forth words without any prompting. Again, there was nothing for him to do but listen, all the while knowing that all he was doing was guaranteeing that he'd get a pretty severe beating at the hands of the older boy. But still, he couldn't seem to stop himself.

"You stupid, redneck *jerk*!! You don't care because all you want is a chance to prove how tough you are!" He paused, then almost screamed "Well, c'mon, show us! Be a tough guy!! Show everyone how you can pick fights with smaller kids!! C'mon, show us!! SHOW ME!!"

His mouth finally closed, but only part of the way; his lips remained apart, baring his grinding teeth. His vision became blurred as his eyes began to water with tears borne of rage and fear and frustration. Silently praying that he wasn't about to start crying in front of everyone, he looked over at Jared. For the first time since Jacob met him, there was no laughter in his eyes. It had been replaced by uncertainty, but only for the few seconds it took for him to decide that there was too much to be lost if he backed down. Those ice-blue, glittering jewels began to gleam again in an instant, but now only with bitter hatred. Yet for all that hatred, they paled next to the rage in Jacob's eyes.

Jacob shifted his eyes to Stevie, who was still peeping out of the trailer but no longer grinning, long enough to think *You pathetic little . . . flunky*, then finally brought them back to rest on Mike.

Mike, who seemed to have been coolly considering Jacob's first comments (they *were* all true – not that it mattered), did not react well to being called a stupid, redneck jerk (perhaps because, on some level, he understood that these accusations might also be true). He took a long, break's-over-time-to-get-back-to-work drag on his cigarette, then threw it to the ground and made a big production of grinding it out with the toe of his motorcycle boot. He shook his head a little, wearing a thin smile that spoke before his mouth even opened: *You poor little putz, I didn't really* want *to beat the tar out of you, but now I gotta.* When his mouth opened and he *did* speak, he did say pretty much that, with just a touch of rationalization.

"Boy, all I wanted was to make sure that Jared got a fair shot at settlin' his score with you. But you had to run yer big mouth off and start insulting me. For that, you will be sorry." He began walking toward Jacob, and Jared fell in line behind him, his eyes laughing again in a perfectly contented little smirk.

Jacob knew what was coming, but *still* he raged, determined to do as much damage as he could before he was beaten to a pulp – something he knew wouldn't take long. He set his feet firmly in the ground, just as he had two years ago when Cliff had come stalking up to him wearing a wilder but somehow less threatening "it's time to pay the piper" look on his face. This time, though, Jacob was suddenly gripped by an urge to charge, screaming and fists flailing, into Mike's waiting arms. And he probably would have, if David hadn't stepped up beside him and placed a firmly restraining hand on his left shoulder.

"You can't fight him, Mike," he said in a voice that was still a notch or two tighter than normal, but determined none-the-less. "You're five years older and you're way bigger and it's not right."

Mike paused for a second, but not to consider David's words. He had simply forgotten that the other boys were even there. He shook his head and gave David the kind of look parents sometimes give their children before handing out a simplistic *that's just the way things are* answer to the children's simplistic question.

"Dave, you and your other friend can stay and watch or you can go, but you best keep out of it. This little punk is gonna eat some dirt, he's gonna hurt, and he's gonna bleed, and I promise you, if you get in my way you will too." He paused a moment to let David consider.

Jacob, teeth still gritted, finally looked over at the two boys beside him. Greg was still sitting on his bike. His mouth was hanging open a bit, and his expression showed that he simply didn't believe that any of this was really happening. Jacob expected that he'd cut and run at any second.

Then he turned to David, who was still standing to his left with his hand on Jacob's shoulder. His face wore a look of grim determination and Jacob knew he wasn't leaving, even if it meant he too would be eating dirt shortly. And suddenly Jacob felt, could almost see, a bond forming between them. It was like nothing he'd felt before; a greater trust, respect, and . . . *love* . . . than he'd ever felt for a friend.

David hadn't run away with the other boys last Saturday, when Jared had thrown the rock. Even when Jim had come tearing out of the trailer, David had stayed. David had gone with Jacob to the library to help his friend look for evidence of something that he'd *dreamed* about, for Pete's sake! David believed in the reality of Jacob's strange dream now, but even before he'd believed, any jokes he'd made had been good-natured. And Jacob now believed that

David would stand by him, not only to face the threat that presently loomed before them, but the unseen threats that surely awaited them as they tried to resolve whatever mystery was hidden behind that strange dream he'd had.

Jacob loved the boy standing next to him, more than any friend he'd ever had. Suddenly, he had a new understanding of what love really was. He turned back to Mike and incredibly, his mouth turned into a bitter smile.

"I'm not leaving, Mike," he heard David say.

Mike looked sincerely puzzled, but it didn't shake his resolve. There was no way in heaven or on earth that he was going to be cowed by a couple of sixth-graders. And in front of his little brother? *You've got to be kidding*!

"Well Davy, if that's what you want, that's fine by me." And he charged.

Jared and David stepped up together, meeting him head on.

Had either of them been even a few years older, they might have had a chance. But they were both only twelve, and both were beginning to suffer that physical awkwardness that accompanies early adolescence. Mike was seventeen, wiry and tough. By the time he was fifteen, he'd been in more fights than the two younger boys would in their entire lives combined. It was the way he'd been brought up, the way he'd lived; it was one of the many gifts passed on by his father, and it was a gift both he and his father had passed on to his younger brother. It was simply their way of dealing with anger or shame, their way of dealing with people who looked down on them, or insulted them, or even frightened them; it was their way of getting in the last word when they couldn't think of anything else to say. It was how they kept other people in their place. If Mike had ever pondered the *reason* for it, his conclusion would have been *that's just how it is, that's all.*

David was half a step ahead of Jacob, and tried to throw a punch with his right arm. Mike simply reached forward with both hands, grabbing David by the collar of his shirt and absorbing the half-deflected punch in his left shoulder. He pulled David in close, shook his head as if he had never seen anything so pathetic in his entire life, and made to push him away with enough force to send him sprawling.

At that moment, Jacob grabbed Mike's left arm with one hand and punched with the other, catching the older boy just below and behind his left armpit. There was some pain, but Mike was more enraged by the fact that these two little idiots were actually fighting back. He released David with his left hand and quickly grabbed Jacob by the wrist. Holding firm to Jacob's wrist, he turned back to David, who was struggling to get away, and pushed him backwards with as much force as he could muster with one arm. David went sprawling backwards, crashing into his own bicycle and landing in a heap at Greg's feet. Greg remained astride his bike, clueless as to what he should do, what he *could* do, to somehow help his friends and avoid getting his own tail whipped in the process.

Jacob was still struggling wildly, but was helpless now that he had Mike's full attention. He was spun around, and suddenly found himself face to face with the older boy, who now had a very firm grip on both his shoulders. Mike flashed him a little smile, just enough for Jacob to realize *yes, this guy definitely shares Jared's blood*, and whispered, "Get ready, little Mr. Smartmouth, it's hurtin' time." He had drawn back a fist, letting it hang in the air for a second, when a hard-as-granite voice suddenly echoed like thunder through the small clearing.

"Son, if you touch that boy, I will crack your skull wide open!"

Everyone froze; all eyes turned to where the path opened into the clearing. There, looking approximately fifteen feet tall and with his dark eyes blazing, stood Jim Hanes.

Six pairs of eyes threatened to pop from their sockets. Six mouths hung open wide enough for a flying insect to enter, explore a little, then leave again unhindered. It's unlikely that any of the boys would have noticed if one did. Mike had released Jacob's arm and taken one step back, but it didn't occur to the younger boy to run for safety. He just stood and stared with the rest of them. He really wasn't as frightened by the sight as the rest were, but was definitely more surprised.

Jim remained standing at the edge of the clearing. He was wearing a different t-shirt, this one a dull, washed out black but every bit as worn, frayed, and full of holes as the others they'd seen him wear; the collar hanging loosely around his neck, exposing his jutting collar-bones, the sleeves hanging sparsely around the knobs of his shoulders. The jeans he wore may or may not have been the same, but the work boots were the same dingy, mud-crusted ones he was wearing when Jacob had first seen him at Dee Dee's (it had not yet been a week, but seemed almost another lifetime). His arms hung loosely to his sides, and in his right hand he held what looked like a wooden axe handle. For a brief moment, every one of those boys was unified in a prayer of thanksgiving that there wasn't a blood-stained blade affixed to the end. But judging by the looks on everyone's faces, there might as well have been.

Jim took one more step into the clearing, then watched with some amusement as David scrambled to his feet and quickly backed away, not realizing that he was moving closer to Mike (or maybe just not caring, as Mike was now definitely the lesser of two evils). Greg, who had finally jumped clear of his bike, was backed up against a tree at the edge of the clearing, to Jim's left. He appeared to realize that he was essentially cut off from the rest of the boys, and seemed to be trying to shrink away – the way a puppy will sometimes cower into a corner to avoid a child's clutching hands – or maybe just somehow disappear into the tree.

Jim took a moment to survey all of the boys as they stood there, barely breathing and waiting to see what he'd do next, then he finally spoke again. The amusement had left his eyes; the old, familiar glare was back.

"Ain't 'nuthin sorrier than a older, bigger guy beatin' up on a smaller one." He raised his right arm, pointing the axe handle directly at Mike. "You need to get outta here, boy. Go hang out with yer hoodlum friends, and leave these boys alone."

The moment Jim pointed that piece of hickory at Mike, Jacob found himself backing away, almost involuntarily. Mostly because he didn't want to be in the line of fire between Mike and Jim, but he also had the strange idea that Mike might make a grab for him, as if to take him hostage and use him as a shield against Hanes. Once clear, Jacob finally looked over at the older boy.

Mike's face was flushed and caught in a bizarre expression, hanging somewhere between confusion, the fear of being humiliated in front of the rest of the boys (including his little brother; Jacob could almost hear David's words echoing in his ears – Jared *worships* Mike), which would surely happen should he tuck tail and run; and the greater fear, deeply ingrained from the time he was in first grade. The fear – the terror, really – that Jim Hanes was a raving madman who probably *would* crack open his skull without much concern for the consequences. And although that shroud of mythical fear seemed to Jacob somehow lessened, somehow thinner, because he now thought he knew who Jim Hanes really was – *had been* – he too believed that Jim would do it.

"This ain't none of your business, old man," Mike finally managed in a voice that was dry and not quite steady. He seemed to want to say something more, but nothing else would come out.

Jim took another step, and his eyes were almost glowing. Jacob was again awed by the power of this old man. His complexion was sickly, he was dirty and mangy looking. He was practically a skeleton with skin and hair, but he still had a power about him – perhaps born of the bitterness and rage that had led him to the life he now lived; and maybe it still fed on that bitterness and rage. Whatever the source, it *was* power, thick and raw.

"I'm makin' it my business, son. And I'm tellin' you, you ain't gonna touch that boy. I guaran-dang-tee you that." He had lowered his right hand again, and glared at Mike, piercing him with all the force, all the *power* of that bitterness and rage.

Mike seemed to be on the verge of wilting under those eyes, but still couldn't bring himself to back down.

"It ain't your business," he insisted, and it seemed to Jacob that Mike could hear the pathetic futility in his own voice just as clearly as the rest of the people in that clearing. His large but fragile ego was desperately clinging to something that had become water in its hands.

Jim had heard it, too, and was nodding now, and when he spoke now it was with the voice of a grandfather urging his child's child to move ahead with a task that may be bitter, but was for their own good.

"Go on, son, just go on. I don't want to have to put you down, but I will if you make me."

Those last words sent a chill up Jacob's sweaty back that actually made him shudder. They reminded him of the way an old man might describe shooting a dog that was in great pain or rabid or deathly sick: I had to put Ole Blue *down.* He looked again at the older boy and saw that fear, and (for once in his life) good sense would finally prevail. Mike took one step back, made to turn around, and then his eyes fell on Jared. His younger brother *who worships Mike*

was staring at him with dazed, uncomprehending eyes. For a moment Mike looked as if those eyes frightened him more than Jim's had; for a second he looked as though he wanted to try to speak to Jared. Then his face flushed to a dark crimson. He looked around at the rest of the boys, realizing that all eyes were on him, all eyes were now witnessing what was happening to him, aware of how he was somehow shrinking right in front of them but especially

worships

in front of Jared. He jerked his head back to Jim, his eyes filled with the same malice Jacob had seen earlier in Jared's eyes. As he began slowly stepping backward, finally walking away, he pointed at Jim with one finger and started to scream in a shrill voice, spit spraying from his trembling lips.

"I'M GONNA *KILL* YOU, OLD MAN! *KILL* YOU!! YOU OLD, WRINKLED, DRIED UP FREAK, I'LL *KILL* YOU!!"

Instead of getting angrier at the sound of Mike's shrill voice, Jim actually seemed to relax a little. His eyes were still glaring (Jacob had only seen something other than a glare in those eyes once), but they no longer seemed to blaze with the fiery intensity they'd had since he first stepped into the clearing. He just stood there, wearing the standard Jim Hanes glare and nodding his head gently.

"Son, if you ever decide that you wear jockeys instead of panties, I'll be ready and waitin'."

David, who was standing between Mike and the tree into which Greg was still trying desperately to disappear, snickered. Jacob cut him an angry *shut up right now* look; Mike's pride had been pummeled already, and his anger was now thankfully focused on someone besides the younger boys. David caught the look and nodded (he almost looked ashamed of himself), but kept right on snickering. He held up a hand, palm out, and kept nodding his head apologetically while staring at the ground; knowing that he really needed to get it under control, but simply unable to do so.

Mike looked first at David, then at Jacob, then at Jim again. His rage enveloped them all like a blanket. The laughter finally died on David's lips; only Jim seemed untouched by the wave of malice that now flooded through the clearing. When Mike spoke again, he didn't scream but only whispered.

"I'll kill every *one* of you. Every . . . freakin' . . . one of you."

He turned to leave, then froze, realizing the only way out of the clearing was the path behind Jim. He turned again, now trembling with his impotent fury, and walked, head down, as quickly as his wounded pride would allow, past Jim and up the path. The crunching sound of his footfalls seemed to echo hollowly in the silence of the clearing.

Jacob watched as he disappeared into the woods, then his eyes fell on Jim. He thought at first that Jim was now glaring at him, then realized the old man was looking past him. He turned around, saw Jared, and nearly reeled as if from a blow to the head. Jared's eyes were boring into his own with an unmasked hatred and bitter fury that he'd never seen before, even on Jim's face. His gray eyes weren't dead, as they'd been in reaction to the "Joe Mama" joke; they were frighteningly alive. They danced brightly, wildly, feverishly in his pale face. The two boys stared at each other; each seeing into the other, sharing an understanding that no one else in that clearing could see, save for Jim. It lasted only for a few seconds, then Jared broke the spell by looking away. He looked around at the other boys in the clearing, sparing each only a quick glance of contempt, then followed in his brother's footsteps. Unlike his brother, however, Jared walked casually, almost proudly, with his chin up. He finally passed Jim without a look or comment, silently vanishing up the path.

Jim watched him go, then turned to look at the three remaining boys (Stevie was hiding in the back of the trailer; his face ashen, his heart racing, and his bowels threatening). His eyes, still glaring, came to rest on Jacob, and he opened his mouth hesitantly. And Jacob knew, he *knew*, what Jim wanted to ask him (*how do you know*? *How could you possibly know*?). But he also knew that Jim wouldn't ask that question, not here, not in front of the others. Jacob's head whirled from the heat, from the fight, and from fear, but mostly with realization that he was right. He didn't just *think* he knew who Jim Hanes really was, he *definitely* knew. Jim closed his mouth and continued to glare, but his eyes were also tinged with curiosity.

How do you know? *How could you possibly know*?

Jim stared a moment or two longer, then finally shifted his gaze to the other two boys.

"You fellas'll want to stay away from this place," he said in a voice that was both gruff and yet somehow tinged with an almost parental concern. "It ain't safe no more." He paused, looking almost thoughtfully around the woods; looking beyond the clearing. "Really never was."

He nodded as if someone else had actually spoken the words and he was in complete agreement, then turned and slowly walked back up the trail. His arms hung wearily to his side, dragging the tip of the ax handle in the dirt. As he watched Jim vanish behind the trees, Jacob briefly forgot everything that had just happened, everything but the last three words the old man had spoken. And his only confused thought was *what did he mean by that*?

For a full minute, the boys did nothing but stare at each other. Greg finally stood up and walked over to his bike. His face showed more shock and disbelief than the others, possibly because he had been absent during the last get together that Jim had been a part of. David finally broke the silence.

"What the . . ." was all he managed, but it still seemed to sum everything up nicely.

Greg nodded, and turned to Jacob.

"Yeah, I thought he tried to kill you Saturday. Now he comes trotting along and saves you? What's going on?"

Jacob only shrugged. He glanced at David, searching his face for any signs of suspicion, but saw only curiosity. This came as a huge relief. For some reason, telling David about his suspicions (now all but confirmed) about Jim's real identity suddenly seemed like a bad idea.

"Don't ask me," he finally answered. "I'm just glad he came when he did."

"No kidding." Greg was shaking his head. "I thought Mike was gonna kill you guys." Then a funny thing happened. His face blushed, and he looked down, suddenly very interested in either his feet or maybe some insects crawling around on the ground. It took a few seconds for Jacob to realize that Greg was ashamed. Not because he had cowered in fear when Jim had shown up; they'd *all* done that. It was because he'd been afraid to stand beside Jacob and David when they'd refused to back down before Mike.

Jacob also realized something else – he wasn't angry, or even disgusted at Greg because he understood somehow that Greg wasn't *supposed* to be involved. He wasn't a part of what was happening; he was little more than a spectator. Jacob wasn't sure he understood *why* he believed this, but he did. He was beginning to believe that everything that had happened to him since arriving in this city was happening for a reason; maybe something was making all of this happen, and like it or not, he had become a part of it. He thought it had been his decision to bring David into it by telling him about the dream, but now he wasn't even sure of that. Maybe David was *supposed* to be a part of it. David had been the first boy he'd met, and they'd met at Jim's trailer, of all places. He and David had hit it off almost immediately. David had been the only boy not to run off after Jared had set Jacob up at Jim's trailer Saturday. Jacob felt a little comforted by the fact that David might have been drawn into whatever was going on, and he was certain that whatever it was, Greg wasn't a part of it.

He looked back at David, who seemed preoccupied with what Greg had just said, but oblivious to his embarrassment. His trademark grin was back, bigger than ever.

"Did you see Mike's face? He was scared to death!" As if David hadn't been.

"You shouldn't have laughed at him," Jacob replied. He had seen Mike's face, all right, and had read more in it than any of the others, save maybe Jim.

"I couldn't help it, man. I'd never heard that one before, 'wear jockeys instead of panties.' Besides, he deserved it. He's a senior in high school; we're in sixth grade. And he knew Jared didn't have any real reason to be mad at you! It should be the other way around."

Jacob just shrugged again, than looked around the clearing. He was feeling uncomfortable again, especially when he remembered Jim's final words.

"Whatever. But I think Jim was right; we don't need to hang around this place anymore."

Greg looked as though he was in complete agreement, but David was shocked and angry. His grin vanished.

"What, you mean just give it over to Jared? You've got to be kidding!"

"It's not safe here, David! I think we need to clear out and let Jared have her!" Jacob stopped as his own words reached his ears.

Let Jared have her! He hadn't meant to phrase his sentence that way, but it somehow seemed perfectly appropriate. As he pondered why that might be, another chill seemed to run down his sweaty back.

David was still shaking his head. "No, I'm *not* just going to let Jared have the Ice House. It's mine, too. Half the stuff in there is mine!" He stopped for a moment, and his eyes studied Jacob for a moment, trying to get a read on the strange new expression on his friend's face. "Besides, you've got a guardian angel now. He may smell like an outhouse, but he's pretty fearsome. Hey, if his looks don't scare someone off, the smell will."

Greg smiled at the joke, but Jacob couldn't. Just being in the clearing was making him more uncomfortable by the second. He found himself wondering if Mike and Jared had just pretended to leave, and would come back now that Jim was gone. And what was David's hang-up about this place, anyway? It had seemed cool to Jacob when he'd first seen it, but he'd found almost nothing but trouble here. David may have some happy memories of this place, but Jacob didn't. He tried to think of another argument to convince David.

"What if Mike comes back with some of *his* friends, older guys? Jim's an old man! What do you think he can do against a gang of high-schoolers?"

Greg needed no other convincing. His face twitched for a moment, and his eyes began to dart nervously around the clearing. Jacob thought he might jump on his bike and split right then, maybe without waiting for the other two boys. David was still shaking his head, but his face seemed less certain. Jacob decided that was good enough for now.

"Look, we can decide later, but I think we should take off now, at least for today. Mike and Jared are really mad, and they might come back. I've gotta call you tonight anyway, about the other thing. We can talk more then."

David considered this a moment, then finally nodded. Jacob glanced at Greg, afraid that the other boy might want to know what "the other thing" was, but Greg seemed entirely focused on getting away from the clearing and didn't even appear to have even heard the words.

Jacob and David walked over to where their bikes lay. As David reached down to pick his up, Jacob saw that his elbow had been bleeding. It had probably been cut when Mike had sent him sprawling backwards into the bicycles. Jacob stopped to check himself out, and found that he didn't have a single scratch.

Unbelievable, he thought.

"Your right elbow's bleeding," he said. David, looking surprised, twisted his arm around to look at it. He winced, but Jacob couldn't tell if it was from pain or just the sight.

"I'll live," he said, then smiled, adding, "I ain't got time to bleed!" in a husky voice.

Jacob grinned back. He'd heard that line in a movie before, but couldn't place it at the moment. The two boys hopped on their bikes and fell in line behind Greg, who was starting to look like he was going to have an accident in his britches if they didn't hurry up. Suddenly, David stopped, turned, and called out in a loud voice.

"You can come out now, Stevie. Big, bad, scary man all gone-gone!"

Jacob turned in time to see Stevie's thin arm stick out of the trailer door, his middle finger pointing skyward. Even Greg joined in the mirthful laughter, and the three boys finally turned and rode away from the clearing.

Stevie watched them go from the safety of the trailer, then turned and sat in one of the old lawn chairs. He decided it would probably be best to wait at least a few minutes before making his own exit from the clearing that was home to the Ice House. He wasn't thrilled at the idea of coming upon the other three boys on the path without Jared to back him up, and he sure didn't want to face that crazy old psycho Hanes all alone.

He grabbed a comic book from the table and looked at it absently while his mind went over the vast changes in the small group of boys that had taken place over the past few days. David and Jacob seemed to have practically become blood brothers, and Greg, as always, preferred David's company. Worst of all, Jared was in a cruddy mood all of the time these days. All he ever wanted to talk about was getting back at Jacob. And after what had just happened, Stevie expected it to get even worse.

He could understand Jared's dislike of the new boy. He didn't much like Jacob, either. After all, the boy had just breezed in out of nowhere, immediately bonded with David, and then expected to just come in and practically take over the Ice House. And David was letting him. Yeah, he understood why Jared might dislike the boy, but he didn't understand Jared's hatred of him. He had been as shocked and scared as the other two boys when Jared had thrown that rock and broken the trailer window Saturday, but more out of the worry that they could get in serious trouble than concern for Jacob's safety. And anyway, the new boy had somehow come out of that one smelling like roses: the terror of every kid in Stratford County was now apparently his bodyguard.

Hanes had made Jared's big brother look like a punk, like a little *girl*, for cryin' out loud. Stevie figured Jared would be angrier than ever. He and Mike were probably hunkered down somewhere together, plotting some sort of revenge; Greg and David were probably rallying around the new boy, no doubt laughing about the whole thing (including little Stevie, who had been hiding in the trailer). And where did that leave him? Alone, that's where. And not just physically – he felt as if he'd been completely shut out from the rest of the group. The idea wasn't just an uncomfortable one; it was downright scary.

He decided right then and there it wasn't a place he was going to stay for very long. And so his brain went to work, and double-timing it at that. His daddy had always jokingly (and oddly enough, almost lovingly) called him a little schemer, but had no idea just how detailed and calculating some of his son's plans really were. Stevie decided that his best (safest) course of action would be to approach

Mike and Jared, maybe later this very afternoon, tomorrow at the latest, and . . .

Stevie . . .

It was just a whisper, but Stevie was sure he'd heard it. Had Jared snuck back to the trailer? It had sounded more like a woman's voice, but he'd been deep in thought when he'd heard it. He stood up, walked to the door of the trailer and looked out. There was nobody there. And there wasn't a sound to be heard. A thick, stifling silence filled the small clearing.

Nobody here, thought Stevie. *I'm still alone*.

He suddenly realized just *how* alone he really was. He didn't like being alone anytime, but in this strange, sudden silence, he wasn't just nervous; he was downright terrified. He looked back into the trailer, and it seemed to him that it looked deeper and darker than he had ever remembered.

It's a coffin. The thought came into his mind unbidden, and he felt his fear multiplied. *It's not a trailer; it's a big coffin*!

He panicked, turned, and ran out. His bike was right where he always parked it, beneath the huge old oak that stood beside the Ice House. As he jogged toward it, a small root, jutting up only one or two inches from the ground, snagged his foot, tripping him. His momentum carried him forward into the larger twisting, knotted roots that bulged along the base of the tree, where he fell. His hands, held out in front of him to help break the fall, were torn open as they slid across the coarse bark of one of the largest roots, as was one of his knees. He rolled over, looking in horror at the torn skin of his palms, able to see *inside* of his hands for a split second before the blood began to flow.

He turned angrily back toward the smaller root that he had tripped over, ready to give it the kind of tongue-lashing people usually dish out at inanimate objects after, through their own clumsiness or inattention, they've stubbed their toes or barked their shins (you stupid, pain-in-the-rump coffee table, sidewalk, tree root, etc.).

Unfortunately, there was no small tree root for Stevie to vent at. He stared at the spot where he'd tripped for a few empty seconds, his head tilted slightly like a puppy trying to figure out those strange, kissing noises its new owner is making, then got carefully to his feet. He looked down at his hands for a moment. They were both still bleeding, but not profusely, and he could see dirt and little specks of bark mingled with the blood of the open wounds. He winced at the sight, then closed both hands into loose fists, and crossed his arms, snuggling both hands into the security of his armpits. He took a cautious couple of steps toward the spot where he'd tripped on something that simply wasn't there.

His mind tried to argue that maybe he'd just lost his footing, but the throbbing big toe of his left foot was telling him something else. He took another step and saw that an almost foot-wide section of the hard earth between the trailer and the tree was broken and crumbly. He leaned over the small patch of broken ground, squinting his eyes in careful study, just in time to see the tip of that small root, which obviously had been birthed out of the ground for the sole purpose of tripping little Stevie Varnado, disappear back into the dry, crumbly, powdery earth. His mouth fell open in disbelief as a small wisp of dust *poofed* out of the ground where the root had been.

Stevie looked up, his eyes darting wildly around the small clearing, suddenly aware again of how silent the woods had become. Then his eyes, drawn either by faint motion detected by his peripheral vision or some other sensation; perhaps the vague sound finally permeating the heavy silence, looked up into the branches of the old oak as they reached across the blue, cloudless sky above him. They seemed to suddenly be reaching, groping, expanding; almost as though the tree itself was stretching after a long nap. The large, rough trunk of the old oak seemed to be bulging and swelling as well.

For a brief, heart-stopping moment, everything seemed to freeze; time itself stopped and seemed to just hang in the air. Then there was a long, deep sighing noise. To Stevie, it seemed as though the patch of woods around him were somehow alive, it had been holding its breath, and was now releasing all that air through the tree towering above him. He stood watching, frozen in place, as the branches swayed and the leaves fluttered, despite the absence of even the slightest breeze; none of the other trees around the clearing moved at all. Then a terror seized his heart, gripping it tightly enough to make it almost stop. It was a fear alien, yet somehow familiar, old but somehow new. And now Stevie wanted nothing but to be gone from this place, never to return. He looked back down from those swaying, whispering branches and realized with dismay that he'd have to approach the old oak, that ancient monument, in order to retrieve his bike. He stared at it for a few moments, torn between his fear of the tree, which had somehow become a living, angry being, and his fear of coming across Jim Hanes on the trails, and having to outrun *him* on foot.

Stevie took a deep breath, then shouted at the tree. His voice was shrill and terrified: *leave me alone*! Then he ran for the bike, clearing the fifteen feet separating them in three long strides. He seized the handlebars with his wounded, bloody hands, oblivious to the pain, and jerked the bike away from the tree, suddenly afraid the roots themselves would come to life, writhing and twisting and clutching at his feet. He ran alongside the bike, taking long strides and building momentum, then hopped on the seat and pedaled harder than he ever had in his life. Behind him, he could hear the sound of the whispering leaves, and as he left the clearing, never to return, it seemed to him that the old oak was laughing at him, mocking his fear and daring him to ever come back. He never would. As he sped recklessly up the path, away from the clearing, the Ice House, and the mocking, whispering laughter of the old tree, he swore to himself that he would *never* go back. He was the first of the group of boys that Jacob had met on his first full day in Logtown to make that oath, but not the last.

Maybe Jim's words about the small clearing, which was older and more significant than any boy who'd ever played in the Ice House or claimed it as his own could possibly know, had been more prophetic than insightful: *It ain't safe no more. Really never was*. Of the boys present, each of whom had heard Jim's words, only Jacob had perceived that there was something beneath those words, something deeper, but not too deep – something that was just below the surface. He did not yet know enough to understand just what was hidden, or just how deep (or shallow) it was buried.

But maybe time was finally ready to tell. It always does, sooner or later. Whether *we're* ready for its secrets doesn't really matter. For time, if nothing else, is the great custodian of secrets. It rolls along, oblivious to our wants or our needs. It sees us born and sees us die, but its steady, flying footsteps never falter. It hears our every vow and every lie; it watches us impassively as we make our plans and live our lives. It watches, and we pretend not to notice that all the while it is looking over our shoulders, waiting.

Not to claim us, to take us suddenly or slowly from all that we know and love to all that we fear or hope; that is the duty of another. No, time only watches: the great, dispassionate observer who knows that nothing, not even our deepest secrets, remains hidden forever. And when those secrets finally come forth from their old, sunken, unmarked graves, time doesn't contemplate whatever follows after; it doesn't even smile at wrongs righted or justice finally found. It simply watches and waits. The earth is filled with the countless corpses of secrets – they outnumber even the rotted bodies of the people, many now long dead, who buried them. Some secrets rest peacefully in their graves. Most do not.

14

The three boys had finally reached the vacant lot where Greg had stumbled across the other two earlier that afternoon. As they were saying their ‘see ya’s and ‘later’s, Jacob noticed Greg kept looking over his shoulder. His face, which had shown relief at getting away from the clearing, now wore an expression of concern. David seemed to have noticed, as well.

“What’s wrong, Gregory? You look like you’ve got the squirts.”

Greg looked back at the other two boys and managed a half smile, but it didn’t seem very sincere.

“I was just thinking about riding back into town. You know, by myself.” Now he almost winced, shame again reflected on his face as he shifted his gaze to the ground. “And Mike was pretty mad. I’ve never seen him or Jared that mad. And he’s got a car, you know. I just don’t wanna ride back to town by myself.”

“Yeah, I didn’t even think about that,” David replied. He was silent for a moment, then said, “He’s probably not even mad at you. Me and Jacob are the ones who tried to fight him.”

Jacob was shaking his head. “You heard what he said, about killing all of us. He looked like he’d gone insane.” He looked David in the eyes. “He’s as crazy as Jared, but it’s worse because he’s older and bigger.” He paused for a moment.

“Maybe none of us should go anywhere alone, at least for now.” Jacob took a deep breath and ran his fingers through his sweaty hair. How had things gotten so far out of control? As if it hadn’t been enough for him to worry about his strange dream, now he had to worry about a death threat from Jared’s older brother.

Greg was nodding vigorously. “Jacob’s right, man. They’re both a couple of psychos. Jared told me last year that Mike got suspended for a week for threatening a teacher. And he was always gettin’ in fights when he still lived here. Remember that time when he broke that boy’s arm at school?”

Now David was nodding as well. He’d heard both stories at the same time as Greg – both had come from Jared, who’d almost been bragging when he’d told them. David had never really worried about Mike because he and Jared had always gotten along. Greg, on the other hand, had always been wary of Mike. On his rare visits to the Ice House (by the time David and his friends had begun hanging out there, Jared’s older brother had gotten his driver’s license and moved on to better things), Mike had picked up on Greg’s nervousness and usually singled him out, picking on him more than he did the other younger boys. David was beginning to understand the likely consequences of not only severing their friendship with Jared, but also of taking part in the older boy’s humiliation as well.

“Yeah, y’all are right. We need to stick together whenever we’re out.” He turned to Greg. “We can ride with you back into town, then we’ll ride back here together.”

Greg seemed relieved, and nodded vigorously, but Jacob wasn't as confident. Mike had handled two of them easily enough before Jim had shown up. Why would next time be any different, especially after Mike had been humiliated and infuriated to the point that he'd threatened to kill them, *all* of them. And it had been a real threat, not just some tough "hey, don't mess with me, man, or I'll have to kill ya" talk. Mike had *meant* it when he said he'd kill them all. Even if Mike had time to calm down before the next time he saw the three boys, Jacob was sure that there'd still be enough of that rage left for him to dole out some pretty serious hurt. *Still*, he thought, *two or three of us against him are better than just one*.

He looked down at his watch. Ten minutes after four.

"Well, if we're all going, we need to get movin'. If my Dad passes us on the highway on his way home from work, I won't be going *anywhere* with you guys for at least a week."

"Yeah, let's rock-n-roll, dudes!" David cried, doing Keanu Reeves yet again. The three boys turned their bikes toward the street, and headed for the highway.

They rode hard and spoke little. Greg's demeanor had changed completely; he looked as if he were riding alongside two muscle-bound bodyguards, both of whom were packing firearms, rather than a couple of sixth graders. In just twenty minutes, they found themselves on his driveway.

As David had told Jacob a few days before, Greg lived on the street that ran directly behind First Baptist Church. Although not as grand in appearance, most of the houses on this street were almost as old as the one that the MacDonald family lived in. Greg invited the boys in for a drink, but Jacob insisted that they didn't have time. His father would be getting off work in less than half an hour, and Jacob didn't want to run the risk of Mr. Hunter seeing them on the highway. So the boys said their goodbyes, and Jacob and David double-timed it back the same way they had come.

Even so, Mr. Hunter technically beat Jacob home. When the two boys reached David's house, Jacob was again invited in for a drink. This time, being safely back within borders of *The Pines* and therefore no longer in danger of being spotted "out of bounds" by his father, he accepted the offer. They parked their bikes beside the driveway, and headed into the house through the garage. As it did at Jacob's house, the door from the garage led directly into the kitchen, where they found David's mother preparing supper. She grimaced when she saw the two boys' appearance.

"Hello, boys. What have you two been up to?"

"Just ridin' with some of the guys," David answered with the typical vagueness that most boys save for their mothers. "Can we have something to drink before Jacob goes home?"

"Help yourselves. There's tea and lemonade in the refrigerator." She finally noticed David's bloody elbow. "What happened to your arm, honey?"

David glanced at it casually and answered "Nuthin', I just had a little bike wreck on the trails, that's all."

Jacob almost smiled as he listened to his friend deliver the same lie he'd used with his own parents after his run-in with Jim last Saturday.

Mrs. Phillips grimaced again. "I wish you'd wear your bike helmet, especially if you insist on doing stunts on those trails."

David looked at Jacob and rolled his eyes.

"I saw that, David Arthur Phillips!" Mrs. Phillips arched her eyebrows, but didn't really look upset. "And I'm serious. I knew a boy when I was younger, who had a serious bicycle wreck, and hit his head just the right way . . ."

Jacob looked at his friend and made a valiant effort not to laugh, but failed. The two boys broke up completely while David's mother watched, shaking her head.

"Fine. You two go ahead and laugh. If you don't want to wear a helmet because it doesn't look cool, that's just fine. But don't blame me when you crack your skull open, go into a coma, and end up having to eat your food through a tube."

David was still laughing as he stepped to the refrigerator. "If living with my idiot brother doesn't put me in a coma, nothing will. Where is the little booger, anyway?"

Mrs. Hunter was still frowning, and looked a little more serious. "David, I'd rather you call your brother by name."

"I thought I just did," David replied, grinning at Jacob.

"I'm serious, David. I know you're just picking, but it really bothers me." She was now wearing a look Jacob clearly recognized

– it said "don't make me embarrass you in front of your friend." David must have recognized the look as well.

"All right, all right." He looked back at Jacob. "Yo, Jacob, tea or lemonade?"

"Lemonade, I guess."

"Me, too," David replied, grabbing the appropriate pitcher and filling two plastic cups. "So, anyway Mom, where's *Dillon*?"

"He's upstairs, in our room, watching TV." She made a dramatic sniffing sound, widened her frown at David, and continued, "You smell like a locker room! You need to clean up before supper."

David handed Jacob one of the cups, then stuck his nose under one of his armpits and inhaled deeply. He then breathed out again with an expression of pure bliss.

"Aahhh, the delightful aroma of masculinity after a hard day in the sun."

Mrs. Phillips shook her head and turned back to the stove as the two boys laughed together. Jacob drank half the glass in one gulp, then looked across the table at his friend and grinned even bigger.

"David *Arthur*?" he asked in a voice just above a whisper.

"Yeah, David Arthur!" his friend replied, also speaking quietly. "And if you tell anyone, I'll personally hand you over to Mike!"

"Yeah, yeah." Jacob was quiet for a second, then asked, "Can I call you 'Artie?"

"Can I call you jerk-wad?" David shot back.

They both started snickering, drawing a suspicious look from David's mother. Jacob finished off his drink and stood.

"Well, I better get goin'," he said, then glanced at Mrs. Phillips and added "thanks for the drink."

"You're very welcome, Jacob. Bye."

He looked back at David and lowered his voice again. "I'll call you later tonight, after I talk to my dad."

"Coolness. See ya, man."

Jacob didn't want to seem too eager about the next day, and somehow managed to keep from asking his father about it until halfway through supper. Mr. Hunter had already made it home by the time Jacob arrived, and was in his room changing clothes. Mrs. Hunter gave Jacob the same look that David had received from his mother, followed by the same instructions – clean up before supper.

"That includes washing your hair!" she called out as he headed to his room.

He took a quick shower, threw on a t-shirt and some sweat-shorts, then stopped by the bathroom a second time to brush his damp, tangled hair. When he got to the table, his parents were already seated, and his place was set. His father said grace and dug right in, while Jacob eyed the food on his plate suspiciously. It held peas, corn bread, and another one of his mother's experimental chicken casseroles. Mrs. Hunter was notorious for her casseroles, which seemed to always contain chicken, yet always taste different. If it bothered Mr. Hunter, he never showed it; he tore through each meal like it was a rare and exotic treat.

Jacob played with his food half-heartedly and waited for his father to mention how he'd talked to Mr. MacDonald and gotten the green light for tomorrow, but he never did. Instead, he talked about how football season would be starting soon and they probably wouldn't make any University of Memphis games this year, but he might consider going to a Saints game, depending on how well they were playing. After all, he reminded his wife, New Orleans was only a thirty minute drive, and Jacob had never been to an NFL game before, etc, etc.

Mrs. Hunter looked a little uncertain. She'd grown up in a small town in north Mississippi, and had an aversion to any city bigger than Memphis, where she'd gone to college and met her husband. On top of that, all she knew about New Orleans was its reputation as a party-town: Bourbon Street, Mardi Gras, not to mention higher than average crime stats. She wasn't sure that that was the kind of place she wanted to take Jacob.

Jacob listened to his parents going back and forth for as long as he could. Finally, when he could stand it no longer and his father had finally stopped talking long enough to stick some food in his mouth, Jacob asked, "So, did you get to talk to Mr. MacDonald?"

His father looked over at his son with a bewildered expression. He swallowed his food, and answered "Of course. He's my boss; I talk to him every day."

"Well, what did he say?"

"About what?" His father still looked confused, and Jacob's heart sank.

"About tomorrow!! About me and David coming in to look at old newspaper stories!!"

Mr. Hunter's face reflected a look of recollection, which was immediately replaced with a look of apology.

"Oh. Ooooohhhh. Son, I'm sorry," he said. "I had a hectic day, and just completely forgot about it."

"Dad! You promised! You said you'd . . ." Jacob's voice trailed off. His father no longer looked apologetic; he was wearing that irritating, cheesy grin again.

"Gotcha!! He said there'd be no problem, as long as you boys behave yourselves. People come in to do research from time to time, so it's not that big a deal."

Jacob was relieved, but he was also angry and was now glaring at his father.

"That wasn't funny!" he grumped.

"C'mon, relax! I was just pickin'," Mr. Hunter replied, but now his wife was coming to Jacob's defense.

"Maybe you shouldn't pick on him so much, Alex. Sometimes it gets old."

Mr. Hunter was about to decry his innocence again and tell his wife she should lighten up as well, but after one look at her face decided against it. He shrugged, looked back at Jacob, and said, "Sorry, buddy. I was just messin' with you, you know that."

Jacob nodded, and went back to picking at his supper. Now a cheesy grin was growing on *his* face. His father's prank wasn't that big of a deal, and the important thing was that he and David would be getting to look at those old newspaper articles tomorrow.

He picked at the food and daydreamed about going to the newspaper office for another five minutes before his mom informed him that he wasn't getting up from the table until he finished his supper. He nodded, took a deep breath, and finally dove into her latest experiment.

Jacob called David around seven-thirty, again using the cordless phone so he could make the call from the privacy of his bedroom. Mrs. Phillips had answered on the third ring, greeted Jacob, then yelled for David. After a few moments, David picked up an extension and yelled, "Got it, Mom!" He waited for the audible *click* of his mother hanging up before speaking again.

"So, are we on, man?"

"Yep. Dad said we'll be there to pick you up around seven forty-five, so make sure you're ready."

"I will. I already told my dad to get me up before he leaves for work; around seven-fifteen."

"Cool. Dad says we'll have until lunchtime to look for whatever we're looking for. That should be plenty of time."

"It better be. I don't want to spend the whole day there."

"Don't worry, King Arthur, we won't." Jacob smiled to himself, feeling proud. He'd spent part of his time in the shower coming up with what he considered to be pretty clever nicknames for David, all variations of his friend's middle name. He planned to use one a day for as long as he could keep thinking them up.

"Well, gawly-dang, you sure are a funny guy!" came the reply. "Yessir, I'm just bustin' a gut over here. Wah-hoo!"

"I bet you are, Artie! Don't worry, I won't tell too many people!" Jacob was having a jolly time, but David didn't appear to be.

"So what's *your* middle name, fool?"

"Jacob." And the funny part was, he was telling the truth.

"Okay, so what's your *first* name?"

It was Christopher, but Jacob had no intention of telling. It wasn't that he was embarrassed, or even worried about any potential ridicule; he was simply having too much fun knowing what David didn't. So he replied accordingly.

"Wouldn't you like to know?"

"Not really. It's probably something like retard, or barf-for-brains. No, wait, I bet its spaz-a-tron," David suggested.

"Nope, nope and nope," Jacob said, grinning.

"Whatever," David said. "I don't want to know."

Jacob saw that the joke was running out of gas, and decided to let it go. For a little while, anyway. He casually switched gears, returning to the original topic of conversation.

"So, what are we gonna do when we find out the rest of it . . . you know, my dream, was real. Where the house was, I mean?" The question, which summed up what his greatest fear had become over the last few days, felt thick and heavy as he spoke it, and immediately chased away the light-hearted mood that dominated the conversation thus far.

There was a long silence on the other end of the line that multiplied Jacob's suddenly exposed discomfort. But he had expected it, really. *For heaven's sake* he thought to himself once again. *We're a couple of* kids! *What* are *we gonna do*? When David finally responded, it was no better and no worse than Jacob had expected.

"I don't know."

The phone line again grew silent, as did Jacob's mind. He had no desire to dig up memories of the dream, or to re-hash any of David's theories, which seemed both absurd and yet perfectly logical – just as his dream had seemed absurd and logical.

"We'll figure something out," he heard David say, and he heard conviction in the other boy's voice. That childlike, almost illogical optimism was still there, and even if Jacob couldn't share it, at least it was something to cling to. He decided to do just that and to forget that nagging voice, the one that had grown louder and more persistent over the past week.

For now, he would hold to the hope of a twelve-year-old boy – the hope that, in the end, everything will be okay. After all, there *was* a God, and He looked out for His children. Maybe bad things *do* only happen to other people; and maybe, if you're a good boy, only good things will happen to you. Jacob remembered those little nuggets now, dispensed throughout his life by older (and therefore, surely wiser) people – namely grandparents and Sunday school teachers. And so he focused on those words, concentrated on them until they almost drowned out that other, determined voice, the one that made him feel so young, so small and helpless. He decided to drop the topic while the happy voices were still on top.

"Yeah, you're probably right," he finally said (hoped). And he suddenly only wanted to be done with this conversation – off the phone and doing something else, anything that would take his mind off of a subject that he could never really escape, especially at night, when the possibility of revisiting that strange other place he had discovered last Saturday night was greater than ever.

"Listen, I gotta go," he told David. "My dad needs some help with the computer; some new software or something." The lie had come easily, and was delivered with smooth tones of a professional.

"All right, I guess I'll see you in the morning." David hesitated a moment, then added "Don't sound so worried, man, . . ."

Jacob knew what David was about to say, and he would be furious when he heard those words: *it was just a dream*. Because, dream or not, it was always there, following him, *haunting him!* Even in the daylight it was there, pushing him to search ever deeper, to find that secret, to *dig up them bones*.

David must have sensed, even over a phone line, Jacob's tension, because he didn't finished the sentence that way. The word 'man' hung in the air for a brief moment, and David finally finished the conversation with an alternate ending.

" . . . We'll think of something. We'll figure it out, man. Anyway, I'll see ya tomorrow."

Jacob released the breath he hadn't even known he was holding and replied, "I know, man, you're right. See ya." He pushed the off button on the phone.

He stared at it for a few moments, then took it to the den and set it on the coffee table. His mother was on the couch, slaking her endless thirst for chick-flicks by watching a movie on the Lifetime channel, which Jacob was convinced had an infinite supply of such movies, all centering around eating disorders, date-rape, or a cheating husband, and all of which he was forbidden to watch (as if he'd want to).

He wandered back to his bedroom, thinking that if anything would take his mind off that haunting, nagging voice, which was still struggling to come out on top, it would be a good dose of Spiderman, basketball, or maybe Pokemon, courtesy of Nintendo. Unfortunately, his parents had pretty strict rules, not only about how much time Jacob could spend in front of the television playing video games, but when he could play them as well. Late evening was one of the times Mrs. Hunter had designated as a video-game-free zone.

So Jacob went back to his bedroom and just sat on the bed. That other voice was getting loud again: it was urging him to drag the library book out from under the bed and look at those pictures again. He resisted, knowing full well that he could draw those pictures up in full detail just by closing his eyes. He looked around the room desperately, finding nothing that seemed even remotely interesting to him; nothing to quiet that ever growing voice.

Finally, he got up and went to the bookshelf that stood beside the small desk he used for doing homework when school was in session. He studied what was a pretty decent collection of books for a twelve-year-old, and finally selected *The Lion, The Witch and The Wardrobe*. He had received the first three books in the Narnia series the previous Christmas, and he had read through them twice already. He'd enjoyed the second reading of this book just as much as the first, and now decided he might like it even more the third time. Especially if it took his mind away from those fears that seemed to dance in the growing dark outside his window and, better yet, quiet that alien voice in his head, the one that insisted that he pursue the dream, while at the same time telling him that there was nothing he could do to stop whatever was happening.

Jacob grabbed the book, hopped on his bed and dove right in. Within ten minutes, that voice was finally silenced as Jacob became lost in a world of Fauns, talking animals, and an ice-cold queen with powers as dark as her heart. An hour passed, and just about the time that Edmund had returned from his own visit to Narnia, Mr. Hunter knocked on his son's bedroom door and stuck his head in.

"You need to be getting ready for bed if you plan on getting up and going to the office with me, Jacob," he said.

Jacob looked up, struggling with the desire to read at least a little further – after another chapter or so, all four of the kids would finally find themselves entering the forest through the back of the wardrobe, and poor little Lucy – the first to find the passage, though she'd been unsuccessful in convincing her siblings of its existence

– would finally be vindicated. But he decided tomorrow was too important. So up he hopped, grabbing a trading card to mark his place, and set the book on his desk. He brushed his teeth, then trotted off to tell his parents good night. His mother was still parked on the couch, her eyes watering as the chick-flick drew toward its banal conclusion. His father was parked at the kitchen table with a bowl of ice cream and a Tom Clancy novel.

"Good night!" he called to both. Then to his father: "Don't forget to get me up!"

"I won't, just make sure you *do* get up. Good night, ace."

"Good night, sweetheart," Mrs. Hunter said absently, her wet eyes still glued to the television screen.

Jacob shook his head and returned to his bedroom. He pushed the door almost closed, leaving an inch or two just to be safe, then turned out the light and hopped into bed.

The closet light remained on, which was probably just as well. As it turned out, the voice and the dreams weren't quite through with Jacob Hunter just yet.

15

The first dream had been bad for Jacob. There was no question about that. But it hadn't started out badly. In fact, it had begun on an unusually pleasant note – just a peaceful walk in the woods amid the gusty, cool breezes of an October night. Even when he had wandered upon a burning house, he hadn't been frightened. To the contrary, it had been an awe-inspiring sight. To see that house, so large and so grand, billowing smoke and painting the sky and the woods and even Jacob in a deep, red-orange hue while the flames danced and the sparks glittered in the sky as the chilly wind scattered dead, dry leaves around him had been – not necessarily exciting, but almost . . . exhilarating. Even as he stood before that terrible but somehow beautiful scene, he understood that what he was watching had really happened, and it had been important.

Jacob had not become uneasy until he had felt the presence of that strange, forlorn boy. And he had not felt real fear until the woman had spoken to him. All that had followed after had been sheer terror for the twelve-year-old. And in the days that had followed, his young mind had tried to reason out, as best it could, exactly what he had seen, which parts – if any – had been real, and what it had meant. The entire experience had been bearable, however, simply because it had built gradually, from the moment he first realized he was taking a "midnight stroll" in the woods while dressed in his pajamas until he had all but flown back to his house, feeling death at his heels all the way. And throughout, there had been that strange, illogical logic of a dreamscape, permeating his mind and his surroundings.

Now, he and David were finally making a quick and (to Jacob, anyway) risky trip to the Ice House. David had been adamant about collecting what he referred to as *his property*, which consisted mostly of comic books and magazines. The racecar poster was also his, and he wasn't about to let Jared, or even worse, Stevie, claim ownership of anything classified as David Phillips' Property. Jacob had finally conceded upon the conditions that they go early, so as to avoid the possibility of meeting any of the other boys there; and David's vow that they wouldn't ever return. The second condition had been much more difficult to obtain.

David loved the Ice House. It wasn't just his *clubhouse* – for two and a half years it had been his refuge; his sanctuary, and he felt he had earned the right to hang out there. Jacob understood this. He remembered well how, just one week before, he had been dazzled by the place, thinking it was one of the coolest places he'd ever seen. He had dreamed of being accepted among those who called it their own. But no more. Perhaps it was because the old refrigerator trailer had been the starting point of both of the two serious confrontations he'd been a part of, each of which having the potential to be the most dangerous situations he had experienced in his short life. Maybe he was just afraid of eventually running into Jared and/or his older brother there. But in his heart, Jacob knew the real reason he was beginning to fear the place. It was the warning that Jim had delivered the day before.

You fellas'll want to stay away from this place, he had said. *It ain't safe no more. Never really was.* Jacob had sensed then and believed now that Jim hadn't just meant because of the half-crazy older boy. Nor had he been referring to the possible dangers of children playing in an old refrigerator trailer. Jacob was becoming convinced that there was something wrong about the place itself. And now, as he and David walked the trails through the woods on a bright, cloudless morning, he could feel his fear of the place growing. With every step the two boys took, drawing ever closer to the Ice House, his unease and anxiety grew.

Why didn't we bring our bikes? he wondered. *What in the world made us decide to walk?*

He looked over at his friend, who was uncharacteristically silent; his face was staring impassively at the path before them. Jacob wanted to assure him that they were doing the right thing, that the place just wasn't safe for them anymore. If for no other reason, it had just yesterday been the scene of a sincere death threat levied at them by a seventeen year-old boy who might not be technically crazy but, at the very least, certainly had some serious issues. But he said nothing, because he knew it wouldn't do any good. David's soul was burning at the notion of surrendering the Ice House to Jared and Stevie, but Jacob felt certain that his friend would get over it soon enough. Maybe they could find another place to call their own, and . . .

Jacob looked up, and was surprised to see that they had already reached the clearing. How could they have gotten here so quickly? It seemed to him that it hadn't taken them any longer on foot than it usually did when they were riding bikes. He turned, looking suspiciously at the trail behind him. It looked exactly as it always did. Had he been so deep in thought that he just hadn't noticed how far they had actually walked? He shrugged. That was apparently the case.

He turned to David and said, "C'mon, lets get this over with. It shouldn't take more than a couple of minutes to grab all of your stuff."

David, his face still impassive, simply nodded and began walking toward the trailer. Jacob watched him, and now his own face was a study in puzzled confusion. David was acting really weird, and Jacob was beginning to wonder if it was more than just being angry at having to give up his personal little "fortress of solitude." As he watched his friend step up into the trailer, it occurred to him that David hadn't spoken at all, not once since they'd been on the trails. And now Jacob was beginning to wonder if David had spoken to him at all *today*. He seemed to remember David agreeing to the specific conditions that Jacob insisted upon before they set out on this ill-fated trip. But now he was wondering if he hadn't just been *thinking* about making those demands before agreeing to accompany his friend back here to the clearing.

Jacob's discomfort was growing quickly now, much too quickly; it was approaching panic at a dangerous speed. He looked up at the trailer, but could no longer see his friend. He knew that David had to be inside; he had just watched the boy enter. Maybe he was in the back, by the table.

"David?" he called out, sounding more timid than he intended.

There was no reply. Jacob looked around the silent clearing, at the old tree, at the Ice House. Everything seemed so dim. Not shadowy, but *dim*, as though the sun had been eclipsed, but not by the moon. Panic had not seized Jacob yet, but he could feel it getting close. *Jim was right,* he thought. *This place* isn't *safe. At all.*

"David, c'mon, man, what are you doing? Let's go!"

Silence. And now Jacob was becoming very upset with his friend, with himself, with this place. Because something was clearly wrong here. David was acting weird, everything, even the air around Jacob *looked* weird, and he was beginning to feel very much alone in a place that *ain't safe no more, never really was.*

"DAVID!" Jacob's shout made it worse, because it went nowhere. It seemed to just kind of fade away as it left his mouth. *No, it didn't fade*, he thought. *Something swallowed it; something ate it up, right out of the air.*

He walked on reluctant legs to the entrance to the Ice House, but couldn't bring himself to step inside, even before he realized it wasn't really the Ice House anymore. He peered inside, hoping to see David in the process of gathering his precious belongings. David would look up at him, wearing the same expression he'd worn when Jacob had first told him about his dream about a burning house and a sad young boy with an empty heart. He would make one of his playfully scornful faces and say something in one of his voices – something like "If you get too tired of just standing there and watching me, you can come on in and give me a hand," or better yet, "No worries, mate."

But Jacob wasn't looking into the Ice House, and David was nowhere to be seen. Instead, Jacob found that he was looking into a passageway he'd never seen. The walls, which should have been insulated fiberglass dotted with scuffs and stains and scratches and decorated with a poster or two, were instead made of dark strips of wood. The floor was also wooden, and three feet or so into the trailer there were stairs leading down into a deep, warm, thick darkness.

Now he could hear a man's voice, raised in anger. But though the voice was deep and strong, its quality seemed faint and weak, as though it was reaching Jacob's ears from a great distance. He couldn't quite make out most of what was being said, but was certain that he heard the words "little whore" more than once. Soon the voice was raised to an almost fevered pitch, but Jacob still couldn't quite make out the words; they were just too . . . far away. The man's voice seemed to reach a climax, almost a scream. Then Jacob *did* hear a scream: two voices, a woman's and a boy's, joined together in a piercing harmony of fear and horror. The sound stopped his heart and froze his blood. For a moment there was silence, then Jacob could hear a guttural, almost rhythmic grunting sound, which seemed to diminish rather than fade, as though the sound, which had seemed far away to begin with, was simply drifting away, until

Jacob could hear nothing except his own heartbeat, which seemed to throb in his ears.

Only then did he remember David, and wondered if his friend had gone down those steps and into that darkness. Had that been David he'd heard screaming in terrified unison with the woman? Jacob leaned a little closer to the entrance, hesitated a moment, then called his friend's name in little more than a pleading whisper.

"David?"

This time the sound of his voice didn't fade; it wasn't swallowed or soaked up. Instead, it seemed to grow: the sound swelled and bounced as it echoed for an eternity along the corridor leading down into a dark, bad place that Jacob, no matter what might have happened – might *still* be happening – to his friend, couldn't even imagine going. The magnified sound of his friend's name finally just stopped; it didn't fade but simply ended, and he listened to the heavy silence, praying for David to respond. There was finally a response, but not from his friend.

The sound, somewhere between a groan and a wail, came from far below, possibly the foot of the stairs, stairs that Jacob was now quite certain led straight to the gates of hell itself. The sound started as little more than a whisper, growing slowly but steadily until it seemed to fill the whole world around him (surely it could be heard back in his neighborhood, maybe even in town), then it slowly died away. Jacob was certain the sound had become a growl before it was gone.

Now the darkness from inside the corridor seemed to swell and overflow, spilling like a black mist out of the trailer and into the already dim, vague clearing. And Jacob heard footsteps on the stairs, slow and heavy, but steady. He understood from the sound that it was too large, too massive, and too powerful to be just the dead, skeletal woman from his dream climbing up to meet him. But his mind simply would not let him imagine what it might be. He wanted to run, but his feet were determined to remain right where they were. And Jacob suddenly understood that it didn't matter that he couldn't run, anyway. He knew that whatever it was slowly making its way to the top of the stairs would find him, no matter where or how fast he ran. And because he couldn't run from it, Jacob would have to stop it. His eyes (which felt as if they'd somehow shrunk inside of his head) began to franticly yet almost dispassionately take in his surroundings. They came to rest on the open door of the trailer, and he stared at it as if noticing it for the first time. Jacob had a sudden epiphany that seemed somehow both brilliant and ridiculous at the same time.

Of course, he thought. *I'll just close the door, and it will be trapped there on the other side. I won't have to see it, and it won't be able to get me*. The idea that just closing the door would be sufficient to stop whatever monstrosity was slowly climbing the stairs, drawing closer with each step, close enough now that Jacob could hear its deep, ragged breathing, seemed both absurd and at the same time perfectly acceptable. So he lunged for the door, grabbed it firmly in hand, and pushed. It wouldn't budge.

For a moment he panicked, and he almost turned to run, even though he understood that whatever was coming would surely find him. Then he remembered the wedge that held the door open. He reached around the door with his left leg and kicked at it, loosening its grip, but not knocking it free. He could hear the breaths of whatever horrible thing he had awakened clearly now. He'd be able to see it soon, and he knew that the sight would freeze him where he stood, helpless as it reached out with a clawed, malformed hand; with a single swipe it would tear the life and mind out of young Jacob Hunter. He refused to look up, staring instead at the stupid wedge as he kicked at it, over and over. Finally it came loose, and Jacob pushed on the door with all his might, slamming it shut and hearing with great relief the loud *click* of the lock as it latched securely in place. He stepped back from the door, breathing hard and sweating, but feeling satisfied that the door had been shut, the door was locked, and he was now safely beyond the reach of whatever stood beyond it. But a part of Jacob knew that sooner or later someone – perhaps even a little boy like himself who didn't know any better – would come along and open that door, releasing whatever it was that waited on the other side.

David! his mind suddenly shouted at him. He looked around the clearing, which remained dim and vague, even though the sun was climbing ever higher into the sky. What had happened to his friend? Had he *really* gone into the trailer? Had Jacob just locked him in with whatever it was that was trying to get out, trying so desperately to finally be free?

"David, where *are* you?" he called, and his voice sounded as if he were on the verge of crying. It was the desperate voice of a child who had become separated from his parents in an unfamiliar place; surrounded by people whose faces he didn't recognize.

And once again, Jacob was answered. Once again it wasn't by David. But this time he recognized the voice. Oh yes, he knew *this* voice. His heart sank and despair washed over him at the sound of its coldness.

Child, I *am here*.

Don't look, don't look, don't look, just turn around and leave or maybe just close your eyes and think about something else, something happy and safe, or pinch yourself, yes, slap yourself and you'll wake up and you'll be in bed and maybe you can sneak into Mom and Dad's room and sleep on the floor beside their bed because you'll be safe there and anything is better than being here and being alone with her because she's dead but she's here and she wants you and if you look at her she'll have you so just DON'T LOOK!!

But of course he did, just as he knew he would. Just as before, he wasn't sure if it was something he had to do, something he needed to do, or if it was even his decision to do it. Because that voice, which now seemed always to be there in the back of his mind, the *deeper* part of his mind, always urging him on, told him he had to. And as he listened, it slowly grew louder and louder, more and more determined. It never shouted or screamed. It never became shrill or threatening. It simply spoke firmly, with an almost maternal love and assurance, saying over and over: *you* must *look, you* must. And

Jacob understood that the voice was right, the voice would guide him, and maybe the voice would protect him.

He finally turned toward the source of his terror, facing it with the desperate prayer that if he can just get it over with, it might not be as horrible as he expected it to be. He faced it the way a man sentenced to die might face his executioner, knowing that there is always a chance, no matter how small, that the phone will ring with the saving grace of the governor's pardon. It took all of a split second for Jacob to wish he hadn't looked; to wish he hadn't listened to that second, more insistent voice; to wish, even, that he'd been struck blind rather than see what he now beheld.

The old oak, once so picturesque, had become a thing of obscene horror. Instead of bark, the skin of the tree was just that – skin, old and rotted flesh that seemed to throb and pulsate. The trunk was spotted with running sores and gaping wounds that oozed: in some places a thick yellow-gray, pus-like slime, in others it oozed blood that was dead and black as midnight. As the trunk of the tree continued to thrum and pulse, the skeletal, leafless branches slowly swayed in the breathless air. But there was no rhythm, no harmony in the movement: only madness and discord.

Jacob became aware of a pattering sound, like that of raindrops, on the earth around his feet. He looked, and if only it *had* been water falling to the ground upon which he stood. But there was no rain, only slugs and leeches and countless other things for which he knew no name. They were falling, dripping from the ends of those fleshless, swaying branches. He knew that when one landed on him he would scream, shrill and mindless, at the feel of its unclean, slimy, oozing gray body on his skin. But somehow, miraculously, none of them did. They fell all around him, but not on him, landing instead on the dusty ground with a light *plop*, then slowly wriggling and rolling in every conceivable direction, sometimes oozing and sliding over each other, but none came within a foot of Jacob.

At the base of the tree, the trunk had split open. The tear was nearly six feet high and as wide as a cavern at the ground, where the roots of the tree were writhing and twisting like serpents. A stench poured forth from the opening, and when it reached his nostrils, Jacob gagged. Never before had he been exposed to such a foul odor, and the sheer power of the thick, heavy, fetid reek made him gag, dream or no. It was the stench of rotting flesh cooking in the sun, baking and roiling with maggots and insects. It was the scent of decay. It was the smell of death.

And now he *could* see maggots, boiling out of the gaping hole before him; he could see flies and worms and beetles. They were chittering and buzzing and crawling, flooding the ground before him as they spilled forth from the open tree, over the coiling, entwining roots.

Then Jacob was looking into the cavern. Although he had moved no closer (the most evil, yellow-eyed and fanged demon-spawn from hell could not have urged him to step any nearer to the horror he was witnessing), he could see clearly into the darkness of that evil place. And he beheld her – the woman, the evil, and the power. She was still clothed in that ancient black dress, a statement from an era past long before even Jacob's father was born. Her dark hair still hung in clumps around her pale, dead face. And he understood that she was the center from which all the foulness of that dark cavern had come.

Yet she was now untouched by the rot and decay. Her face, which before had been little more than a few dried strips of flesh clinging to a yellowed skull, was now beautiful and terrible: her skin was like the smooth, poreless texture of a porcelain doll and colored the cold luster of pearl. Her eyes, which may have once been hazel, now burned with the fiery red of the most heart-stopping of sunsets, and the whites of her eyes were a hot yellow. She was certainly still dead: there was no life-bearing blood flowing through that cold body. And yet she was now whole, untouched by the decay that time brings to all things lifeless. Only her heart had succumbed: it was a foul, black worm-feast.

She smiled at him with a cold, beautiful, deadly and barely perceptible movement of her almost white lips. She raised her arms slightly, as though in a gesture of welcome, and Jacob could now see two boys standing to either side. They stood lifelessly, arms dangling, shoulders slumped, jaws slack and lips slightly parted. They stared at Jacob with white, sightless eyes, and he knew them both. To her right was the young boy from his dream: Jim Hanes from a childhood where he lived a different life under a different name. To her left was Mike, Jared's older brother. Both seemed even to be further along in death than their hostess. As Jacob stared in mute despair, both boys began to wither away before him. Their flesh became dry and powdery, their eyes disappeared into dark, hollow sockets, and their hair thinned into feathery wisps. Then they simply disintegrated, until all that was left were two small piles of gray dust, which somehow scattered in the motionless air.

Come to me, child. She spoke to him without moving her cold, pale lips, and her voice completely filled his head. And Jacob realized with utter disbelief and terror that, without having taken a single step, he now stood before her. The image of her face wholly filled his sight, and still she wore that terrible, deadly cold smile on her pale lips. The smell filling this tomb, her abode, was unbearable, but he was unable to gag, unable to even breathe, as he stood staring with wide, unblinking eyes into her dark, soulless gaze. Again the sound of her voice filled his mind, driving his own thoughts effortlessly before it. But there was another voice as well: the kinder, gentle but firm voice that had urged him to look at the beautiful horror that stood before him; the voice that promised to somehow protect him from the inescapable promise of death he now witnessed. The two voices completely filled his mind, intertwining promises of his part in what was to be.

I am close, child She is close, so very close*, and I will not be hindered, even by the one who has opened the door.* You can stop her. *My day of reckoning is here, and there will be justice.* You must go to him. *The costs of retribution will not be too great* You must help him understand, *for are not the sins of the father visited upon his sons?* It wasn't his fault. *But the father lies now beyond even my reach.* YOU MUST *The cost* MAKE HIM *shall not be* UNDERSTAND *too great, it shall be just. See to yourself, child,* I will help you *that you are not part of the price to be paid.*

And now she *did* smile at Jacob – an icy, terrible smile that held no joy. She reached out to him with her cold, colorless hands. In his mind, he screamed with madness and despair, but his body wouldn't move, and no sound came from his mouth. He now stood as still and lifeless as the two boys who had stood beside her only moments before, his own face expressionless with what he saw as she drew to him. Only his mind echoed with the shrill screams of his terror as her arms began to close about him, as if in a mocking mother's embrace.

At that exact moment, Jim Hanes sat bolt upright from where he had fallen into a nightmare-filled sleep on the couch. He sat there for several minutes, trembling and breathing hard and drenched in his terror-induced sweat as his wild eyes searched frantically around the filthy den of his trailer. Even after he had oriented himself and confirmed his place in reality, the horror of the dream held him. There was more of that sense of lingering than usual, and he twisted around more than once to look over his shoulder, certain that he'd find himself staring into her pale, dead face; into those burning eyes. And although he saw no one, still he felt the heaviness in the air. Something *had* been here, and was taking its time about leaving.

When the thick air had become breathable again, Jim leaned forward, bony elbows resting on his bony knees, and put his face in his hands. The terror he had felt wasn't subsiding, yet it was not now the dominant emotion. A great sadness was welling up in his heart. This was an emotion he'd long thought to never experience again, and it had been long indeed since he'd last experienced it. The sadness and the terror seemed to be almost interchangeable now; they seemed to somehow be feeding each other.

Until last Saturday, there had been guilt, and there had of course been some fear when they'd come to visit. But Jim was old, and growing older daily, and it seemed that more than anything he was tired. He had accepted *their* visits, and while he had feared those visits he still almost welcomed the guilty fingers that pointed at him, always reminding him that it *was* his fault. But now, something was changing, there was a power growing in one of his visitors, and the other two were growing weaker. And as he sensed *her* growing power, he began to suspect two things: perhaps *her* spirit *wasn't* just given life by his guilty soul, and he wasn't the only one who was seeing her.

He remembered thinking that the boy knew who he was. Now he was beginning to suspect . . . had *she* told him? And if that was the case, why? What was so special about that boy? What exactly had happened between them last Saturday, when Jim had sat astride the terrified boy, holding a knife to his young, tender throat with – he now almost shuddered to realize – the earnest intent of cutting. What had passed between them that had somehow served to bond the two? And had this strange and unlikely bond been formed for their purpose and benefit, or for *hers*?

Sweet Heaven above us, would you just listen to yourself he thought. *You sound like a lunatic!* This thought struck him as being not only poignant, but downright hilarious, and he laughed aloud. But the sound of his laughter was frightening – it *did* sound awfully like that of a madman, and as it choked off in his throat, he found himself looking over his shoulder again, making sure he was really alone.

I'll tell you what the problem is, old man. You need a drink! This is what happens when you fall asleep without saying goodnight to the only faithful friend you've ever had. And it was true; he *had* fallen asleep without his ineffective but very necessary last glass of drink. He had gone to the kitchen to pour it, but for some reason the mere thought of drinking had made him feel so sick to his stomach that he had actually gagged. He had staggered back to the couch and lain down, and had eventually fallen asleep, pondering this new development instead of nursing his usual wounds.

He had eventually fallen into a shallow sort of sleep, and then at some point had found himself standing before her unmarked (and he might say "forgotten" but for the fact that it was never known, save by himself and one other) grave, standing and watching. He had seen the boy walk into the clearing, talking to someone that Jim couldn't see. He had felt, along with the boy, the unnatural quiet that had settled even more heavily than usual upon the clearing. When the boy had looked with confusion and fright into the trailer, Jim had also looked, and realized with growing horror that he recognized not only those stairs, but also the sounds that had come drifting up out of the dark (past). And when the tree that he had known when it was maybe half of its present size came to life, and split open to reveal its secrets, he'd known before he even looked who would be waiting in those dark shadows. What he hadn't expected was how *alive* she'd be, even though she still was just as dead as ever.

No, she wasn't alive he corrected himself. But she was now endowed with something almost as powerful as life, something that let her prowl unhindered in that place just beyond the waking world. And when she had spoken, her eyes had looked right through the boy and into his own eyes, and Jim understood that the words she had spoken were meant for both man and child. He recognized, of course, the two lifeless boys standing on either side of that not-quite-living nightmare before him. One was that older boy whom he'd rebuked and sent away with his tail between his legs earlier that very same day. But much greater was his horror when he realized who the other boy was. He was looking at himself – Jim Hanes, at the exact age when his life had changed forever; Jim Hanes at a time when the name "Jim Hanes" didn't even exist. It was a young James Stockton II from an era in his life that Jim still remembered; remembered in even greater detail than what he'd had for lunch the day before. He had watched in mute horror as the two boys had stood briefly at her side, both staring at Jim through those grotesque, white, sightless eyes. Both already as dead as Julius Caesar himself. Then they were gone, withering and dissolving away into nothingness like some terrible portent. Finally, as he watched her embrace the terrified young boy, he had felt *himself* pulled into and wrapped up in that cold, suffocating, deadly embrace before he had finally awakened to the sound of his own cries of terror. And the worst part was that, like Jacob, he wasn't sure how much of what he'd just seen had been a dream, and how much had been real.

It had been a lifetime since Jim had even considered uttering a prayer to the God he had been raised – on one side of his family, anyway – to believe in. It had been long indeed since he'd felt anything but bitterness for whatever entity it was that might have created not only the universe, but in Jim's mind at least, the circumstances that had led the old man to where he now was. And even if he had, at any point in his long and bitter life, felt inclined to utter up a prayer, who was he – a wretched drunk – that God would even listen? But, despite that lifetime of bitter resentment that he felt toward The Creator, a prayer found its way past Jim's lips early that dark morning.

Oh dear Lord, he almost sobbed, *just make it go away. Please make them go away.* He didn't wait for an answer, though. In his experience, there had always been only one thing that had ever helped. He was afraid to try again, but more afraid not to. He told himself that it was a chance worth taking, even if it only brought him a short time of forgetfulness and rest.

He slowly stood up and began padding his way across the dirty floor to the kitchen; cautiously peering into every shadow to make sure he really was alone. He reached with shaking hands to grab the jug and a glass from the sink. This time, he didn't bother to rinse it out before filling it up. He brought the glass to his lips, meaning to toss back half of it before even returning to the den, but no sooner had the first swallow passed through his mouth and into his throat than he vomited it right back out, partially into the glass and partially into the sink. He dropped the glass into the sink where it shattered with a sudden, sharp crash, splashing the cheap, foul-smelling drink on his face, the sink, the walls.

Jim gripped the counter with both hands as his empty stomach heaved four or five more times. When it was over, he sank to his knees and, resting both forearms on the edge of the counter, hung his head over – almost into – the sink and began to weep. He remained like this for another two or three minutes, waiting for his strength to return, waiting to get himself under control, and trying to understand what was happening. The drink tasted just as it always had (not particularly pleasant, but something he had long grown accustomed to), but now the very smell of it was threatening to make him gag again.

When he finally felt enough strength in his legs to believe he could make it to the sofa without collapsing, he turned away from the sink and its nauseating odor, staggering along and holding the walls and doorframes for support. He went to his knees about seven feet from his intended destination, and was crawling on all fours by the time he finally made it. Then he climbed up and lay on his side, curled up like a child, still crying and wondering over and over: *what's happening to us? What's happening*?

16

Mr. Hunter had no trouble getting his son up early Thursday morning. Jacob was already awake when his father came and knocked gently on the door around six-thirty. In fact, Jacob had awakened long before his father – sometime around three a.m. to be exact. He had not jerked back into the waking world with a sudden start, as he had at the end of his first dream. This time, he had sort of pulled himself out of the dream. The sensation was akin to having been trapped deep underwater, struggling and finally squirming free; breaching the surface of the water just as he felt he could hold his breath no longer. He had actually gasped aloud upon waking, sucking in that fresh oxygen greedily, just as one might do upon breaking free of suffocating water into cool, clean air.

He had found only a little comfort in the fact that the closet light was already on and he therefore wouldn't have to tempt fate (or whatever else might be out there waiting) by venturing forth from the safety of his bed and blanket to turn on its reassuring, shadow dispelling light. Indeed, the faint light peeking through the crack in the closet door seemed very frail, and Jacob had found himself wishing in vain for the courage to hazard forth from the bed and turn on the overhead light, sending every hint of shadow, dark, and nighttime that prowled his room into exile. But the terror of this latest dream held him much too strongly. He could still feel the deadly cold of that strange, pale woman's embrace, he could still see the burning fire of her eyes; his nostrils were still filled with those horrible, sickening smells of death.

And so there he had lain, wishing for and yet desperately afraid of sleep, as the few remaining hours of dark slowly ticked away. The situation had given him more than ample time to try and decipher the dream and perhaps even ponder its meaning, but he wouldn't dare attempt to willingly draw up those images, still so fresh in his mind that they seemed to flash before him every time his eyes closed, even in the split second of a blink. Only one conclusion would Jacob allow himself to ponder, and this thought echoed in his mind over and over – the woman in his dream was definitely *not* the woman in the picture from the library book.

And so, when Mr. Hunter opened Jacob's bedroom door expecting to have to coax his son out of bed, he was surprised to see Jacob all but leap up and onto the floor as if a cluster of firecrackers had just gone off underneath him.

"Whoa! Up and rearing to go, huh?" Mr. Hunter shook his head, smiling with surprise. "Too bad you can't pop out of bed like that during school."

Jacob sort of shrugged, wearing a half smile. He started to search his mind for a sarcastic reply, but after the night he'd just spent, it didn't seem worth the effort. His father, still smiling, shrugged right back at him.

"Anyway, you need to hurry up and get dressed and get some breakfast. We need to leave in no more than forty-five minutes so we'll have time to pick up David."

Jacob was dressed in under five minutes, and could hear his father in the shower as he walked to the kitchen for breakfast. His mother was obviously still in bed, because with the exception of his bedroom and his parents' bathroom, the only light in the house was that of the pale early morning seeping through the curtains and blinds over the windows. He made a point of turning on almost every lamp he passed on the way to the kitchen, and then the big light over the dinner table for good measure.

Jacob was halfway through his second bowl of cereal when his mother and father finally came into the kitchen. As usual, she was bleary-eyed and still dressed in her pajamas; he was chipper, upbeat, and dressed casually in a pair of dress slacks and a polo. While Mr. Hunter poured a couple of glasses of orange juice, his wife fetched a couple of breakfast bars from the pantry. Both sat in their usual places at the table and started eating.

"I told you Jacob was up and at 'em. I didn't even have to wake him, he was out of the bed as soon as I opened his door." Mr. Hunter was doing the same smiling headshake he had done a few minutes earlier in Jacob's room.

Mrs. Hunter was also smiling at Jacob, but like Sunday morning there was a look of concern behind the smile.

"Are you feeling okay, honey?" she asked. "You look really tired."

"Yeah, I'm just nervous or something. I guess I didn't sleep very good last night." This was all perfectly true. And for some reason, Jacob wanted to laugh. He had just summed up everything that was wrong without revealing a single thing. It *was* funny in a way, but his desire to burst out into what would probably be peals of lunatic laughter frightened him.

"What in the world are you nervous about?" Mr. Hunter asked. Now he too was beginning to look a little concerned.

"I meant excited," Jacob said quickly, trying not to stammer or hem-haw in his attempt to come up with a plausible lie on the spot. "You know, about going to the newspaper office with you today." He turned his attention back to his cereal, hoping the matter would be dropped.

His parents looked at him a moment later, faces still mostly concerned but now tainted with a touch of skepticism, then looked at each other. Mr. Hunter shook his head again, this time with an expression that said *kids: why do we even bother trying to figure them out?*

Mr. Hunter and Jacob pulled into the driveway at David's house at seven-forty. Jacob hopped out of the car, but didn't even make it halfway to the front door before it opened, and out came David. He flashed a big grin at Jacob, clearly looking forward to this important step toward solving the big mystery. The two boys got into the car, both in the back seat so they could easily chat, and off they went.

David wasted no time, quickly and easily slipping into what Jacob now thought of as his friend's "impress and delight the adults" modc.

"Good morning, Mr. Hunter. I really appreciate you letting me and Jacob visit the newspaper office. We'll probably be able to find more there in one morning than a whole week at the library." He smiled sincerely in the rear-view mirror, and Jacob found himself praying that his friend wouldn't lay it on too thick.

"You're very welcome," Mr. Hunter replied. "I have to say that I've never seen two sixth-graders who were so fired up about doing school work." He flashed his own look in the rear-view mirror, a perfect blend of amusement and suspicion.

"Oh, yes, I cherish any opportunity to do school work, even in the summer." David's voice was clearly sarcastic, but just to be sure, he added "Just kidding."

"Yeah, I figured you were."

"Actually, this was Jacob's idea," David went on. "He saw a library book I had checked out, you know, just for research, and was looking at the pictures and reading a little, and came across the story about how the founder of Logtown had built a huge house, like a mansion, and it had burned down. He got really interested and wanted to find out more about it, and I told him about how we're gonna have to write a report this year about something historical in the area or the state. He said we ought to check out the newspaper office and see if we could find some old newspaper stories about it, but we knew we wouldn't be able to do that when school starts up, so we decided to go on and see what we could find as soon as we could."

Jacob listened with nervous fascination as David spun out this yarn. He looked back and forth between his father and his friend. The former was nodding as he listened with kind of curious amusement. The latter was just rambling on, his face perfectly sincere, as if he himself believed every word that was spilling so effortlessly from his mouth. Jacob suddenly understood that his friend was babbling like this because he was nervous. He wondered if David was making up this story as he went, or had crafted it the night before. Either way, it sounded perfectly believable to Jacob.

"Well," Mr. Hunter began, as soon as David had stopped talking long enough to take a breath, "like I told Jacob, you boys should talk to Mr. MacDonald while you're at the office. He's lived in Logtown his entire life, and can probably tell you just as much, if not more, than you'll find out looking at old newspapers."

David didn't miss a beat.

"That's a pretty good idea, Mr. Hunter, thanks. 'Cause we were wanting to find out where the house was, and the book didn't say anything about it. It looked pretty big in the picture, so we thought it must have been in the countryside instead of in town."

Geez, will you please just shut up before you make him suspicious? Jacob thought. He willed this thought at David as forcefully as he could without changing his facial expression, but his prayer went unanswered.

"I know from my dad that there wasn't much outside the city limits besides farms and stuff until maybe the late seventies, so I was thinking that maybe it used to be where something else is now, you know, a new business or maybe a subdivision. Maybe even where *The Pines* is now, or around where the woods are behind it."

Jacob finally reached over and thumped his friend on the leg, giving him a dirty look that clearly conveyed a *will you please just shut the heck up* message. David gave him a sincere look of innocence look while Mr. Hunter answered David.

"Well, like I said, if anyone can answer that question, it'll be Mr. MacDonald."

At that point, Jacob did his best to take over the conversation. He started talking as casually as possible about video games, movies, and the upcoming trip to Ship Island – anything he could think of besides the errand they were on. The last topic seemed to be the most effective. David was obviously excited about the trip and took the opportunity to impress Mr. Hunter, who had heard of but never been to Ship Island, with his limited knowledge about the place and its history. Five minutes later they were parked in a small lot that sat adjacent to and south of the building that housed the newspaper offices. Jacob began to feel excited again for the first time since David had gotten into the car and started babbling uncontrollably. Surely he and David would be able to find the information they sought without arousing any suspicion. Surely they would find some answers.

The two boys followed Mr. Hunter through glass double doors beneath a large sign that read *The Logtown News*, written in bold calligraphy. Beneath those words was the newspaper's logo – a young boy, dressed in the style of the 1920s, holding up a folded newspaper and shouting (presumably something to the effect of *Extra, Extra, read-all-about-it*, although the only thing coming out of his mouth were a couple of squiggly lines, which served to assure anyone looking at the sign that the boy *was* shouting and not just yawning).

After stepping through the doors they found themselves in a small waiting room. There were only four chairs for anyone doing any waiting – two against each wall on either side of the doors they'd just entered. Before them was a large desk shaped like a lopsided horseshoe. It was equipped with a computer monitor, a telephone, a typewriter, and an adding machine. Scattered across the surface of the desk were a couple of files, several unsteady stacks of paper, and a couple of message and Post It pads. Mounted on the wall behind the desk was an upright box that looked to Jacob like a large, wooden tick-tack-toe board. The box was about five inches deep. A sheet of paper with the word *messages* scrawled across it was taped to the top of the box, and under each square was a name written on a small label. Jacob saw that all of them, including his father's, were empty.

Mr. Hunter walked up to the lady sitting behind the desk. She had been pecking away on the computer's keyboard, but she looked up and smiled as he approached. Jacob had to catch his breath. The lady appeared to be in her mid-twenties. She had a stunningly beautiful face that was accentuated by that dazzling smile. Her straight blonde hair was pulled back in a ponytail, and her make-up, while applied tastefully, still gave her a somewhat seductive look. Her lips were painted ruby-red, and she wore a tight, short-sleeved sweater that fit snugly around a perfectly proportioned frame. Jacob figured that she could give the woman on the pin-up at the Ice House a run for her money.

"Good Morning, Alex. Brought in some extra help today, I see."

Mr. Hunter returned the smile.

"Good morning, Jenny." He looked at the two boys, then back at the receptionist. "Yeah, we got some new help. Jerry told me he was looking to try and make the newspaper more appealing to younger readers, so we decided to give these boys their own column. They'll be writing about video games, movies, girls; stuff like that."

Jacob and David looked at each other and half-smiled at the feeble joke, but Jenny looked thoroughly confused.

"I'm just kidding, Jenny. This is my son Jacob, and his friend, David Phillips." Both boys raised their hands in a half wave, and David flashed the young lady a toothy smile. "They're here to do some research. Is Jerry in his office?"

Jenny was smiling again, but now it was an uncertain smile. She was obviously aware that everyone got the joke except for her.

She finally answered "Yes, sir," then went back to typing.

There were two doors leading away from the reception area, one on either side of Jenny's desk. Mr. Hunter pointed to the one on the right.

"That's where the papers are printed; it's mostly machinery on that side. The offices are on this side."

As the two boys followed his father through the doorway to the left of Jenny's desk, both turned to get one last look. The receptionist had gotten out of her chair, and was bent over, digging something out of a filing cabinet. She was wearing skin-tight jeans, but the fact of the matter was that there were probably no jeans in existence that wouldn't have been skin-tight on her.

The bottom half of Jenny was as bulky as the top half was petite. The sweater was untucked, but there was absolutely no way for it to hide the bulging hips, rump, and thighs that were packed tightly into the slightly faded Levis.

Jacob and David looked at each other. Both faces expressed horrified disbelief, and David mouthed the words *Oh . . . my . . . gosh* to his friend. As they walked through the doorway and into the corridor beyond, Jacob took one last fascinated look at Jenny and marveled. It was as if her top half and bottom half had at one time actually belonged to two different people, one thin and the other overweight, and the two halves had been surgically attached by some deranged scientist with a sick sense of humor.

Jacob's first emotion upon entering the newspaper building was one of hopeful excitement (of finding the information they sought), his second was of shock (upon seeing Jenny's disproportionate bottom half), and now, as the two boys followed his father down the corridor, he felt a kind of disappointment. Despite his father's profession, Jacob's only experience with newspaper offices was the same as most other experiences of a kid his age – what he'd been exposed to on TV. In the land of Hollywood, newspaper offices were made up of huge, bustling rooms filled with cubicles; the sounds of typewriters and keyboards clicking, phones ringing, and printers printing; men and women yelling frantically at each other as they ran to and fro, trying to *beat the deadline*. In every show Jacob had ever seen, reporters were always barely able to *beat that deadline*, getting their exposés in just under the wire and then successfully meting out justice by the power of the pen.

This place, on the other hand, was more like a doctor's office. There was no shouting, no running, and very little to be heard in the way of office machinery. The threesome only passed one other person in the hallway (and that exchange consisted only of "Hey, Alex," and "Hiya, Bill") before reaching the open office door of, according to the nameplate, *Jerry MacDonald, Editor-In-Chief.* Mr. Hunter knocked on the open door. Mr. MacDonald, who was holding a telephone to his ear, smiled at the trio and waved them in.

There were three empty chairs in Mr. MacDonald's office. Two were in front of the big desk where he now sat and the third was in front of a small, antique writing desk that sat in a corner of the room. Jacob and David sat in the two facing Mr. MacDonald's desk, Mr. Hunter took the third in the corner. Jacob glanced at Mr. MacDonald – who was still listening to the phone stuck to his ear while holding one hand in the air, conveying a *give me just a minute* message to his guests – then began to study the office. The man apparently had a severe case of civic pride, as most of the pictures hanging on the walls were devoted to Logtown in one way or another. On one wall hung a painting of the First Baptist Church in the twilight of some evening, looking much more magnificent than Jacob could possibly imagine. The wall directly behind Mr. MacDonald's desk boasted a poster announcing the upcoming first centennial of Logtown (in 2003), and was flanked by several pictures of Mr. MacDonald posing with either celebrities or politicians, none of whom Jacob recognized.

The last wall, to his left, really caught Jacob's attention. There were between fifteen and twenty framed photographs of different sizes and quality of early Logtown. He recognized several of them from the library book he'd read, and at the center was a large photograph of the Stockton Estate, taken at a great distance and height so as to capture the entire house. Jacob stared in fascination: except for the daylight and the fact that it wasn't burning, it looked exactly as it had in his dream.

"Look, Toby, I agree a hundred percent," Mr. MacDonald was saying. "And I don't think there'll be any problem." He listened for a few more seconds, then added, "Well, listen, I've got some people in my office, so I'll let you go. But I should have an answer for you by tomorrow afternoon at the latest." Another pause, then "You got that right! All right, I'll talk to you tomorrow." He finally hung up the phone, then looked at his guests with a smile.

"Sorry 'bout that," he said, and leaned back in his chair. "Mr. Alex and Jacob Hunter, and Mr. David Phillips. How are you gentlemen today?"

"Doin' great, Jerry," Mr. Hunter answered. "Sorry to barge in on you like this, but I thought you might be able to answer a few questions for the boys before they got started with the micro-film."

"Be glad to, if I can." Mr. MacDonald was still smiling. "Fire away, gents."

The two young boys looked at each other for a moment, then David took the ball.

"Well, we're trying to find out about the big house owned by the guy who built Logtown . . ."

"Stockton," Jacob interjected. "James Stockton."

" . . . right, Stockton," David continued. "We read in a library book about how it burned, and we just wanted to find out more about it, you know, how it happened and all, and maybe where the house used to be."

Mr. MacDonald, looking pleased at the opportunity to tell a good story, crossed his arms and leaned back even further in his chair. From the creaking, groaning sounds it was making, Jacob began to fear that it would tip over or even collapse at any moment, spilling their cheerful and dignified host into a very undignified heap on the floor.

"Well, boys, I can tell you mostly everything that happened, but you'll want to look at the old newspapers, anyway. You know, to get all the names and dates right.

"What I know is this: it happened in the fall of '33. The fire happened at night, and it started in the basement. They thought maybe a servant or someone might've left a lamp or lantern or somethin' burnin' down there, but, you know, they didn't have the technology like we do now, so they never knew for sure. But when a fire starts in a basement like that – back then, in those old houses, nuthin' was fireproof or non-combustible – the house is a goner if the fire ain't put out mighty quick. There was coal down there, and probably a lot of stuff stored in wooden boxes and all, so it was up and burnin' in no time. Most of the household staff, the servants and all, also lived there. They had to be available at any hour, you see. Well, they had their own small wing at the, I think it was the south end of the house. The fire was already goin' pretty good by the time anyone noticed. So they all got each other awake and headed outside through one of the doors on their side of the house. Two of them were sent off in the direction of town to try and raise help from the closest neighbors, which weren't very close at all – back then, it was all farms and pasturelands along the highway, though I guess it wasn't really a highway back then. Anywho, the others started shoutin' for Stockton and his wife and boy, tryin' to rouse them up and outta the house.

"The problem was that the fire was eatin' right up through the middle of the house and spreadin' outward, so nobody could get up to where the family bedrooms were on the second and third floors. A couple of men said later that they'd broken down a door on the north end of the house, where the kitchen was, and tried to get up that way, but the fire, like I said, was getting too big too fast. Supposedly, one of the men tried anyway, but was turned back by the flames and heat, and he ended up burnt pretty badly. So all they could do was holler and scream for the family, and watch the house burn.

"Now, the crazy part was that right about the time help from some of the neighbors and townfolk showed up, here comes Mr. Stockton and his son, around the north end of the house. They say that Mr. Stockton looked pretty sick when he found out his wife hadn't been seen, but the boy just went berserk. Some of the servants carried him off, away from the house. You know, to calm him down and get him to safety and all. Some of 'em were afraid he might bolt right into the burnin' house after his momma, even though it was an inferno by now."

Mr. MacDonald paused for effect and leaned forward, placing his clasped hands on the desk in front of him.

"It was just as well they took the boy away, too, because they say that Mrs. Stockton appeared at the window right after. She wasn't screaming or panicked or anything. She just walked slowly up to the window and stood there, looking down at the folks gathered below. Well, of course everyone started yellin' and hollerin' for her to jump; she was only on the second floor and probably would've survived without much injury, and besides, anything's better than just stayin' up there and burnin' to death, right? But she only turned, and walked slowly away from the window. No one ever saw her again."

Again, Mr. MacDonald paused for effect. The two boys could only stare at him, open-mouthed. Jacob was both thrilled and horrified as once again what he'd seen in a dream was verified in almost every terrible detail. He looked over at his friend who, for only the second or third time since Jacob had known him, appeared speechless. Then David's eyes met his own, and he knew he was mistaken. If the adults hadn't been present, David wouldn't have been speechless; he'd probably be making some kind of vulgar exclamation.

Mr. MacDonald, clearly pleased with their reaction, finally continued.

"Well, that's pretty much it. The house burned to the ground, except for maybe a wall or two and maybe the chimneys. Everybody was amazed that only two people died, as big a fire as it was, and bein' so far from help and all, plus . . ."

"*Two* people?" Jacob interrupted. "The library book only said his wife, Mrs. Stockton, died!"

"Nope," Mr. MacDonald answered. "There was also one of the servants, a young lady. I don't know what her name was, but she turned up missin' when everybody first gathered outside. They knew she wasn't in her room, 'cause they checked there when the servants first woke up and were roustin' everybody to get out of the house. But she wasn't seen by anyone ever again, so they figured she must've burned up in the house with Mrs. Stockton. But they never found any remains other than Mr. Stockton's wife.

"A lot of folks thought that maybe she was the one who started the fire down in the basement. Some said on accident, some said on purpose. There was a rumor started floatin' around that she and Mr. Stockton had a little thing goin', if you know what I mean, but nobody knew for certain. You know how people like to talk and gossip, and they were just as bad about it, if not worse, back then. Especially the servants, and a rumor started that she – the young lady, that is – was all distraught because Mr. Stockton had broken it off, and so she started the fire then ran off, or maybe killed herself, or maybe just accidentally got burned up in the fire she started. Either way, her body wasn't never found, but like I said, they didn't have the kind of technology like we have now, and if she burned up in the basement, where the fire was so hot, and maybe the house collapsed on her – well, that could be why they never found her."

Jacob's father had listened with quite a bit of interest to most of the narrative, but unlike the boys, he'd become skeptical when the story turned and began following the trail of legend rather than fact. Especially the parts about the wife turning away from the window and walking to her own fiery death, and a love-stricken maid who may have burned the house then killed herself.

"Well, that's a great story, Jerry, but how much of it is just legend and myth?"

Mr. MacDonald looked over at Mr. Hunter with raised eyebrows.

"Not too much," he replied. "You see, my grandfather was one of the neighbors who showed up to help. My dad was too young to help out. He was only six or seven; I'd have to do the math to know for sure. But my granddad was there, and he told me more than once exactly what he saw."

Mr. Hunter seemed a little surprised by that, and leaned back in the chair with a thoughtful expression on his face. Jacob looked at him for a moment, then back at Mr. MacDonald. For himself, he believed every word of the story so far, and with good reason: it was almost identical to what he'd seen in the dream. And perhaps most importantly, he had discovered that someone else, a young lady who was *not* Mrs. Stockton, had also died in the fire.

"Does anyone know why Mr. Stockton and his son weren't in the house when the fire started?" he asked.

Mr. MacDonald turned back to the young boy.

"Oh yeah, that's what I was getting at when I said everyone was surprised that only two people died in the fire. Well, according to Mr. Stockton, he and the boy had stayed up a little later than usual; they were up reading or talking or somethin', and had heard a noise, maybe down in the cellar. So they went out to see if someone had broken into the cellar from the back of the house, where they took coal deliveries."

Jacob's father interrupted again. "If he thought someone was breaking in, why would he take a young boy with him? Why not get one of his servants?"

"That's what a lot of people wanted to know. He said he figured it probably wasn't nuthin' but an animal anyway, but he took the boy to run and get help while he kept watch, just in case it was a break-in."

"That seems a little strange to me," Mr. Hunter said.

"It seemed a little strange to a lot of people, but remember, that Stockton fella wasn't from around here, and there was a lot of things he did that people thought was a little strange. He was known for doin' things his own way. He was pretty stubborn about that, which is probably why he was such a great businessman. And keep in mind, he practically built Logtown from the ground up, so there weren't too many folks that were likely to question him. More'n three-quarters of the town worked for him. You don't bite the hand that feeds you, and most folks were smart enough to know that."

Mr. MacDonald was leaning back in his chair again, and had re-crossed his arms. The chair still creaked dangerously every time he moved, but Jacob was so absorbed into the story that he no longer noticed.

"So anyway, Stockton said that he and the boy smelled smoke when they got around to the back of the house, so he sent his boy to start working on gettin' water from the well while he checked to see how bad the fire was. But he said that when he opened the back door to the cellar, the fire was already burnin' too big and so he and the boy gave up trying to put it out after only a little while. When they heard the crowd of neighbors coming along, they came 'round to the front to make sure everybody was out and safe. Well, a lot of people thought his story was a little fishy, but he and the boy were both pretty dirty and sweaty, like they'd been hard at work, which seemed to jive with Mr. Stockton's story. And like I said, he was the big dog around here at the time. So if anyone had any real suspicions, they must've kept it to themselves."

"You mean some people thought Mr. Stockton started the fire?" Jacob meant to ask the question, but David beat him to it.

"Sure," Mr. MacDonald replied. "After all, the Great Depression was really settl'n in about this time, and the timber business had been kinda laggin' even before that. Some folks – especially those who no longer had a job – said he did it for the insurance money, and for an excuse to get out of town. But there wasn't any more proof that *he'd* done it than there was that the servant lady had. Anyway, he – Mr. Stockton that is – packed up shortly thereafter, sold his business and properties to whoever'd buy 'em, and left town. Nobody's heard from any of those folks here in Logtown since." He took one last pause, leaning forward on the desk with his hands clasped before him again, and smiled. "So how's that for a campfire story?"

The two boys looked at each other and smiled in unison. Mr. Hunter glanced at his watch, then stood up and stretched his arms behind his head.

"Well, we've taken enough of your time, Jerry. I'm gonna go ahead and take them down to the microfilm machine and get them started so they'll be through by lunchtime."

Mr. MacDonald and the boys stood together.

"Thanks for your time, Mr. MacDonald," said David. "And thanks for letting us look at the old newspapers. It will be very helpful when we write our papers."

Jacob found himself hoping that David wasn't about to start babbling again, but to his relief, David seemed content to drop just one reminder as to why the boys were so interested in a house that had burned seventy-five years ago.

“You’re more than welcome,” the big man said as he reached across the desk and shook hands with both boys. “And if you have any more questions, feel free to ask.”

The boys turned to where Mr. Hunter stood waiting by the door, both trying to discreetly wipe Mr. MacDonald’s sweat from their hands, when Jacob remembered his biggest and probably most important question, which he had somehow forgotten to ask. He turned back toward his father’s boss.

“Oh, yeah, I almost forgot. Where was the Stockton’s house before it burned down?”

Mr. MacDonald smiled his jolly, Santa Claus smile once again.

“Right, I’d forgot that myself – I’d meant to tell that at the beginning of the story. See, the homestead is the one piece of property that Mr. Stockton didn’t sell off when he moved. It stayed in the family, all three hundred and sixty odd acres of it, until it was put into some sort of family trust, in the sixties I think. A land developer out of New Orleans finally got a decent sized chunk of it in the late eighties, and built *The Pines*, where both you boys now live. But the trust won’t sell no more, especially the part where the house was, which is now all grown up woods, behind your subdivision. If the house were still there, Old Highway forty-three would run right through the front yard. Son, if any Stocktons still lived in Logtown, you’d practically be neighbors!”

17

The microfilm room wasn't much bigger than a storage closet. In fact, it appeared to be serving in that second capacity as well. Three of the four walls were lined with desks, filing cabinets, and cardboard storage boxes. The fourth wall was occupied by the microfilm machine itself, which rested on a small table. Against the wall to the left of this table was a cabinet, which stood about four feet high. In it were five rows of small drawers, five drawers per row. On the front of each drawer were little cards showing the beginning and end dates covered by the microfilm in each drawer. Mr. Hunter grabbed a chair sitting under a desk and placed it beside the chair already sitting under the table where the machine rested.

"Okay, guys, I'm gonna get you started real quick, then I've got to get to work. First of all, tell me again when the fire occurred?"

"October of 1933," Jacob answered.

"All right." Mr. Hunter began running his finger down the rows of drawers, and quickly found the one they needed. He opened the drawer, which contained five small boxes lined up in a row. Each box had a label with dates, neatly hand-written, stuck to its top. Mr. Hunter selected a box with the dates Jan.7 '32 – Nov.12 '36 printed across the top.

"Okay, here we go. I want you boys to pay close attention to these instructions. This machine is very expensive, and Mr. MacDonald is doing you a huge favor by letting you use it. I don't want anything to happen to it."

As he was speaking, Mr. Hunter seated himself in the chair closest to the table and flipped on the power switch. The machine began to hum faintly, and Jacob took his first real look at it. It looked to him like an oversized computer monitor that had been placed on what looked like a small platform. At the center of the "platform," directly beneath the monitor, was a plate of glass. Mr. Hunter pushed a button to the right of the screen, and a light came on beneath the glass plate. Then he opened the small box that he'd taken from the cabinet, and took out a narrow spool, which was about four inches in diameter. As he attached the spool to the machine, he began speaking again.

"Now, as you might have noticed, this spool contains newspapers printed between January seven of thirty-two and November twelve of thirty-six. Back then, the *Logtown News* only printed one paper a week, and it was only one sheet of paper, folded, so there were only four pages per edition. So it shouldn't take you too long to find what you're looking for. Alright, here's how the machine works." He slid his chair back a little and motioned for the two boys to move closer before continuing. Jacob saw that the line of microfilm ran from the rod where his father had attached the spool, under the glass plate, then to another spool that was actually built onto the microfilm reader. Both the machine's spool and the rod to which the microfilm spool had been attached had handles. From beneath the monitor, extending down to within an inch of the glass plate was what looked to Jacob like the lens of a large microscope.

While Jacob studied the machine, his father began turning the handle on the machine's spool. After maybe five turns, a newspaper page appeared on the monitor, moving from left to right. Mr. Hunter began speaking again.

"As I hope you noticed, turning this handle on the right moves the microfilm forward. You'll probably have to do that for a good minute or so to get to the month and year you're looking for. Now, this tray moves forwards and backwards." As he spoke, he began to demonstrate by moving the tray supporting the glass plate back and forth. As he did so, the newspaper on the monitor screen began to move up and down. Mr. Hunter adjusted the tray so that the date of the newspaper was visible at the top of the screen.

"You'll want to leave it right here until you find the date you're looking for. Now, this," he continued, reaching for a knob located directly beneath the center of the monitor, "is how you focus." He turned the knob to the left, and the date they'd been looking at immediately became thick and fuzzy. He turned it back a few notches, and the print returned to normal.

"I doubt you'll need to adjust the focus too much, but in case you do, that's how." He paused a moment, looked over the machine as if to insure that he'd given the boys all the information they'd need, then stood up.

"That's pretty much it. Please remember to be very careful with this thing. Turn the handles carefully; slide the platform carefully;

adjust the focus carefully. Even look at it and breathe around it carefully."

"We get the idea, Dad," Jacob said, and took the seat his father had been using. David grabbed the other chair, and slid it up to the table next to his friend.

"You better get the idea," Mr. Hunter replied, but he was smiling. "Also, don't forget what I said about there being only one newspaper published a week. That means that if there is anything about the fire, it may not have been published until a week or two later."

"Thanks for pointing that out, Dad. We might have never figured that one out by ourselves." Jacob followed up his comment with a smile so his father wouldn't think he was just smarting-off (which, of course, he was).

"You're very, very welcome, Jacob." Mr. Hunter was also smiling. He reached over and gently thumped his son on the ear.

"When you guys finish up, just leave everything like it is and come get me in my office. Don't try to turn off the machine or anything. I'll do that." He paused a second, then added, "And by the way, you need to be careful with that thing!" He grinned as if he'd just managed to score the final point over his son, then quickly turned and left the room before Jacob could respond. Having been denied the opportunity to roll his eyes at his father, Jacob turned and did a head-shake/eye-roll combo for David. They both grinned, and turned their eyes to the screen before them.

"I guess we need to get to October of thirty-three first." David said. Jacob nodded and began turning the handle on his right. Pages of newspaper began whizzing across the screen, moving from left to right. It took nearly two full minutes of constantly turning the handle, stopping every twenty seconds or so to check the date, before they got to 1933. It took another minute to reach October, because Jacob had slowed down to check the dates more frequently.

"It shouldn't take too long, since your dad said there were only four pages a paper, and one paper a week," David continued.

"It won't even take that long," Jacob replied. "It happened at the end of the month, close to Halloween, so I bet it'll be in either October's last paper or November's first." He spoke with complete confidence, but David looked doubtfully at him when he said it.

"How do you know *that*?" he asked.

Jacob just shrugged. "I guess it's just how it felt in my dream. I remember thinking at first that it actually *was* Halloween night, but I don't know why." He paused a moment, searching for a way to explain the unexplainable to his friend, before continuing. "It might not have actually been Halloween, but it was close to it." He shrugged again, and turned his attention back to the monitor screen.

David shrugged back and made a face.

"Oh, yeah, I forgot that you're psychic." It was pretty obvious that he was horsing around, but it still grated on Jacob's nerves. Maybe he was just too keyed up about finally actually being here, hopefully about to find detailed documentation about the source of his nightmares, which had taken on a new, frightening twist the night before. No matter what they found today, he felt sure that he needed to tell David about the second dream, as well as his suspicions concerning the former identity of Mr. Jim Hanes. He looked over at David, who was still rambling on with his new "psychic Jacob" spiel.

"Hey, maybe you should get a '900' number on TV, you know, a psychic hotline deal. You could tell people who call about the history of the town they live in, which houses may have burned, where the houses were before they burned, and who lived there. You know, useful info like that. Oh, and you'll need a cool name. Maybe something like The Stupendous Maha-Jacob-san." At this point, David's voice took on the tone and inflexion of a professional TV commercial announcer.

"Need to know if a house burned in your town? Let Jacob dream about it for you! He can tell you where the house was! He can tell you who might have lived there, and what they thought about the fire! He can even tell you which holiday the event might have transpired on! So call right now: 1-900-DREAM-4-U!!" David began nodding as if this was a good, workable idea he'd just come up with. "We can charge twenty dollars for the first five minutes, then one dollar for every extra minute." He nodded his head and raised his eyebrows at Jacob, as if to say *not bad, what'cha think?*

Jacob tried to glare at his friend, but the goofy expression on David's face made it impossible.

"Please do me a favor and pretend you know how to shut up. Just for a little while. Please," he finally said, then turned his attention back to the microfilm reader's screen. He began to crank the handle again, watching as October of 1933 went spinning away before his eyes. After eight pages had passed by, he stopped to check the date. Thursday, October 26, 1933. The headline spoke of the ever-growing depression. There was a political cartoon in the center of the page which also seemed to be focused on the failing economy. Jacob studied it for a moment, noticing how much more detailed it seemed to be than its counterparts in the late nineties. He seldom read political cartoons, mostly because he never got the punch lines, but he didn't even know where to start with this one. There seemed to be a hundred things going on all at once, and he didn't recognize any of the names assigned to the various buffoon caricatures. It took maybe ten seconds for him to get tired of looking at it.

Carefully (his father would have been proud), he pulled the tray supporting the glass plate toward himself, watching as the newspaper page moved slowly upward on the screen before him, revealing the bottom half of the front page. Still, the two boys saw nothing about the fire. Jacob was about to advance the microfilm to the next page when David spoke.

"Hold on, look at that."

The headline read *Ten Released From Parchman for Participating in Tests*. Jacob looked closer. According to the story, ten prisoners (neither their names nor their crimes were listed) were released from the state penitentiary, receiving either full pardons or suspended sentences for participating in tests involving encephalitis. Jacob looked over at his friend, who was studying the story intently.

"Yeah, so?" he finally asked.

"So, what do you think the tests were?"

"I dunno, they were probably trying to find a cure, or trying out some new medicines or something."

David was indignant at the reply.

"Aw, come on!! I bet you anything the government was trying out some type of biological weapon, testing it on the prisoners!" David's eyes were glowing, much as they had when he'd first started floating theories about Jacob's dream a few days before while the boys were riding back from the library. Jacob made a face.

"What in the world makes you say that? Why would they?"

"For the war! The war with the Nazis – World War Two!" Now David was making a face, like he just couldn't believe that his friend could be so naïve.

"World War Two wasn't 'til almost ten years later, nineteen forty-one or two!"

"No it wasn't, it was the late thirties!" A brief pause. "Wasn't it?"

Jacob shrugged, not knowing and not really caring.

"I don't remember. I've been out of school for over two months. I don't remember hardly anything. Anyway, who cares? I want to find out about the fire, not CIA tests on prisoners. And why would the prisoners have volunteered to have war weapons tested on them? They were released from jail, so the tests must not have been *that* bad."

Now David was rolling his eyes.

"The government doctors probably lied to them about what kind of tests they were doing. Then they let them go home so that they could monitor the effects." He was nodding as he spoke. Yes, it all made perfect sense! Jacob shook his head and looked back at the screen, working the handle and advancing to the next page.

"You've been watching too many weird TV shows," he told his friend.

"Yeah, well you've been having too many weird dreams," his friend replied. They looked at each other and began snickering.

The next three pages told the two boys plenty about the agricultural and livestock prospects of South Mississippi in nineteen thirty-three, but nothing about a fire. Jacob advanced the film again to the next edition of *The Logtown News*. This one was dated November 2, 1933. The headline didn't just jump out at them. It seemed to *attack*!

FIRE AT STOCKTON ESTATE: TWO DEAD!!

Beneath it was the byline: *House burns to the ground, Mrs. Stockton among dead.*

The two boys looked at each other, eyes glittering with excitement. David, grinning a fool's grin, said, "Oh, yeah, brother-man! Jackpot! This is it!"

Jacob returned the grin, and turned back to the screen. A very grainy photograph beneath the byline reflected a perfect match of Mr. MacDonald's description of the charred remains of what had been, at the time, the grandest home in this part of the state since the Civil War. Only part of one wall and two chimneys remained standing. The rest was just a mountain of brick, stone, and charred wood. There were people in the photograph milling around through the remains. Some were probably official, most appeared to be neighbors and townsfolk.

Jacob again pulled the tray toward himself, revealing the bottom half of the front page, which appeared to be completely dedicated the story of the fire. He and David leaned in close and began reading.

A late-night fire on October 31 leveled the magnificent home of Mr. James Stockton, killing two people, including Mrs. Melinda Stockton, wife of Mr. James Stockton and daughter of successful New Orleans businessman Henry Brooks. Mr. Stockton and his son, James II, escaped unhurt. Also believed to have been killed in the fire was Miss Della Hanes, a maid who had been in the employ of the Stocktons for about two years. A second servant, Mr. Clayford Wiggins, was badly burned while attempting to rescue Mrs. Stockton. He was taken to Charity Hospital in New Orleans, where his condition is reported as stable but guarded. While the remains of Mrs. Stockton have been recovered, the search for Miss Hanes' body is ongoing.

According to Sheriff Danny McQueen, the fire is believed to have started between ten and eleven o'clock the night of October thirty-first, and is believed to have started in the cellar. This theory is supported by the accounts of Mr. Stockton, who stated that he and his son had been up reading when they heard noises in the back of the house. Mr. Stockton, with his son, went to investigate and discovered the fire through the back doors to the cellar. Mr. Stockton and his son attempted to extinguish the fire themselves, and by the time the servants became aware of the fire, it was burning out of control. Help was then immediately sent for, but by the time the neighbors arrived, the fire had consumed the entire middle section of the house.

Rumors have surfaced that the missing and presumed dead maid, Miss Hanes, may have actually been responsible for the fire, but Sheriff McQueen refused to confirm this report, saying only that the search for the missing body and cause of the fire are still ongoing.

Both boys barely breathed while reading the account, which appeared to confirm what they'd been told by Mr. MacDonald, but Jacob's heart almost stopped when he saw the name of the missing and presumed dead maid.

Hanes, he thought, *was* her *last name! HE TOOK HER LAST NAME!!* He tried to take a moment to reflect on how important this new fact might or might not be, what it might or might not mean, but his mind was a whirlwind and he found it almost impossible to concentrate.

Jacob turned his attention back to the newspaper displayed on the bright screen before him, but as his eyes skimmed the rest of the page, he was disappointed to find that the rest of the story concerned Mr. James Stockton's timber empire and his contributions to the city. The last paragraph of the story stated that Mrs. Stockton would be buried Saturday, November fourth, at the Holy Meadows Cemetery.

After he finished reading the article, Jacob pushed back from the table and stared blankly at the glowing screen. His mind was kicking into overdrive again, just as it had a few days before when he'd reasoned out the former identity of Mr. Jim Hanes. The images from the two dreams were once again spinning and whirling before his eyes, as the screen of the microfilm reader had done just minutes before. And then three of those images seemed to stand out from the rest: intertwining, meshing, then separating again like dreadful shapes and pictures from some evil kaleidoscope.

. . . The boy, looking at Jacob with those stricken, hopeless eyes, whispering *I only wanted to help. I was only trying to help.*

. . . The man, so filled with rage that he seemed to be on the verge of going mad, screaming at his grief-stricken and terrified son.

. . . The woman in the tree: dead and yet not dead, cold and beautiful and terrible as she had somehow spoken to him inside his head.

The images, each filled with its own special version of horror, continued to swirl before Jacob's eyes. He waited and wished vainly for them to snap together like pieces of a puzzle into a coherent picture, but they wouldn't. Something was still missing. Something that had served to form an evil, time-spanning bond between the boy, the man, and the woman.

Dear Lord, he thought/prayed silently to himself, *what* happened *that night?*

"Yo', Jacob, you still with me?"

Jacob started, as if from a trance (which was pretty much where he'd been). He turned to David, who was looking at him with concern and amusement.

"You looked totally zoned out, man. What, were you having a vision or something?"

Jacob considered answering in the affirmative, but only for a second. Admitting to having dreams and nightmares about events from many years past was bad enough. Admitting to having visions was unacceptable. The jokes would be harsh and without end.

"Sort of," he finally replied. "An angel appeared unto me and said I shouldn't waste my time hanging out with losers like you."

David sneered. "Hoo-ah, the Jacob-meister makes another funny. Whatta guy, what . . . a . . . guy."

Jacob turned back to the screen, and when he spoke again, his voice was hard and firm.

"Seriously, though, I think I have figured a few things out. Let's make sure that there aren't any more stories about the fire, then we've gotta talk."

Instead of returning his attention to the microfilm reader, David continued to stare at Jacob.

"What do you mean, 'you've figured a few things out'? A few things like what?"

"We'll talk about it later. Not here."

David made a big production of looking around to see if anyone might be eavesdropping on two twelve-year-olds looking at old newspapers on microfilm.

"Well, why *not* here? What's the big deal?"

Jacob immediately regretted that he'd said anything. He didn't want to talk until he had a guarantee of more than just a few minutes of privacy. At the same time, it was clear that David wasn't going to drop it until he got at least *something.*

"Okay," Jacob finally said after a few moments of considering. He pointed to the screen, and David looked.

"Did you notice the name of the maid who also died in the fire?"

David hadn't. He looked at the screen where Jacob was pointing.

"Della Hanes. Yeah, so what?"

"So, who else do we know with that last name?" Jacob watched his friends face, and could almost hear the click when David's mind made the connection.

"Jim Hanes?" He paused a moment, then made the next logical conclusion. "You mean he's the maid's *son*? No way!"

Jacob shook his head, reminding himself that David hadn't been with him on his second trip to Jim's trailer, and was unaware of the conclusion Jacob felt certain that visit had verified.

"No, he's not the maid's son, but he *did* take her name."

David, who'd just looked quite pleased at making a connection between Jim and the maid, now looked thoroughly confused. He shook his head.

"But . . . well, why would he do *that*?"

"That's why we need to talk later, after we leave here. I think I've figured a bunch of things out, I just don't know why they happened." He paused a moment, looking for words to better explain what he meant, but found none.

"Anyway, let's just see if there are any more stories about the fire, then we'll talk later."

David studied his friend's face for a moment then shrugged. Both boys turned once more toward the softly humming machine on the table, and Jacob began to advance the reel again. They found nothing else about the fire on the three remaining pages of the November 2 edition of *The Logtown News*, and Jacob quickly moved on to the November 9 edition. A very small story on the front page briefly recounted the major points of the November 2 story, adding only that, after investigation, the fire had been officially ruled an accident, cause unknown, and that the body of the missing maid still had not been found. According to the story, she was now officially declared dead, and her family, residents of the city of Port Sulfur, Louisiana had held a memorial service for her earlier in the week.

The two boys quickly scanned the remaining pages, but found nothing else. Jacob was relieved and more than ready to get out of the small, cramped room. He felt certain that whatever remained to be discovered about that October night more than sixty years past, it wasn't part of any written history.

He rewound the spool as quickly as he could, and both boys sat silent and thoughtful as the years and images flew by on the screen before them. When it was finally rewound, Jacob carefully removed the spool from the post where it had been mounted, placed it back in its box, and put the box back in the drawer where his father had first gotten it. He then turned off the microfilm machine, and as the hum died away, turned off the lights of the small room. Then the boys set off down the hall, searching for Jacob's father.

18

In its own way, Jared's morning was almost as productive as Jacob and David's. It wasn't an *active* morning for Jared. In fact, it was much less active than usual. He spent the entire morning – from the time he finished his breakfast of generic-brand cereal until his lunch of a ham and cheese loaf sandwich, chips, and a soft drink – in his bedroom, lying on the bed and thinking. Jared had never been one to spend much time pondering the circumstances of life, so this was indeed a big moment for him. But there was so much going on, and he was beginning to feel very confused. Maybe he had made an unconscious decision to actually take some time to sort it out; it certainly hadn't been a cognizant, "hey, I need to take a few minutes to slow down and reflect" decision.

All Jared knew for sure was that he no longer felt certain about any part of his life. Things that had once seemed absolute now seemed to be fading before his eyes like a mist. His place among friends and family had also begun to vanish, and for the first time in his life, he was beginning to feel completely and utterly alone. And behind those feelings of uncertainty and loneliness, not quite visible but only thinly veiled, lay the darkest, deadliest, and most merciless of his emotions: fear.

He thought about having to repeat sixth grade next year. School had never been much more to Jared than a place to horse around with the few friends he had. He'd never felt motivated, either by internal or external pressure, to excel, and though he'd never failed a grade before, his grades rarely averaged higher than "C." He'd once gotten a "B" in spelling on a report card. It hadn't been acknowledged by either parent until he'd pointed it out, and even then their reaction had been feeble enough for him to decide it wasn't really that important, after all, and therefore not worth the effort.

To the contrary, his final report card last year, when accompanied by a letter informing his parents that he'd be required to repeat sixth grade and requesting a conference, had evoked some pretty impressive reactions. His mother had begun by screaming at him; the usual tirade about everything she tried to do for him, how she worked non-stop, day and night, squeezing in as much overtime as she could to keep him clothed and fed, and this was how he was thanking her: by failing school. He had listened to her rant for almost fifteen minutes, and had even begun to feel a little remorse – maybe, he had thought, she was right about him being unappreciative and selfish. Then she'd concluded one of her sentences with the phrase . . . *and you'll end up just like your father*. At those words, his defiant temper had immediately flared, and he never even paused to consider if there might be any truth to her words. Instead, he let loose with a tirade of his own, peppering his sentences liberally with the type of words that he only occasionally heard from his mother, but frequently heard from his father. She stared at him in disbelief until he had finished, then, lip trembling and eyes watering, she began to lament that she was treated this way by everyone; that nothing she ever did was good enough.

Instead of guilt, Jared now felt only disgust. It was the same whining, poor me *trash* he had listened to for thirteen years: she had whined it to him, whined it to his brother, and whined it to his father. Even after his father, with no prior warning (at least that Jacob had been aware of), had packed his bags and walked out the door the year before, all she had done about it was whine and cry and occasionally bad-mouth the man when he wasn't around. She had never even taken the man to court to get a divorce, or at the very least some sort of child support, which was why Jared now had to live in this stinking little trailer.

And so here he was, once again listening to her useless and irritating whining, but only for a few seconds before muttering, "You're pathetic," and turning to walk out the door. His mother's response was quick enough to almost impress him.

For the last year or so, Jared had been on eye-level with her, and therefore too large for her to even try to spank. So instead, she had taken to just swinging at him with whatever she may have handy. On this occasion, it was a broom. By the time she laid her hands on it, Jared had already reached and was opening the front door to the trailer (and thus was out of swinging distance), so she hurled the broom at him as though it were a javelin. The broom's handle struck the wall maybe six inches to the left of the door with enough force to leave a scuffed indention and knock down a small picture (a family portrait taken three years before). Jared heard the glass break just before slamming the door behind him. He hopped on his bike and rode away, not knowing or caring where he went (he'd ended up riding the trails for a while, then going to the Ice House), as long as it was away from here. As he rode down the narrow, twisting street, he heard the trailer door open, followed by his mother's shrill, whiney voice, first demanding that he come back, then telling him he was a no-good little piece of trash and he didn't need to *ever* come back. He shot her the bird over his shoulder without ever turning around. Even now, two months later, he still smiled proudly at the memory.

Jared also spent part of Thursday morning thinking about his friends. He had never been the type of kid who'd had too many friends to begin with, but now that everyone else was moving on to junior high, all but Stevie (*very* small conciliation) seemed to have abandoned him, keenly aware that hanging out with a sixth-grader could damage their reputations, no matter what his age might be. Furthermore, although none of the guys he hung out with were particularly bright and had often joined him in making fun of the "smart kids", at least they'd *passed*. Dumb had always been a joke to Jared and his friends, but now that he'd been held back while they'd moved on, the others had apparently decided that he was just a little *too* dumb to spend any more time with. That left him the boys who hung around the Ice House, all of whom (with the exception of Stevie) were younger than Jared, and none of whom seemed to like or respect him very much, especially lately.

He thought about living in the trailer for the past year. Until then, he had lived in a real house in a real neighborhood. Sure, it had been an older neighborhood with older houses that weren't all that big, but it was still a *real* house with a *real* yard, and therefore he and his family hadn't been what some people (ironically, his mother had been one of them) called "trailer-trash." Now, Jared supposed, that's exactly what he and his mother were. They currently lived in a small, two-bedroom trailer on a small lot in the Sundance Court Trailer Park. The only yard was the remaining twenty feet of the lot running along the rear and two sides of the trailer; a balding strip of ground that offered no privacy from the other trailers, all of which were packed into the "mobile home community" (according to the sign fronting on Old Highway 43) like cars in a parking lot. There was, of course, no carport or garage. A small patch of gravel at the front of the lot served as his mother's reserved parking space. When it rained, his bike got wet.

Jared thought a lot about his older brother. He hadn't seen Mike since Wednesday, shortly after the big blowout at the Ice House. As soon as he was sure that he was out of Hanes' and the other boys' line of sight, he'd broken into a run, catching up to Mike quickly. His brother continued his stiff march up the old trail, and together they'd walked, past the race course Mike had helped to build, through the woods to the highway, and finally to Dee Dee's, where Mike had left his car earlier in the day. All the while, Mike hadn't spoken a word, despite Jared's attempts to build him up by running down the old man and the new boy. When they'd gotten into the car (his brother's pride and joy: a 1988 Mustang 5.0; black with white racing stripes; dual pipes that let you know of his approach almost a full minute before he arrived; and a sound system that let you know of his approach almost three full minutes before he arrived), Mike cranked it, revved it up a few times (the noise was sufficient to rattle the windows of the quick stop), popped the car into gear, and punched it, slinging rocks and dirt as the car spun out of the gravel parking lot. When they arrived at Jared's trailer a few minutes later, Mike finally spoke to Jared.

"Get out," he'd said, without even looking over. Jared opened his mouth, but couldn't think of anything to say except "Mike, c'mon, man."

"Go on, get out," was Mike's only reply. His eyes were still stuck to the windshield, and he remained motionless but for the clearly visible clenching of his jaw.

"Whatever," Jared had muttered, getting out of the car and slamming the door. Mike punched it again, and Jared felt the sting of sand and gravel on his face and neck as his brother sped away.

When his mother inquired about Mike later that evening (he was supposed to be staying with them at the trailer until Friday), Jared told her that his brother had decided to go back to their father's house in Gulfport. He considered calling his dad to see if Mike *was* there, but was afraid of getting his older brother in trouble – he wasn't sure *where* Mike had gone, but the more he'd thought about it, the more certain he was that it wasn't back to their father's in Gulfport.

All of these random, intangible memories and thoughts swirled and flitted through his mind like transparent phantoms that he couldn't quite touch or feel, and all seemed to lead to one particular realization: he no longer understood how he felt about the most important people in his life. He loved and hated them all, but this concept didn't make any sense to him. How could he could he feel such strong and yet conflicting emotions?

His father was everything Jared thought a man should be – good-looking, funny, and above all else, tough. He'd been a football hero in the small high school he'd attended, but had never gone to college after failing to get either an academic or athletic scholarship. Instead, he'd begun working as a mechanic, and he discovered he was good at it. He'd worked at a couple of local shops in town for a several years before finding a partner with whom he'd opened his own shop in Gulfport. That was when the problems had started.

Jared's father had always been a little short-tempered, but – and he'd always been quick to remind the rest of the family – he was head of the household, so it wasn't that big a deal . . . right? And he'd always liked to have a few beers now and then, but that particular hobby had usually been saved for the weekends. Over the past couple of years, however, it had become three or four beers every night, and his fuse had gotten a lot shorter. His temper seemed to flare over even the smallest matters; Jared, his brother, and his mom had each been popped across the cheeks on more than one occasion for "mouthing off."

Eventually, Jared's father had taken to spending a couple of nights a week at his shop in Gulfport with the excuse that he was swamped with business. When his wife began to complain, he had shouted and cursed at her, saying she ought to be grateful and appreciate him instead of nagging and whining all the time, complaining about how he didn't help out enough at home while he was out earning the money that *paid* for their damned house in the first place. She said the stress from his work was getting to him, and he was taking it out on his family. His cold reply was that it was his family and the way they (especially his wife) were always popping off, being disrespectful, and never appreciating him that caused his stress. As usual, Jared's mother had relented and apologized. She explained that she understood the responsibilities that came with owning a business, but that she and the boys missed having him around. A fragile truce was made, and he agreed to spend more time at home.

Then, not three weeks later, a friend of Jared's mother had seen his father at one of the coast's casinos with another woman. She had dutifully reported it to his mother (after dutifully reporting it to half of the town first). The confrontation the next day had been terrible, and was made worse by the fact that both boys were at home when it happened. Mike had stormed into his room and turned up the stereo as soon as the fireworks started. Jared had knocked on his older brother's door, almost desperate in his desire to not be alone while his parents screamed and called each other names he had never heard before (which was a surprise; until then, he thought that his father and brother had used every word in the book on him already). Mike hadn't responded to his knocks or pleading voice, so Jared finally went into his own bedroom, closed the door, and somehow ended up sitting on the floor of his closet with the light off while his parents raged at each other for another forty-five minutes or so. And the whole time, all Jared could think about was how he wasn't sure which of his family members he hated more at that moment. One and a half years later, he still didn't know.

In the end, Jared's father simply moved out of the house in Logtown and into one he'd had in Gulfport for nearly six months without anyone (save his girlfriend) even knowing about it. With only their mother's meager income now available to pay the bills, the Logtown house was eventually lost to foreclosure. At that point, Mike had moved into the Gulfport house with his father, and Jared and his mother moved to Sundance Court.

The brutal truth that Jared now faced was that his father had *chosen* to live his life away from Jared and the rest of the family. Sure, he let Mike live at the house in Gulfport, but for two reasons only: his estranged wife couldn't support both boys by herself, and Mike had reached the age where he required little from his father other than a place to sleep and food to eat. And to Jared, the most confusing and therefore worst part of it was that, when he spent those weekends in Gulfport, his father seemed to enjoy having him. He, Mike, and Jared played cards together, watched 'R' rated movies together, went to car and truck shows together. On those occasions when Jared got to visit his father's shop, the man really did seem proud of his son, bragging on him in front of the other mechanics and letting him help out, just as if he actually worked there. On some occasions, after Jared helped change the oil in a car or played gopher for the mechanics, fetching whatever they might need from the supply room, his father even paid him!

But he didn't want to *live* with his son. He was too busy to be burdened with the boy for more than just two days a week. Or maybe he was just too taken with his new, worry-free lifestyle to return to his wife and family so that they could live together again.

After his father left, Jared's mother apparently made up her mind that all men really were pigs. None of them appreciated the things she did for them. And since Jared was now the only one who lived with her, he was the one who got to listen to the bulk of her whiney complaints. These were always more frequent and intense just before and after his weekend trips to his father's house. She clearly took it personally that Jared wanted anything to do with the man who had abandoned her for a new woman and a carefree life. But for all her complaining, she never *did* anything about it.

About the time Mike had moved in with his father, she had visited with a lawyer and had divorce papers drawn up, but she never followed through with it. She never even attempted to take him to court for child support, which again was why Jared now had to live in a stinkin' trailer, nestled snugly in between other stinkin' trailers in this stinkin' trailer park. Instead, she worked double shifts and overtime, bringing in just enough money to make the monthly payments on their "home", buy generic food to eat (mostly in the form of cans, boxes, and microwaveable plates), and keep Jared and herself dressed in cheap clothing, mostly purchased at no-name, discount stores. She whined and complained all the while, but *never did anything about it*.

And yet, Jared had to admit, sometimes it *did* seem that everything she was doing *was* for him. She worked those double shifts and overtime, but never took an evening out for herself, even on the weekends when Jared was in Gulfport. She never dated (sure, she was still technically married, but that didn't stop his father from playing the field), even though Jared was sure she could. The harsh life she'd lived for the past few years was beginning to take a toll, but she was still an attractive woman, and Jared was sure there were plenty of men who would love to take her out, even if the reason was less than honorable. But she never did anything for herself.

And after every tongue-lashing she delivered over his grades at school – after laying yet another guilt trip on him – she would follow up by getting on the phone with his teacher to schedule a conference, usually during her lunch hour in the middle of another double-shift. At those conferences, she would proceed to chew the *teacher* up one side and down the other, explaining how it wasn't Jared's fault that he was failing and explaining in a little too much detail all the stuff going on in their personal lives. Each time she would end the conference by pleading for just one more chance for her son, which she almost always managed to get. It seemed that no matter what Jared did, his mom would defend him (after the initial, whiny guilt trip). But for all that, she still never really did anything that mattered enough to make life better for herself and her son, nothing that ever amounted to anything more than making excuses and putting off the inevitable.

Finally, Jared's mind returned to Mike – his older brother, his mentor, and his hero. Mike, who'd taught Jared how to ride his bike, how to play football and baseball, and eventually helped construct the racecourse that Jared and his friends still used. Mike, who frequently picked at, and had, on several occasions, seriously beat up on his younger brother. But no matter what kind of arguments or fights they'd had, even if the fights were ongoing, he'd never (until yesterday) failed to step up and defend his younger brother from another guy, young or old.

Mike had taught him every cuss word and slang term he knew; let him look at his first Playboy when he was in second grade (which was well before most of Jared's friends had ever seen anything of the sort); shared every new vulgar joke he learned, and had given Jared his first cigarette (only ragging him a little as he choked and coughed and gagged, trying to figure out how to smoke the thing). They had gone camping together, hunting and fishing together, and vandalizing – everything from knocking over mailboxes to breaking windows to spray-painting vulgarities on the sides of bridges – together. And Mike had allowed Jared to start hanging out at the Ice House when he was only eight years old. Granted, Jared had usually felt more like the older boys' mascot than their friend, but to his knowledge he was the youngest boy to ever have been allowed to frequent the place, which was one of the reasons he felt that he had a claim to the unofficial title of leader of the group that hung out there now.

Things had begun to change when Mike had started high school. Almost overnight, he began to spend more and more time with older boys, and less time with Jared. Jared was no longer asked to join Mike when he went camping, or to the movies, or to a pick-up game of football. And Mike was no longer contented to just look at pictures of girls; he began dating them. This was, of course, the natural order of things. But like most little brothers, Jared would not have felt comforted by that knowledge even if there had been someone to explain it to him. All Jared knew was that the guy he had known and admired all of his short life no longer wanted to spend much time with his little brother. It wasn't that Mike seemed to dislike him; he just didn't seem to *care* much about him anymore.

Ironically, things were actually a little better now that Mike lived with their father in Gulfport. Although it meant that there were only two days a week for the brothers to hang out, Mike usually spent more of that time actually doing things with Jared, especially on Sundays. On those days they'd usually sleep late, then get up, have a late breakfast (usually leftover pizza from the night before), then just horse around – playing cards, throwing the football, or watching TV. Sometimes Mike would take Jared riding around in the Mustang, just cruising up and down Highway 90, along the coastline, with the windows down and the stereo blaring. It was during those times that Jared thought that things might turn out okay after all, even though he knew he'd be headed back to Logtown and the small, cramped trailer by day's end. And it was on those long, lonely Sunday nights, after Mike dropped him off at the trailer and Jared stepped back through that door and into his real life – back to the resentful sounds of his mother complaining about working all weekend while the men in her life played and goofed off without sparing her a single thought; back to another long week with no real friends to talk to and the prospect of another long year of sixth grade looming on the horizon – that Jared felt how *fragile* it all was, so *very* fragile. It was on those lonely Sunday nights and Monday mornings that he missed his father and especially his brother so *much*, and deep in his heart, always taunting and threatening, was the fear that it wouldn't take much to sever away all ties to that other life – that escape, that *hope* – that he was somehow able to cling to by the tips of his fingers for two days a week.

And now, finally, it was actually happening. The thing he had dreaded for so long had finally come to pass, all because of that *rotten old psycho* and that *snotty little jerk!* Just the thought of it made the fear and rage swell up inside of Jared, and he suddenly jumped out of bed, began pacing around his room, swearing aloud and swinging his fists at unseen threats and foes. And as he stormed around the small trailer, making his own threats and swearing vows of revenge, it occurred to him that he had been wrong. There were two people in this world about whom he understood *exactly* how he felt.

He stomped back to his room and sat on the floor, his back to his bed, and began to cry in his rage. The rotten old psycho and the little jerk hadn't just made *him* look bad, they had made Mike look bad. They had made him look like a little punk sissy in front of Jared and everyone, and now Mike seemed to be blaming Jared for the whole thing! Nothing Jared had said to Mike on the way back from the Ice House had made a bit of difference to the older boy. It was all slipping away, just as Jared had long feared it would, all because of those two *stupid* . . . Jared suddenly jumped up, opened his mouth, and violently screamed out every obscenity, every vile and hateful word he could think of. None seemed strong enough for the rage he now felt.

Then Jared sat – almost collapsed, really – back onto the floor, his legs drawn up to his chest and his face buried in his arms, and cried out his fury and hatred and fear. For nearly ten minutes his body was wracked with the bitter sobbing and wailing. It eventually subsided into snubbing and hitched breaths. And then, finally, he looked up, his normally cold, gray eyes now angry, red, and swollen. He took a few deep breaths, and felt better. His unexpected fit of helpless weeping seemed to be over, and he felt both his strength and a strong sense of determination returning. Now he stood up, and took a few more deep breaths with only an occasional hitch and snuffle.

He was *not* going to let it happen – he would die first! There was no way – absolutely *no way* – that he would let it! Now he was nodding as he began slowly pacing the room, and he felt a soothing calm settle over his entire body. There was no way that he was going to stand by and watch what he'd dreaded for so long happen right in front of him! And as the plan began to form in his mind, as he nodded vigorously and stalked his room, he began to speak aloud: to himself, to the room, to no one and everyone. He swore – to God, to himself, and to the entire world – that they would be sorry. Both of them! The old drunk psycho and the little jerk who were making all of this happen – doing everything they possibly could to make him loose all he had ever cared about – they would both pay for what they'd done, and they would pay big.

19

After lunch at the local Sonic Drive-In, Mr. Hunter dropped the two boys off at David's house and headed back to work. Jacob was careful to steer conversation away from their research at the newspaper office, and as Mr. Hunter wasn't terribly interested in the doings of two twelve-year-olds researching for a school paper that wouldn't even be written for another several months, the task wasn't very difficult.

The moment Jacob's father had backed out of the driveway, David started pestering his friend to spill whatever new theory he had alluded to at the newspaper office. Jacob refused, insisting that they needed to be somewhere private to talk, somewhere without the threat of interruption, and both boys knew that Dillon was nothing if not an ever present threat of interruption. David tentatively suggested the Ice House, but Jacob refused, reminding his friend (unnecessarily, it seemed, David appeared almost relieved at Jacob's refusal) that a seventeen year old had threatened to kill them at that very spot the day before. They finally decided that Jacob's house would be as good a place as any to talk, so the two boys set out. David brought his bike, and offered to ride Jacob double on it. Jacob declined, explaining that he was afraid he might fall and hit his head *just the right way*. The boys had a good chuckle, and continued down the street, both walking on either side of David's bike. It took just under fifteen minutes to walk the distance between the two boys houses, and after the laughter from Jacob's little joke died away, neither boy spoke.

When they finally arrived, the boys found Mrs. Hunter in the back yard, dressed in cut-off jeans and a red, sleeveless t-shirt, hair pulled back in a ponytail, toiling over her flower garden project.

"Hey, Mom," Jacob called from the back door. "We're back."

Mrs. Hunter looked up and managed a smile, despite the fact that she was bathed in sweat and had potting soil on both knees and up to her elbows.

"Hi, sweetheart. Hello David." She stood up, took off the dirty gardening gloves, put her hands on her hips and stretched her back. It was all David could do not to gawk. Mrs. Hunter let out a long sigh, and finally dropped her hands to her side.

"So, how was the research expedition? Did you find what you were looking for?"

"Yeah, I guess." Jacob answered, shrugging indifferently to covey a "no big deal" attitude. David remained uncharacteristically silent.

"Have you two eaten lunch yet?"

"Yeah, Frito-chili pie. Dad took us to Sonic."

Jacob's mother made a face. She was not a big fan of fast food, and there were some meals at some restaurants that she absolutely refused to eat. Jacob couldn't resist egging her on. He made a big show of patting his belly and licking his lips.

"I think the chili had some rat-meat in it, too. Yum, yum." He turned and grinned at David, who finally managed to pull his eyes away from Mrs. Hunter and grin back.

"That's gross, Jacob." She wasn't amused, but both boys kept right on grinning. "So, what do you two have planned for this afternoon?"

Uh-oh, Jacob thought. He recognized the tone. It meant that she was either going to put them to work, or insist that they play outside and get some exercise. He quickly responded with what he hoped would be a satisfactory answer.

"Well, we were gonna play Nintendo for a little while, you know, to let our food digest before we came back out into the heat." *Let my food digest* was an excuse he'd heard his father use many times. Mrs. Hunter obviously recognized it, because her mouth formed a wry smile.

"Okay, but I don't want you spending all afternoon in front of a TV."

"We won't," Jacob assured her, and the two boys turned toward the house.

"Honey, do me a favor before you crank up the video games and get me some more water." She indicated a water bottle sitting on the patio table.

"Sure." Jacob grabbed the bottle on his way to the door. "Do you want any ice?"

"Please, but not too much."

The two boys went into the patio door, which led into the den, then to the kitchen. While Jacob took a pitcher of filtered water from the refrigerator, David stood staring out of the kitchen window into the back yard. Jacob quickly filled the water bottle, replaced the pitcher in the refrigerator (without refilling it), then added a few pieces of ice and screwed the lid back onto the bottle. When he turned around, David was still looking out of the window.

"What are you staring at?" Jacob asked, suddenly suspicious.

"Your mom." David answered in an uncharacteristically serious voice. He finally turned away from the window. "I never really noticed how hot she is before."

At first Jacob thought his friend was referring to the fact that she was outside, working and sweating in the hot sun. When, after a second or two, it dawned on him what David had actually meant, was horrified. He knew that his mother was an attractive woman, but to have a friend try to discuss how "hot" she was disturbed him in a way he couldn't and wouldn't explain or define. Nor did he think it *necessary* to have to explain or define. He remembered David's description of the library assistant a few days before, and decided that this conversation would go no further.

"Aw, man . . ." he said, disgust clearly showing on every inch of his face. " . . . please, just shut up and don't say another word!"

David's hands went up, palms out defensively. "I didn't mean anything, I'm just saying."

"Yeah, well, I'm not sure I can hang out with some perv who is gonna be lusting after my mom and having weird fantasies and stuff." His tone carried a slight hint of jest that wasn't reflected on his face at all. David got the message.

"Alright, alright, I hear ya." David raised his hands again then added, "She's not my type, anyway."

Jacob glared, and David knew his light-hearted jest had fallen flat.

"Wait right here. And turn around. You can stare at the TV or the fireplace or something, anything but my mom, ya perv," Jacob instructed before stepping back out through the patio door to deliver the water. He was back in a flash, and led the way back to his bedroom. Once there, he closed the door and turned the television and Nintendo on so that they'd be able to quickly start up a game in case his mother came in before they finished talking.

David sat in the chair parked at his friend's desk and watched as Jacob set up the props. Finally, Jacob sat down on the floor with his back to his bed and looked over at his friend, who was staring impatiently.

"All right, dude, let's hear it. What exactly do you think you've figured out?"

Jacob took a deep breath and dropped his eyes to the floor. When he spoke, his words were slow and carefully selected. He was determined that David should understand his reasoning, and believe his story when it was finished.

"Okay, first of all, do you believe my dream? That what I saw really happened, I mean?"

"You know I do, man. I mean, it's kinda weird and all, but geez, after all that stuff we've found out, why wouldn't I?"

"Yeah, I guess. But it still seems hard to believe even to me. What I was going to say, though, is that . . ." Jacob's voice trailed off. He knew that David believed what he'd heard so far, and he was finally ready to tell about the rest of the first dream, about that skull-faced woman who'd chased him through the woods, and maybe even tell him about the second dream. But now that he was coming to it, it was harder than he had imagined. Maybe it shouldn't have been, but it was, because deep down he knew that if it was David having the dreams and telling *him* about it, he might just seriously consider whether his friend was mentally stable. More importantly, to openly speak of the reality of what he'd dreamed was to admit the possibility that things he'd always been taught were fairy-tales and kid stuff might somehow actually be a part of the waking world around him. This was an idea that most kids his age might sometimes discuss in a "what if" or "wouldn't it be cool if" kind of way from time to time, but only as a temporary distraction from other, more important things, like video games and movies and climbing trees and racing on your bike. It was one thing to consider those possibilities while swapping ghost stories around a campfire or while watching a scary movie late at night; it was another to find yourself earnestly discussing them in broad daylight.

Jacob looked back up at David, and their eyes met. He was surprised to see a patient, reassuring look instead of the eager, ready-to-make-a-joke expression David usually wore. His confidence returned, and with a deep breath, Jacob plunged forward with his story.

"All right. First of all, remember how I told you that the library book said that the lady, Mrs. Stockton, died in the fire? That was in the newspaper, too, but the newspaper and Mr. MacDonald also said that another lady, a maid, also died in the fire."

David was nodding. "Yeah, the Hanes lady. You said that was where Jim got his last name, but he wasn't related to her. But why does he have the same last name if he's not related?"

"I'm getting to that, just hold on." Jacob paused again for a few seconds to organize his thoughts. He was still determined, despite David's assurances that he believed what he had heard so far, to present this new argument in a way that his friend would *have* to believe as he did – not only about Jim, but also about the two mysterious women.

"All right. First of all, I left out part of the dream when I first told you about it because . . . well, it's a little out there. But after I saw the man screaming at the boy, I saw a woman, dressed in old fashioned clothes, and she said something to me."

David was immediately hooked. "Which one was it, the Stockton lady or the maid?" he asked eagerly.

"I don't know, she was between me and the burning house, and it was too dark to see her face. At first, anyway. I think . . ." he paused again, and his eyes fell to the floor again as he almost unwillingly brought the image up in his mind. " . . . I *think* that it was *both* of them, that at first she was Mrs. Stockton, *then* she was the maid."

David looked thoroughly confused. "I don't know what you mean," he said. "You're saying that it started out as one, then changed into the other?"

"Sort of. When she first started to talk, I couldn't see her face, but she sounded normal. She sounded kind of sad. She said something like *help him* and *it wasn't his fault*. I think she was talking about the boy."

"The boy you already told me about, who watched the fire with you and was so sad?"

"Right, the one who said he was trying to help." Jacob was pleased that David appeared to believe the story so far, and seemed to be getting excited. In fact, the more he talked, the more Jacob felt *himself* getting excited. He looked back up and continued.

"Well, after she said it wasn't his fault, she stepped closer and screamed *Help me*! But her voice had changed, you know, and not just because she was screaming. It was a different voice, really angry and full of hate, and she sounded like she was . . . insane or something. And then I *could* see her face, and geez, man, you should have seen it! It was like something in a horror movie! Instead of a face, all she had was a rotten skull-head! She still had hair and all, but no eyes, and just a little bit of skin that was just kinda hangin' on her face."

David was nodding now, and his mouth was hanging open a little. He looked like he believed every word, and even if he didn't, it was making a heck of a good story.

"Well, she started chasing me through the woods, back toward my house, only I didn't know if the house would even be here, because it wasn't at the beginning of the dream."

"Wait, I don't remember that part." David interrupted. "When was your house not here?"

"At the beginning of the dream. I don't think I mentioned that part when I first told you. I didn't think it was that important, and besides, I wasn't sure how much you'd believe, anyway."

David shrugged and nodded as if he understood completely.

"Well, at the beginning of the dream, or at least the first part I can remember, I was on the trails behind the house, but when I turned around and looked, there weren't any houses here at all. It was just a big, empty field. I think maybe that was how this place looked back then, you know, before *The Pines* was even built. But later, when the skull-chick was chasing me and I ran back through the woods, the houses were here again. So I climbed the fence and tried the back door, but it was locked, of course, so I ran around to my window, my bedroom window, and looked in. And here's the really freaky part. I saw myself lying in bed, asleep. So I started banging on the window and yelling, but the dream me just lies there, fast asleep. Then I felt something grab me on the shoulder, and I woke up in bed, right where the dream me was!"

Jacob paused a few seconds, then looked up at David again, wearing a shamefaced grin and eyes that pleaded not to be ridiculed.

"Pretty bizarre, huh?"

David nodded slowly, and Jacob was relieved to see nothing but belief on his friend's face. *So far, so good* he thought, and pushed ahead.

"Well, after I read that library book, and read about the lady, Mrs. Stockton, getting killed in the fire, I figured that she was the skull-chick who had come after me. But I couldn't figure out why she'd ask me to help the boy, whoever he was, then come chasing after me."

"Maybe she wanted to scare you into helping?" David suggested.

"I don't think so, because I've found out a few things." Jacob stood up and began to pace around the room as he was speaking.

"Okay, the biggest thing I've figured out, or at least I *think* I've figured out is who Jim Hanes really is." Jacob paused a moment, and looked David in the eyes again before continuing.

"Do you remember what I told you the boy in the dream said to me? About how he was only trying to help?"

David nodded wordlessly. The boy was completely spellbound.

"Well, that wasn't the first time I heard those words. *I was only trying to help* was exactly what I said to Jim when he had me on the ground with the knife to my throat!"

David started shaking his head. "Maybe that's why you dreamed about a boy saying it, because you had said it yourself earlier on that same day."

"No, I thought about that, but it doesn't cover all of the other stuff in my dream, the stuff that really happened. And besides, when

I said it to Jim, you should have seen his face! He totally freaked!" Jacob paused a moment, then shook his head. "No, he didn't really freak, but his face just looked . . . almost dead, man. He just totally zoned out, and he looked scared to death, more scared than I was. And that was when he let me go."

Jacob paused again to see if David had any questions, but got only a *go on, what else* look from his friend.

"Well, I already told you that the boy in the picture from the book was the same as the boy in my dream, Mr. Stockton's son – James Jr. or whatever. So I looked up his birthday in the book, and it seemed about right. The fire was in 1933, and the boy was born in . . ." Jacob paused, trying to work out the math. "Okay, I remember thinking he was twelve at the time of the fire, so that means the book we got at the library said he was born in . . . 1921. And that means that he'd be . . ." Jacob reached past David to grab a calculator from a drawer in his desk. He worked out a few quick figures and then continued.

"That's right, he'd be about 78 years old now. And the way Jim looks? That sounds about right, doesn't it?"

Now another look was dawning across David's face, an odd blend of comprehension and suspicion. He started to speak, paused a few seconds with his lips still parted, then asked "Dude, are you saying that Jim Hanes is the same person as the Stockton boy, the boy in your dream?"

Jacob was nodding, and began pacing the room again, excited by his theory all over again now that he began to explain it to a second party.

"Yeah, that's what I'm saying! I think that's why he let me go; because I said to him the same thing he said to his father when the house burned, and I think that's why he lives on that spot, 'cause that's where it happened. Also . . ." and here Jacob took a Jerry MacDonald-like pause for effect, looking David right in the eye, "I went back and talked to him again."

David's face could finally be officially described as flabbergasted (which was the effect Jacob had hoped for during his dramatic pause).

"You've gotta be kiddin' me!!" David cried in a hoarse voice that could only be accurately described as a screaming whisper. "By yourself? Are you completely outta your *mind*?"

Jacob grinned at the irony of the question before he answered.

"For a while I thought I might be, but not because I went back to Jim's trailer. I wanted to see if I could get any info out of him; you know, to see if he'd admit that he was James Stockton."

"Did he?"

"Not really, but I didn't really just come out and ask him 'hey, man, is your real name James Stockton, II; and if so did your house burn to the ground when you were a kid; and if so, who died in the fire?' I told him that I went there to fix the broken window; told him I was sorry and all that."

"I can't believe he didn't do anything, like maybe *kill you*? Or at least cuss you real good."

"Well, he *was* pretty grumpy, as usual, and he did cuss a lot, as usual, but he didn't run me off at first. He ended up fixing the window himself, then told me to get lost. I was kinda nervous about being there, and I almost left without asking him anything."

David, still shocked at his friend's daring, was nodding appreciatively.

"But just before he went back inside, I finally got up some nerve and asked if he lived in Logtown when he was a kid."

"What'd he say?"

"Well, he *did* get really mad then, and told me to get off his property. But I could see his face, man, and I knew I was right. I think that's why he got so mad at me, 'cause I was right. He looked at me again the same way at the Ice House yesterday, after Jared and his brother left, kind of a real suspicious look, you know?"

Jacob finally sat down on the edge of his bed while David tried to digest what he'd just been told. It seemed that part of him wanted to believe what he'd heard, but part of him, the part that had spent most of his life in this town and grown up with the legend of the old man in question, couldn't believe that the notorious Jim Hanes, town drunk and resident terror to local children, was actually the heir to the founder of the City of Logtown. He eyed Jacob suspiciously, trying to find holes in the story.

"If he's that Stockton guy's son, he should be pretty rich. Why does he live in that disgusting little trailer and wear old rags for clothes? I mean, *look* at him! He looks like a bum. He *lives* like a bum!"

Jacob only shrugged and shook his head.

"I don't know, maybe for the same reason he changed his name. Maybe his dad kicked him out of the family after they moved away from here. But think about this: Mr. MacDonald told us where the old Stockton house had been, and that's about where the trailer is. And he told us that the property is still owned by the Stockton family, and they won't sell any of it. How do you think Jim got his property? You think he just went up to the Stockton family or whoever, up in New York or wherever, and asked then for some of their land so that he could park a trailer on it?"

David was nodding as if in agreement to what Jacob said, but the whole idea was still difficult for him to accept.

"But I still don't see why he even *lives* in a trailer and looks like he does if he's rich."

Jacob shrugged, but his face showed his excitement: he was finally beginning to believe that the two of them might be able to figure out this mystery after all.

"I don't know, but I'm tellin' you, I bet it has something to do with why he changed his name. *And* I bet it has something to do with whatever happened that night, when the house burned!"

Now David was nodding, and his face finally showed that he believed Jacob was right. It also showed that, now that he accepted Jim's secret identity as fact, his conspiracy-oriented mind could begin exploring the possibilities of what had really happened on that night, sixty-six years before, when a house had burned to the ground and two people had died – both, arguably, under suspicious conditions. Now his head was bobbing up and down excitedly, and he looked over at his friend.

"You know," he said with a slight smile, "Jim is sort of like a knick-name for James. Like Jake for Jacob or Dave for David."

Jacob smiled back. He was halfway there, but the hard part still loomed before him – what *had* happened, why was Jacob dreaming about it, and what could they do about it? But David seemed to be with him, so he decided to keep pushing forward. And that meant telling his friend about the other dream; something that was still difficult despite the fact that David seemed to be one hundred percent on board so far. *Okay, man*, he thought to himself, *just do it*! He took another deep breath, and started talking again.

"There's more, dude. I had another dream. Last night." He took another pause to gauge David's reaction. It was somewhere between astonishment and exhilaration.

"We were at the Ice House; me and you, I mean. You went into the trailer, then you disappeared. I looked inside to see where you were, but the inside of the trailer – instead of the chairs and table and stuff, there were just some old wooden stairs leading down into the dark. I started calling you, but you didn't answer. Then I heard a man yelling, then a scream, and something started walking up the stairs. It sounded giant, like a . . . I don't know, like a monster or something, so I closed the door to the trailer."

David's expression of excitement had undergone a dramatic transformation: his face was now almost comically distorted with horror. The legitimacy of Jacob's dreams seemed to have become very important to the boy.

"Wait a minute!" he almost yelled. "What happened to *me*? Was it *me* that screamed? Did I *DIE* or something?"

Jacob started waving his hands, and made a face of his own.

"Shhhh! Quiet down, man! Mom'll hear us!"

He got up, opened the door, and stepped out in to the hallway. The house was quiet; his mother was obviously still outside. He went back into the room, pulling the door shut, and looked up at David, who was still wearing a stricken look on his face.

"WELL?" David demanded.

"No, I don't think you died or anything. I think that you just kind of disappeared because you weren't really an important part of the dream; or at least part of what was about to happen."

David looked doubtful, but Jacob couldn't think of any other explanation that might satisfy his friend, so he went on with the dream.

"So anyway, after I closed the trailer door, I heard a voice. It was a woman, and I think it was the second woman from my first dream, the one that chased me. The voice came from that tree; you know, that big old tree next to the Ice House. When I looked, there was an opening in the tree trunk, like a cave or something. There was a really gross smell coming out, like the smell of a dead animal. I thought I was gonna barf when I smelled it. And when I looked inside . . ."

Jacob's voice trailed off, and he shuddered at the memory. When he spoke again, his words were slow and unsteady as he tried to describe what he'd beheld.

"You should have seen her, man . . . she was . . . she didn't look *dead* anymore, but she wasn't . . . she wasn't *alive*." He looked helplessly at his friend, searching for the right words, but unable to find them.

"What I mean is, she had a real face, not a skull, but she was all white and . . . cold. And she was pretty, you know, but she was so . . . horrible . . . or maybe just evil."

David was now literally on the edge of his seat; all of his fears about what may or may not have happened to him in the dream apparently forgotten.

"Kinda like a vampire?" he suggested.

Jacob gave a slight nod, but his face was still scrunched up as he searched for a better way to describe what had been the most frightening, and yes, the most evil thing he'd ever seen. He shuddered again.

"Maybe," he finally muttered. "Only worse. A lot worse."

He finally shook his head, disgusted at his inability to verbalize the image, and then went on with the story.

"Anyway, she was standing inside the opening – inside the tree – and two guys were standing next to her, one on each side. Jared's brother was on one side, and Jim was on the other, but it was Jim when he was a boy, like in the first dream. And *they* both looked dead, too. But not evil, like the lady. Just dead – their eyes were really creepy, man, all white with no pupils or anything. Then they just kind of . . . dissolved away. They both just turned into dust, and blew away in the wind. Then the lady started talking to me. Her mouth wasn't moving, but I could hear her voice, you know, in my head. And there was another voice, too, at the same time. I could hear them both, at the same time. I think the other voice was the first voice I heard in the first dream."

"The one that said *help him*?" David interrupted.

"Right," Jacob answered, nodding eagerly. "And, like I said, I could hear them both at the same time. The evil voice was saying something about "the sins of the father" and "revenge on the son." The . . . I don't know . . . *gentle* voice was still talking about "help him," and then said I have to stop her. I guess stop *her* means the other lady, the evil one."

Another pause. Jacob had been sitting again, but now he stood up with the air of someone who has decided the time for talk was over and the time for action was nigh. *Carpe Diem*, boys! Up and at 'em! Forward march!

"Okay, so here's the deal. I think that the two women are Jim's mother and the maid, the Hanes lady. They both died that night, but I'm not sure if they both died in the fire. The maid lady wants revenge on Jim, but not for something he did, for something his father did. And his mother, who says it wasn't his fault, whatever that means, wants me to stop the Hanes lady." Jacob stopped speaking, and looked at his friend hard. Speaking the words seemed to have made all of the difference; and he now believed every supernatural moment of both dreams.

"I guess maybe I *do* believe in ghosts, because I think two of them have been talking to me, at least in my dreams. I don't know if they are, like, in the real world or not, but the bad one *is* getting stronger – getting more . . . real. And I'm afraid that if I don't do *something*, she *will* be real. And I'm tellin' you, man, she is evil." Another short pause. Another pleading expression on his face. "Will you help me?"

David stood, his face wearing that rare, somber look Jacob had seen only once or twice before, and nodded.

"Heck, yeah I will, man. You should know that. But . . . help you do what? What are you gonna do?"

Jacob didn't answer for a few seconds. He stared out of the window for a moment, then turned back to face David again, shaking his head.

"I don't know, man. But I think first we need to find out what really happened, and there's only one way I can think of to do that . . . we gotta talk to Jim."

20

Somehow, as always, the August sun managed to beat through the white haze of the afternoon sky – the kind of sky that, when you looked out at the horizon or over the treetops, you couldn't tell where the clouds ended and the sky began. The shade of the trees did little to relieve the heat. Not even the slight breeze could do that; it was as warm as the air blowing from a hair dryer. Both boys were sweating heavily as they peddled their bikes along the path, following its gentle slope to the clearing where the Ice House stood.

Mrs. Hunter had run them out of the house thirty minutes earlier. It was too hot to do anything except maybe swim, but the boys didn't want to swim; they wanted to talk and plan. The likelihood that David's mom wouldn't want the boys loafing around in his house (along with the ever-present threat of Dillon) ruled out going there, and both boys were reluctant to confide to anyone about the situation, despite the very real danger that it imposed. Certainly, one reason for this was the fact that they were dealing with the supernatural, and chances were that anyone they spoke to about it would likely think they were playing some stupid joke. But the truth was that they had somehow become strangely possessive of the situation; both believed that, for good or ill, it was theirs and theirs alone to deal with. This ruled out going to Greg's house. And that left only one option: the Ice House. The two boys had spent most of the thirty minutes since being kicked out of the house arguing about whether or not they should do this.

Jacob was totally against it. Although he claimed that his main concern was the risk of running into Jared and his older brother (a real possibility that David had to admit), it was clear that the images from his most recent dream were still vivid in his mind, and that those images were in fact his foremost motivation for avoiding the place.

David argued that, while Mike and Jared *were* a threat, they weren't likely to be at the Ice House because Jim had clearly frightened them both. And besides, on Wednesday he, Jacob and Greg had been caught by surprise, talking amongst themselves and walking right up to the clearing before they were aware that anything was up. This time they would be more careful, David insisted, riding quietly and not talking. They could even get off of the bikes and walk just before they got to the clearing, looking and listening to make sure that they were alone.

"And anyway," David had said "I want to get my stuff out of there before the other guys, especially Stevie, can get their hands on it."

Jacob took the opportunity to remind David that this was the exact reason he had given for returning to the trailer in the second dream. This thought seemed to give David pause, but only for a moment.

"I thought you said that nothing happened to me; I only disappeared because I wasn't part of the, you know, *plot* of the dream."

Jacob had to concede the point, but was quick to observe that the similarities were still pretty creepy. David assured him that they'd only stay long enough for him to collect his goodies and firm up whatever plans they were going to make, then they'd head back. Maybe by then it wouldn't be so hot, and they could play a little football or something.

After crossing over the last makeshift bridge which spanned the last small creek before the path sloped down to the clearing (the bridge being unnecessary; there had been no rain since the short thunderstorm Jacob and David had watched from the safety of the trailer that previous Sunday, and the little creek had dried into nothing more than a cracked layer of grayish dirt), the two boys got off of their bikes and cautiously walked into the clearing. As they approached, both strained their ears for any hint of sound, but it was pointless. There was none. It seemed as if they had the Ice House to themselves.

David hurried forward into the trailer to begin gathering his things, but Jacob lingered outside for a few moments. He was suddenly mesmerized by the old oak, which stood beside the trailer. As he stood there staring, forcing himself to recall the images from the night before, it suddenly seemed to him that he wasn't looking at an old, wizened tree, but rather a monolithic monument that stood not only to serve as a memorial to some great event from long ago, but also as a sentinel and a warning. But what was it guarding against? What was the warning? What did an old tree standing beside a refrigerator trailer used by neighborhood kids as a clubhouse have to do with a woman who died in a fire almost seventy years ago?

Jacob took a deep breath and stepped nearer to the tree, waiting for an epiphany or revelation to come bursting into his mind, but there was nothing. The only images were the memories of the dream, the woman's red and yellow eyes burning in her cold face; the sickening odor of rot and decay; and the dichotomy of the two voices speaking simultaneously inside of his head: one soothing and reassuring, the other cold and portending. *I will not be hindered* one voice had told him. *Only you can stop her,* the other had countered.

You must help him understand, it wasn't his fault.

Jacob shook his head in frustration. *What* wasn't his fault? That's what it all came down to, wasn't it? He had to know what had happened the night of the fire, what had *really* happened. He had read in books and newspapers about the fire, but the fire was really only a consequence, wasn't it?

I was only trying to help young James had told Jacob in the first dream.

It wasn't his fault the gentle voice had assured Jacob.

The sins of the father the cold voice had insisted.

Jacob suddenly began to suspect that all three phrases *did* have something in common, they *were* all connected somehow, but until he knew what had happened . . .

David's voice suddenly came rolling out of the trailer, and the spell was shattered.

"Yo, partner, think you can gimme a hand?"

"Yeah, I'm coming."

Jacob turned toward the trailer, then stopped to give the tree one last look. It seemed ordinary enough now; in the daylight (and outside the magical, mysterious world of his dreams) it seemed to be just another tree. The woods were full of 'em. His eyes went back to the trailer, and as he approached it a thought popped into his mind out of nowhere; a slight variation of an old maxim occasionally repeated by his father.

Guess you can't see the forest for the tree, Jacob.

Despite his unease at coming to the Ice House, Jacob had to admit that barring an air-conditioned lounge it was probably the best place to be on a hot day. He noticed once again the slightly stale, dank feeling of the place, and the perpetual cool that seemed to linger, despite the open door. He supposed the sun was simply unable to penetrate the insulated walls.

David stood at the back of the trailer, beside the small card table. He had already gone through the magazine/comic book stack and sifted out his own, making a separate stack on one end of the table. Now he had pulled the box out from under the table and was rummaging through it, clearly determined that nothing of his would find its way into the wrong hands.

"So, what do you want me to do?"

David looked up from the box.

"Just stand there staring while I do all the work, like you're doin' now." Then he grinned. "But if you get tired of that, you can take my racecar poster off the wall. But be careful! We had to use tape, and I don't want it torn."

"Oh, yessir!"

Jacob stepped up and began to carefully remove the poster from the wall. It came loose much more easily than he expected. He then took a seat in one of the old lawn chairs and gently began trying to remove the tape that was still stuck to the poster without tearing it. As he worked, his eyes wandered around the inside of the Ice House. He almost hated that they wouldn't be returning here, at least any time soon, and yet he was relieved at the same time. As cool a clubhouse as it might be, there was something wrong with this place. And it wasn't just because of his dream that Jacob believed this. The words that Jim had muttered after the big fight with Jared and Mike came back to Jacob yet again.

This place ain't safe . . . really never was.

Jacob remembered thinking at the time that Jim hadn't meant the fact that a bunch of boys were using an old refrigerator trailer for a clubhouse. He was pretty certain that, while most of the boys' mothers would probably go into conniptions if they found out about the Ice House, Jim Hanes probably didn't give much of a rip one way or another. And while the situation with Mike and Jared could have been pretty serious if Jim hadn't shown up when he did, Jacob was pretty sure that the older man hadn't been speaking about older boys beating up on younger ones, either. Maybe it had something to do with the night of the fire, and whatever had happened that, according to one of the voices that had spoken to Jacob, wasn't young James Stockton's fault. Maybe it had something to do with the sins of the father.

It was right about this time that Jacob first begin to feel bad – like something wasn't quite right. He looked back down as he worked the tape with his fingernails, trying not to tear the poster. He looked up again, and his eyes fell upon the flashy smile of the woman in the centerfold, that incredible, bare-bodied woman which he had somehow forgotten about.

"I must be more uptight than I thought," he muttered.

David looked up from the box, where he was apparently scrutinizing every item, no matter how small.

"You say somethin'?" he asked.

"The centerfold," Jacob said, pointing. "Is that yours?"

David glanced at it, shaking his head.

"Nope." Then he cut Jacob a little smile. "But I think I'll take it anyway!"

They shared a grin, and then went back to their respective tasks. Two minutes later David, finally satisfied that he'd missed nothing, put the box back under the table. Then he grabbed his stack of stuff, which consisted of most of the magazines and the lantern that had always sat on the table and placed them near the door of the trailer. He looked outside for a few moments, perhaps checking for revenge-minded older boys who might be seeking payback. Seeing none, he sat down in a chair across from Jacob, holding his hands out for the poster.

"Here, I can do that."

"Good idea, since it's yours anyway," Jacob replied as he handed it over.

David acted as if he hadn't heard anything. Instead, he pulled a small pocketknife out of his shorts and began gently working at the tape on the poster. Jacob leaned back in his chair and looked out through the open door of the trailer. The glaring heat outside made him squint his eyes, and he became vaguely aware that his stomach didn't feel so hot. Maybe Frito-chili Pie hadn't been such a grand idea on a hot day like this. Once again, David broke in on his thoughts.

"So, what's the plan for the Jim Hanes deal? You still really want to try and talk to him?"

Jacob shrugged. "I don't see any other way to find out what happened. He's the only person who knows."

"And you really think he's that guy, James Stockton's son?"

"Yes. You don't?"

"If you say so. You're the one having all the visions." David looked up from the poster long enough to convey a smirk and a "just kidding" look, then went back to work.

Jacob knew that his friend was just messing around, but his sense of humor was fading fast. And it wasn't just his stomach; now his entire body was beginning to feel blighted. He tried forcing a belch, to see if he could relieve any pressure. It didn't help. David, oblivious to his friend's growing discomfort, kept talking.

"So, if he's the last Stockton, he's probably rich, huh?"

"I guess. Yeah, probably so, if his dad didn't kick him out of the family or disown him or anything like that." He tried taking deep breaths, and it seemed to help a little.

"Well, like I said before, if he's rich, why does he live in a trailer? And not just any trailer, but one of the grossest, nastiest trailers I've ever seen?"

"I don't know. Maybe it has something to do with whatever happened. Maybe he's on some sort of major guilt trip. Remember, he said, 'I was only trying to help', but the first lady said, 'it wasn't his fault.' And think about it. He doesn't work, and you guys said he's not on welfare. How does he pay for stuff? If he isn't a Stockton, how did he manage to get some of their land?" Jacob paused as a new idea struck him, and he looked over at David.

"Here's something else. Your aunt is a mailman . . . or mail-woman, whatever . . . and you guys said that *she* said all he ever gets is a big envelope from New York once a month. I bet he's getting money! And Mr. MacDonald said that all the property was put into a family trust. Maybe the money was, too, and Jim gets a certain amount each month to live on – like an allowance or somethin'."

David was shaking his head in bewilderment.

"Well, I still don't see why he lives like a bum."

"Cause he feels guilty, man. He thinks that whatever happened is his fault. And that's what the lady said we have to show him – it *wasn't* his fault!"

David looked back down at his poster.

"So, Jim Hanes is actually the son of James Stockton, founder of the City of Logtown, and owner of no telling how many businesses. The creepy, smelly, ugly, drunk old man down the road is probably richer than anyone else in town." He paused, smiled, and glanced at Jacob. "You think he'll give us some money – you know, for figuring all this out?"

Jacob didn't return the smile, and it wasn't just because he wasn't feeling good. He was beginning to understand that maybe he was right. Maybe Jim *had* chosen to live this way, maybe as a kind of penance for whatever he felt responsible for. He started to say something to that effect, but didn't. He knew that David hadn't really meant what he'd said. Instead, he shifted in his chair and tried belching again. Once again, it didn't help. In fact, he almost gagged this time. He took another deep breath, then leaned back in the chair with his eyes closed. He had no desire to hang around this place, but neither could he imagine riding his bike in the thick, oppressive heat while feeling like this.

David glanced over at his friend, and seemed to notice for the first time that something was wrong.

"Dude, you okay? You look sick or something."

Jacob shook his head. "I don't know. I think it's my stomach. No . . . it's more like my whole body. Maybe I shouldn't have had that chili for lunch."

David was nodding. "Yeah, I know what you mean. Frito-chili pie always gives me the rooty-toots. Why don't you try this; it always works for me." And with that, David reared back in his chair, lifted both legs, and let one rip. It was one of the most impressive sounds Jacob had ever heard. The duration alone, almost seven seconds, was enough to make him grin in spite of his discomfort, but it was the sound that really got to him. It was as if the world's smallest bugle player was trying, unsuccessfully, to sustain a single note on the world's smallest bugle. Both boys were howling long before the note finally dwindled.

When he could finally speak, David said, "I'd like to dedicate that one to Stevie, Jared and Mike. It pretty much sums up how I feel about 'em."

Jacob laughed some more, and began to wonder if all he really needed to do in order to feel better was maybe engage in a little rooty-toot therapy himself.

"So, what do you think the other guys would say if they knew Hanes was rich?" David asked.

Jacob turned to his friend immediately; ready to explain that even joking about telling anyone wasn't the least bit funny. Nobody needed to know unless Jim said so, and even then he wasn't sure it would be a good idea. He opened his mouth to say as much, but no words came out. His eyes had fallen on the centerfold hanging above David's head, and now his face was blanched with horror. In an instant, his mind had finally managed to associate the strange, sick feeling he was experiencing with a specific source; he had felt exactly this way once before – when he'd stood before that unholy woman in his dream just last night! For a few moments, the only sounds that his throat would make were strange croaking noises. Finally, he managed to choke out the words "Oh, dear God, help us!!"

David turned to his friend, took one look at the horror-stricken face, then turned again, following Jacob's eyes to the centerfold that had hung on the Ice House wall for almost a year. What he saw on the wall directly above him froze his heart in terror and disbelief. For a second he was completely paralyzed with fear, then he half leapt and half staggered out of his chair with a shrill cry. He crouched low against the wall beside Jacob's chair, both arms raised as if to ward off a blow. A noise like a low groan escaped him before he finally spoke.

"What is . . . Jacob, what *is* it? *WHAT IS IT?*"

Jacob, frozen in his chair beneath that terrible gaze, could only whisper through barely parted lips. The sound was barely audible, as though he were speaking only to himself. Maybe he was.

"It's her. Oh please no, it's her, it's really *her*."

Before the two boys, on a full-color, foldout piece of paper that had once mesmerized every boy to set foot in the Ice House, the unclad model had metamorphosed from a figure of grace and delicate form into the hideous mockery of beauty from Jacob's dream. The dark, healthy complexion was gone. Now the bare body was a mass of purple bruises on white, lifeless flesh. The pearly, poreless skin was splitting in several places with deep cuts and sores, each oozing something thick and yellow; each crawling with tiny, hungry insects. The hair, once blonde and full of body was now dark and dank; it hung limply down to her shoulders, though some of it seemed to be stirred, as if by a light breeze. And the eyes, which once gazed so seductively out at the boys, now burned yellow and orange with an angry fire as she glared down at them. Only the smile remained unaltered: a slight, hinting turn of the mouth. But now the smile seemed horrible and mocking.

How long the boys remained where they were, neither would be able to say. It seemed like an eternity before David finally screamed.

"Go, Jacob, go!! Run!! *RUN!!*"

Jacob started, jerked suddenly from his paralysis by his friend's shrill voice. But even as they stood, both boys paused a moment more, unable to pull their eyes from the obscenity before them.

In that moment, the lips of the woman parted ever so slightly, and there was a sighing sound. It was almost the sound of ecstasy. And as the sigh reached their ears, a warm puff of breath filled the trailer. It was a foul reek that Jacob at once remembered; it had filled the air around the tree in his dream. Rot, decay, death. It was the smell of all those things, and now it seemed to be even more. It was the smell of an abomination on the face of the earth; the smell of all things evil and foul, of festering rage and hate.

It was the terrible stench that finally brought the two boys back to life. Hands over their faces in a vain attempt to block out the smell, they bolted, gagging, from the trailer. Empty handed (neither boy spared a single thought about the personal effects of David that they had come to collect), they sprang on their bikes and pedaled up the path and away from the Ice House as fast as they could. Soon the sound of their coughing and gagging faded into the distance, and once again silence enveloped the Ice House. It was, in fact, as silent as the proverbial grave. And from behind the old oak, as silent as the clearing itself, stepped Jared. He wore a strange expression on his face.

For a few moments Jared simply stood beside the tree, unsure whether he felt amused, excited, or just confused. After a long morning and afternoon spent alone in his bedroom, licking his wounds and nursing thoughts of revenge, he finally decided that he just wanted to get away for a while. He was tired of thinking and tired of being alone, but still didn't know where Mike was, and no one had answered when he called Stevie's house. This left him one option, a place he had always been able to go to forget about all those things that confused and enraged and sometimes frightened his young mind – the trails and the Ice House. He wasn't overly excited about visiting those places alone, but he was beginning to feel almost desperate to escape the trailer park, if only for a little while.

The racecourse, which he felt was a safe enough distant from the Ice House – and more importantly, Jim Hanes's trailer – was where he'd ended up. It had kept him occupied for almost forty-five minutes. In that time he raced, jumped ramps, and performed stunts with greater energy than he ever had before; he attacked them all with a vengeance, so to speak. As he did so, it seemed that his body grew more relaxed and less tense, as though a lot of whatever had been bottled up inside was somehow finally released. He still felt a lot of anger, hatred, and resentment, but not the blind, impotent fury he'd been feeling for most of the day. And he was starting to get tired. Not just physically, but emotionally as well. The draining away of that pent-up fury left him almost exhausted. His thoughts went to the Ice House, and he slowly began pedaling in that direction.

Like Jacob, he'd felt a certain apprehension about returning to the scene of yesterday's embarrassing confrontation between his brother and that old drunk Hanes. His hatred of the old man was matched only by his fear of him. But in his exhausted physical and emotional state, he felt strangely drawn to the site in a way he wouldn't have understood even if he had stopped and tried.

When he reached the fork in the path and turned left onto the trail leading to the clearing, he unknowingly mimicked the actions of the other two boys who were already there, deciding that if he got off of his bike and approached the clearing quietly, he could determine if anyone was there, who it was, and whether he should stay or go.

He was able to make out voices by the time he was halfway down the trail, and by the time he had reached the last curve before the clearing, he knew exactly who the voices belonged to. He stopped, and almost turned back for two reasons.

First, he wasn't about to subject himself to whatever jokes and jibes the boys may have ready for him after yesterday's failed plot to humiliate and yes, hurt – maybe even severely hurt – the new kid. Second, although he would have dearly loved to beat the snot out of either of the boys, he knew that he couldn't take on both of them at the same time.

But he couldn't leave. Something wouldn't let him; something was drawing him to the clearing. And before he really even knew or understood what he was doing, Jared found that he had left the trail, taking his bike with him, and was stealthily approaching the trailer from the thick woods surrounding the clearing. He approached the trailer from its left, backhand side. At the halfway point between where he had abandoned the trail and the clearing, he gently laid his bike on the ground behind a large pine and continued the rest of the way without it. When he reached the old oak that stood beside the trailer, he stopped and began to listen.

What he heard amazed him. The two boys were talking about the old drunk Hanes, but they were describing him with a word Jared never expected to hear used in the same sentence with the name of Jim Hanes: rich. They discussed a few other things that Jared didn't understand at all – something about a woman and what she'd told Jacob; a name – James Stockton – that he'd never heard before; and some sort of plan to go and talk to Hanes about what the two boys knew. But the only part of their discussion that Jared was able to comprehend and therefore focus on was the fact that Jacob and David seemed to have discovered that Jim Hanes had some sort of secret identity or secret past. The smelly old drunken freak was *rich.* And from what the boys were saying, it seemed to Jared that they had some sort of evidence to back this theory up. As he listened, somewhere in the back of his mind an idea – not quite a plan, just a question that might lead to a plan – began to form: how could he use this information to his advantage?

Jared remained hidden and continued to listen, almost laughing in spite of himself at the impressive bugle-sound produced by David's bowels, then fuming when the boy dedicated it to Stevie, himself, and his brother.

Then something happened that had confused him greatly. The two boys had suddenly freaked out, *completely and totally* freaked out, and had come tearing out of the trailer, gagging and coughing. They had nearly killed themselves as they ran madly for their bikes, hopped on, and taken off at breakneck speed, almost running into each other and the trees lining either side of the path as they sped away.

At first, Jared thought that he had been found out, though he could not imagine how. Yet as he had watched the two boys fleeing recklessly up the path from behind the tree where he had been perched, he realized it must have been something else that had frightened the boys so badly, but he simply couldn't imagine what it might have been.

After they had passed beyond hearing, he stepped out from behind the tree, and for a few minutes just stood there, wearing his strange expression of confusion and suspicion and watching the trail to make sure the two boys wouldn't return. When he was sure that they were really gone, he turned and began to cautiously approach the door to the Ice House. As he got nearer, his eyes carefully scanned the entrance to the trailer and the surrounding clearing. What *had* made the two boys run off as they had? Was it a wasp nest? He knew from experience that wasps occasionally tried to build nests around the old refrigerator trailer, but he'd been in the trailer just yesterday and had noticed nothing. Then Jared remembered the way the two boys had coughed and gagged. Had it been a skunk? He was all too familiar with *that* smell; those stupid things usually managed to get themselves clobbered by a truck or car out on Old 43 at least once a month, and the smell would carry for at least a mile in all directions. But he had never seen a skunk in *these* woods, especially in the middle of the day. And surely the odor that David had just released into the trailer couldn't have caused a reaction like *that*, no matter what he'd had for lunch.

Jared tentatively lifted his chin and cautiously sniffed at the air, but smelled nothing. He shook his head in bewilderment, and took a few more tentative steps toward the trailer, peeking inside the doorway. Just inside the opening, Jared could see evidence not only of the two boy's quick exit, but also of what they had been doing there in the first place. Just inside the doorway, in front of two lawn chairs which now lay on their sides, was a tumbled stack of magazines and comic books; a tipped over lantern, and the now partially crumpled racecar poster that had adorned one of the walls of the Ice House. David had come to grab up all of his stuff, and had brought new-boy with him in case Jared or any of the other guys had been here. After gathering up his junk, they had sat down to talk a little, which was when Jared had arrived, but then something had scared the boys enough that they had run off without even taking the stuff they'd come to get. Jared laughed aloud at the thought of their failed mission, but it was a hesitant, almost timid laugh. He still couldn't imagine what had frightened the boys so badly, making them run off in the empty-handed panic that he'd witnessed.

"Whatever," he said aloud in an attempted to buck himself up and recapture his confidence. "They ran off empty-handed like a couple of fag babies, and they won't get another chance."

The sound of his voice mostly accomplished what he'd hoped, and now he stepped confidently into the Ice House, stopping just inside the doorway to stoop over and pick up what they'd left behind. The magazines and comics went back on the table, as did the lantern. In a sudden, unforeseen burst of anger, Jared tore David's racecar poster into shreds, then balled the remains up into a wad and threw it onto the floor between the table and the rear wall of the trailer. Then he walked back to the entrance, picked up one of the spilled lawn chairs, and sat down heavily in it. He took a deep breath and, as he stared out into the clearing, allowed his mind to begin replaying the discussion he'd overheard.

Jim Hanes, according to David and Jacob, was rich. He wasn't just not *poor*, as everyone in town believed; he wasn't financially lower class or even middle class (as Jared's family had once been, before his daddy left them); the man was, if Jared was to believe what the other two boys had been saying, actually *rich.*

So why did he live like a drunken bum? Why give up all that money in exchange for living in a nasty, smelly old trailer, wearing nasty, smelly old clothes? Why did he look the way he looked – like a homeless wino slumped against the wall of some side street or alley in the French Quarter? Jared's mother didn't know it, but the three men in her life occasionally made the hour or so drive from Gulfport to New Orleans during Jared's weekend visits. They seldom stayed late, and he and his brother weren't allowed inside any of the establishments that their father sometimes visited, but he had walked Bourbon Street many times, and had seen his share of extremities up and down both sides of the spectrum – women who would cheerfully lift their shirts in exchange for a drink; men dressed (often very poorly) as women; people staggering down the street, sometimes stopping only long enough to vomit on the curb before going on their way; and, of course, the many winos and homeless people, huddled along the sidewalks and against the buildings, dressed in rags picked up at some charity and usually wearing coats or jackets, even in the summer. They would look up from whatever they stared at on the ground only long enough to sometimes beg for and sometimes demand money – a dollar, a couple of dollars, spare change. Mike usually got a kick out of telling those people to get a job or rummaging through his pockets as if searching for money to give, then walking away in laughter, equally amused both by the ones who cursed him and the ones who just wore a shocked and disappointed expression. Jared, after being a little frightened the first two or three times Mike pulled this stunt, usually laughed along with his older brother, never speaking aloud how being near those people terrified him in a way he didn't understand.

Jim Hanes's *appearance* was certainly akin to those Jared had seen crowding the darker streets of the French Quarter, but his demeanor was very different. There was an angry fire in Jim's eyes, and yesterday it had flared in a way Jared had never seen before. Before this moment, he, like most of the people in Logtown, had just assumed that Jim was a grumpy, bitter old man. But after hearing the words spoken by David and Jacob, he was starting to think there might be more to the old drunk. The other two boys certainly believed it. And if they had discovered something that no one else in the town knew, Jared was beginning to think that maybe he and Mike could find out what, and they'd have leverage enough to . . .

Jared . . .

It wasn't a whisper, this voice that Jared heard, but was somehow faint, distant. It had come into his mind out of nowhere, clearly heard, but not by his ears, and it frightened him badly. He jumped out of the chair, caught his breath, and peered cautiously out into the clearing. There wasn't a sound to be heard in the thick, hot air outside. No breath of air, no birds singing, no distant rumble of a gravel or logging truck barreling up the highway.

"Who's there?" Jared's voice sounded very small and timid in his ears, and it frightened him. He made an angry, frustrated face and tried again with a little more force.

"Who's *there*?"

Jared . . .

His heart stopped and he spun around, nearly losing his balance. The voice had come from behind him, from *inside* the trailer. Except that wasn't possible, no one else was in the Ice House with Jared. At least no one that he could *see*. An icy cold seemed to grip his heart and chill his skin. It actually hurt, and he convulsed uncontrollably for a brief, horrible moment.

In an instant, he decided that he really needed to do exactly what the other two boys had done: bolt from that trailer like he was being shot from a gun, get on his bike, and ride like the freakin' wind.

But when Jared left the Ice House (much later, after she had spoken at great length with him), it wasn't in a bolt as though shot from a gun, and he didn't ride like the freakin' wind. Instead, he took slow, almost unsteady steps to his bike. And, walking alongside his bike, he took slow, unsteady steps up the path, down the trail, and alongside the highway, all the way home to the small, two-bedroom trailer where he lived, nestled in among the other small, unkempt trailers of Sundance Court. Jared moved as if in a dream; he didn't seem to notice much of anything as he stepped inside the trailer and walked back to his bedroom, where he locked the door and lay down on his bed. He didn't even notice when his mother got home late from work, called out his name a few times, and finally began hollering and beating on his bedroom door when he didn't answer. And he would never be able to remember exactly what it had been that had made her cry out a few muffled screams of agony and horror before she would finally *SHUT . . . UP . . .*

Jared was *unable* to notice any of those things. His mind was simply too full of the images of that cold face and those burning eyes. And his ears heard only the words that, even now, she continued to whisper.

21

Jacob and David sped up the trails like a couple of madmen, both nearly losing control of their bicycles several times as they raced around the curves and along the unsteady terrain without ever slowing down; both somehow resisting the urge to look back over their shoulders. Only when they reached the path running along the backyards of Jacob's street did they allow themselves to slow down. When they reached the vacant lot used to gain entry to the trails, they finally stopped. For a while, neither boy spoke. Instead they struggled to catch their breath, all the while staring fearfully into each other's eyes or occasionally taking hurried glances into the woods behind them. It was David who finally spoke.

"Jacob, what . . . what *was* that?" he asked in a weak and unsteady voice.

"It was her." Jacob's own voice seemed almost to reflect more awe than fear. "The woman I told you about, from my dream. She's alive, somehow. She's *real* now . . ." His voice trailed off into silence as his mind tried to grasp what he'd just said.

"HOW? How can she believe *alive*?" David's shrill voice began to rise with panic. "She's a dream, she's not *real*!! How can she be REAL? Jacob, please help me!! WHAT'S HAPPENING?"

David had grabbed Jacob by the arms and started shaking him violently as he almost screamed those last words. His eyes and face showed only terror and shock.

"STOP IT!!" Jacob shouted at his friend, who was completely falling to pieces as his mind tried to comprehend was his eyes had just reported. "David! Stop! Stop it! We're okay now! She didn't follow us; I really think we're okay."

David didn't seem to hear at first, but gradually began to calm down. He quit shaking Jacob's arms, and after a few moments let them go completely. But his eyes, still filled with terror and looking like they could easily slip back into panic, never left Jacob's. When he spoke, it was a pleading whisper.

"*How*, Jacob? *How* can she be alive? How was she in that picture? How could we see her and hear her, and smell her? Was that *her* we smelled?" David turned away, and when he spoke again, Jacob was sure his friend was not just using the name of the Almighty in his fear, he was actually pleading with Him. "Oh my God, please, what's happening?"

Jacob shook his head and glanced back to the woods again. He had no answers to any of the questions his friend had asked, with the possible exception of one. It *had* been her that they smelled. He knew because he had smelled it before, in the dream. And he knew that it wasn't just death that they had smelled. It was death and hatred and rage and evil, and it had somehow found its way out of that world he had walked in his dreams and into the world where the two boys now stood, alone and afraid.

Jacob looked back at David and could see that although the mighty demon of panic had released its hold on his friend, it was still hanging just over his shoulders, ready to take possession again. His eyes were frantic with fear when he spoke.

"What are we gonna do? I mean . . . I don't know what to *do*, man! I don't know what . . . what are we gonna *do*?" He looked fearfully over Jacob's shoulder into the woods for a few seconds, and when his eyes returned to Jacob's, they were suddenly wild with a look of desperate hope.

"We gotta tell our folks, man! I'll tell my mom and dad; they'll know what to do! They'll help us, man; they'll keep us safe!"

Jacob was shaking his head now, almost desperately. David's suggestion seemed almost to frighten Jacob more than the horror they'd just witnessed.

"No, man! No way! We can't tell *anyone*!"

Instantly, that evil panic spirit seemed to take possession of David's soul once more.

"*Forget you*, man!" David shouted. "We've got to! What else do you think we're gonna to? Have you lost your mind?"

"That's exactly what our *parents* are gonna think, if we tell them! Or they'll think we're playing some kinda joke on them! C'mon, man, think about it!" Jacob lowered his voice and stared hard into David's eyes as he continued.

"Think! Do you really think they'll believe us? Would you, if you were them? You didn't believe me when I first told you about my dream, and you're not even a grown-up. They don't believe anything, man! Nothing like *this* kind of stuff, anyway!"

David's look of panic melted away into plain, unmasked fear. Tears began to well up in his eyes, and he spoke in a pleading whisper, his voice hitching every few words.

"Then what are we gonna do? Huh? What are we gonna *do*, Jacob?" There was only the briefest pause before he finished. "I'm *scared*, Jacob. I'm really scared."

Jacob was nodding, not so much to reassure his friend as to show that he, too, was scared. But he did have at least some idea of what they had to do. He wasn't excited about it at all; in fact, he was dreading it worse than ever. But he knew it was the only thing they could do. When he spoke, it was in slow, measured tones; a desperate attempted to sound confident.

"We've gotta go talk to Jim. We've got to find out what happened, and we've got to make him see that it wasn't his fault. That's what the lady; the other one who wasn't, you know . . . bad, evil, whatever . . . that's what she said to do. And if what we just saw was real, then what the other lady said in my dreams has to be real, too. Right?"

David's countenance fell sharply when he heard what Jacob was suggesting, partially with fear and partially with the grim and very dismal certainty that his friend was right. No one, especially a grown-up, would believe the two boys if they tried to tell about what had happened. They'd probably just laugh it off as a lame joke, no matter how much the boys insisted. Only weeks of extremely paranoid behavior would convince their parents that maybe something really *was* wrong. And the most likely conclusion for the grown-ups would be that the two boys had gone mental: maybe traumatized by some pervert child molester. But never, not in a million years, would their parents believe that the boys had seen – what, exactly? A haunted centerfold pin-up? A picture of a naked woman that had been possessed by an evil spirit? Please! It sounded crazy to David at this very moment, and he'd *been* there; he'd *seen* it, just moments before!

So what options were left? There was nothing that David could think of, other than what Jacob had suggested. And surely his friend was right, wasn't he? Didn't it make some sort of sense that if what Jacob had seen in the first dream had really happened, however many years ago it had been; and if he had seen an evil woman in both dreams who had promised vengeance on a young boy named James Stockton; and if young James Stockton had grown up to become Jim Hanes (as bizarre as that still seemed, it was nowhere near as bizarre as what David had just witnessed); and if there had been another woman, a kind woman, who had told him what to do in order to stop the evil, murderous woman . . . shouldn't that be exactly what the two boys should do? He had to believe that if what he'd just seen at the Ice House was real, than the solution offered to Jacob in his dream was equally real. He *had* to believe it because there was nothing else; there were no other choices.

David looked back up from the ground and into Jacob's eyes, his face awash with desperation. His gaze then drifted over Jacob's shoulder and into the woods. The shadows had grown long and deep with the coming evening. He finally nodded submissively and spoke.

"Alright. Alright, man, we'll go. But not now." He looked into Jacob's eyes again, his own pleading. "Please, I can't go back in those woods right now."

"Yeah, I know. Me neither." Jacob turned around with a grimace, looking into woods that he *never* wanted to go into again, but knowing he'd have to. And soon. It would have to be *very* soon, because that cold, terrible woman was now here. She had crossed over, somehow, and even if she wasn't quite literally walking among them, Jacob felt pretty certain she soon would be. He didn't even want to consider what *that* would be like.

"But we've gotta go soon, man. She's out, out of the dream somehow. I don't know if we can only *see* her now, or if she's really here. But she's not just in my dream anymore. We have to go tomorrow."

He turned back to David and received another submissive nod. Then David's eyes fell to the ground, and when he spoke, it was not so much with shame as a kind of pleading desperation.

"Jacob, I . . . I, uh . . . I don't want to be by myself tonight, man . . . you know?"

Having spoken the words, David looked up and saw Jacob smiling, but it was a smile of relief, not amusement. David quickly mirrored it. After what they'd just seen, both boys were well past the point of being ashamed to admit their fear.

"Me neither, man. C'mon, lets get out of here. Maybe I can sweet-talk my mom into letting you sleep over. And even if I can't, I bet you can."

David grinned, and even if it wasn't as big a grin as he usually wore, it was as sincere as ever. The two boys turned their bikes toward the street and, after taking a final, nervous look back at the woods they'd just left, headed to Jacob's house.

Permission for the sleepover was granted, to the surprise of both boys, with minimal persuasion. Mrs. Hunter even suggested that they unpack the tent and set it up in the back yard. She was surprised when both boys enthusiastically balked at her idea. Jacob had always enjoyed camping out, even if it wasn't technically in the woods. As long as there was a tent he had always considered it worthwhile, and she assumed most other boys his age felt the same way. This time, however, the two boys had taken one quick – and it seemed to her, almost fearful – look at each other and then both had begun spouting off excuses that ranged from reasonable ("It's still way too hot!") to ridiculous ("the mosquitoes are bigger this year, and have been spreading a lot of diseases!"). She gave the boys a funny look and then shrugged, informing them that they could only stay inside if they promised not to keep the two grown-ups awake, reminding Jacob that it was a weeknight and his father had to go to work in the morning. The two boys gave solemn oaths that the two adults wouldn't even know that they were there, to which she responded with a doubtful, raised-eyebrows look. In her experience, the solemn oaths of twelve-year old-boys were pretty dubious.

Jacob then accompanied David back to the Phillips household. There were two reasons for this. First, his friend didn't want to make the trip alone. After what they'd experienced that afternoon, "alone" wasn't a word either boy liked much. The second reason was that, based on prior experience, they both knew permission from the second set of parents was much more likely to be obtained if both boys were present to assure that permission had already been granted by the first set of parents. The strategy usually paid off – just as it had for their parents when they were kids – and this time was no exception. Soon they were upstairs in David's bedroom, packing a duffle bag with a few necessities while involuntarily watching an impromptu performance by Dillon. The best either boy could guess was that it was a reenactment of a scene from that day's episode of Sesame Street, a sketch that Dillon clearly thought hilarious. In a rare display of tolerance, both boys halfway watched the performance, and even gave up some slight applause when it was over. Dillon was shocked and extremely pleased by their reaction and immediately ran to his room to fetch a couple of hand puppets (Ernie and Elmo). He raced back to David's room, eager to perform an encore, only to discover the older boys had given him the slip. He was bitterly disappointed, but after returning to his own room and performing instead for some stuffed animals and a few other puppets that were set up on the floor as an audience, his disappointment was forgotten.

When the boys got back to Jacob's house, they found that Mr. Hunter was already home from work. Jacob's mother had called ahead to warn him, and he had picked up a pizza on the way home. The two grownups took one slice apiece, to go with a couple of large salads that Mrs. Hunter had prepared, and the boys got the rest (which, despite their rather subdued mood, they devoured, along with drinks and an entire bag of chips) off of TV trays in the den as they watched an action flick on the tube.

At ten o'clock, the boys were sent to Jacob's room for the night with a few gentle reminders to make sure they kept the noise level down. Both boys lay in sleeping bags on the floor, side by side, and they whispered long into the night, making plans for their visit to Jim's trailer, and discussing how he should be approached. One subject they studiously avoided was that of the hideous spectacle they'd witnessed earlier that day. Regardless, sleep was slow in coming that night.

At about the same time the two boys were settling in front of the television with their pizza, Jared stood in the narrow hallway of the small trailer where he lived, gazing down at the lifeless body of his mother. For a long time he stood there, motionless – barely breathing, it seemed – and staring at the black and purple marks around her throat, the way her mouth hung slightly agape as if it had been frozen in mid-conversation, the unnatural angle at which her neck and head were bent, and her empty, staring eyes. In a vague, distant way, these images disturbed him. But that eager and persistent voice was still whispering to him, assuring him that everything was as it should be. Over and over it insisted that his mother was better off as she was, and Jared finally decided that the voice was right. The voice *had* to be right. After all, the woman whose voice he heard knew things that no one else knew. She knew *secrets*. Secrets about life and death; secrets about what those things *really* were. She had told many of these secrets to Jared, and what she had shown him had at first terrified him beyond the most hideously gruesome nightmare he'd ever had. Eventually the images had gone, and there was only the sound of her voice, whispering endlessly. Sometimes gently, sometimes urgently, but it never stopped, and it left him in a state of confused submission.

All that really mattered, he now understood, was that she had a plan. She had explained the plan to him carefully and completely, making him realize not only how important the plan was, but how important his part in it would be. But time was short, and there was much to do. The small part of his consciousness – that part of *himself* that she still allowed – suddenly remembered this and seemed to kind of snap to attention. She had told him that Mike would be home soon, and everything had to be ready.

Time to get it in gear he told himself. He stepped over his mother without a downward glance and walked into her bedroom. The small lamp on the dresser had already been turned on – probably by his mother, when she first got home (before she started banging on the door and yelling out his name and then . . . something . . . something else). He walked to the head of her bed, which despite the fact that they lived in a rather flimsy old trailer which rested in a very flimsy neighborhood, was always neatly "made" every morning: pillows tucked neatly under a bedspread that hung exactly one and a half inches from the floor on all sides; an old quilted throw folded neatly at the foot of the bed; and a few old decorative pillows added for just the right touch. The bedspread, throw and pillows were all inexpensive yet tasteful, as if she was saying *sure, we live in a trashy old trailer, but only until something better comes along.*

Jared grabbed the bedspread and top sheet, and with one mighty tug pulled both all the way back to the foot of the bed, scattering pillows in every direction. The decorative pillows were left on the floor where they fell, the other two – *why exactly does she bother with two*, came a hazy and bitter thought, *when she hasn't shared her bed with anyone for over a year and a half* – were placed back at the top of the bed. He then returned to the hallway and, sliding his wrists under her armpits, began to drag his mother's body down the hall. Although those open, staring eyes never moved, her head began lolling back and forth on her limp neck, as if she was slowly shaking her head; begging him *no, don't do this . . . please, don't.* Again, it was an image that was vaguely, distantly disturbing. That small part of him that was still his had a sudden desire to reach down and close those sightless yet somehow still accusatory eyes. But maybe it was just a silly, pipe-dream type of wish: that fuzzy, far-away part of him that was really just *watching* all of this happen understood that to reach down and actually touch his mother's dead eyes would be horrible beyond endurance. That one little act, which ought to have been simple when compared to the chore of dragging her corpse down the hallway, would drive away that last remaining part of him like dead autumn leaves in a strong wind. So instead he just turned his head and concentrated on where he was going instead of what he was doing.

When he got to the bed, he found that, to accomplish his mission, he actually had to climb onto the bed himself in order to get the leverage he needed. He pulled her up as far as he could in this fashion, then let go, listening to the upper part of her body hit the mattress with a soft *thump*. He got off of the bed and walked around, allowing himself to survey the scene as dispassionately as possible. The back of his mother's knees rested on the corner of the mattress, leaving her legs to hang loosely to the floor. She looked like a drunk who had just barely made it to the bed before passing out, and was now sleeping off the night's festivities. *Except for her eyes . . .*

Jared, agitated with himself for his inability to keep his eyes away from hers, shook his head angrily and got back to work, grabbing both legs and swinging them up onto the bed. Then, crawling back onto the bed himself, he pulled her up to the headboard. By the time she was pretty much situated, Jared found that he was quite winded from the heavy lifting, pushing and pulling.

I guess that's what they mean by dead weight a thought (Jared wasn't sure if it was his own) seemed to mutter in his mind. The thought excited him and terrified him at the same time, and he found himself giggling with all of the heartfelt sincerity of a madman. After his little outburst was over, he added the finishing touches – laying her head, facing away from the doorway, on a pillow and pulling the bedspread up to her neck. Then he kicked the pillows left lying on the floor into a small pile at the foot of the bed, turned off the lamp, closed the door, and walked down the short hallway and into the den. There he sat down on the small, inexpensive hide-a-bed sofa to catch his breath and wait for Mike.

Thirty minutes passed before his older brother arrived, right on schedule (*her* schedule, anyway). During that time, Jared only got up once, to turn on the television so that Mike wouldn't come home to find his kid brother sitting and staring at the walls. A sight like that might make Mike suspicious, and suspicion of one thing could lead to suspicion of other things, including why their mother was in bed at seven-thirty in the evening. Except for the fifteen seconds it took to get up and turn on the TV, though, Jared remained on the couch, quite motionless and unaware of anything going on around him. He still heard only the sound of her voice; now speaking to him about their plans (she called the plans *their* plans, and he liked that, but he still understood the planning was her responsibility; his job was just to *do*); now speaking about things he didn't understand, couldn't understand, and didn't really *want* to understand. These latter things were just too big, too powerful for his mind to grasp, even if he'd wanted to. He thought maybe he wasn't *supposed* to be able to understand such things. After all, he was still *alive*. Such mysteries weren't supposed to be shown to the living. But her voice was forever there, filling up his mind, speaking about those things whether he was ready to hear them or not. And so he listened, grateful that it was only words and not images that filled his head.

As usual, Mike's arrival was announced well before he actually got there. First came the distant roar and rumble of the Mustang's healthy 5.0 liter V-8 through its twin chrome pipes. Soon that sound was accented by the deep and heavy *thoom . . . thump-thump, thoom . . . thump-thump* of his stereo. The odd harmony grew, occasionally accompanied by the sound of squealing tires, until the windows of the small trailer vibrated and rattled enough to sound like they might actually shatter or fall loose from their frames.

The car finally came to rest directly behind their mother's car, parked at an odd angle half on the patch of gravel that served as a driveway and half on the narrow road leading through the trailer park. Mike turned the key, the engine died almost unwillingly, and the world seemed to breathe a sigh of relief. Jared waited patiently, listening to the sounds of the car door opening and closing, his brother's heavy footsteps on the gravel and then the steps of the trailer, the key in the lock. Finally, in stepped Mike. He was wearing the same rumpled clothes he'd been wearing the day before, had an extra days worth of growth added to the stubble on his face, and the bleary, reddish eyes of someone still battling a hangover from the night before.

Mike shot Jared a quick glance before closing the door behind him. Without a word he strolled into the kitchen, first grabbing a soft-drink can out of the refrigerator then a bag of chips out of one of the cabinets. He walked over to the small table, which sat in the small dining area off to one side of the small kitchen. He plopped down in a chair, popped open the can, and took a mighty guzzle. Then he opened the chips, crammed in a mouthful, and chased it with another hearty swig of drink. He finally let out a tremendous belch, which gradually faded into a contented sigh, and spoke.

"Where's mom?"

"In bed," Jared replied.

Mike made a face.

"Already? It ain't even eight o'clock yet!" He looked at the watch on his wrist to make sure.

Jared's answer was ready, and he marveled out how casually it came out.

"I guess she didn't feel too hot when she got home. She just banged around a little, didn't really say much, and now she's in bed with the light off." All of which was perfectly true, Jacob realized as he spoke the words. He was surprised at the fact that part of him had wanted to say *she* was *banged around a little* instead of *she* just *banged around a little*, and wanted to laugh with a mad cackle about such a clever little joke. Even now it was hard to suppress the little giggles that were building up inside of him. It was that same strange sensation he'd felt earlier: excitement and terror. Thrill and horror. Joy and revulsion. Something was happening to him, to his mind and his soul. The two emotions, each of which had always existed on opposite ends of the spectrum, were now mingling and blending in a way he never would have thought possible. And as that hazy, distant feeling of discomfort tried once again to assert itself, she began to whisper even louder and more urgently, drowning out the voice of his own thoughts once again. He looked over at Mike, suddenly aware that the older boy was speaking. Her voice immediately grew quieter, and Jared suddenly understood why there was even a little of himself left in his head. She was deciding what was to be done and said, but needed Jared in order to understand what was being said, what was being seen, what was being done by other people. She was a stranger here; she didn't belong. He had become her translator, her envoy, her ambassador. And even though she had left him a small piece of his own true self so that his job could be done effectively, there was nothing he could do but go along for the ride. Trying to think his own thoughts was what led to the odd, discomforting sensation of finding pleasure at things that ought to have horrified him.

Better just hunker down his remaining self whispered quietly, just beneath the sound of her voice. *Just watch and wait and think happy thoughts and this will all be over soon, and maybe she'll go away and you'll be okay again.* Please *let that be exactly what happens. Please . . .*

So hunker down he did, all but shutting that small and growing smaller vestige of himself down with the decision to do what he was told when he was told, and hopefully, when this was all over, maybe *oh, please* he would find his way back.

"Hey retard, what's the *matter* with you?"

Jared looked over and saw that his brother was glaring.

"Huh?"

"Whatareya, in a coma or somthin'? I asked what's on TV?"

And with his decision finally made to not question what he did and saw and heard; to rather just follow the directions given to him without questioning why; to just, essentially, curl up in a little, protective ball and wait out the storm, there was a sudden harmonious blending of her thoughts with his own. And he had been right: things began to roll right along, much more smoothly and easily than they had when he tried to think about and understand exactly what was happening.

So now, in entirely Jared-like fashion, he turned back to the television, gave a little shrug, and said "Simpson's re-run."

"Nothin' else on?" Mike asked, already knowing the answer. Their mother couldn't afford cable or satellite, and the only channels they got were the big networks out of New Orleans and the Gulf Coast.

"I dunno. Haven't really looked."

Mike looked at his younger brother with an expression of annoyance that only older brothers can convey.

"So what are you doin', anyway, medatatin'?"

Jared looked over and sort of smiled.

"Nope. Just thinkin'."

If there was a change in Mike's face at all, it was maybe the annoyance giving way a bit to suspicion. He had never seen Jared smile like that; it almost changed his little brother's face into someone else's. The face of someone Mike didn't know and wasn't sure if he wanted to know. Just for an instant, then it was gone.

"I found out a few things today, and I think you'll want to hear about 'em," Jared said as he hopped up suddenly from the sofa and walked into the kitchen.

Mike watched as the younger boy approached, once again looking like the same Jared he'd known for the past thirteen years. Except now it seemed that maybe there was *more* of him. There was a brief moment of panic then, as his mind raced back to the events of Wednesday afternoon at the Ice House, of standing in the clearing before Jim Hanes and Jared and the other boys. Of the horrible sensation that the rotting old freak-show Hanes was growing while Mike was shrinking. Right in front of Hanes and those other boys and especially Jared, he was just shrinking away, and if he couldn't make it stop he'd shrink away into nothing.

NO!! his mind answered, trying desperately to boost him back up. *That's crazy! Just a couple of kids and an old man! If they hadn't all teamed up; if he hadn't come along, toting that piece of hickory, and stuck his crusty nose in something that was none of his business, then . . . what? It would have been a fair fight?* Mike knew the answer to that question, so he chose to ignore it, or at least justify it with the idea that those two little punk kids would only have gotten exactly what they deserved . . . if Hanes hadn't come strolling along and stuck his nose in and made Mike feel like he was . . . shrinking . . . just shrinking away. The same way he now felt when he looked at Jared?

NO!! his mind screamed, and now it was almost a panicky sound. With some effort, Mike pushed those thoughts away, because that *had* to be exactly what it was – just a bunch of crazy, head-shrink bull. Still, he had trouble looking his younger brother in the face.

So he grabbed the soft-drink can, pushed back in his chair, and took another hearty gulp and let out another hearty belch as Jared sat down at the table across from him. He finally responded to the younger boys comment, but looking at the television as he did so.

"You found somethin' out, huh? Well, I just can't wait to hear it."

Listening the sarcastic tones in his own voice made Mike feel a little better, a little bigger; the way an older brother is supposed to feel around younger kids, especially his own little brother. But not quite big enough to look Jared in the eye yet; not quite big enough to act interested in whatever it was that a thirteen-year-old might think is interesting.

"It's about Jim Hanes," Jared said casually.

Mikes face flushed when he heard the name. On some level he figured that Jared had some new gossip about the old drunk, maybe even some joke or wisecrack about him. But Mike was past the point where just bad-mouthing the guy was going to make him feel even a little bit better about what had happened, about how he'd been . . . *shrinking . . . shrinking* . . . right in front of his brother and everyone else. Now his eyes finally found their way back to Jared's face. He glared at his younger brother.

"I don't wanna hear one thing about that crazy old drunk bastard!" Mike hissed. "Not one stinkin' thing, so you better just shut yer pie-hole!!"

He pushed his chair back from the table, still glaring; daring his brother to say another word. But Jared's face was undaunted by Mike's harsh words.

Shrinking . . . still shrinking . . . just shrinking away . . .

Mike turned away, feeling another hot rush of panicky anger. He stormed away from the table, unsure whether he should even stay the night or just load up in his car right then and head back to Gulfport. He hadn't taken two steps when Jared spoke again.

"He's rich."

The older boy froze in his tracks, turning around only enough to deliver another red-hot glare at Jared. He expected to see a smirk or grin or *something* like that on the younger boy's face. Instead, he saw the same relaxed, confident and . . . *knowing* look that Jared had worn from the moment he had gotten up from the sofa and walked into the kitchen. The same look that made him seem . . . *bigger.*

"What?"

"Jim Hanes is rich."

"Really." The word was uttered flatly, conveying a *what a cute little joke* message. But Mike saw no smirk in Jared's face, no grin or twinkle of the eyes that would serve to say *gotcha!*

Instead, Jared's face remained knowing, confident, and almost cheerful as he simply replied "Really."

Mike stepped back to the table and sat down slowly, eyeing his brother suspiciously.

"What are you blabbin' about? Is this some kinda stupid joke?" Mike tried to display the angriest glare possible. "I guess he's livin' in that gross, run-down trailer 'cause it's more convenient than a mansion, huh? And, oh yeah, most rich folks dress like he does, right? It's a fashion statement; he has his clothes tailor-made with holes and stuff in 'em. And the fact that he smells like a funky, mangy dog . . . that must be some new, expensive cologne, right?" Mike shook his head as if Jared's comment was the most ignorant thing he'd ever heard (which in fact it was).

Unfortunately, what he considered to be a withering glare and stinging remarks had no apparent effect on Jared, who withstood the little tirade with that same confident, knowing look on his face throughout. Everything seemed to just roll off his back.

Shrinking . . .

"What are you *smirking* at?" Mike demanded.

Jared put his arms on the table and leaned forward. That ghost of a smile formed around his lips again, just enough for Mike to see the shadow of someone else's face as a shiver ran the length of his spine. Then Jared began to speak, and the sensation was gone.

"If you can just sit there for a little bit and listen, I've got a heck-of-a story to tell you."

22

Jared told Mike very little of what he now knew, which was substantially more than Jacob or David. Instead, he stuck to the true identity of Jim Hanes and what that meant: the old smelly drunk was, without question, the wealthiest person in Stratford County. And although his story remained fixed on Hanes' wealth and identity, Jared was able to divulge more than enough details to convince his older brother. Carefully woven throughout the entire tale was the idea that Jim Hanes was a man with a terrible secret, but Jared disclaimed any knowledge of what that secret might be.

Once Mike was convinced that Jared's story was true, the younger boy subtly planted the seeds of revenge – how could they turn what they now knew to their advantage? Of course, *She* already had a plan (sitting here and talking to Mike was a small but important part of it), and Jared understood that allowing his brother to feel like he was a part of the process, maybe even allowing him to think that it had *all* been his idea would serve to draw him deeper and deeper, until Mike became determined that a visit to the old man at his trailer was absolutely necessary.

"You think he keeps all his money at that trailer?" Jared asked.

Mike looked thoughtful for a moment, and it was all Jared could do not to smile.

"I guess he must, as hard as that is to believe," he finally said. "I mean, I think everyone in town would know if he had a bank account, 'specially a big one. Can you see him walkin' into First National, dressed like he does and smellin' like a mountain of garbage, checkin' on his CDs or askin' for a cashiers check for a couple of thou'?" The idea was enough to make Mike snort with laughter, and Jared laughed right along with him.

"Yeah, I guess he must keep it all right there in the trailer with him so he'll have it handy for food and booze," Jared suggested, watching his brother carefully.

"Maybe. It's just hard to believe he'd just keep it there, if there's as much as you say." Mike paused again, his face visibly strained with the effort of thinking, of actually trying to reason something out. "You know, he might have it all in a bank or somthin' in another city, and just have what he needs sent to him, like a monthly allowance." Mike nodded at Jared, clearly proud of himself for reasoning out such a complex theory.

This simple and perfectly logical idea, although expected, was not one that Jared wanted Mike to pursue. So he looked at the table, nodded, and scrunched up his face, as though it *was* a really good theory and he was seriously considering it. When he looked back up and spoke, his voice had the tone of an inexperienced youngster who was looking for guidance and explanations from an older, more experienced boy, like he was asking his big brother about sex or smoking or getting drunk – *what was doing that kind of stuff really like?*

"Yeah, that sounds right. I bet that's it, he's got the money in another bank somewhere far away from here and just gets a check in the mail once a month, like you said, just enough to get what he needs." He looked at Mike as though he was the smartest guy in the world, as though he was lucky to have such a tough *and* smart fella as a big brother.

But Mike shook his head at Jared as he spoke. He looked prouder than ever of his theory, but still managed a disdaining look as he quickly pointed out flaws in his younger brother's idea.

"Naw, man, they wouldn't send a check. He'd have to go to a bank to cash it, remember? Then everybody in town would know he's loaded, just the same as if he had his money at a bank here. They must send cash; a certain amount each month or week or whatever."

"Dad told me one time that only an idiot would send cash money in the mail. Said when you send a check, a person had to have I.D. to cash it, but if they get hold of cash, it's theirs to spend, and anyone who loses money 'cause they mailed it gets what they deserve." And this was a true story. Once again, Jared had given *Her* exactly what was needed to push Mike in the right direction.

Mike listened thoughtfully and nodded; he seemed to remember hearing his father say something along those lines once himself. And it stood to reason, he thought, that if someone were sending cash several times a year (maybe even several times a month), sooner or later someone would get suspicious and start snooping around. According to his little brother, those two little wise-guy jerks, David and the new boy, had found out that not only was Jim rich, but he apparently had a dark secret. Wouldn't it be in his best interest, therefore, not to draw any attention to himself? Isn't that why he lived in a trailer and kept to himself all of the time? This thought led to other stranger and deeper questions – what kind of secret was it that would make a man who is rich change his name and choose to live in poverty in a little town in south Mississippi? Why not live in the Bahamas or France or someplace like that?

Mike's brain slowly churned the ideas and possibilities up and down, round and round. Were there people after him? The mob? The government? Was he, for this reason, afraid of leaving a paper trail? Mike supposed that one couldn't get much more anonymous than living in a trailer in south Mississippi; that would practically make him a needle in a haystack. But to have that much money, if the story he'd just heard was true, and not enjoy any more of it than what it took to keep him fed and drunk . . .

What was the secret? And how bad was it if it was powerful enough to make him live such a squalid lifestyle? Mike supposed that the only way he'd ever know the answer would be to hear it from the old man himself. If Hanes really did keep all of his money there at the trailer, and if Mike showed up to inform him that he knew who Jim Hanes really was, and if he could somehow bluff or even beat the old man's secret out of him . . .

Finally, the seed *She* had planted through Jared began to take root. And, through Jared's eyes, *She* could see it happening as Mike's eyes suddenly seemed to swell in his face, growing excited and, more importantly, almost greedy. She smiled with Jared's lips once more, but this time, Mike didn't even notice how his brother's face almost became someone else's. His mind was completely preoccupied with the opportunity for something that had, just yesterday, seemed a world away.

Revenge!

Payback for what the crusty old drunk had done the day before, coming along from out of nowhere and sticking his nose into something that was none of his business. There he had stood, threatening Mike with a hickory axe handle and calling him names right in front of all those younger boys. Mike told himself that, if Jim hadn't had that weapon, he would have beat the old man half to death with his bare hands; would have taught him to mind his own business, and he almost had himself convinced. But at the time he'd been so shocked by the sudden appearance of a legend he'd been taught to fear in his youth by older boys, and had subsequently taught other younger boys to fear, that he had honestly been too afraid to do anything. Even against a man who, as it turned out, was closing in on the *very* ripe old age of eighty.

Now, out of the clear blue, an opportunity had been laid before him for true, sweet, and possibly long-term revenge. When he left the clearing the day before, Mike had earnestly wanted to kill the old man. And he knew he had the means to do it, too. But after he'd dropped Jared off at the trailer and gone on that extended road trip, which gave him time to drink a few beers and toke on a few sweet ones and cool off, he'd decided it was a bad idea. He even decided that beating up on the old man was a bad idea, because there were too many witnesses to the confrontation at the Ice House. Mike knew that Jared wouldn't tell if he did something to the old man, and he was pretty sure that the Varnado kid wouldn't, either. But those other three boys would point the cops in his direction, sure as anything. So he'd spent the night alone, stoned and driving around in impotent fury as he thought over and over about what Jim Hanes had done, how he'd made Mike (*shrink*) look bad in front of all those other boys, especially Jared. And he'd understood that there was nothing that he could do about it without getting himself into more trouble, the kind of trouble that includes jail time.

And now this, handed to him on a silver platter. Mike couldn't help smiling; the possibilities were almost endless. They could blackmail Hanes, and maybe not just for a lump sum. If it turned out that the old scrod actually kept a huge stash of money on site, Mike probably *would* go for one big payoff. If Hanes got his money on a weekly or monthly basis, then Mike could demand a cut of the stipend. And now that he thought about it, he probably *could* slap the old codger around some – with the threat of exposure, there wasn't much of a chance that the old man would report it.

Mike's smile grew to a full-fledged grin. He felt like he'd just won the lottery – he was even debating whether to take the cash in a lump sum or in smaller, annual payments.

"What are you smiling about?" Jared asked, although he knew full well what the answer was: Mike had taken the bait and was hooked.

"Because we're about to get our payback on that sorry old jerk-wad." Mike replied, his face as smug as ever, "and we're gonna get paid some spending cash while we're at it."

Jared continued to smile, and tried to look a little excited as well.

"Whatcha got in mind?" he asked.

Mike kicked back in his chair, and for the first time since Hanes showed up uninvited at the clearing surrounding the Ice House to rescue the two little smart-mouthed jerks the day before, he looked like his old self – cool, collected and cocky.

"We're gonna pay Hanes a little visit, tell him what we know, and inform him that we can keep his little secret if the price is right. If he keeps his money there at the trailer, we'll find his stash and take as much as we want. If he don't, we'll just take a cut of his monthly allowance."

Mike paused a moment, then leaned forward onto the small table. He was still grinning, but his face became almost thoughtful for a moment.

"And you know what? I think I might just put my boot to his tail anyway, even after he pays us. A little payback for yesterday, and a warning not to mess with me."

Then he kicked back in his chair again and smiled at the ceiling, nearly bursting both with pride at having come up with such a clever scheme and the thought of the money he would soon be spending.

Jared was smiling too, but his was cold and calculating. The hard part was over, and it really hadn't been too hard at all. People with hearts set on vengeance are easy to manipulate. *She* knew that as well as anyone. After all, hadn't *she* allowed herself to be manipulated; to be used? Wasn't she *still* allowing herself to be used? She knew it was so, but that hadn't mattered for a long time. And the torment she'd suffered for so long, for what seemed like so many lifetimes, an eternity even, would finally end. The door had finally been opened for her, just as she had once opened a different door for another.

There *was* a price to be paid, and the costs of retribution were *not* too great. She had also heard whispering voices, so long ago, and in her rage and despair she'd believed them, and so made her choice. Then she had herself given what was necessary for that retribution, and now that the long waiting was finally over, it was time that check was paid. The costs were *not* too great. They were necessary, a part of the price to be paid in the name of justice.

It was time for Jared to take charge and lead the way, but it still had to be done carefully, lest Mike realize there was more at stake than his own petty retribution. So Jared spoke again, carefully selecting words that were spoken so casually that Mike would never really understand how easily he'd been led.

"That sounds like a plan and a half, man," he said, and his eyes shone with excitement and admiration. "When are we gonna do it?"

"Soon as we can," came the reply. Mike was still staring at the ceiling, probably already spending the money he believed was as good as his. "Maybe later tonight."

"We ought to wait 'til tomorrow," Jared cautioned.

Mike finally drifted out of his shopping-spree daydream and looked his younger brother in the eye.

"Why? We can't just go stormin' his trailer in broad daylight, somebody'll see us."

"If we try to bust in there in the middle of the night, we'll get shot. You know he's prob'ly got guns in there, and he'll prob'ly answer the door with one if we show up in the middle of the night." Jared paused, looking Mike carefully in the eyes to get this important message across. It would do her no good to have her link to this place blown away before she could accomplish what had to be done.

Mike frowned, not only at the words Jared spoke, but also at the expression on his face. It was so intense, so powerful, and once again Mike felt like he could almost swear it was the face someone he didn't know, someone who almost frightened him, peering out at him through the younger boy's ice-blue eyes. He found that he had to break eye contact with Jared before he could say anything. He shifted his eyes toward one of the windows, and opened his mouth, but before a single word came out, Jared was speaking again.

"Your gun won't do us much good if Hanes is waiting on the other side of the door with a shotgun."

Mike's eyes shot back to Jared's face involuntarily, and saw that his brother's eyes were almost dancing with laughter and amusement. He had been planning to bring the gun, of course, but only as extra insurance – part of Jim's notoriety was built on the generally accepted idea that the man had guns out the wazoo and, being a drunken madman, would likely use them as retaliation for the even the smallest of infractions.

Mike's gun, a forty-five caliber revolver, had been purchased at one of the many pawn shop in Gulfport that had sprung up and thrived since the arrival of casinos on the Mississippi Gulf Coast. The buyer was the father of one of Mike's friends who, for a "finder's fee", strongly believed in the right of every American – even those under the legal age – to bear arms. Only the closest of his few friends knew about the gun. This didn't include Jared or their father.

"How'd you know about that?" Mike demanded. He tried to speak with authority, desperate to keep the feeling that he was once again in charge, the feeling that he, not his thirteen-year-old brother, was in control of the situation. *He* was making the plans and calling the shots.

Jared's smile remained fixed and placid. He (she) knew more than this ignorant, teenaged redneck could possibly comprehend, but now wasn't the time to show him. She had a task to complete, and the moment was finally here. But until she had what she wanted, she would have to keep leading and pushing him in the direction she wanted him to go.

"I saw it in the glove compartment of your car a few weeks ago when I was looking for a CD," he lied. "Don't worry, I didn't touch it and I won't tell Mom or Dad."

Mike eyeballed his brother for a few moments, trying to decide if he was hearing the truth, but he couldn't read the expression on Jared's face and soon looked away. The story seemed likely enough, and Mike was sure he would've heard from one or both parents by now if Jared had told. He wasn't happy about the idea of anyone, even his own brother, snooping through his car, but he let it go. He was still too pumped about the little scheme he was cooking up to get sidetracked right now. He took a few moments to think about what Jared had just said.

"Well, I can guaran-dang-tee you he *does* have guns, and I don't plan on letting him use one on me. But if he sees that it's us, he'll probably come out shootin' whether it's day or night. We're gonna have to take him by surprise, and that means breakin' in. We can't do that in broad daylight."

Jared's expression never changed, and Mike felt unnerved every time he looked at the boy. *It's like he already knows what I'm gonna say even before I say it*, he thought. He looked away again and clenched his jaws, irritated at himself for being so nervous around a boy whom he had once seen dig the poop out of his diaper and smear it on his own face at age one and a half, whom he had caught picking his nose and eating the booger at age four, and until last year, when Mike had moved to Gulfport to live with their father, had thumped upside the head and sucker-punched on the shoulder whenever the urge struck him.

I'm just a little nervous, that's all, he thought. *This is a pretty big thing we're planning here, and we're both a little nervous and excited, and that's all it is.* He finally managed to look in Jared's direction again and realized the boy was talking.

"Maybe we won't have to break in," he said. "What if he don't know its us trying to get in the trailer?"

Mike made an exaggerated scoffing noise.

"And how do we do that? I think he'll probably recognize us when he sees us."

"Jacob and David will prob'ly want to talk to him, and soon. If he sees that Jacob boy at the door, he'll let him in. And if we're there when they show up, we'll get in, too."

Mike considered this for a few moments, which was all it took for him to decide that once again, Jared was right. Hanes had come to the new boy's rescue, so obviously he liked the kid (as difficult a concept as that was for Mike to believe – Hanes liking anyone, especially a kid), and if that was the case, it meant that Hanes might trust the boy enough to let him in the trailer. He and Jared could hide in the brush or maybe around the side of the trailer. Jim's guard would probably be down when he saw that it was Jacob knocking on his door, and then Mike and Jared could charge in, taking everyone by surprise.

He looked back across the table and was relieved to see that old, familiar look on Jared's face; the look a younger brother is supposed to have when scheming with his older brother. Excitement and admiration. Gone was that strange, knowing, almost ominous look. Now he was once again just Mike's kid brother, and the older boy was almost able to convince himself that he had imagined those other looks – it had been just a bad case of nerves and self-doubt after the disastrous confrontation at the Ice House yesterday.

"We ought to leave pretty early in the morning," Jared suggested, with just the right amount of excitement and nervousness in his voice. "David and Jacob might show up there anytime, and besides, we need to be outta here before mom gets up for work so she won't think we're up to something."

Mike nodded, blissfully unaware that his mother wouldn't have to worry about getting up for work ever again.

"Right-o," he said. "We can leave a note; tell her we left early to go fishing or somethin' like that." Now Mike was grinning as he nodded. It seemed to him that it was a pretty good plan with the potential for a really good payoff if everything worked. He was feeling good again and finally managed to push those feelings that had been haunting him relentlessly for more than twenty-four hours straight down deep; so deep that they were almost forgotten. After all, most of the plan had been his idea, right? Mike wasn't too sure about the answer to that question and decided not to pursue it. What mattered was that there *was* a plan, and the big payoff would be tomorrow.

Jared suggested it was time for bed since they would have such an early start. Mike agreed, and was surprised when Jared offered to let the older boy sleep in his bed. Mike usually slept on the couch whenever he visited, but tonight Jared offered to take his place. Mike readily accepted, taking the offer as yet another sign that he was still king-of-the-world to his younger brother; he wasn't *really* shrinking – it was all just in his mind, an unpleasant side-effect from the day before. He left Jared sitting on the couch and headed to the small bedroom, closing the door behind him. He kicked off his boots and flopped down on the covers, lying on his back with his hands behind his head and staring at the ceiling. Despite his excitement over the upcoming festivities, he was asleep in under twenty minutes. After all, the past day and a half had seen plenty of excitement but little rest.

After Mike closed the door to the bedroom, Jared walked to the television, turned it off, then took a seat on the couch. He sat exactly as he had been sitting before Mike had arrived, staring straight ahead but seeing nothing. Her voice continued to whisper, always relentless and urgent and filled with hate. But now her whisper had a different quality as well – excitement. After what had seemed like an eternity of waiting, her moment was finally at hand. Jared almost left the safe little place he'd found in a desperate attempt to discover what exactly her plans held for him and was immediately nearly swept away forever in the violent, swirling typhoon of urgency and seething rage that had consumed her. He was pulled, twisted and torn by the power and images he beheld as he stood at the edge of his own thoughts and barely out of reach of hers. He screamed and despaired over what he saw for a brief moment that would stay with him forever. Finally, with a strength born of utter desperation, he wrenched himself away from what had been exposed to him in such honest, terrible, vivid detail, fleeing blindly back to that small, safe place he'd found before. Jared vowed that he'd never leave that small, safe place again.

23

Although sleep had not come easily for either Jacob or David, it had eventually come. It was the vague, shallow sort of sleep that sometimes precedes big events like Christmas, especially for children. And in that shallow sleep they'd each dreamed shallow dreams, all centered around the perilous undertaking that awaited them when the sun came up. In each of these dreams, Jacob and David had already left on their daunting quest, sometimes ending up on the trails, sometimes the Ice House, and once making it as far as Jim's trailer. In each case, that strange, evil woman was already there, waiting for them. She had smiled that cold, evil smile of hers as if mocking the futility of what they sought to accomplish; her fiery eyes had burned through them as they stood paralyzed before her, leaving them horribly exposed to both her power and their own insignificance in a place that was hers alone.

It was from one of these daunting and frightening images that Jacob finally awoke. In that last dream, the boys had successfully reached the trailer, and had been allowed by Jim – who was wearing the same thirties-style clothing he'd worn as a boy in Jacob's first dream – inside. Jacob had begun to try to explain to Jim what he'd experienced; what both he and David had witnessed the day before, but Jim simply ignored him. Instead, he had scurried about the trailer, picking up garbage off the floor, straightening pictures on the wall and dusting off the tables and furniture as if he were trying to tidy up the place for an important visitor. Jacob had finally begun to plead urgently with Jim, trying to make him understand the danger they all now faced. Jim then sat on the couch and began sobbing like a child, his face in his hands, and suddenly his father, James Stockton, stood before Jacob. He began to scream at Jacob the way he'd once screamed at his own son, telling Jacob to mind his own business – to see to himself, so that he won't be part of the price to be paid. "Her day is here," he had finally whispered to Jacob, as if telling an urgent secret. "There will be justice." And with those words he had leaned into Jacob's face, leering like a jackal, his eyes burning with her yellow flame. That last image served to jolt Jacob much more fully awake than he'd been since first drifting off into the first of these strange, thin half-dreams.

He was able to affirm his return to reality by looking over at David, who was lying on the floor beside him and snoring loudly. It was a little comforting to know that he was not alone in the semi-dark room, but not as comforting as he would have hoped. He pushed himself up on his elbows and glanced nervously around his bedroom. Something didn't feel right; everything seemed dim and vague, the way the clearing around the Ice House had felt in his second dream. This thought was very disconcerting to Jacob, and for a moment he was torn between the urge to actually get up and do something, anything, to convince himself he was really awake and everything was just hunky-dory, and the urge to lie back down, pull the cover over his head, and pray a mighty prayer that he'd just go back to sleep.

He would gladly have pursued this second option except for the way he felt: he was awake, he *knew* he was awake, but his alert mind would not reject the reality of the strange, twisted-up feeling that now hung heavily in the air. Mingling with that feeling was a sense of urgency that Jacob could neither deny nor define.

He finally sat up completely and studied his surroundings again, peering cautiously into every shadow, seeing nothing but feeling everything. And though the strange, unnatural look of the world remained the same, that sense of urgency continued to grow exponentially by the second, until Jacob was near panicked. He tried to calm himself by taking slow, deep breaths, but it didn't seem to help much at all. He looked at the clock on his bedside table. It was 4:30; surely the first traces of daylight couldn't be too far off. Still, it was much too distant for Jacob, who was now afraid to even try to go back to sleep. Something was either happening or about to happen; the very air in Jacob's bedroom was pregnant with possibilities, and while he was terrified of whatever it might be, he was more terrified of lying down, closing his eyes, and turning his back on it. He stared at David for a desperate moment, trying to decide if he should wake the boy up now or wait just a moment more, wait to make sure he was awake and not having another crazy half-dream.

At that moment, he detected a slight movement out of the corner of his eye. He looked up, and was horrified to see his bedroom door swinging slowly open, as if pushed by a hand. He braced himself, ready to either indignantly chastise one of his parents for coming in and scaring him at 4:30 in the morning, or – and he thought this second option much more likely – scream David awake because it would be the woman; that cold, dead, terrifying but somehow beautiful woman standing in the doorway, her bright eyes burning; her lips barely parted in that now familiar mocking half-smile.

An eternity seemed to pass as Jacob waited for the door to swing open fully and reveal whatever awaited him on the other side, but the time still passed much too quickly. His breathing became quick and shallow again, he could feel his heart throbbing behind his eyes, and his entire body broke out in gooseflesh. And still the door crept along, taking its time; it seemed to relish the suspense, reveling in the knowledge that, at this moment and at this time, it was the star of the show. Finally, it was fully open, stopping just an inch shy of the small, brass-colored doorstop at the base of the wall. And there, standing in his doorway, Jacob saw . . . nothing at all. The frail beam of the nightlight in the hallway flowed gently into his room through the doorway; the stronger light from Jacob's closet spilled into the hallway. Their crossbeams intersected right in the doorway leading into the hall, illuminating it more than enough for Jacob to see that there was simply nothing there.

Jacob stood slowly, trying to get a sense for what he was witnessing and feeling; still trying desperately to decide if he was really awake and seeing what he was seeing, or if he was still asleep and having another crazy dream. Until a week ago, dreams hadn't been much of a factor in his life, but now they seemed to be dictating every waking moment. And the first two had been so powerful that, once night fell and the magic began, he was no longer sure what was real and what was simply a sleep-induced hallucination. The one thing he couldn't deny was that, real or imagined, that sense of urgency had continued to grow and had now reached an almost fevered, maniacal pitch.

Incredibly, Jacob became aware that he was now taking careful, measured steps toward the doorway. He was frightened, yes. Moments before, in fact, he would have sworn to being paralyzed with this fear that had frozen his insides. But it was something he *had* to do. It wasn't the same sensation he'd experienced in the dreams, a feeling that he had no control over his actions and subsequently no choice in the matter. Instead, he was now very much in control. His heartbeat seemed to resonate throughout his entire body; his breaths still came in short, shallow gasps; every inch of his flesh was still covered in goose-bumps, causing every hair to stand on end. But that sense of urgency had prevailed; he knew that he *had* to do this. Because she was coming; he understood that she was almost here already. She had first come to him in his dreams, growing and filling them until they could no longer hold her. Then she had pushed hard against the wall of reality, and both he and David had seen her when she had almost broken through. Jacob knew that she wouldn't stop until she walked among those who lived and breathed. And then there would be nothing to stop her from doing whatever she wanted to Jim, to David, to Jacob.

Another thought occurred to Jacob as he slowly approached the open doorway. He suddenly remembered the words she had spoken to him in the second dream. *I will not be hindered*, she had said, *even by the one who has opened the door*. The first part of that phrase had immediately registered with Jacob; how could it not – it had been a clear warning. The second half didn't register until this very moment.

He had opened the door to her; he had allowed her, albeit unwittingly, into his dreams, and now she threatened to break free. This realization caused a sudden surge of two very unexpected emotions – guilt and anger. She had used him, or rather she had used that strange, inexplicable bond that had formed between Jim and himself when he had stared into Jim's rage-filled face and uttered those fateful words that the old man himself had uttered once upon a time. Maybe she'd always been there, waiting for a fertile, innocent, imaginative mind to feed upon. Maybe she'd tried to feed upon Jim's mind that way, but it was too dulled and clouded by countless years of drunkenness. Whatever the reason, Jacob now fully realized the weight of those words – he was the one who had opened the door to her.

The unexpected surge of anger tinged with guilt now firmed his resolve. He steeled himself and resumed walking, passing through the open doorway and into the faintly lit hall. He glanced briefly to his right at his parents closed bedroom door, and vainly wished for a fleeting moment that he was there, tucked safely in bed between the two of them. Another thought occurred to him at that moment, one terrible enough that he pushed it down deep immediately – if she succeeded in breaking through into the living world, what could his parents possibly do to protect him or themselves? He shuddered, then turned left. He took a few not-quite-steady steps to the end of the hallway and turned right, stepping through the opening into the den. His heart stopped.

There, standing in the center of the room, was the woman he'd seen in that photograph from *The Glory Days of Logtown, A History,* the woman identified by the caption beneath the picture as Mrs. Melinda Stockton.

Jacob stared, barely breathing, knowing what he saw couldn't be possible, but almost casually accepting that it was. This casual acceptance was almost as strange to him as the figure that couldn't be standing in the center of the den, returning his stare. He almost *wanted* to be shocked and terrified; *wanted* to be afraid, *wanted* to disbelieve this phenomenon that instead, his brain simply acknowledged as being just as real as the television and VCR perched on the entertainment center to his left. Because she *was* there, she was real. She didn't shimmer, she wasn't transparent, and she didn't hover above the floor on invisible legs. She was simply there, really there – although it *did* seem somehow that *her* "really there" was a different kind of "really there" than the rest of the room. Perhaps it was her pale skin, which seemed to be bathed in moonlight, even though the rest of the room was dark.

Like the other woman from his dreams, she was dressed in a style of clothing that hadn't been worn outside of the movies for sixty years, though the dress she wore was somewhat more ornate than the one worn by the other woman. Her eyes reflected the same sadness Jacob had seen in the old photograph, but her face wore a look of reassuring love and concern – it was almost a look of maternal love. It was a stark contrast to the mocking smile he'd seen on the face of the other woman, and it made the memory of that other face, beautiful but icy cold, all the more obscene.

Another sensation that contrasted this figure from the other he'd seen was one that Jacob would remember forever. In every movie he'd seen and every book he'd read, the presence of ghosts and spirits was invariably announced by a cold chill in the air; a drop in the temperature so drastic that those experiencing the phenomenon could actually see their foggy breath, even in the summertime. But now, standing before this apparition with his breathing and heartbeat on the verge of red-lining; with his nerves so alive and aware they felt as if they were screaming, Jacob was suddenly enveloped with a sense of warmth and security such as he'd never known. It was as if she'd reached out to him with her heart and mind, cuddling his soul the way a mother will cuddle her infant. He stared at her with unblinking eyes, never wanting to lose the feelings that now held him – this immeasurable feeling of love and promise of security. Such intense feelings he had never before experienced, and he found himself, for just a moment, wishing with all his heart that this woman was *his* mother. And at that moment a strange thought popped into his mind – *am I looking at a ghost, or an angel*? Then she opened her mouth as if to speak; the strange notion disappeared from his mind, and everything – the entire world – seemed to slide into slow motion. Every movement made by the figure before him, every movement made by Jacob; the ticking of the clock and the soft hum of the air conditioner. The entire world became slurred and leaden, slow and monotonous.

The woman was clearly speaking to him, and the expression of urgency was now the dominant emotion on her face. But no sound came from her lips. Jacob began to feel that sense of urgency himself, just as he'd felt it moments before in his bedroom, but he had absolutely no idea what the woman was trying to tell him. He felt his arms rising slowly up into the air, his palms upward, and he slowly shook his head. *I can't hear you*, he thought at her as hard as he could.

The woman's face became both more urgent and sort of strained as she began to speak again; it was as if the act of speaking and maybe even just being here, visible to Jacob, came at a great price. But still no sound came from those lips. Jacob, his hands still hanging in the air before him, his own head slowly shaking from side to side with frustration, whispered, "I can't hear you. I don't understand what you're saying." The words seemed to float out of his mouth, drifting slowly through the air.

Now her face became desperate as her eyes pleaded with him. She stood for a moment longer, those despondent eyes begging him to understand. Then she turned slowly toward the kitchen, motioning for Jacob to follow. They both began to move to the kitchen, both still in slow motion, both seeming to almost glide through the air though their feet never left the ground. He followed her through that still, dream-like air until she finally stopped, of all places, in front of the refrigerator. There she stood, looking back at him and pointing to the refrigerator door. Jacob, still feeling like he was floating rather than walking, approached her and looked carefully to where she pointed. There, on the refrigerator door, was the magnetic note-board that his parents used to jot down grocery lists and phone numbers. A narrow felt marker was clipped to the top, and it was this to which she pointed.

Jacob looked back at the woman, and she nodded. Suddenly he understood. His hand slowly reached up and took the marker. At that moment, the woman reached out and took Jacob's hand in her own. His arm immediately went numb from his shoulder down, and he watched in shock and amazement as she began guiding his hand. The message, printed in his own unsteady script, was as urgent as the expression on her face.

GO TO HIM NOW

Jacob looked from the message to her urgent face, then through the kitchen window into the darkness outside. His own eyes, now shocked, desperate, and terrified, returned to hers and he shook his head violently. Up to now, the task Jacob had laid out for himself and David was only bearable because they had planned to do it in the daylight. He knew he wouldn't be able to convince David to make the trek in the dark, and he wasn't about to go into those dark woods by himself.

Now her face became even more desperate than his own. This time she seized his hand almost forcefully. His arm immediately became numb again, and he watched helplessly as new words were formed, though now they were scrawled violently across the message board as his hand jerked out her urgent message. Jacob's blood turned to ice as he read

SHE KNOWS WHAT YOU'RE DOING SHE'LL BE WAITING IF YOU DON'T GO NOW

Jacob looked back at the woman, his face awash in despair. Her face seemed to relax, trying to reassure him as she silently mouthed words he finally understood, though he wasn't sure he believed.

I'll help you, she told him.

Suddenly the woman's head jerked, and the reassuring look in her eyes was replaced by a fearful awareness. For a moment she seemed to be looking past Jacob, looking *through* not only him but also the house and maybe even the entire world around them. Then she looked into his eyes again, and with an urgency greater than any she'd yet demonstrated, screamed silently at him *GO! NOW!* as she not so much vanished as faded away, as though she were being pulled against her will back to wherever it was she had come from. In an instant she was completely gone, as if she'd never been. Jacob stood alone in the kitchen breathing once more in short, shallow gasps, heart racing, trembling all over as his mind tried to grasp what he'd just seen and what he now had to do. He glanced over at the message board on the refrigerator and saw that, unlike his visitor, the two messages he'd scribbled were still there.

The second message, barely legible because it had been scrawled rather than written, commanded his full attention. *She knows. She'll be waiting.* Panic seized him, and he was torn between taking the time to convince David to come with him in this, the darkest hour before dawn, or of facing that dark hour by himself, utterly alone. He hesitated a moment longer, calling up the memory of the last words the woman had tried to speak to him: *I'll help you* and *go now*. If he believed that the strange figure, whether or not the ghost of a woman now almost seventy years dead, had actually been here (and he did), then he must believe what she had told him.

Jacob hesitated a moment more, his face contorted with an unnatural blend of fear and desperate determination, then took a deep breath and stepped out through the kitchen door.

Mike's sleep had been deep, but not particularly restful. There had been no dreams that he could remember, only a growing, almost subconscious sensation of discomfort, such he sometimes experienced after passing out when too much cheap beer had been consumed and his soured stomach was threatening to send it all back up.

He drifted out of his heavy sleep to the slowly intensifying impression of being shaken. When he finally grudgingly opened his eyes, the vision that now filled his sight blasted away what remained of sleep.

Stooping over Mike, his face only inches away, was Jared. He was leaning right into Mike's face as if carefully studying the older boy with bright, burning eyes. They were no longer gray, those eyes, but as yellow-orange as a flame, as though red-hot coals smoldered behind them. At that moment Mike clearly heard the words *my soul for his* – although it seemed to him that he heard them spoken in his head rather than his ears, and he hadn't seen Jared's mouth move at all. Furthermore, the voice had definitely *not* been that of his younger brother. It was a woman's voice, filled with an icy malice and hate.

"*WHAAT*?" Mike yelped, bolting from the bed on the opposite side from where Jared stood. He looked around the room wildly for a second or two to get his bearings, then looked again at his younger brother. The eyes, once again gray, stared out at Mike with only the faintest traces of surprise and amusement from an otherwise expressionless face.

Just dreamin', Mike told himself. *Just havin' some freaky-deaky, crazy dream, that's all.* He was almost able to believe that was all it had been, but he found himself shuddering nonetheless.

"*Jerk*!" Mike finally whispered harshly after catching his breath, "you scared the stinky cheese right outta me." He tried to form an indignant scowl as he half-heartedly rebuked the younger boy.

"What the heck is the matter with you? And why the heck are you waking me up at –" he paused long enough to look at the clock beside Jared's bed, "– four-forty in the stinkin' morning?"

"We have to go right now," Jared said matter-of-factly, as if no explanation was necessary, and turned to leave the room.

Mike tried to keep glaring, but his confusion over this announcement combined with the lingering effect of the strange vision he'd had upon waking made it difficult.

"Hey, hold on a second," he called softly after his younger brother, who was passing through the doorway, "What are you talking about?"

Jared paused, and for a second, he didn't turn around. His body language was that of someone trying to mask or at least control emotions that they wanted to remain hidden, but when he did finally turn to face the older boy it appeared as if he wasn't having much luck. His eyes seemed to blaze much as they had when Mike had first awoke, and when he spoke, the words were spat out in a hiss.

"I'm saying we have to go right now. The boy is on his way to see Jim, and if we don't go *right now*, it will be too late!"

Jared glared at his older brother with terrible animosity and intensity, and Mike was shocked at the power and authority in his younger brother's face. It was even greater now than it had been the night before. Jared saw that Mike saw, and he nodded with a smirk. He spoke again, now taunting Mike with carefully chosen words.

"If you're too afraid to come, then get back in the bed and I'll go alone. And I *will* be taking your gun."

Mike continued to stare at a face that was no longer entirely Jared's, and for a moment was unable to speak. For the first time he wasn't just confused by what he saw, he was really afraid. Maybe it *wasn't* all in his mind . . . that shrinking sensation that had been plaguing him since the confrontation with those boys and Jim at the Ice House. Only now, shrinking didn't frighten him half as much as that thirteen-year-old boy who stood so boldly before him now, eyes burning as he taunted Mike into doing whatever it was he commanded. Mike suddenly panicked at the realization that he was afraid of *Jared*; afraid of what the boy would do to him if he failed to play his part in whatever the younger boy had planned. The idea of getting his hands on Jim Hanes' rumored fortune was now taking back seat to the idea of what Jared might do should Mike fail to help him carry out his plan.

Mike *tried* to glare at the younger boy; he *tried* to growl as he spoke.

"You touch my gun and I'll whip yer scrawny tail! And there ain't no way you're goin' out there alone. Hanes 'd prob'ly blow your ignorant head off as soon as you stepped in his yard. If you can keep your panties on for five seconds and let me get my shoes on, we'll go." Mike paused for effect before adding, "If you're wrong about this, I'll stick my boot so far up your rump that you'll be flossin' yer teeth with my shoe strings."

As he spoke, Mike could hear how frail and hollow his words sounded; he felt as if he was standing on a beach, shaking his fist at a hurricane. Jared saw this even more clearly than Mike, and gave the older boy another smirk before turning and walking down the hallway.

Mike put on his boots with trembling hands; it was all he could do to tie those slippery, squirmy little strings. Then he strode with a frail, hollow husk of confidence, which was all he seemed capable of gathering, into the den where Jared waited, glaring and impatient. Mike walked past him without so much as a glance (he was trying desperately for a look of arrogance that might somehow mask his growing fear), grabbed his car keys from the kitchen table, and the two boys slipped out the front door.

Thirty seconds later, Sundance Court echoed first with the rumbling sounds of Mike's Mustang as it pulled onto the narrow road that wound through the trailer park, then with a sudden roar and scream of tires as it sped onto the highway and into the night. The sounds went mostly unnoticed by people who were used to hearing large trucks and unmuffled cars rambling up and down the highway throughout all hours of the day and night.

24

Jacob was riding his bike along the trails at a clip that was better than just walking or even jogging, but not much.

In the garage, he had pulled on the old, dirty pair of shoes that he used for yard-work and, grateful that he had gone to sleep wearing a t-shirt and shorts instead of the usual pajama bottoms (which he would never have worn in front of David), snuck his bike out of the garage through its back door. He was on the trails just five minutes after his mysterious visitor had left him so abruptly, standing alone in the kitchen, shivering with more than just the cool, conditioned air. And, as it always seemed to these days, the time had somehow both flown and crawled by.

Both the door to the garage and the gate leading out of his back yard had, it seemed to him, been loud enough to wake up the entire neighborhood. He had cringed at the clicking of the latches and the groaning and scraping of the hinges, sounds he would have been prepared to swear popped in the still night air like firecrackers. After each such noise he would pause and glance around nervously, certain that the lights in his parent's room would come on at any second, he'd see his father peeking out the window, and the jig would be up.

Added to this were the worries of a neighbor hearing what they would probably assume were the sounds of a burglar and calling the police, and the growing sense of dread – dread of going into those woods alone at night and dread of what probably awaited him, if not in the woods then surely at the abode of Jim himself. By the time he reached the road and hopped on his bike, his nervous, almost excited fear was so great that his entire body was shaking with waves of small convulsions. It was a miracle he was able to ride at all in this state, but ride he did; down the street to the empty lot which served as the gateway to the trails that awaited him.

Even that empty lot seemed daunting; in the yellow glow of the street light, it seemed foreign and exotic, but Jacob never hesitated, understanding that the faster he rode, the more difficult it would be for any of the bugaboos that might very well be lingering behind the trees or crouched down in the tall grass to lay hands on him.

He zipped over the uneven ground and was quickly on the path, where he turned left, back toward his house, and rode quickly to the trail leading into the woods. It was then, looking deep into the darkness that awaited him – looking, in fact, into the darkness that was now completely surrounding him – that Jacob realized something rather important. He hadn't thought to bring a flashlight.

He paused at the edge of the woods and stared hard into what seemed at first like an almost pitch-black wall of darkness. The pale but better-than-nothing glow of the streetlights was completely cut off by the houses that stood behind him, but he realized with just a little gratitude that it wasn't a complete blackness he was looking at. Whether because his eyes were becoming adjusted to the dark, or dawn was finally approaching, Jacob realized that he was able to make out the darker shapes of trees and shrubs, as well as the lighter shades of the path in the thick gray world around him. But still he didn't move, not just yet. He simply sat on the bike, shivering as he stared into that thick gray darkness – shivering with the damp morning air on his skin, shivering with fear, and somehow shivering with the terrible thrill of the moment. It wasn't excitement, at least in the sense that Jacob usually considered things to be exciting, but still he felt an almost electrifying buzz with the great fear of being at this jumping-off place where he would cross over to the point of No Turning Back.

He stared in to the darkness a few seconds more, breathing deeply to work up his nerve the same way he had both times he had approached Jim's trailer, then closed his eyes and whispered into the quiet air.

"God, help me. Please. Guide me and help me."

Jacob believed in God with all his heart, and had for as long as he could remember. He'd been brought up by parents who were not fanatical, but still firm in their beliefs and, most importantly, lived their lives in accordance with those beliefs. They were not perfect, but could be counted on to do the right thing most of the time, and this was something Jacob had picked up on long ago. And so, although he sometimes used language that he figured would send his mother into convulsions if she overheard him, and although he might not always be able to resist the temptation of looking at what Jared had so eloquently called *porno mags* if the opportunity presented itself, and although he had many times participated in activities that would have gotten him in serious trouble had his parents found out (and in some of those instances he had told them bald-faced lies about his involvement), Jacob believed with all his heart in a loving God that had sent his son Jesus to die for the sins of humanity. And he now hoped that that God would, despite all of Jacob's shortcomings, see him safely through whatever lay ahead. He then opened his eyes, took one last deep breath and, only slightly comforted by the short, desperate prayer he'd just uttered, plunged into the woods.

Now he was almost halfway there, riding at a slow pace in the pale dark so that he wouldn't lose the trail or wreck his bike. He tried desperately to keep his eyes on the path before him, but the occasional rustling in the underbrush caused him to involuntarily jerk his head in whatever direction each sound came from, certain he'd see the deathly pale woman from his nightmares gliding through the woods beside him, ready to swoop down upon him with that evil smile and steal away his mind and soul. Instead, he saw only the dark shapes of trees and wild undergrowth, though each time he looked he was sure, just for a moment, that those dark shapes looked more like a woman in a flowing black dress than tree trunks and shrubs. There seemed to be faces in those leaves and branches, some sneering, some snarling bitterly, and Jacob's heart would leap into his throat each time he looked.

It wasn't until he had reached the fork in the trail, one path leading in the direction of the Ice House, the other to Jim's trailer, that Jacob first heard the heavy sounds of thunder. It sounded far off, but not *too* far off. In this part of the country and at this time of the year, thunderstorms could pop up at almost any moment with little or no warning, but Jacob hadn't been expecting it; there still had been no rain since that Sunday afternoon he and David had spent at the Ice House.

Well, that's just great, Jacob thought. *I really need this to top off everything else! Maybe I'll get lucky and there'll be a tornado, too, or maybe an earthquake and a swarm of killer bees.* He almost added *or some other act of God*, but the thought made him shudder. He was pretty sure that none of what had been happening, and what might still happen, was an act of God. If anything, it was an act of His opposite number. He shook off the thought and began riding again, turning right and onto the path that led to Jim.

The disused, overgrown trail leading to Jim's trailer was hard enough to maneuver in broad daylight, but Jacob quickly discovered it was nearly impossible in the gray dark that now surrounded him, and he ended up having to abandon his bike sooner that he had on the previous trips. And to make matters worse, although he had been prepared to swear that the light had finally begun to grow a little, now it seemed to be getting darker again – possibly because of the approaching storm – and he found himself having to work his way carefully through overgrown shrubs, weeds, and briars that were little more than black shapes until he was right on top of them. The rumbling thunder had become constant and was definitely closer. Jacob had no doubt that the storm was headed this way, and it would be a whopper.

He redoubled his efforts, struggling through the darkness and the undergrowth but becoming more and more desperate. He should have been to the fence behind the trailer by now, and Jacob suddenly realized with horror and desperation that he must have gotten turned around somehow in the dark and was no longer even on the small trail that led to the trailer. He turned, hoping to see his bike and be able to use it as a point of reference to orient himself, but saw nothing except the dark shapes of the undergrowth, all of which now seemed to be filled with those vague shapes of faces he'd seen along the trail. They seemed to snarl as they reached for him with wet, leafy hands. Jacob panicked, turned, and ran blindly into the thick of it. Small branches slapped at his face; thorns from long, tangled briars pulled at his clothing and tore across his bare skin. The sound of the thunder continued to grow, warning him to turn back as it boomed through the gray air. And the rustling sounds made by his struggle through the almost impenetrable growth were like taunting whispers and laughter, mocking him and daring him to go on.

With a final, desperate lunge, Jacob broke through and ran headlong into the fence. He quickly swarmed up one side and down the other into Jim's yard, desperate to get away from the clutching, grabbing undergrowth. Only after he had set foot on the ground inside the fence did he stop to get his bearings.

He found himself standing a few feet from the lonely pine, the only real tree on the entire lot, only a few feet from where he had crossed over (or, more accurately, under) on his two previous visits. Once oriented, Jacob realized that he must have drifted toward too far to his left, and come alongside the fence on the side of the lot rather than running upon the part of the fence that bordered the back of the lot.

He turned and studied the thick undergrowth he'd just fought his way through, convinced that he would still hear that whispery laughter and see those clutching branches, maybe reaching over the fence to grab at him again and pull him screaming back into the woods. But there was no sound or movement. They were, after all, just plants, right? He had been nervous to begin with, and had become panicked at the idea of getting lost; the approaching morning was getting darker instead of lighter (but that was just because of the coming storm, he was certain), and his young, imaginative mind had simply gotten carried away, making him think he heard all those voices, whispering and taunting him. That had to be it. And anyway, here he was, safely on the other side of the fence, so ha-ha-ha! He looked at the undergrowth a few seconds more and, seeing nothing supernatural, confidently hawked and spat over the fence in into the thicket of shrubbery.

When he turned back toward the trailer, however, that small boost of confidence immediately left him. The thunder was still booming and crashing, and now that he was clear of the trees and overhang of the woods, Jacob could just make out the dark, rolling thunderheads as they sailed across the sky. The wind was beginning to pick up as well, and felt chilly sweaty skin. The sudden, powerful gusts whipped all around him, stirring up clouds of dust. It would be raining soon, likely it would be a downpour, and if he kept just standing here, he would either get drenched, struck by lightning, or both.

He began walking quickly toward the trailer through air that was almost popping with electric possibilities. As it had when he had seen that strange, unnatural figure in the den earlier this morning, the world seemed both real and dream-like at the same time. Maybe it was the black storm that now hung heavily over the city of Logtown, turning the dark shapes around him a dull shade of gray-green; maybe it was the impossible, supernatural errand on which Jacob had embarked; maybe it was the fact that he felt as though this gathering tempest was part of that errand – a gathering of the power of the dark force he had found himself pitted against.

This last idea was the most terrifying, and it grew with every step he took toward the trailer. He was once again gliding through the air at a pace that seemed both fast and slow, and he was again unsure if his feet were even touching the ground. The thunder didn't just boom and roll, now it was roaring at him as the gusts of wind whipped up the dusty ground and stung his eyes. He finally broke into a run, and reached the cinderblock steps of the trailer in five long strides. He made a fist, beat on the door three times, then stepped back, waiting.

It was at this point that Jacob realized that he had no idea what he was going to say to Jim. His last visit hadn't exactly gone as planned, but at least there *had* been a plan. All he had to work with this time was a ghostly message to deliver – he was supposed to help Jim understand that *it* (whatever *it* was) wasn't his fault. Exactly how he was to do this, Jacob had no idea. He still didn't know what had happened on the night that Stockton Manor burned to the ground, taking the lives of two young women, and therefore didn't know why Jim blamed himself. All Jacob had to work with was that, in the first dream, young James Stockton had said he was only trying to help, and in both dreams, his mother said that it wasn't his fault. Jacob decided that all he could do was relate to Jim exactly what he'd experienced and seen (both in that world of dreams and in this world of the living), and hope that would be enough.

These thoughts raced through Jacob's mind in the space of maybe five seconds before the door of the trailer slowly opened and there, half in the shadow cast by a light behind him in the trailer while at the same time lit from the front by the flickering strobe of lightning flashes, stood a very, very old James Stockton II.

Jacob was stunned by what he saw. Jim seemed to have aged ten years in the day and a half since Jacob last saw him. The pale skin of his face was now ashen; it was almost the same grayish-green as the storm-light around them, and seemed to barely cling to his skeletal face. The once fiery, glaring eyes were now dull and vacant, and appeared to have sunken deeper into his skull. His arms hung listlessly at his sides, and his shoulders slumped as if all the weight of the world had been heaped upon them. Most surprising of all was the fact that Jim did not seem at all surprised to see Jacob standing at his doorstep at this ridiculous hour of the morning while the storm of the century appeared to be brewing all around them – he might well have been expecting his young visitor.

For a few moments they just stood there staring at each other, Jacob wearing an expression that was a blend of several emotions, mostly shock and fear, and Jim looking like the half-dead remains of a man who had been dragged face down through a hellish pit of despair and didn't care that he had somehow survived the ordeal. Jacob eventually became aware of the look of shock he was wearing and immediately dropped his gaze, feeling that familiar burning of embarrassment in his ears. When he looked back up, Jim was still staring at him, his expression unchanged. He either had missed Jacob's blush in the dark or, more likely, simply didn't care.

Jacob swallowed hard and, speaking loudly against the rumbling skies said, "Can I come in? There's something I've got to tell you."

Jim didn't seem any more surprised by this than he had been at finding Jacob on his doorstep. He simply nodded, then turned and plodded back into the depths of the trailer. Jacob followed, pushing the door shut behind him.

When he reached his battered old couch, Jim lost whatever it was that had kept him on his feet. He didn't really collapse, but looked as if some invisible hydraulics that had been holding him up suddenly depressurized. Once seated, he leaned forward, putting his face in his hands in a manner that struck Jacob as both childish and pitiful, and said nothing.

Jacob stared at him for a few moments, waiting to see if the old man would say anything – at the very least he expected to be asked why exactly he was here at whatever o'clock in the blasted morning. But Jim said nothing; he did nothing. The only sign Jacob had that the old man was still alive was the occasional hitch in his breath, as if he kept starting to say something, then kept changing his mind.

After a few awkward moments, Jacob looked around the smelly, filthy den of the trailer for a place to sit. He could have sat next to the old man on the couch, but was afraid to get that close to him. After all, despite whatever bond may have formed between the two, part of Jacob was very aware that he *was* still Jim Hanes, the crazy old drunk of Logtown, Mississippi who had shot at kids who came a-knockin' at his door, even in broad daylight. And besides, the couch itself was ragged, smelly, and looked as if several generations of a very large family of rats had spent a decade or so gnawing on it and using it as a toilet.

He finally spotted a rickety old chair sitting in a corner next to a pile of half-full plastic trash bags and old, half-collapsed boxes that were draped with nasty, mildewy rags that may or may not have once been clothes. He recognized it as the chair he had stood on while trying to tape up the broken window a few days before, and since it had no cushion (and therefore no visible pee-stains or rat droppings) he decided it was his best bet. He walked over, picked it up, and carried it to a spot maybe six feet from Jim. He set it down, hesitated a moment more, then sat down in it.

Jim showed no sign that he was even aware that the young boy was still in the trailer. This made Jacob even more uncomfortable, and he was at a loss as to how he should even begin saying whatever it was he was going to say. Confiding in a friend that one was having psychic dreams and visitors from beyond the grave was bad enough, sharing such things with a grumpy old drunk now seemed ludicrous, despite the urgency of the situation. He finally decided to start with something simple and obvious.

"Mr. Hanes, are you alright?"

For a few seconds Jacob wasn't sure the old man had even heard him. Then Jim finally began to raise his head, just enough so that Jacob could see his eyes. They were red, and looked weary beyond words. When he spoke, it was through his hands, which still covered the bottom half of his face.

"No, son, I'm not. I'm a dern far cry from alright, but thanks for askin'." Despite how he looked, Jim's biting sarcasm was still healthy and intact.

Jacob's eyes went to the floor, and he wasted a few more moments trying to find a response to what Jim had said. He decided that it was exactly the kind of answer he should have expected, and there really *was* no proper response. And, remembering the urgent message he had helped scrawl across the message board in his kitchen, Jacob finally decided that there was really nothing left for him to do but get to the point of his visit.

He took another one of those deep, confidence building breaths and spoke again, raising his voice against the ever-growing storm outside.

"Mr. Hanes, I've gotta tell you something. It's gonna sound crazy, but I swear, it's the truth."

Jim continued to stare at Jacob, and when he finally let his hands fall away from his face, Jacob saw he was wearing a bleak grin that contained no joy; it looked every bit as weary as his eyes. Even behind the tinfoil lining the windows of the trailer, the bright lightning was flashing through the poorly lit room, creating shadows where there had been none, illuminating corners that had been dark, and dancing across the creased, bearded, weary-but-grinning face of Jim, making him look like the psychotic-killer star of some cheap slasher film. Jacob again wondered if he had done a smart thing by coming alone to visit Jim at the trailer, and found himself calculating how many running strides it would take for him to reach the door should a quick escape become necessary. Then Jim's smile melted away and he spoke again.

"Lemme take a stab at guessin'. I bet I can tell you exactly what you're gonna say." He paused a moment, and that awful, weary smile returned to his face. "You've had yerself a ghostly encounter, right? A beautiful young lady, but just as dead and cold as winter. Except for her eyes . . . her eyes burn like a hot fire, right?"

Thunder boomed again, as if right on cue, and the entire trailer trembled along with Jacob as he stared, shocked and open-mouthed, at Jim's somnolent, smiling face.

Jim barked a humorless laugh at Jacob's expression and shook his head scornfully. His hands finally dropped completely away from his face, and he leaned wearily against the back of the couch, now staring at the water-stained ceiling of his trailer. Still wearing that bleak grin (which now looked more like a smirk) he spoke again.

"Shoot, boy," he said, "she's been comin' to see me for years. More years'n I can count. Smilin' that icy smile of hers and whisperin', pointin', laughin', teasin'. But she couldn't ever touch me. Scary as she is – and yeah, she does look like she come straight outta hell itself – she's never been able to do more'n just taunt 'n tease . . ."

Jacob was suddenly terribly agitated by what he thought he was hearing, and cut Jim off, blurting out, "But she *can* do something! She's *real* now, Mr. Hanes, she's really real! I've seen her . . ."

Jim leaned forward on his knees, and now the old, familiar glare was finally back.

"Shut up and let me finish! I can't tell you nuthin' if you're gonna be interuptin' me the whole time. Just shut up and let me talk."

Jim leaned back again and shook his head at the ceiling. He was silent for a few seconds, but Jacob said nothing. The rebuke, along with Jim's sudden change in temperament, startled him enough that, despite the sense of urgency that was growing in perfect unison with the storm outside, he quickly decided it was best to let the old man have his say before relating any more of his own personal experiences with the supernatural.

He watched Jim pensively, but instead of gathering himself, Jim seemed to be on the verge of losing control. His eyes had begun to water, and his jaw actually trembled a little. This seemed to make him angry all over again. But it was an empty anger, and there was no one in the trailer for Jim to direct it at, so he spoke to the ceiling again, growling out the words as he talked.

"I *know* she's real now, boy. Don't you think if anyone would know, it'd be *me*?" Another brief pause, and then the floodgate opened.

"Everything changed when I met *you*! On the day you and those natural-born-fools you call friends decided to play your little prank and broke that window. When I almost cut your little throat. You don't know how close I came, boy. Maybe I should've, and none of this would be happening."

Jacob shifted in his chair and yet again reflected on the wisdom of coming here alone. There was simply no way of telling whether or not Jim was jesting, and he took another measured look at the door leading out of the trailer. When he turned back he saw that Jim was looking him directly in the eyes. He clearly understood exactly what Jacob was thinking, and that old look of scornful amusement was back for a few seconds.

"Don't worry, son, I ain't gonna kill you now. It's a little too late for that, ain't it? And anyway, what's done is done."

Another smirk, then the look was gone and his eyes drifted back to the ceiling.

"Yeah, everything changed that day, but I don't know why. She's been gettin' stronger ever since. I expect you may be right; she may be real as you and me by now. She's gotten so strong . . . I can't sleep anymore; can't eat or even drink . . ." here he paused and shot an almost embarrassed look at Jacob, as if he hadn't meant to say quite so much " . . . and I don't really know if she's just in my dreams anymore. I don't *see* her like I used to when I'd dream at night, when I'd see *all* of 'em, but I *feel* her now. I feel her even when I'm wide-awake. And something else has been happening to me." He paused yet again, and again Jacob sensed that Jim was embarrassed to be saying these things, and especially a twelve-year-old.

"I think I feel her like this because I *can't* drink anymore. The blasted stuff 'bout makes me puke if I even *smell* it! And so I can't hardly sleep no more. And when I see her – when I dream about her, she's not just *here* anymore, hauntin' me and tormenting me, she's other places. Tormenting you. Something is different, but for the life of me, I can't understand what . . . or why."

Jim finally stopped speaking. He looked down from the ceiling and directly at Jacob, and for the first time ever, Jacob saw a truly human emotion in Jim's face. It was so unnatural on Jim's face that Jacob was frightened all over again – what he saw was a kind of pleading fear. Jacob had come to Jim's trailer with the belief that Jim would be able to explain exactly why all of this was happening. Now, Jim seemed to be asking Jacob that same question, and expecting the young boy to be able to answer. It was not a role Jacob felt at all comfortable in, but he remembered what his spectral visitor had told him, not only this evening but in both nightmares, and he hoped that the clues she'd left would be enough for Jim and he to put the puzzle together before it was too late. But he had a question to ask Jim; probably the second most important question he'd ask this evening. He was sure he knew the answer, but he had to hear it from Jim's mouth before he could go any further. He waited for the latest tear of thunder to die away, and finally spoke.

"Before I tell you about all the stuff that's happened to me, I've gotta know this." He paused, evenly meeting Jim's staring eyes, and asked, "Is your real name James Stockton?"

For the first time since Jacob had ever seen him, the traces of a real smile flitted faintly across Jim's mouth. He leaned back on the couch again, but his eyes never left Jacob. They studied him as carefully as they had a few days before in the clearing at the Ice House, after he'd rescued Jacob and his friends from Jared's older brother. When he spoke, his head was nodding slightly.

"I knew you knew. I don't know how you figured it out, but I knew you did. That's why you came 'round here the other day, actin' like you wanted to fix that window you and your little buddies broke. So you could ask your questions and see if I'd be dumb enough to answer. Right?"

Jacob started to shake his head, but didn't. He was beginning to feel frustrated at Jim's ability to ask those questions – the kind that, no matter how you answered, your answer seemed wrong.

Jim leaned forward again, and the sneer returned to his face.

"So, what else do you already know about, smart-boy?"

Jacob was finally beginning to tire of trying to work around Jim's constant and drastic mood swings – one minute he seemed a broken, desperate old man, the next he was back to being the grumpy old jerk everyone in town thought him to be. He finally decided that they would get nowhere if he let Jim's jibes and cutting remarks dictate his own actions, and he hadn't forgotten the message that had sent him on this desperate errand at this desperate hour. If anything, Jim's bizarre temperament was finally making him angry.

The thunder had continued to grow, and was now almost a constant, so instead of waiting for it to fade, Jacob simply raised his voice, almost to a shout, and began to tell his own story.

"I know that the house you lived in when you were a kid burned down on Halloween night in 1933, and that the house was somewhere close to where this trailer is now. I know that your mother and a maid named Della Hanes died in the fire. And that your father blamed you for whatever happened, even though you were only trying to help."

Jacob could see the rage building in Jim's eyes with every word that was spoken, but still he plowed onward. Then he got to the part about *only trying to help.* As soon as he said those words, Jim's face once again became stricken. It was the same expression he'd worn on the day they'd met, when he'd held a knife to Jacob's throat. This time, however, the look almost instantly melted away as Jim completely fell apart. He hid his face behind his hands again, just as he had when he'd first sat down on the couch, and a low moan came up from somewhere deep inside. It was horrible to listen to; stretching out for a seemingly endless span of time, and it sounded almost inhuman. Then it finally ended, and Jim's entire body began to shake as he sobbed uncontrollably.

The crying fit was like nothing Jacob had ever seen before, and it frightened him badly – Jim seemed to have lost all control. A part of Jacob wanted to go to him, to try and console him with what he was pretty sure would be empty, useless words, but he was still afraid to go near the old man, whose state of mind was clearly questionable; his mood could become angry again at any moment. So he watched and listened as both the thunder and Jim Hanes boomed out in the small den of the trailer, almost as if trying to outdo one another.

Jacob finally decided he had to finish, To tell Jim what he'd been told to tell him, and he hoped it wouldn't send the old man over the edge of whatever cliff he was already teetering on.

"I think I've seen your mother, too," he said, barely hearing his own voice above the racket of the storm outside and Jim's own personal storm inside.

Jim looked up, his red, streaming eyes shocked but this time not stricken. He snubbed and gasped for breath like a child for a moment, and finally managed to weakly choke out the word "*What*?"

Jacob raised his voice only a little, still afraid, still uncertain if this news would bring relief, joy, or another fit of anger.

"I've seen your mother. I saw her in a dream, and I saw her tonight – I *really* saw her, at my house. It had to be her, because I saw a picture of her in a book, and whatever I saw looked just like her. She's the reason I came here this morning. She said I had to hurry; that I had to tell you . . ." Jacob trailed off for a brief moment as Jim's pleading face strained forward in desperate amazement at the words he was hearing, that he desperately needed to hear – the message this boy was about to deliver from the woman whose death he truly believed he'd caused. Jacob was stunned that Jim so obviously believed every word that was now being spoken. He hesitated one second more before finally voicing the words he now understood Jim had waited over sixty years to hear.

"She said it wasn't your fault, Mr. Hanes. Any of it. She told me that I had to help you understand that, because that was the only way to stop that other woman. The evil one."

Jim stared open-mouthed, his eyes wanting desperately to believe the words just spoken to him, but still tinged with doubt. Years of listening to the cold, blaming voice of his father, followed by many more years listening to his own accusatory voice and the voices of those ghostly dreams he himself had conjured still held him. Maybe they now only held him by the tips of their bony, clawed fingers, but still they held. Jacob wondered if the words of a young, frightened boy delivering a message given to him in a dream could possibly be enough to finally break that grip. Then Jim put his face in his hands and began to violently weep again.

At that moment there was another thunderous crash, much louder and heavier than any so far, and the front door flew open. For an instant Jacob thought it must have been blown open by the gale-force winds that had been shaking the trailer for the past few minutes, and the possibility of being caught in a tornado drove away all thoughts of his errand. According to every news report he'd ever seen, the one place that a person could be sure of getting wiped out by a tornado was in a trailer – the stupid things were like severe-storm magnets. An instant later Jacob realized that the weather was now the least of his worries.

In through the open door stormed Mike and Jared, both soaked to the skin from the pouring rain. To his horror, Jacob saw that Mike was brandishing a gun. He came running through the small arch leading into the den, gun raised, and struck Jim, who had just caught Jacob's expression and begun to turn his to see what had so completely engulfed his young visitor's attention. The blow caught the old man just behind his left ear. Mike's arm had swung in a full arc, and the sound of the gun-barrel striking Jim was a dull, sickening crack. Jim fell soundlessly to the floor as blood immediately began to flow from the side of his head. Jacob let out a cry, and leapt to the floor beside him, afraid the old man was either dead or unconscious. Before he could reach the bleeding figure, Mike leaned over and dealt him a vicious, backhanded slap to the side of his face. The smacking sound seemed to travel the entire length of Jacob's body. His head reeled, and he collapsed on the floor next to Jim. His left cheekbone immediately began to burn and throb, but he was too shocked and afraid to even consider crying out from the pain.

To his left, he saw Jim struggling up into a sitting position. He held a hand to the side of his head, but the blood was streaming freely between his fingers. His eyes glared out from a pale face at the teenage boy who stood above them, pointing the gun. If he was afraid, Jim wasn't showing it.

Jacob, on the other hand, was absolutely terrified. He looked up at Mike, who was pointing the gun and grinning. It was a wild grin, as if the boy had worked himself up into some sort of frenzy in order to make this daring assault on the trailer. He was absolutely beside himself with the notion that he had the notorious Jim Hanes, who had sent him away cowering just two days before, sitting helpless and bleeding on the floor of the trailer. The boy stood there, grinning like a raging idiot, and finally began to giggle – the same irritating, spastic sound that Jacob had heard Stevie make.

"Well, would you look at this! Two for the price of one! Ain't that just peachy?"

He giggled again, and there was enough of a psychotic edge to the sound that whatever hope Jacob had of ever leaving the trailer simply vanished. Jim was still struggling to his feet. He needed both hands to do it, and now didn't seem to even notice the blood running freely out of his head, staining the left shoulder of his old, frayed t-shirt a deep crimson.

"You little chicken-turd coward," he growled as he finally managed to stand, albeit unsteadily. "If you got the guts to put down that gun, I'll be more'n happy to put . . ."

Jim's mouth hung open and his words were cut short by his sudden gasp. His eyes, still red and swollen from his interrupted crying fit, grew in dumbfounded amazement and terror, and his face had returned to a deathly pale hue. Jacob watched this drastic change with a sense of dread before finally turning to see what had caused such a radical effect on the old man. His eyes fell on Jared, who had stepped up beside his older brother.

Jared was wearing a closed-mouth smile that was as cold and deadly as a glacier. But the boy's expression, while frightening, wasn't the source of the old man's despair. There was something else, something new, in the other boy's face, and when Jacob saw it, he too despaired.

Because when Jacob looked into the other boy's eyes, he didn't see the glittering, ice-blue gems that had always been there. He saw burning, yellow-orange flame. He saw the eyes of another, the one who meant to have Jim's life and soul. The eyes of the one who had promised Jacob that, if he didn't look to himself, he would be part of the price to be paid.

Those burning eyes looked from Jim to Jacob and back again, seeing the recognition and understanding that was clearly written on the face of old man and young boy alike. The icy smile grew.

"So," Jared finally said in a voice that was not entirely his own, "here I am. Here we all are."

REVELATIONS

"But in the end she is bitter as wormwood,
sharp as a two-edged sword.
Her feet go down to death, her steps lay hold of Sheol.
She does not ponder the path of life . . ."

Proverbs 5, verses 4-6

25

I

It may well have been coincidence that brought those three people, each with drastically different agendas, together late one night back in 1933, but Jim would never be convinced of it. It certainly wasn't a coincidence that he had been there, in a place he almost never went. He had been there only a few times before, and once only he'd gone there by himself. That last time, the one time he'd gone by himself, he'd found something that had confused him mightily. He'd questioned his father about it later, and had been even more confused by his father's reaction. The elder James Stockton had rebuked him and instructed him never to go down there again, especially alone. Then the man's face had softened a little upon seeing little James' confusion. "It's dangerous down there, especially at night. You've no business down there, anyway." It turned out that his father was quite right; it was *very* dangerous down there.

As a child, James Stockton II spent most of his time alone, but until just a few days before the worst night of his life, he never realized that he was lonely. He knew that he was rich – or at least, his family was rich – but he was kept sheltered enough that he never understood how being rich in a poor southern town during the early to mid nineteen-hundreds, especially after the onset of the Great Depression, sometimes brought hard feelings and unpleasant circumstances. While those circumstances could never have been as bad for him as it was for those who were black during that same era, it could, at times, run a close second. Just how close a second would depend on who was asked – and *when* they were asked. Certainly Jim would never be beaten or lynched or have his place of worship fire-bombed, but had he tried to interact socially with the other children of the small community, he would have found himself grudgingly accepted at best. At worst, if there were no adults around to make sure the only child of the town's largest employer was treated well by their own children, he would likely have been teased and ridiculed and ostracized. On a bad day, he might have even taken a few lumps (so long as those involved had their alibis straight or could make it look like an accident).

Young James had never actually been *discouraged* from playing with the children that lived in Logtown; the opportunity simply never presented itself. He had been in the full-time care of a nanny from birth through age six, and then had been schooled at home by a tutor his father had brought up from New Orleans. Most weekends had been spent with his mother in the Garden District of New Orleans, at the St. Charles Avenue home she had grown up in. His father never accompanied them on these trips, but Papa Brooks seemed more than happy to fill that role, taking his only daughter and grandson to the trendy shops that lined Canal Street, dining at the finest restaurants in the French Quarter, and to Sunday Mass at the Saint Louis Cathedral. Sometimes it was just grandfather and grandson, going to see the New Orleans baseball team play at Pelican Stadium in mid-town, or just sitting on one of the piers owned by Mr. Brooks's company, watching the barges as they lazily crept up and down the Mississippi. Once in a while Mr. Brooks would even take him to a boxing match or a horse race, something his mother was not at all fond of but let pass without much comment because it was time spent with a father figure, something her beloved son seemed to enjoy more than anything.

But during that last year, it seemed as though it was more and more often just grandfather and grandson; Melinda seemed to be dropping slowly but surely out of all social activity. She still seemed to want to be with her son, but only when they were at the Logtown home or at her family's house in New Orleans, never out in public. Young James noticed the change in his mother, but never spoke to her about it, mostly because he didn't know how, but surely there was at least a small part of him that was afraid (his fault) of what she might tell him.

And such was the life of James Stockton II, heir-apparent to the Logtown timber fortune, at least until October 28, 1933. He had no friends his age – no other children in his life to go swimming or fishing in the creek with or to play baseball, tag, or whatever else with. And, to be perfectly blunt (and maybe even simplistic), he honestly didn't know what he was missing because he had never been exposed to it. Then, on the afternoon of October 28, Mrs. Stockton and her son made a rare trip into Logtown.

Melinda had, once upon a time, gone into town at least once a week, usually to have dinner with her only close friend, one Mrs. Kathleen Clement, wife of Jack Clement, who worked for Mr. Stockton as the foreman of the Logtown saw mill. She was probably the closest thing the small city had to a blue-blood – a native of Natchez, Mississippi, she was able to boast not only of a father who owned one of the larger banks in that city, but a grandfather who had fought in and survived what she still referred to as The War of Northern Aggression. And although Melinda had married a *Yankee*, Mrs. Clement recognized her as a true Southern Belle from a wealthy family in New Orleans, whose husband paid her own much better than he did most of the townsfolk who labored and toiled for the Stockton Timber Company.

Two factors, closely related (though young James wouldn't understand their close relationship until later that week), made the trip unusual. The first was the fact that Melinda was even making the trip – her weekly dinners and teas with Mrs. Clement were among the activities that had been forsaken during his mother's gradual, yearlong withdrawal from society. The second was the fact that she had taken him along. Mrs. Stockton usually went to see her friend alone, viewing the time they spent together gossiping about the other town-folk and reminding themselves of how important they were as personal and valuable time a small town with almost no real society. But James had noticed that along with her withdrawal had come a sort of paranoia, at least where he was concerned. She rarely let him out of her sight these days, at least while they were in Logtown. It was as if she were afraid that to do so might mean she would lose him, or at least lose the closeness that they had once shared.

Mrs. Stockton had seemed more nervous – almost upset – than her son had seen so far in what had been a year of anxious melancholy for his mother. Upon arrival, after a greeting that seemed rather subdued, she asked her hostess where her own children were.

"They're out back, playin' at some game or other. The Lee boys are over, too."

Mrs. Stockton looked down at her son with a smile that seemed forced and somehow almost tragic.

"Honey, why don't you go on out there and play with the other children for a little while so me and Kathleen can talk a bit?"

James was not quite dumbfounded, but he was very surprised. Playing with other children was simply not something he did. Sure, there was the occasional child of a relative or friend of his grandfather's that might be visiting during one of his weekend stays in New Orleans, but the games they were allowed to play never got any closer to athletic than hide-and-seek.

Mrs. Clement took one look at her friend's eyes, then nodded and began leading James to the back door with an arm around his shoulders.

"That's a good idea, honey," she told him. "I believe the boys have a game of baseball going, and I'm sure they'd love to have another player."

When they reached the back door and stepped out, James saw that the boys did indeed have some sort of baseball game going.

One of the boys was pitching, one stood about fifty yards behind the pitcher, ready to field any hits, another stood at bat, and the fourth was squatted down behind the batter, playing catcher. None of the boys had gloves, they were using a heavy stick to hit, and the ball in question was dingy brown in color; the cover barely held on by the frayed and tattered stitching. To James' left, on the far side of the back porch where he now stood, the Clements' two daughters – ages nine and five – were hosting some sort of doll tea-party. Both paused just long enough to see who it was visiting, then returned to their world of make-believe society.

Mrs. Clement gently pushed James down the steps from the porch and out into the backyard as she called out to the other children, "Boys, this is James Stockton. He and his momma are visitin' for a little bit this afternoon. Y'all let him play too, alright?"

The boys all stopped right in the middle of a play and turned in unison to stare at their young visitor. Something in that look made James uncomfortable, and he decided he'd really rather stay inside with the womenfolk, maybe reading a book or something. He looked up at Mrs. Clement with pleading eyes.

"Can't I just stay inside, please? I won't get in the way or anything, I promise."

Mrs. Clement smiled down at him, her eyes touched with a trace of sympathy, and for a moment he thought she might relent. Instead, she waved the other boys over. They dutifully dropped their makeshift equipment and walked over. All but one of them stared at him sulkily, and James wondered again why his mother hadn't just left him at home and come by herself, the way she usually did.

"James, these are my boys, Henry and Jake. The other two rascals are Billy and Clay Lee." She looked at one of the older boys, the one she had identified as Henry, and said, "I want you to let James play, and I want you to play nice, understood?"

Henry, who was the only boy who hadn't been scowling, now actually gave James a kind of curious smile, and stuck out his hand. James took it cautiously, and Henry's smile widened into a grin as they shook.

"Hiya, James. You know how to play baseball?"

"Yes," James replied, then added cautiously, "I mean, I've seen people play. I've never played myself."

The scowls worn by the other boys quickly became smirks. Henry seemed to be truly surprised, but he kept right on smiling.

"No foolin'?" He shook his head. "Well, I bet we can teach you how pretty quick." He looked at James' tall, skinny frame and said, "I bet you'd make a pretty good infielder. How old are ya, anyway?"

"Twelve," James answered, certain that the fact that he'd reached the ripe old age of twelve without ever having played a game of baseball would earn him another hearty dose of smirks. Instead, all the boys now gawked at him; he had at least half an inch on Henry, the tallest of the others. Even Mrs. Clement seemed surprised.

"James Stockton, are you only twelve years old? Why, my Henry here is fifteen; so is Billy, and you're taller than both. Clay there is thirteen, and Jake is twelve, same as you." She paused a moment and smiled, apparently reaching the conclusion that James would be able to handle himself just fine simply because he was the tallest. The fact that he was as lean as a bean-pole didn't seem to matter, at least to her. "Well, you boys play nice, now, and don't get too rough." She gave James another pat on the shoulder, then turned and walked back into the house.

Henry gave James another grin, then his young face grew serious again. After all, this was baseball they were playing, not some little kiddy game.

"All right, boys, let's go, let's go!" he shouted, like he was manager of the New York Yankees and the team was taking the field for game five of the World Series. "Billy, it's your at-bat. Clay, you're catching; Jake, you're outfield. James, you play infield behind me."

Although he had never played, James had watched enough baseball with his grandfather that he had an excellent academic understanding of the rules and theories of baseball, and he quickly jogged to where a makeshift second base was lying, maybe twenty feet behind where Henry, the pitcher, was standing. His nervousness gave way to excitement, and he was determined to show these boys he could play just as well as any of them.

Thirty minutes later, James was running as hard as he'd ever run, but not to beat a throw to first base, or from third about to slide into the makeshift home plate. He was running down a dry, dusty dirt road, tears stinging his eyes, his back drenched with sweat, and jeering voices ringing in his ears. October afternoons in the deep south aren't much better than those in August – just a little less humid with temperatures in the upper eighties instead of the upper nineties – and that afternoon, the sun was beating down hard on his back. But still he ran, harder than he'd ever run in his life. It wasn't the run of someone who is trying to get somewhere; it was the run of someone who was trying desperately to get away. Where didn't matter, as long as it was away. It was as though his body thought that, if he ran hard and far enough, he could somehow leave the words he'd just heard far behind. But his mind knew better. His mind understood that those words were going to be with him forever.

He hated himself for believing, even for a few moments, that he wouldn't be ridiculed when those boys saw him trying to play. But then, how could he have known the heights to which the hateful insults hurled at him by those other boys would climb? He had expected the laughter when he'd tried to throw the ball and it had traveled maybe ten feet before it just kind of died and fell to the ground. Or when he'd been clonked by the ball – on the chest, stomach, or head – every time he'd tried to catch it, whether it was hit or thrown.

Finally, it had been his turn to bat. He'd picked up the heavy old stick, which looked like it might have been a broom-handle in a past life, and stepped up to a home plate that might have once been a roof shingle (also in a past life). As he did so, he actually prayed – *God, please let me hit the ball, please, just one hit.* He never even got close.

After the sixth or seventh miss, Billy – who had laughed louder and more frequently than any of the others, and was now laughing so hard he'd had to sit down – called out, "Why don'tcha get yer rich daddy to buy you some talent?"

Both Clay and Jake thought that was just about the funniest thing they'd ever heard, and both joined Billy on the ground, rolling around like a couple of imbeciles as they laughed. Even Henry, who had to this point been the only boy not laughing at James, had to smile at Billy's wit.

James, who was embarrassed and angry that God had chosen not to answer his one request (one little hit, even if it went foul, was that just too much to ask for?), yelled right back at Billy, "Shut up, you stupid . . ." but then couldn't think of a name to call the boy. Not that it mattered; apparently the word *stupid* did the trick all by itself. Billy, who'd been playing infield, stood up straight and tall and began to approach the younger boy.

"Did you just call me stupid? Huh, you little stringbean rich-boy? Is that what you just called me?"

Henry stepped up between them, telling Billy to stop before they all got in trouble. Billy's legs stopped, but his mouth didn't. His mouth was just getting warmed up, and the more it said, the more energized it seemed to get.

"Smart little rich-boy calls *me* stupid, but at least I can catch the ball! At least I can hit the ball, and throw it! Why don't you go play dollies with the girls, rich-boy? Go put on a dress and sit on the porch and play with the little girls instead of standing around out here, trying to look pretty!"

Again Henry stepped between the two boys, again he told Billy to stop it before they all got in trouble. Of the boys present, only he seemed to realize that Billy was out of getting control and they'd all more than likely get the strap if he didn't stop. But the other boy *was* on a roll, and just as Henry feared, Billy finally went too far.

"Calls *me* stupid! Well, maybe my daddy ain't rich, but at least he ain't doin' it with no niggers!"

Henry face was stricken as he cried out, "Billy, *stop* it!"

Billy stopped long enough to look at the other boys, all of whom seemed as shocked as Henry. And to James, whose own face had grown ashen, the worst part was that the other boys didn't look shocked so much by the accusation as the fact that it had been uttered. Then Billy started again.

"Why? Everyone knows it! Y'all know it, Mom'n Dad knows it! Everybody knows it!" He turned back to James, anger and disgust struggling to be the dominant emotion expressed on his face. "You prob'ly know it too, don'tcha? Your daddy may be rich, but he sure does like screwin' that nigger maid. I bet *my* daddy never messed around with no niggers!"

"SHUT UP!" James had finally screamed in desperation, then turned and ran, wishing he hadn't waited quite so long to do so. He tore around the side of the house, hearing the sounds of Henry calling out for him to wait, to come back; the sound of the back door opening and the voice of Mrs. Clement shouting "What's goin' on out here? Where's James?"

He had run away from the house to the road, run past a schoolhouse he'd never set foot in, and past the church and the drug store, never slowing down. He'd run past the barber shop, where a couple of old timers sitting out front in rocking chairs had gawked at the well-dressed young fella running down the road like the devil was at his heels. He'd run all the way out of town, and he was still running.

When his house appeared on the horizon, James finally began to slow down. He didn't want to go there. He didn't want to be anywhere other people were, especially the two that had just been the topic of Billy's wrathful scorn and the source of his own burning anger and humiliation. So he left the road, climbing the wooden fence that bordered the family's property on this side of the road, and ended up wandering the fields until it was almost dark.

The mysteries of the past few months were suddenly mysteries no longer. In fact, given what he now knew, they all seemed to make perfect sense, and all served to confirm his awful new discovery. James thought of his mother's behavior over the past few months, and suddenly wondered if she knew. Of *course* she did; why else would she behave the way she now did, both sad and afraid, all of the time? Sad, James could understand. But afraid – why? Was it fear that his father was going to leave them? James stopped to consider this possibility. *Would* his father leave them, so he could marry this other woman and start a new family? If that were to happen, James supposed that he and his mother would go to live in New Orleans with his grandfather, a thought that didn't bother him one bit. Why should it? He had no friends here, and when he'd been foolish enough to try and make some this very afternoon, the results had been disastrous. *So what? Who cares about any of them? Not me, that's for sure*, his angry and humiliated mind burned. He'd never needed friends before, why had he even tried to make them now? James had no problem at all with the thought of leaving this place forever and never coming back. The very idea was enough to excite him.

But his mother – she would be devastated. And James somehow understood that it wasn't just the idea of losing her husband; although the loss and betrayal would hurt, why would anyone want to be with someone who didn't love them? Maybe it was the idea of people – anyone or maybe even everyone in town – knowing that her husband had left her to be with the maid, a lowly servant. And to make it worse, she was, as Billy had put it, a *nigger* maid! James had known immediately to whom the other boy had been referring (the family had several maids, but only one was not just attractive, but truly beautiful), yet he had never really thought of her that way, as a *nigger*. Now, after careful consideration, he supposed the other boy was right. The maid – Della was her name – wasn't as dark as most of the other blacks James knew, and maybe her hair wasn't quite as kinky, but her smooth, beautiful skin was much too dark for her to be anything else. But was that beauty enticing enough to lure his father away from the family? James pondered this possibility a few minutes before dismissing it as ridiculous; he understood instinctively that his father would never in a million years leave his wife to marry such a woman – not just a maid but again, as Billy had so diplomatically phrased it – a *nigger* maid. Still, the humiliation his mother must feel at the situation must have been almost unbearable.

Another mystery that had suddenly been resolved was that strange discovery he'd made barely a month before, during the only solitary trip he'd ever made into the basement of the huge house he lived in. He'd just finished reading *King Solomon's Mines,* which he'd received as a gift from his grandfather on his last visit to New Orleans. It had been by far the most exciting and suspenseful story he'd ever read, and now *he* was Allan Quartermain, ready for adventure and danger; ready to set out on his own quest for lost treasure hidden somewhere in the dark, secret places of the world. But where to look? Where to find such a place in his own small world of rules, limits, and borders? Ah, elementary, my dear Watson – the cellar! That deep, dark, dank-smelling place full of shadow and mystery – a place surely brimming with secrets. Also a place that had always frightened him, even though he'd been accompanied by an adult the few times he'd been there (actually, he had accompanied the adults – servants, who were the closest thing he'd had to friends in the city of Logtown – when their duties required them to venture down into the cellar. For some reason, the servants disliked going down into the place almost as much as little James had). But now adventure called, and James was feeling more than equal to the challenge. After all, when one was on a quest for adventure and treasure, one must be willing to face down any and all prospective danger.

At this time of day, most of the servants were busy performing the duties for which they'd been hired, and James was easily able to gain access to the cellar unnoticed. Soon he stood behind the closed door, looking nervously down the stairs and into the darkness that awaited him. He was armed only with a small lantern that seemed to barely cut through that thick, dark air of the cellar (FDR's Rural Electrification Administration wouldn't bring electricity to this part of the world for almost another ten years), and a short wooden stick that served him as a makeshift sword. But his nervousness quickly gave way to excitement, and soon he was down in the thick of it, deftly dodging imaginary booby-traps and fighting off every type of treasure-guarding warrior and supernatural beast his young mind could conjure up. He was determined to search every inch of these catacombs until he had found every last doubloon left by some marauding pirate and every last golden statue cleverly hidden by the wealthiest, iron-fisted king ever to reign.

His adventure lasted a good forty-five minutes, in which he fought many battles and found several locked chests that he decided *must* contain valuable treasure. Why else would they be locked? Then, in the furthest, darkest corner, in a small space almost completely sheltered from view by crates and boxes, James had made his confusing discovery. Tucked against the wall was a small, stained mattress, complete with a single bed sheet and pillow. All of his games were instantly forgotten. For a moment, little

James was convinced that he had come upon the resting place of some mysterious Guardian of The Cellar, and he whirled around frantically, searching out every nook and cranny illuminated by his small lantern. But he was still alone; no secret guardian leapt out of the shadows to challenge the young boy's presence in a place that suddenly no longer seemed dark and mysterious due only to the efforts of his fertile imagination.

He turned back toward his discovery and carefully squeezed between the boxes and the cool, damp wall of the cellar. Once inside the small crawl space, he held the lantern aloft and began to study the scene carefully. Sure enough, his eyes hadn't deceived him; there were the mattress, pillow and sheet that he'd thought he'd seen when he'd first peeked around the corner. All were old and dirty, and James decided someone would have to be pretty tired to sleep in such a place. He moved the lantern slowly before him, watching the shadows slide and dance across the floor and wall, but saw nothing else to indicate who it was that used this little hide-a-way or why. Then he raised the lantern again, and his eyes fell on the wall at the head of the small makeshift bed. James caught his breath.

The wall was painted with strange symbols and figures, the likes of which he'd never seen. Some of the faces seemed almost comical with their exaggerated features and expressions, but here, alone and in the dark, James was terrified by the very sight of them. His heart leapt into his throat for a moment before falling all the way down into the pit of his stomach, and an icy chill climbed the length of his back. Never before had he felt so alone; so naked, exposed, defenseless.

He quickly turned, squeezed back through the small crawl space, and retreated from the cellar as quickly as he dared, all treasure and adventure swept firmly out of his mind by this strange and somehow eerie discovery. Soon he was back safely in his bedroom, carefully pondering what he'd seen. James decided he'd better ask his father about it. He knew from experience that James Sr. ran his household like he ran his business; he liked to know who, what, when, how, why and where at all times. And if his father didn't know what was going on, James knew the man would find out pretty quick
.

Now James was sitting on the ground, his back to a medium-sized oak, the only tree growing in this small clearing in the woods behind the family's grand home. It was a place he came to often when he was tired of being stuck in the house, although he usually brought a book to accompany him. But this time James had no book, only the memories of what had seemed such small but confusing events. And as the words that Billy had shouted this afternoon continued to ring in his ears, James' confusion gave way to complete and total understanding, not only of his strange discovery, but of his father's reaction to it as well.

It was at this moment – a moment in which he desperately wanted to hate his father, but was somehow terrified of such terrible and surely damning emotions – that young James Stockton II made a decision. His resolve was as cold as the panicky fear that had overtaken him earlier. He could not allow this to happen to his mother – the only person who loved him completely and unconditionally.

But he would say nothing to anyone, not just yet. Instead, he would watch and wait, carefully and patiently. If Billy's accusations were true (and James had no doubt that they were), sooner or later his father and Miss Hanes would meet up for a little rendezvous, and James now knew where they'd be meeting. Whether it was tonight or a month from now, he would be ready. His only prayer was that Della would arrive before his father. He'd had ample experience with his father's notorious temper, and he knew that any confrontation with his father would be disastrous. The very idea of trying to face down his father, of trying to stand up to a man that seemed to fear nothing at all, made the pit of James' stomach ache with dread. No, the only way this would work would for him to catch the maid alone, and convince her to leave. He would confront her, plead with her, bargain with or threaten her – whatever it took. But one way or another, he'd make sure that whatever was going on between the maid and his father ended.

II

James Stockton – founder of Logtown, multi-millionaire entrepreneur and, for all intents and purposes, master of all he surveyed – sat at the desk behind the locked door of his office/study, his head in his hands, and despaired. It was a despair born of fear and self-doubt, two things he'd had precious little experience with over the course of his life. Perhaps it was this lack of experience that caused such an overwhelming emotion now; desperation at his inability to defend himself against those two alien emotions as they grew in him like cancer, feeding not just off each other, but everything else that stood in their paths as well.

How could you let matters come to this?

That was the thought that kept returning, over and over, to deride him and browbeat him and grind its heels into him now that he was down and couldn't seem to get back up. He should have seen it coming; should have made preparations to either get out of this particular business and this particular place with minimal loss, or tightened his belt in a big, big way so as to safely ride out the storm.

But he wasn't being entirely honest, was he? Mr. Stockton had never been one to admit his mistakes, but he found himself unable to dodge this one, now that the inevitable consequences loomed so clearly before him. He *had* seen it coming; for almost five years now he'd watched as the country's economic train sped down the tracks to a ravine with no bridge to help it safely cross. Everyone on board was having the time of their lives; it was a regular orgy of excess, and hardly any of the passengers seemed to have noticed the small sign alongside the tracks that read, in great, bold lettering, DANGER AHEAD, BRIDGE OUT! Mr. Stockton, along with a few other unusually perceptive passengers had noticed it; but only casually, only in passing. All seemed to believe that they could ride that train just a little longer before jumping to safety, as though none of them understood that trying to jump from a speeding train will either get you seriously hurt or, more likely, killed. And so on they rode, until the train finally plunged into that ravine when the stock market crashed in 1929. Many of the men that hadn't jumped from the train ended up jumping from the windows of their Wall Street offices. Mr. Stockton hadn't rode the train into the ravine, but he had waited much too long before jumping off, and though he'd tried hard to cover it, the jump had hurt him badly. Sure, he'd salvaged a large part of his fortune by getting out before the big crash, but in his arrogance, his feelings of infallibility that bordered omnipotence, he'd honestly come to believe that he could ride out the coming storm without having to sacrifice a single thing. But who could have known that the coming storm would build into a raging hurricane?

You! You should have seen exactly *what was coming; the inevitable downturn on the horizon; the cliff that was looming at the end of the tracks.*

Again, he understood inside that he was still deceiving himself with half-truths and hollow reassurances that he wasn't to blame;

he was still trying to convince himself that it wasn't his pride and conceit that had led him where he was now, waiting for the bottom to fall out. And the bottom *was* going to fall. He could see his own folly quite clearly now; he had tasted its bitterness, just as he now saw that it was too late to somehow stop it. It would all collapse, and it could happen any day now. There were no lessons to be learned now from *should have*. The lesson was perfectly obvious – he had see it coming, and had believed himself untouchable – just as it was perfectly obvious that he had been grossly mistaken, and this particular lesson had been learned much too late.

You watched it coming and did nothing!

It was something that he could no longer deny. Almost since the end of the Great War, he'd watched it coming, but he'd jumped on that bandwagon right along with everyone else, riding it as long and hard as he could, milking it for all it was worth. Now it was time for him, like so many others had already done, to pay the check.

Sure, he'd managed to jump ship mere months before the stock market had crashed four years earlier, and he'd salvaged most of the money he'd invested. But then he'd turned right around and invested most of it right back into his company, proudly and greedily watching as it continue to grow even as the rest of the country had begun to falter. Perhaps he *had* been too eager (greedy) to grow his empire, almost to the point of obscenity, while the rest of the country's institutions continued to dwindle and crumble. But it was how he'd always attacked business; daring the odds and rolling full steam ahead. Just as he'd always defied fate or whatever else might be out there watching over mankind – perhaps benevolently, pouring grace and mercy upon those who sought to better serve not just themselves, but all of mankind as well; perhaps malevolently, moving each and every person on this planet around like pieces on a giant chessboard, creating war and havoc, peace and prosperity, strictly for amusement – to even try and stop him. Business, life, pleasure – Stockton had always faced them all head-on with the same attitude of all-or-nothing, believing in his heart that any other approach was a sure sign of weakness.

And so he'd continued to grow, laying endless lines of railroad tracks deeper into the depleting wilderness of South Mississippi; building two more sawmills along the Pearl River from the ground up, and buying another two existing sawmills – one in Gainesville and another in Pearlington. He remembered disdaining the men who'd sold him these last two sawmills as being spineless cowards, lacking the courage to stand up against the tide.

And yet throughout all of his deal-making and expansion and growth, he'd seen it, hovering just on the edge of sight like a specter waiting for its moment to strike. The rampant inflation and excesses in the stock market after the war; the lack of safeguards in the financial institutions of this country – safeguards that could have at least helped to control all that free-flowing money.

Sure there was still *some* hope, as far as it went. Hoover had spent these last four years being manhandled by congress, neither side able to agree on how best to open the treasury and get jobs to the suffering people of this country; but now he was gone. His successor, Roosevelt, at least showed some promise. Every word that came from the man's mouth seemed to exude hope, but Mr. Stockton was at a place where he desperately needed more than just hope. *Hope* wouldn't pay the huge debt that would soon be coming due. *Hope* wouldn't save from ruin the world he'd spent so many years building for himself. He needed concrete assurances, and no matter what this new president did, Mr. Stockton understood that real relief would be years in coming. If nothing changed for him in the meantime, it would be miles past too late.

Ironically, the greatest source of his despair didn't even come from the threat to his business empire, the thing he'd spent almost every waking hour of his life to build. It came instead from the threat to his personal life, his family; something he'd never spent much time building at all. For some reason, Mr. Stockton had always held to the assumption that one's personal life was supposed to just happen, naturally and with minimal input or effort. One's family was supposed to just grow by itself, almost organically, and always be there, steady and strong, to support the necessary image society demands. On the rare occasion that one needs moral buttress from a source other than oneself, one's family should be at the ready, a firm and strong support. His own family hadn't turned out quite that way.

Of course James had been proud at the birth of his son, who wouldn't be? A boy, who would one day be a man and carry on not just the Stockton name, but its legacy as well. It didn't take Mr.

Stockton long to discover that destiny seemed to have other plans for his namesake.

Young James seemed to have absolutely zero interest in carrying on the family empire. The boy was smart enough, there was no question about that; he excelled at his studies. But when he wasn't at his studies, you could safely bet the house and lot that his head was either stuck in one of those ridiculous books that his grandfather insisted on giving him, or he was off by himself, roaming the fields and woods behind the house – lost in his outlandishly fertile imagination, doing nothing productive whatsoever.

His wife Melinda was also something of a mystery and disappointment. She was certainly beautiful, in a wholesome kind of way. She'd entered their marriage as an excited, carefree young woman – a young woman who'd grown up the privileged, almost spoiled only daughter of one of the wealthiest ship magnates in New Orleans. But that seemed to have changed almost overnight after their son had been born. She now had ideas and expectation of their marriage and family life that Mr. Stockton not only couldn't understand, but to be honest, didn't *want* to understand. She wanted James to spend more time with his family; "leisure time" that should be spent building his empire would be wasted on doing nothing even remotely productive. She'd been angry when he'd told her as much, and over the years she'd become resentful and cold toward him, taking their son to New Orleans not just for the weekends, but extended stays that occasionally stretched out into more than a week at a time.

Worst of all, during the time she did spend at their luxurious home in Logtown, she'd taken to sleeping in a separate bedroom, and denying him access to it. To Mr. Stockton, that was the ultimate sin, a deliberate and unrepentant failing of her fundamental duties and responsibilities as his wife. His disbelief at her audacity had enraged him at first, but in almost no time it was practically forgotten. Mr. Stockton simply followed the course of so many other men before him, looking for and finding satisfaction with other women. When a man has enough money and knows the right people, all sorts of pleasure can be easily found and discretion can be guaranteed. So, although he still burned at his wife's recently found chastity, his needs and desires never went unfulfilled and he never felt even the slightest pang of guilt for it.

Enter Della Hanes. She was "introduced" to Mr. Stockton during a glitzy ball at the new and elegant Pontchartrain Hotel one weekend about six years after little James was born. Mrs. Stockton had also been in attendance, but it had been a perfunctory appearance that had lasted maybe two hours before she left, returning to her family's home only a few blocks further down St. Charles.

The gentleman who'd set up the introduction had described her as a Creole beauty, whispering in Mr. Stockton's ear that he could live another two hundred years and not see another woman as stunning. After one look, James knew that the man had spoken the truth. At that moment he didn't give a whit about what her ethnic origins might be, and soon Mr. Stockton, like his wife, vanished from the lively party. Unlike his wife, he did not leave alone.

For almost six years, he'd had no other mistress. He didn't love her – love was as foreign a concept to James Stockton as his own fallibility – but, in time, he had grown to need her like he'd never needed a woman before. She did things for him that no woman before her had ever done; things he hadn't even known were possible. And whatever his mood might be during their lovemaking – tender, playful, aggressive, sometimes even bordering on violent – she had always been a ready and willing partner.

Three years ago (and right about the time he had begun to recognize – at least in some deep, undercurrent flow of thought – that his kingdom might not last forever), he had come to understand that once or twice a week was no longer enough; he needed her to be available anytime and almost all the time. He finally moved her into his grand home in Logtown under the title of "maid", and while he tried to remain discreet, he found it had become harder and harder to do so. His lustful need for her had grown almost out of control, and was nearing obsession. And growing almost parallel with that lust was his need for the aggressive, sometimes violent type of sex they were engaging in more and more frequently. Their "special place" in the basement was being visited at least four or five times a week now, and if he'd had his way, they'd go down there and sweat it out daily. As his wife was spending more and more time away from the home, they probably could have arranged to meet in a more comfortable room in the large house and still maintained at least an illusion of discretion, but Mr. Stockton wouldn't do it. Part of him, down deep in a place where there wasn't cognizant thought, understood that what he was doing belonged in the dirty corners of that dark, dank-smelling place. There was another part of him, too, that found the place where they were doing it just as exciting as the act itself; just thinking about that place was enough to get him excited.

But now, finally, his longstanding affair with Della Hanes was teetering on the brink of collapse, just as surely as his business empire was. She had become dissatisfied, it seemed, with their current arrangement, and wanted more. Where her crazy ideas were coming from, he couldn't imagine, but over the past few months she'd gotten bolder and bolder; not just hinting at the things she wanted – everything from clothing to jewelry to money – but actually demanding these things. The money wasn't that big a deal, he'd always seen to it that she'd had more than a maid's salary to get by on. Furthermore, he'd seen to it that her own room in the servant's quarters were somewhat more extravagantly furnished that those of the other servants, and her duties as a maid had always been light and undemanding (something he knew the other servants had noticed, but were too afraid for their own jobs to mention, at least to him).

But now, for some reason, that was no longer enough, and his anger at her ingratitude burned his very soul. "A Creole beauty" was how she'd been introduced to him six years ago, but Mr. Stockton now raged at that notion; she was an ungrateful, manipulating, half-breed nigger! She'd even been bold enough to suggest things like having her own room, outside of the servant's quarters, and attending parties and other social gatherings at his side. At this rate, she'd soon be suggesting that he divorce Melinda and take her, a filthy half-breed nigger, as his wife! Underlying each of her new demands was the vague hint that the special capacity in which she served him might come to an end if her demands weren't met. And the worst part was that, despite his wrath at her lack of gratitude and her bold, insolent demands, he still wanted her. He wanted and needed her more intensely and with a deeper, burning desire than anything else he'd ever known.

He finally sat back into his chair, and stared long at a spot where the smooth, wood-grained wall met the ceiling. He stared so long and hard that he felt he might burn a hole in that spot while he finally made up his mind. His decision was as firm as it was inevitable – he was not going to be brought down by that little whore anymore than his empire would be brought down by those weak and faint-hearted cowards who'd destroy what he'd spent a lifetime building. He would see to that the next time they met, making it clear to her that she would continue in her current capacity (and in the same grateful, willing spirit she'd once had) or she would go back to the streets of the French Quarter, selling herself to the highest bidder at an age where she was close to being past her prime. He felt confident that he knew what her answer to such a daunting choice would have to be. And even if she surprised him by choosing the latter option, she would, by glory, do for him what she'd always done for him, exactly the way he wanted it done, one last time before he tossed her out the door.

III

If she'd grown up a few decades later, Della Hanes would have been referred to by the learned and wise social intelligentsia as "a product of her environment." If said social analysts had told her as much, she would probably have laughed and asked if they would like to analyze her in private.

The youngest of five siblings (and in her neighborhood, that was a small family), Della learned quickly exactly how the world worked for people who came from a certain place or had a certain name or weren't a certain pedigree. But what she lacked in all of those areas, the incomparable beauty that God had seen fit to bless her with served as ample compensation. Her complexion was flawless, her body was shapely, and her eyes – a deep, almost emerald green – could laugh, tease, and seduce all at the same moment as they sparkled and gleamed brightly in her café-au-lait face. By the time she was twelve years old, she was already turning the heads of any and all men who crossed her path; old or young, black or white, it didn't matter. By the time she was fourteen, she'd learned exactly what most men wanted from her, and just how far they'd go to get it. An uncle had taught her that, and while the experience had been a terrible one, she'd learned something valuable from it: if she could control what, how and when men got what they wanted from her, then she could control them, using them in a much greater and important way than they used her, usually with the men being none the wiser. She learned that, although born and raised in a place far from society, her beauty and the ability to use it shrewdly could be the ticket to a cachet she so desperately wanted to be a part of. It took her much longer to finally understand that more than just a few blocks and dirty streets separated her world and the world she dreamed of being a part of.

Her mother was born only two generations out of slavery; part of a family that had worked a plantation in south Louisiana for a hundred years. She, like so many of the children of the freed slaves who had migrated from those plantations to the city of New Orleans, had ended up as a prostitute, walking the streets of Storyville and the Vieux Carre and struggling to make better a life that was remarkably like the one left behind, wondering sometimes if the freedom they'd been granted was nothing more than just a glamorous word on a fancy document. Della's great-grandmother, who had lived for sixteen years as a slave, wouldn't hear of such talk; she knew full well what had been left behind; and understood that it was going to take time rather than just a war to change people's hearts.

Della had never known her father. According to her mother, he'd arrived on a merchant ship one day, looking for work in a country that seemed to have so much to offer. He'd found work on the docks, a place that Della's mother had always found offered as much opportunity for those in her line of work as it did for merchants, sailors, and roughnecks. She'd found the man intriguing in a way that most men she met were not; he was handsome, spoke faltering English with a thick French accent, and told fascinating tales of the things he'd seen and done while traveling from city to city and country to country, paying his way by working at harbors and seaports and on the mighty ships that had carried him around the world. He'd come to live with her and her four children (each with a different father that had chosen not to stick around), and had stayed for just over a year. Then, two weeks after Della had been born, he'd simply disappeared. And strangely, of all the men who'd left her "holding the bag", he was the only one that her mother never seemed to hold a bitter grudge against, often recounting to Della the stories of his exploits and adventures and wistfully remembering their time together. "Hanes" was the name the man had given, and "Hanes" was the name passed along to his daughter.

Della never walked the streets the way her mother did. She had seen firsthand the risks of such a lifestyle – not just the risk of not being paid, but also the very real dangers of being beaten, or worse. She had also seen how such women, like her own mother, seemed to age almost ten years for every one year they walked the streets. And she knew that, every so often, one of the women turned up missing. Some would be found after a few days, others never were. The stories involving the ones that were found should have been enough to discourage each and every prostitute in the entire city to search for safer means of employment. But above all else, even the potential risk of being beaten or murdered, Della instinctively understood that there was simply no future in this line of work.

Women who walked the streets found only the type of men who wanted to pay as little as possible for what they had to offer. Such women would never find themselves walking through the doorways of the Hotel Monteleone or The Cave, a popular and exclusive nightclub at the Grunewald Hotel (which had, just the year before, had its name changed to The Roosevelt – something Della didn't think she'd ever get used to), entertaining the wealthiest of patrons – men who gladly paid for discretion as well as service. They would never find themselves clothed in anything other than shabby dresses, usually secondhand or homemade, and would never have a street address much different from the one Della herself currently shared with her mother and siblings. Her mother wanted more for her favorite child as well, but while her hopes and ambitions for Della would have probably led the young woman to a better life, it still wasn't the life Della desired. She wanted to be a *part* of society, not just a paid slave of it.

On Della's sixteenth birthday, her mother had presented her with a simple but elegant dress as a gift. She had been working extra for several months, setting the additional money aside for the present, and was almost as thrilled as her daughter the first time Della wore it (both only casually noticed the envious looks of her brothers and sisters). Her mother's plan was for Della to wear this dress as she began looking for work at some of the nicer hotels and elegant homes of the city, perhaps as a chambermaid, cook or seamstress. Della had other ideas.

For a couple of years, Della had been listening carefully to the whispered stories of one Madam Larue. Like Della's mother, she was a woman of color. Unlike her mother, Madam Larue had, as a child, migrated with her family from Saint Domingue to New Orleans in the late 1860s. While the family wasn't rich, they were still better off than most of the recently freed slave families. But, more importantly, they'd brought a kind of prestige. Apparently, her father had been a great vodun priest back on the island of Saint Domingue, and the family had arrived in New Orleans toward the end of the reign of Marie Laveau, the undisputed queen of voodoo in this part of the world for most of the century. Della had heard rumors that Madam Larue's family had taken part in Laveau's "retirement" in order to accelerate its own ascent to power. Whether this was fact or gossip, Della didn't know; nor did she care. What mattered now was that Madam Larue currently reigned as one of the top priestesses in the city. Furthermore, she controlled a select group of ladies who performed services for an even more select clientele. They attended fabulous parties and spectacular balls, dressed suggestively in the newest and sometimes most outrageous fashions. And they satisfied the lusts of some of the most powerful men in the entire city, men who paid generously for their services and the guaranteed discretion they were famous for. Most of these men were, of course, married, and many held important and sensitive positions in the city. All were more than willing to pay Madam Larue's prices in order to guarantee that her ladies kept their mouths shut (except, of course, when they were "at work").

This special group of ladies actually lived with Madam Larue in her stately home on Rampart Street. It was to this address that sixteen-year-old Della Hanes went job-hunting, wearing her new dress and with her hair and make-up done just so (her mother had even helped with the latter after Della truthfully told her that she was going out to try to find work; she just conveniently left out *where*). She boldly knocked at the front door and insisted on seeing the mistress of the house.

Ordinarily, unsolicited applicants were summarily turned away, but it was immediately noticed that Della had a certain quality about her. It was the same quality that Della had understood and already used to her benefit for several years, and she was counting on it to get her in now. That quality – her beauty and the way she used it in a way that was suggestive but never flouting – and her youth (Larue's clientele preferred them younger) once again got Della what she wanted, and by the end of the day, she was officially one of Madam Larue's Ladies. She never went home again.

The next three years flew by. Della became a favorite; even those who'd been regulars over the years began to request her over the ladies with more experience and supposedly, more skill. This earned her some resentment and cold treatment from the other ladies, but Della didn't care. Her rise in popularity with Madam Larue's clientele earned her a special place in the madam's heart, and word quickly spread that to cross Della would certainly mean facing the wrath of the madam. One thing only seemed to mar the success she'd achieved over the past few years. It was something she only felt at night, a thought that kept returning as she tossed and turned, searching for sleep in a lavishly furnished bedroom that was larger than the entire shanty-like home she'd grown up in. This thought was the simple but haunting realization that she still wasn't a *part* of that society she so desperately craved; she was simply entertainment for that crowd – a prop, a sideshow, a dirty little urge that had to be kept secret.

It was about this time that she had been introduced to James Stockton. From the beginning, Della was never certain whether she liked him or not. He was certainly an attractive man, and more importantly, he was rich. Incredibly rich. During that first encounter, he had been so passionate and aggressive that they'd both nearly been overwhelmed. And from that moment forth, she'd had another name to add to her list of regulars who requested her alone when they made arrangements to meet up with one of Larue's Ladies.

What made Della uncomfortable was how Stockton had immediately become possessive of her. He knew exactly what she did for a living (after all, that's how he had met her), but even after just one meeting, it seemed obvious to her that he was disturbed – almost offended – that she'd be doing it with anyone else. Over the next year they'd met at least once a week, every week. And every time, when they were through with business, he would make some sort of comment about having to share her. Such comments had been made to her before by other men, but usually in the context of a joke or comment about how they ought to just quit their jobs, pack up their goods, and move out to a deserted island or to some mountain out in the wilderness where they'd be all alone and could do it all the time. Mr. Stockton's comments weren't like that. He seemed to be sincerely jealous of the fact that other men would be with her during the time between when he left and could return. But what was truly disturbing about these cold comments was how they didn't come across to her as a jealousy born of love or affection. It seemed that, from day one, he considered her to be his property. And Mr. James Stockton didn't like sharing his property.

After a year or so of this, Mr. Stockton made arrangements with Madam Larue: he would pay whatever price she named for exclusive rights to Della. Ms. Larue had never had such a request before, but quickly quoted an almost outrageous sum just to gauge how serious the man was. He had immediately agreed (leaving her to wish she'd quoted an even higher price), and he became Della's only client. Their get-togethers became more and more frequent over the next couple of years, and he finally asked her to come live at his home, across the state line in Mississippi. In terms of wealth and society, a small, rural place like Logtown was literally a world away from New Orleans and the exciting way of life she'd come to love over the past several years. She was, at first, inclined to pass on his offer for this very reason. After all, it was society she craved; what kind of society did a logging town in Mississippi have to offer? Mr. Stockton, however, seemed to have anticipated her concerns, and was standing ready with pre-packaged answers to most of her objections. Yes, her title would be "maid", but she would have her own rooms, as elegantly decorated as the one she now had. Furthermore, she would be paid well in excess of what a maid (not just in Logtown, but even in New Orleans) would be paid. New Orleans was only forty-five miles away, and he would still be visiting the place for various functions and business deals. She could go to visit her friends at those times, and maybe even attend some of those functions with him. He skillfully drew for her a beautiful picture in which she would actually be a part of the society that was entertained instead of being the entertainment. It was this final argument that won her over, and she chose to ignore the little warning that continued to whisper quietly in her ears, an unnamed feeling of worry that always seemed to lead back to his almost neurotic possessiveness of her.

Madam Larue was not at all pleased with the prospect of losing her most lucrative investment, but there wasn't a whole lot she could do about it. Ordinarily, she was not at all averse to making threats (sometimes subtle, sometimes not) or even blackmailing some of her clientele. She tried to keep such practices to a minimum; after all, the assured discretion of both her ladies and herself was one of the reasons for the rapid ascent of the most successful and powerful mistress in the entire city, or for that matter, the entire region. The very nature of her business would make blackmail an easy thing; not only did the activity her clients were engaging in make them easy targets, but many of them frequently felt the need to try and impress the young ladies they had bedded down with. They would often, in a state of drunkenness brought on by both alcohol and the thrill of what these girls were willing to do, chatter almost endlessly about things ranging from inane to potentially earth-shattering; things involving the most powerful government and business officials not just in the city or state, but throughout the entire country. Larue's Ladies were taught to listen carefully, and report back even the smallest detail of who and what might have been discussed. The information reported would literally be categorized and filed away. It would only be brought forth if an important favor was called in by a really big name, or, in the case of city and state officials, if a certain vote or referendum that might affect Larue's business was before the city council or state legislature.

Stockton was different from most of these men. He was, without a doubt, the most brazen man she'd ever seen, both in matters of business, and apparently, pleasure. What other man had she ever known would have first bought exclusive rights to one of her ladies, then have the audacity to move that lady into his own home, to live under the same roof with his wife and family? No, such a man would only be enraged by the very threat of blackmail, and would probably go to battle with her just as eagerly and aggressively as he went to battle, almost daily, in the business world. And so she had released Della from service, assuring the young lady who had once been Madam Larue's brightest star that if this new situation didn't work out, she was always welcome to come back. Neither of the women was sure if they believed this or not.

It didn't take long for Della to realize that the most important of Mr. Stockton's promises had only been made in order to lure her into his home. The money was there, as well as the beautifully furnished room. But the time that wasn't spent with Mr. Stockton in a grubby little hide-a-way he'd prepared down in that dark, dank cellar was spent doing light housework or languishing away in her bedroom, alone. None of the other household staff was even remotely interested in having anything to do with her, as each and every one of them knew exactly why she'd been brought here. Even the occasional visit to New Orleans brought nothing but loneliness; without the title of being one of Larue's Ladies, Della couldn't even *buy* her way into any of the glamorous places she'd frequented before. Perhaps Stockton had forgotten his promise to take her with him to the various parties and gatherings he attended (perhaps this even included the ones his wife didn't attend), but she strongly suspected that the promise had been one he'd never intended to fulfill; it had simply been another clever lure that she had been foolish enough to take.

During her last year as a resident of Stockton Manor, Della began to pick up some very bad vibes, indeed. Some came from the other servants (which was nothing new), some had begun to come from Stockton's wife (who was, unless she was a complete fool, finally beginning to understand the nature of the maid's real services). On several occasions, Della had looked up from whatever light, almost non-existent work she was doing and found the lady of the house staring at her. There was no maliciousness in those stares, only a vague curiosity and sadness that made Della very uncomfortable.

Then, without a word, Mrs. Stockton would turn and walk away. But the worst of the vibes came from the man himself.

He had, over the course of the past two years, reached the point where he insisted on meeting with her at least four or five times a week, and he honestly didn't seem to care if anyone else knew or not. Worse than that, his sexual demands had become angry, abusive and violent during this time, and she was now afraid to offer any protest to the sometimes unnatural and painful things he did to her. She had hoped that her submission might finally get her some of the things he'd promised but had never delivered. But now, when she timidly mentioned these things, he grew angrier instead of simply trying to put her off. Della had finally begun to fear that the man was losing control of himself in some deeply hidden place she couldn't quite see, and she grew more and more afraid that he would one day (perhaps sooner than later) seriously hurt or even kill her if he wasn't somehow brought back to where he'd been, mentally and emotionally, when they'd first met.

About a month ago, she managed to get away to New Orleans for a weekend, and spent the time with her family. Not her birth family; her mother had met yet another man almost three years ago, and had moved with him down to Port Sulfur. She didn't know if they had gotten married or not, nor did she care. No, on this visit she went to see her *real* mother, Madam Larue, and she went seeking advice that had nothing to do with her successful business venture. Della remembered well the stories of how Larue's family had quickly come to power upon their arrival in this city. It had been, more than anything, the result of their almost overnight power-grab and subsequent domination of the voodoo culture of New Orleans. Madam Larue's involvement in that scene was what Della now wanted to discuss.

The lady of the house seemed surprised at Della's sudden interest; all of her ladies had been encouraged rather than forced to take part in the religion, but Della had been one of the very few who had opted out. Upon hearing the young lady's concerns, the madam immediately suggested that Della return to her former employment, but was surprised and disappointed at the "not just yet" response that she got. Instead, Della wanted to know what type of protection might be available to her through the various spells and charms used by those who practiced the curious religion in which her former madam held such power.

Madam Larue stared long and hard at the frightened young woman, but finally relented. She wrote down instructions for a few simple spells, complete with symbols to be used. She then prepared two bags of gris-gris, one to be hung in her bedroom and one to be hung in the basement, where Della and Mr. Stockton met in "secret." Finally she gave Della a small charm hanging from a delicate braided necklace, which she called a Scapular.

"Never take this off," Larue told Della, her eyes almost stony in an effort to convey the gravity of the instructions. "It will repel both negative energy and evil spirits."

The last thing Larue told Della was that these charms and spells would be much more effective if Della came and participated in some of the ceremonies that were performed weekly at a temple just down the road. Della promised that she'd try, but wasn't sure if Stockton would allow her to leave again anytime soon.

The first time Mr. Stockton arrived at their meeting place in the basement and saw the strange symbols and words that had been scribbled on the wall, he came close to being outraged. Della quickly told the lie she'd been planning from the moment she prepared the place, explaining to him that they were spells and charms designed to bring greater pleasure for him during their lovemaking. When he heard this, he relented and allowed the symbols and words to remain on the walls, and though he had scorned the idea with his mouth, she could see the excitement burning in his eyes. Then he'd taken her, just as roughly and coldly and violently as ever, leaving her naked and shivering with more than just the damp chill of the cellar as soon as he was finished.

This routine went on for three weeks. During that time, Mr. Stockton's sadistic attitude got no worse; nor did it get any better. Finally, Della managed another trip back to New Orleans. Larue again met with her, and was shocked at the young lady's appearance. She was pale, unkempt, and had ash-colored circles beneath her eyes. She seemed to have aged almost ten years since her last visit. Madam Larue didn't offer her a job this time; she no longer saw any profit in the young woman. But her heart went out to Della when the young lady – still not much more than a girl, really – finally confided the reason she had thus far refused to return to New Orleans. Larue's face did not reflect the shock she felt upon hearing what Della had to say, but it did reflect the sympathy and even anger that welled up, ever so briefly, as Della told her tale. And once again, the madam gave her what she'd asked for, despite her strong misgivings – the young lady was inquiring about something dark and dangerous; something the madam herself had never taken part in, although she did understand how, in the most extreme of circumstances, some people might want to. It was an art even older than the religion she practiced, although it seemed to have absorbed some of the customs of voo-doo and many other religions into its fold (always perverting and distorting those customs to meld with its own dark purpose) during the countless centuries it had slithered and crawled its way through time eternal, down deep under the comings and goings of countless societies and civilizations. And she knew well the name of a local man rumored to be as dark and deadly as those arts, to which it was said he had pledged his very soul; a man whose name was feared throughout even the murkiest, shadowy parts of the city. A man rumored to be devoid of fear, conscience, and reason. Madam Larue wouldn't speak this man's name, but simply gave Della directions and a warning.

"Be careful, child. He might be able to do what you want, but the price asked of you will almost certainly be great, perhaps even greater than you will understand . . . until it's too late."

The address was deep in a part of town Della rarely set foot in; where the prostitutes worked for things other than money; a place where the emaciated, homeless dregs of the city languished in doorways and alleys; a place where heroin and opium addicts gathered in dark, smoke-filled rooms to sleep and dream and gibber endlessly as they beheld visions of both heaven and hell.

She found the man himself in a small apartment tucked away between one such opium den and a cheap, run-down hotel. He sat on the floor in the center of a dark room, huddling over his busy hands. Crazy, jumbled symbols that seemed frighteningly chaotic in comparison to the methodical, soothing patterns given to her by Larue adorned the walls of the small room, and everything from dead snakes to gourds to what looked like wind-chimes wrought of bones hung from a dark and dirty ceiling.

He looked up and smiled a nearly toothless smile when she entered, a smile that grew at her horrified expression when she realized that the work he'd set himself to involved removing the intestines of a dead cat. He laughed when he saw the Scapular she still wore around her neck, and he laughed when she told her story, and he laughed when she explained the charms and spells she'd tried in order to rectify the situation.

Then his smile grew cold and his eyes flashed brightly and dangerously in his face, as though he found great pleasure in her desperate need. When he spoke, the sound of the man's voice was like booted feet walking through gravel. His voice was heavy with a Cajun accent. Della spoke Cajun French, of course – she'd been surrounded by it her entire life – but she rarely did, except during moments of high anger; the words and musical accent seemed to capture her mood better. There were also times, of course, when certain customers seemed to get a special little thrill when she spoke it to them, but most of the time, she stuck with the regular, New Orleans version of English. This man, too, stuck with English, but his accent was much heavier than her own; it was Cajun English.

"An' so now you finally has to come to me, eh? A dirty old bokor, who dare to use da left han'; who dare to call on de Ge-Rouge when dem pretty little charms won' help none? Oh, lady, I can help, I know who you be needin'. But you bes beware!" He finally stood up, and she was surprised to see his lanky frame reached well over six feet in height. His eyes grew even brighter, reminding her somehow of the dangerous excitement she'd seen lately in Stockton's face.

"Dis ain' no Rada or Petro I call for you! Dis ain' no voodoo spirit at all, oh no, not at all – he a devil, a monster, a loup-garous! He can do what you want, but he may want more den what you wanna pay, eh?" His repulsive smile grew even more; he now seemed pleased by the fear his words were creating behind her river-green eyes. He chuckled a moment before continuing, taking great pleasure at delivering his final warning. "Oh yeah, dis one hungry all de time, an' if he hungry enough, he might jus eat up your soul; your gros bon ange, your ti bon ange an all." He finally grew quiet, but continued to smile, as if daring her to accept what he now offered. She hesitated for a moment, torn between a horrible fear of this unknown he had just described to her and the fear that had led her to this place. She finally reached into her purse and pulled out a bag containing $300.00. It was all the money she had been able to lay hands on, and she told him as much.

The man's toothless smile remained unchanged, but his eyes flicked with surprised pleasure. He turned and walked slowly to a small door at the back of the dark room. He opened the door and stepped inside, almost disappearing from view. Della timidly approached and looked over the man's shoulder as he squatted down She saw a small shelf that had been hidden by boxes, tucked away in the back of the deep, foul-smelling closet. She felt a sudden urge to flee, to just leave the money and whatever the man was about to give her and run back to Larue's house. But she remembered her need again, and felt its great weight steel her heart. So she simply backed a few paces away from the closet, enough to get away from that thick and frightening smell, and waited.

The strange, dark man dug around for a few more moments, then slowly stood, turned, and gimped his way back across the floor. When he stood directly before her, he suddenly reached out and fiercely ripped the small charm she'd been wearing from around her neck and threw it to the floor. He then held up a crystal, which hung from a silver chain. She studied the strange symbols that adorned the charm for a few moments as if hypnotized, but was too afraid to ask what they were.

"You wear dis, an don' you *never* take it off, you hear me? If you hafta call up dis devil, all you do is hold de charm tight an swear to him whatever you think he wan. If he *do* wan what you swear to him, he come and take it. Den he do what you ask, but only in his own good time."

Della stared with frightened eyes at the charm, then took it and hung it around her neck. She looked deep into the old man's eyes.

"Who is this devil? What is it called?"

The old man turned away, sitting on the dirty floor, and resumed working with the dead cat as he muttered, "I don' know his name and wouldn' say it if I did. But you don' worry, he come when you call him. Mebbe you can ask his name den." He began to laugh that gravelly, mocking laugh again. As Della walked out the door, it echoed loudly and frightfully in her ears.

Throughout the entire trip back to Logtown, Della could think of nothing other than the strange and frightening man with the bright and haunting eyes, the mysterious charm she now wore and her next inevitable meeting with James Stockton. She knew she must confront him, no matter how afraid she was. She must be strong and brave as she told him exactly what the situation was and what she expected him to do about it. Surely the man she had begun to hate would see reason; surely he would understand and own up to the fact that she was where she was because of him. And if necessary, she would call upon whatever power – be it spirit or demon – that waited somewhere in the depths of the crystal charm she now wore. She would promise it whatever was necessary, her very soul if it came to that, to see that things were set right.

26

Jacob was still cowering on the floor as he stared in mute terror at the two boys standing before him. His cheek throbbed from the backhanded slap Mike had dealt him, but he barely even noticed. Instead, his panicked mind seemed only capable of two flurried, jumbled thoughts that fought desperately for domination in his young mind – *how can this be happening?* and *I'm going to die; today I'm really going to* die*!*

It was Jared that he most feared to look at, but he couldn't seem to pull his own eyes away from the other boy's, which still burned with a fire Jacob had seen before, but in someone else's face. His only comfort (and it was a small comfort indeed) was that those fiery eyes were fixed unwaveringly on Jim. Jacob felt certain that if those orange and yellow eyes fell on him, he would die of terror.

Mike was still pointing his gun at Jim and grinning like a madman. His wild and almost feverish eyes constantly darted between his two captives, but he was most wary of Jim. Every time the thunder boomed outside, he would flinch, and Jacob thought it wouldn't take much to completely unhinge the older boy. Jacob also noticed that Mike seemed to be, either consciously or unconsciously, avoiding any eye contact with Jared. Mike finally spoke, his voice loud and as wild as his eyes as he raised it against the storm raging outside.

"What'sa matter, Jimbo? Don't you have anything cute to say? Huh? You still gonna crack my skull, old man? Well, where's your piece of hickory? Where's all them guns I've always heard about?" He paused long enough for another insane outburst of giggling before continuing his rant.

"Can'tcha talk, gramps? C'mon, tell me about how you're gonna crack my skull! How you're gonna *whip my tail*! Let's go, I wanna hear all about it!"

Throughout this entire diatribe, Jim remained speechless, staring open-mouthed not so much at Jared as the eyes that no longer belonged to the boy. This seemed to anger Mike, who still had not looked at his younger brother since the two had entered the trailer. He couldn't understand why the old man seemed more afraid of a silent thirteen-year-old than a seventeen-year-old who was brandishing a gun and almost screaming in his face. Another brilliant flash of lightning lit up the room and was followed almost immediately by an ear-splitting boom that shook the entire trailer. Both Jacob and Mike flinched at the sound, but Jared and Jim never moved. Instead, they continued to stare at each other, as though they were the only two people in the entire world.

This agitated Mike even further. His frantic confidence began sliding back toward uncertainty. With that feeling came the realization that, as far as Jim and Jared were concerned, he didn't matter (*shrinking*). Mike could feel the panic rising, and it made him angry all over again. He began shouting at Jim again, but his voice had become more desperate, shrill, and shakier than ever.

"Hey, you wrinkly old drunk, *I'm* talking to you! You gone deaf, or you just don't have anything to say when you ain't got a big ole stick or gun to hide behind?"

Still no response from Jim. Mike finally stepped up and with his free hand pushed the old man in the chest. Instead of resisting even a little, Jim toppled over backwards like a tree felled by some woodsman's axe. The back of his head struck the old wooden chair where Jacob had been sitting before the two brothers had come storming in, knocking it over with a crack that could be heard over the rain and hail that seemed to be beating against every inch of the old trailer. The blow seemed to finally snap Jim out of his stupor, and as he struggled up into a sitting position, now to Jacob's immediate left, he finally turned his attention to Mike. His infamous glare, albeit somewhat weaker and less threatening than usual, finally returned.

"That's right, old man," said Mike, nodding vigorously, the frantic excitement finally returning to his eyes, "We're gonna have us some fun. A boy-howdy, knee-slappin' how-do-you-do good time. But first things first," and here Mike started grinning again as he nodded his head, "Word has it that you've got a little secret, and you know what? I think it's true!"

Unnecessarily (after all, hadn't Jim just seen *her* eyes blazing out from Jared's pale face?), Jacob turned to Jim and said desperately, "I didn't tell them, I swear, I –"

"SHUT UP!" Mike screamed. He turned to glare at Jacob, but kept his gun centered on Jim. "You just keep yer pie-hole shut, you little smart-mouth punk! I'll be takin' care of you before this is over, you better believe that, but if you don't keep that trap shut, I swear I'll shove this gun up yer nose and pull the trigger!"

Jacob shut his mouth immediately, and his eyes began to water. Mike grinned even bigger than before.

"Yeah, you'll have plenty to cry about pretty soon, but if you wanna start now, that's fine, you go on ahead."

Jacob clenched his jaws and quickly wiped at his eyes. He made up his mind right then that he would not cry, no matter what Mike did. No matter how bad a beating he got, he wouldn't give Mike that satisfaction. Then his eyes drifted back to Jared. The boy was still staring right at Jim through those blazing eyes; he was completely oblivious to everything else, including, it seemed, all of the words that had just been exchanged. Jacob suddenly realized that Mike had no idea what was going on with his younger brother; he didn't understand who (what) was now piercing Jim with Jared's eyes. Jacob couldn't even begin to guess how it had happened, but *she* was now somehow *inside* of Jared; she was finally in the world of the living. And Jacob seriously doubted that, now that she was here, she would be content to just rough the old man up a little. She had told him as much in that second dream – she wanted justice; she wanted both Jim's life and his soul. Jacob's terrible revelation was interrupted as Mike began speaking again, his frantic voice still raised against the storm.

"All-righty, then, here's what we're gonna do! First off, Jimbo, you're gonna show me exactly where . . ."

"*Kill him*."

The voice, unfamiliar to Mike but not to Jacob and Jim, had come from Jared's mouth. And although it hadn't been shouted, it seemed to cut easily through the noise of the storm.

Mike hesitated only a moment before saying, "What?"

"*Kill. Him.*"

The unnatural, unfamiliar quality of the voice finally dawning on him, Mike carefully turned toward his younger brother.

"What are you talking abou . . ."

For the first time since they'd entered the trailer, Mike looked into Jared's face. His mouth fell open and his body grew rigid. He took a few careful steps backwards, and he drew his gun away from Jim, now leveling his aim on Jared's chest. He seemed to be trying to speak, but it took a few moments before the shrill words finally left his lips.

"*Jared?* What's wrong, man? What *happened* to y . . . ? *Jared*, man, your *eyes*!"

Jared turned to his brother and grinned so big and grotesquely that it seemed to consume his entire face; the sight was a hideous spectacle that would stay with Jacob for the rest of his life. Then it was gone and Jared leaned forward, his body just as rigid as Mike's, his face strained, and his mouth opened impossibly wide. He looked for all the world as if he were about to projectile vomit across the entire state of Mississippi. But instead of gorge, he spewed forth something unlike anything Jacob had ever seen; something he would never be fully able to describe.

It was a substance that seemed both real and unreal, almost like a thin, transparent liquid that wasn't really there at all. It rushed forth, shimmering in the pale light, and hit Mike full in the face. Into his mouth it went, and up his nose; some seemed to separate itself and wormed its way into his eyes and ears. When it had finally departed completely from Jared's mouth, the young boy let out a weak but hideous sound, a sickening cross between a gasp and a wet belch, then collapsed on the floor without another sound.

Mike, who had started screaming the moment Jared's mouth had opened, became even more desperately rigid the instant that the strange, fluid substance touched him. He began to shake violently, his terrified eyes bulging before they were completely lost from view. His arms went stiffly to his side, and his right hand involuntarily squeezed off a round from the gun into the floor of the trailer. The loud pop of the discharge seemed amplified in the small trailer, despite the ever-raging storm outside and the echoing sounds of Mike's screams, which Jacob thought would never end. He and Jim struggled to their feet, both too mesmerized by the outright horror they were witnessing to even try to run.

Finally, Mike grew abruptly silent. For a second or two he just stood there, arms still held stiffly at his side, breathing hard and trembling violently. Then, just as abruptly as the screaming had stopped, so, too, did the trembling. He looked up into Jim's pale face, and now *his* eyes burned with that bright, angry fire; now *his* lips formed that familiar, cold smile.

Without a word, he raised the gun and leveled it at Jim's chest.

This is it! Jacob thought frantically. *We're going to die, right now! Both of us! And there's nothing left to do or say to stop it. We're both about to die!*

At that moment, even as those frantic, shrill thoughts rang in his mind, a new thunderstorm seemed to break – this one *inside* the trailer. And once again, Jacob couldn't decide if things were happening in slow-motion or fast-forward. A strange *whooshing* sound seemed to fill the air, and Jacob felt almost every bit of air suddenly sucked right out of his body. It was as though the entire trailer had suddenly depressurized like the cabin of a jetliner. As he sank helplessly to his knees, he saw another shape, very much like the one spewed forth from Jared's mouth, forming at the wall behind Jim. It raced forward, gaining shape and substance as Jacob's strength left him; it sped directly toward Mike and the upraised gun. It passed through Jim, who let out a gasp and cry of surprised amazement.

Mike squeezed the trigger, and once again the sound of the discharge cracked loudly throughout the small trailer. Much to Jacob's shock, he actually *saw* the bullet! The bullet didn't seem to be traveling in slow motion, like some techno-enhanced special effect in the movies, but still Jacob *saw* it! It reached the still transparent figure, which was now less than a foot from Mike, a figure Jacob now recognized as having visited him at his house not forty-five minutes before. And as it passed through this form, the bullet somehow changed – its speed, its direction; its very *form*. But whatever caused the change was not enough to keep it from its destiny, and it struck Jim full in the left side of his chest with a dull *thud* that Jacob could swear he actually heard. With a grunt, Jim fell backwards into a pile of garbage bags and old boxes. There he lay, motionless and except for his long legs, completely lost from view.

Jacob, who was still on his knees and trying to steady himself with one hand to keep from collapsing entirely, didn't have a chance to react to Jim being shot. The apparition that he had recognized as Jim's mother had finally reached Mike. A thin and hot sizzling sound joined the other noises in the trailer. Jacob looked, and saw that this second apparition, like the first entity, seemed to be entering the older boy. Unlike the first, however, this spirit never lost its form; it seemed to be simply disappearing as it went into Mike. And at every place where the now almost equally real bodies met, they were somehow joining, becoming one. Jacob realized that the sizzling sounds he heard were a part of that joining; at every place where Mrs. Stockton's spirit touched him, Mike's skin was being seared. Jacob could almost see the skin beginning to smolder, and the trailer began to fill with the sickening stench of charred flesh. Then Mrs. Stockton's form vanished completely, and only Mike could be seen, standing alone at the center of the room.

A ruinous change came over his face. It grew deathly pale, and his mouth fell open, hanging slack as spit and froth began oozing out over his chin. The fiery eyes glazed over like a cataract; they became chalky and forever sightless. And finally, a low, desperate, guttural sound began to escape from his open mouth. It might have been a moan or it might have been a wailing cry, and the sound – like the screams uttered by the boy just moments before – seemed to stretch out into eternity, filling the air around Jacob and freezing his blood.

"*Nnnnnooooooooooooo . . .*"

Jacob, unable to pull his eyes away, watched as forever seemed to have come and gone again, and still the boy stood there, motionless; thick white goo spilling from his chin onto his chest and wide, bulging eyes staring sightlessly; that horrible moaning sound still issuing from somewhere deep inside. Then, finally, the arm holding the gun began to rise. It was trembling violently, the knuckles white as they gripped the handle, but the arc it followed never faltered or slowed. As soon as the elbow bent and the barrel of the gun began to close in on its target, Jacob finally realized what was happening. He squeezed his eyes shut and put both hands over his ears, finally collapsing face down on the floor.

For the third and final time that morning, the sound of gunfire cut sharply through the small trailer. It was followed by a dull thud as Mike's body fell to the floor.

Jacob wanted desperately to keep his eyes shut, to just lie there on the floor until someone, preferably an adult – maybe, miraculously, his own mother or father – arrived on the scene and whisked him away to safety. But now a new sound had erupted in the small room, and he found that he was more afraid *not* to look. He was still laying face down, but when he opened his eyes and looked up, what he saw forced him to gather what little strength he had left and weakly scramble further away to what seemed like the safest place he could go without drawing attention to himself – against the front wall of the small den. He pulled himself into a sitting position, back to the wall, and began to watch, mesmerized, the supernatural drama playing out before his eyes.

Two forms – both of them transparent, liquid, and shimmering like the one that had first entered Mike – danced in the air above the dead boy's prone body. They spun and swirled through the air like a helix, moving together, faster and tighter until it seemed as if there was only one shape. As it rose higher and higher into the air, a whistling shriek drowned out all sounds of the storm outside. Then the spinning shape reached the ceiling, and with an enormous tearing sound, the two forms burst apart. Another cry of desperation filled the air; not the sound of one or two women, but the voices of a thousand tortured souls screaming their rage and desperation as one. As with Mike's screams and final groan of anguish, the sound seemed to stretch out into eternity, and Jacob fell facedown on the floor once more, hands over his ears, screaming his own desperation right along with the other voices. Then, slowly, the sound diminished; like the sounds Jacob had heard at the Ice House in his second dream, it was as though the cries hadn't lessened, but were coming from a great distance. And finally, only Jacob's screams could be heard; the others were completely gone.

Jacob cautiously uncovered his ears and opened his eyes. The only sounds left were those of the storm, still raging outside, and he found himself wondering if it was ever going to end. He pushed himself back up into a sitting position, keeping his eyes fixed firmly on the floor, and realized that his strength seemed to be returning.

He finally forced himself to lift his gaze and survey the scene before him.

Mike, of course, still lay in the center of the room. A large portion of the left side of his head, including part of his face, was now splattered against a wall of the trailer, and his bloody NASCAR cap lay a few feet away beside a fist-sized chunk of scalp. The right side of his head was still intact, although everything inside of it seemed to have spilled out onto the floor through the gaping left side. The one eye that was still in its proper place was no longer glazed, and seemed to be staring quite peacefully and contentedly at the ceiling. At the sight, Jacob felt a rush of dizzying nausea. He turned from the gruesome sight and gagged, but there was nothing for his stomach to send up other than a few strands of a bitter-tasting, yellowish substance, which hung from his mouth like ropes until he finally spit. A few moments of deep breathing helped the sensation to pass, and he finally sat back up and wiped his mouth.

Despite the strain of his fruitless effort to vomit, Jacob's strength – perhaps fueled by a fresh surge of adrenaline – was still returning with reassuring speed, and he finally forced himself to stand up. A wave of lightheadedness swept over him, and he braced one hand against the wall to keep his balance. Then, carefully avoiding the sight of the fallen older boy, Jacob again attempted to scan the room again. His eyes were drawn momentarily to Jared, who was lying on the floor in the far corner of the room, near the entrance to the kitchen. He was curled into a ball; into what was clearly some sort of fetal position, and his thumb was stuck firmly in his mouth. His tightly curled body was trembling violently, and tears were streaming freely from eyes that were wide with terror. Jacob was pretty sure that the boy had no idea where he was or, for that matter, *who* he was.

Then the corner of his eye caught a slight movement, and Jacob finally turned his attention to the other side of the room.

Jim had somehow dislodged himself from the pile of trash he had fallen into, but his head was still resting on one of the garbage bags as if it was a pillow. The once again recognizable shape that looked exactly like the photograph of Melinda Stockton was kneeling before the old man, but she had become transparent again, and even as he watched she was fading. The more she faded, the more Jacob could feel the air or atmosphere of the trailer returning to normal. Even as he watched, he absently began to wonder on some secondary level if maybe the strange, depressurized, suffocating sensation was the result of this spirit or angel or whatever it was breaking through some wall of reality into a world where it (she) no longer strictly belonged. Now that the atmosphere of this world was returning to normal, her place in it was closing, and closing fast.

She leaned in close to Jim, their faces now only inches apart, and began to whisper. Jacob couldn't hear what she said, but as she spoke Jim's face began to relax. His eyes, now glistening as his tears began again, seemed to shine in his face, and his mouth slowly began to form a smile. It was the first real smile Jacob had ever seen on the old man's face, and it was almost childlike in its purity and innocence. For some reason, the sight of it broke Jacob's heart, and the world became a blur as his own tears began.

And still the form of the mysterious visitor faded, until soon she was little more than a vague, shimmering shape in the air. She leaned in even closer to the old man's face, as if to kiss her only child on the cheek one last time, but before her lips could reach him, she was gone.

Outside, the storm raged on. Inside, Jacob, Jim and Jared – now all alone in the small trailer – wept.

It took only a few moments before Jacob realized that he needed to call the cops or an ambulance or something. And it occurred to him that whenever this help did arrive, it was going to be a chore to explain exactly what had happened here. But he'd have to worry about that when the time came; Jim had been shot, and could die if he didn't get help right away. Jacob considered the man's age, and suddenly realized the man might die anyway, no matter how soon help arrived. He jogged over to the old man's side. Jim looked up at him, his watery eyes still shining and, incredibly, his face still very much at peace.

He's already dying! Jacob thought. *It's too late, even if I call an ambulance; he's gonna die anyway!* Jacob's mind again returned to The World According To Hollywood, and he remembered how, in the movies, people always became calm and peaceful when they were about to take that last step over into the Great Unknown. He found himself expecting the old man to start babbling about being drawn toward a great, beautiful white light, and how all of the family and friends who'd gone on before him were waiting. He looked again, and saw Jim still smiling that weak but contented smile.

"Where's your phone?" Jacob asked in a panicky voice. "I've got to call 911!"

Jim closed his eyes and shook his head slowly. Jacob could see that every moment was costing the old man dearly. His fear was rising again, and his feelings of panic continued to grow.

"Where's your phone?" he insisted, his voice now becoming shrill. "You were shot, Mr. Hanes. I've got to get help! You need an ambulance, you need a doctor!"

"Ain't got no phone," Jim finally managed to gasp out, and Jacob's heart sank deep into his bowels. For a second he actually felt angry at the old man – who the heck doesn't have a telephone in nineteen-freakin'-ninety-nine? Less than five months from the twenty-first century? His panicked eyes darted around the trailer again, and he decided he should have expected this bit of news. He shook his head in anger, and forced himself to think calmly and rationally.

Dee-Dees! Of course! They would probably be opened by now, and even if they weren't, he remembered seeing a pay phone under the awning where the picnic tables were. He could ride his bike along the side of the highway and get there in less than five minutes, he was sure. He turned back to Jim, and was alarmed at how pale the old man's face had become. It had always been pretty sickly looking, but now it was deathly white – corpse white. Jacob wondered how much blood the old man had lost, first from the blow to the side of his head, then from the fall against the small wooden chair, and finally from the gunshot wound. But even more alarming than the deathly hue of the man's flesh was his face, which still wore an expression of complete serenity. The man was clearly dying, and he clearly didn't care! Jacob leaned into the old man's face again, and forced himself to speak slowly; to sound calm and confident, almost upbeat: *yeah, yeah, this kind of stuff happens to me all the time; no problemo, I'll handle it, just let me unpack my cape and utility belt and I'll be off!*

"Mr. Hanes, you've been shot! I'm gonna ride to Dee Dee's and call for help. Then I'll be right back!"

On hearing Jacob's repeated declaration that he'd been shot, Jim's face finally curdled into a shadow of its usual glare. *No kidding!* it seemed to say, *so* that's *what happened when the boy pointed the gun, pulled the trigger and the gun made that big bang-bang sound!*

Then, upon hearing that Jacob was about to race to Dee Dee's to call for help, Jim's face finally began to reflect fear. He shook his head violently, and spoke to Jacob in a harsh whisper. Jacob had to lean in closer than ever, straining desperately to hear the dying man's words over the tempest outside.

"No," he finally managed to croak, "You've got to finish . . . it's not just *her* now, guess maybe it never was . . . Mother told me . . ." his voice trailed off for a moment as he struggled for more breath. When he spoke again, it was as though he was speaking only to himself. "That woman, *she* brought in the others and *they're* the ones . . . all this time, it was *them*." He spoke between ragged, raspy breaths that were becoming shorter and more shallow by the second, and his eyes now cut into Jacob, deeper than ever before. "Mother said it's the charm . . . she said it has to be broken, the door will shut . . . but you've got to hurry . . . you've got to go, right now."

Jacob's false bravado shattered into a thousand pieces, each of them scurrying around on the floor like roaches in search of shelter, when he heard these words. He had seen more than enough to last him the rest of his life, even if he lived for another one hundred years. He believed that he'd just witnessed some sort of spiritual duel, and that good had prevailed, banishing the evil into some sort of other-worldly, trans-dimensional chasm from which it could never escape. Now he felt like he was right back where he started, all alone and having to face an evil that he couldn't even begin to understand. He stood up straight and took a step away from Jim, who was still struggling for breath and looking at the young boy with another expression Jacob had never seen on the creased, bearded face. This look said simply, *it's up to you, and only you. It's up to you to end this once and for all.*

Jacob felt desperation wash over him once again. *God, please,* he half prayed and half begged, *isn't this ever going to end*? He looked at Jim's face again, and knew the answer. It might, but it was up to Jacob to make it happen.

Jim saw the decision in Jacob's eyes, and his face finally relaxed again. He gathered himself, then spoke again in that same raspy whisper, which grew weaker and weaker with each passing moment.

"It's the tree . . . the big oak by that trailer you boys play at . . . she's at the tree." Jim took another breath, this one little more than a wheeze. "Hurry . . . and be careful." He smiled weakly, and Jacob, in spite of himself and the situation, found himself smiling back, albeit grimly. Then he turned and ran to the door, pausing one last time to look back. Jim's eyes were closed, but his mouth was moving in a steady whisper. Jacob strained his ears, and realized that, perhaps for the first time in his life, the old man was praying. He was praying for forgiveness of a life of drunkenness, bitterness, and hate. He was praying for the salvation of his old and once-bitter soul. And he was praying that God would help and protect the young boy who now meant so much to an old man who was finally ready to accept love and forgiveness – the two things he'd never felt he deserved to have. As each word was spoken, Jim's face seemed to be more at peace, and Jacob felt a strange sort of peace settle over his own heart. With renewed determination, he turned and passed through the door of the trailer and into the raging storm.

Jacob was soaked through to the skin before he'd even rounded the side of the trailer. His scalp, neck, and back stung from pea-sized hail that was mingled with the rain, but he hoped that once screened by the sheltering tree and overhang in the woods, it wouldn't be as bad. He ran past the lonely pine, flinching and ducking every time the lightning flashed and thunder ripped across the sky, and slipped carefully under the fence. He then turned left, walking quickly but carefully alongside the fence, scanning the earth carefully to make sure he didn't miss the trail. He had no intention of repeating the episode in which he almost lost his way in the woods earlier. Whether it was due to these efforts or because the sky finally contained a little more gray light, Jacob couldn't say, but he found the overgrown trail pretty easily this time, and was able to follow it back to his bike without losing his way. And, as he'd hoped, once under the canopy provided by the trees, he was no longer getting pelted by the rain and hail, although the water-drops falling from the leaves and branches were at least twice as large as those falling from the sky. He had almost reached his bicycle when he had another experience that he almost offhandedly filed away as yet another supernatural event. These events were becoming almost commonplace enough that they no longer shocked the boy.

Just as he had gotten within sight of his bike, a searing flash of lightning had blazed across the sky and into the woods, turning the entire world a bluish white. The thunderous crash had followed immediately afterward, threatening to split the earth wide open. Jacob screamed and fell to his knees; hands firmly over his ears and eyes squeezed shut. Several seconds passed before he dared to open his eyes and stand back up. When he did, the image and shape of the lightning, now a deep blue, still danced before his eyes like spots from a flashbulb. There was a metallic, flinty smell in the air that reminded him of a cigarette lighter. He stood there a moment longer, and as the image of the lightening finally faded something else suddenly caught his eye. He began jogging and saw, hanging from the limb of a small tree next to his bike, a small cross on a chain. He recognized it immediately, although the last time he'd seen it, it had been a fuzzy blur in a grainy, black and white photograph. Purely on instinct, Jacob reached out and grabbed it. He studied the tarnished gold in wonder for a moment, then carefully slipped the chain over his neck and finally hopped on his bike. Soon he was riding as quickly as he dared along the muddy trails.

He kept his head down as he rode in order to keep his vision clear of those oversized water drops that, every time a gust of wind came howling through the treetops, fell around him almost as thickly as the rain. He also discovered pretty quickly that, in some places over the trail, the canopy was pretty thin and in others, it was completely missing. In those places he could once again feel the hail mingled with the cold rain, stinging his face and neck, and he had to shade his eyes with one hand, making it even more difficult to maneuver the slick, muddy trails while at the same time reducing his field of vision.

This was why he didn't see the pine tree that had fallen directly across the path in front of him until it was almost too late. When he finally did see it, he knew immediately that even if he hit the brakes with every bit of his strength and weight, he'd never stop in time; the front tire of his bike would hit the tree, and he'd likely be thrown from the bike. Instead, he reacted purely on instinct – he grabbed the handlebars with the hand he'd been using to shield his face from the rain and hail and hit the brakes hard while at the same time leaning in and turning the handlebars a little to the left. He immediately went down on one side, sliding over the slick mud and pine needles. Just as he'd planned, the bike hit the tree tires first, and he was jerked to a sudden stop without the danger of being thrown. Unlike he'd planned, Jacob (who was still technically astride the bike, even though it was now on its side) took a moderate jolt directly to his privates. A dull but sickening pain started at the point of impact, worked its way up to his belly, and finally stopped in his lower back. For a moment he just lay there, allowing himself a short but heartfelt groan, before he finally got back to his feet. His entire left side was now smeared with mud and grime, and he had a few new scrapes on the outside of his left leg. But, all things considered, Jacob knew it could have been a lot worse (especially the blow he'd taken to what he considered to be, if not the most important, definitely the most sensitive part of his anatomy).

He turned and glared at the tree angrily, as if it had fallen across the path intentionally, just to get in his way, or maybe even injure him. Then he realized that this foolish idea might actually be a real possibility. Although it wasn't a huge tree, maybe two feet in circumference, it was big enough to have ruined his bike and maybe hurt him seriously had he run into it head on. Whether it had been blown down or felled by that same stroke of lightning that had nearly blinded him a few moments before, Jacob couldn't say. And, at this particular moment, he didn't have the time to pause and consider even if he'd wanted to. Instead, he carefully lifted the bike over the tree, then stepped over it himself. Then he gingerly resumed his position on the seat of the bike and began to pedal again.

He had two more spills on his bike as he continued struggling to maneuver the slick, muddy trails with just one hand, but none were as bad as his near miss with the fallen pine. And finally, with the rain still falling as thickly as ever, with the wind howling, and the sky now positively dancing with lightning, Jacob rode his bike into the clearing.

27

He found the calm that enveloped the small clearing both surprising and unsettling. He had expected the scene to be like his last nightmare come to life – the old oak alive and writhing while oozing slimy, unnamed things from its bark and the tips of its branches. And at the center of the clearing, dust and leaves swirling around her like a small tornado, would be the no-longer-quite-dead maid Della Hanes, her beautiful but deathly pale body endowed with some type of power that wasn't exactly life, but rather an evil mockery of it.

Instead, the clearing seemed to be almost sheltered from the storm; although the rain and hail continued to fall and Jacob could still see flashes of lightning streaking across the sky, the sounds – the very power – of the storm seemed somehow distant, unimportant. A scene-setting backdrop.

Jacob finally turned his attention to the old oak standing beside the Ice House, and here he saw that at least one fragment of that terrible dream had made its way out into the real world. The wide trunk of the tree had either split or been torn wide open. It yawned like a cavern, at least six feet high and over three feet wide at the ground. And yes, a darkness that he could almost see seemed to spill out into the air of the clearing.

Jacob almost turned and ran. And later on, he would never be able to say exactly why he didn't. It certainly wasn't courage that kept him there. At that moment, he wanted nothing more than to be safe at home, tucked in safely between his mom and dad. He would even have settled for being back on the floor of his bedroom, listening to David's obnoxious snoring.

David! Jacob suddenly realized he had forgotten all about his friend. From the moment he had struck out all alone on his bike, he had thought of nothing but the mission, believing that, once he and Jim had talked and worked things out, everything would be over and he could head home, mission accomplished, and maybe sit down and tell David all about it over a bowl of Lucky Charms or a Pop-Tart. Then Jared and Mike had shown up, and everything had gone straight to hell. No, that wasn't really right, was it? What really happened was that *she* had shown up, and had brought hell with her. Now Mike was dead, Jim was dying, and Jared seemed to be quite the vegetable. Jacob believed that Jared was now probably much further down the road to madness than Crazy Mary herself could possibly have been.

This last thought, for some reason, almost made Jacob lose it. Desperate, nauseating panic hit him hard in the gut. He put both hands on his head, grabbing and pulling at clumps of his soaked hair and clenching his jaws, trying to force himself to remain calm.

How could any of this be happening? And he didn't just mean the fact that, apparently, the spirits of the dead – and from what Jim had just told him, maybe something worse – were now walking among the living. Mike was *dead*! He was *really* dead! He was completely, totally, beyond all hope dead; no silent candlelight vigil or pray-in down at the church house or modern miracle of science would ever bring him back. Whatever hopes and dreams the boy might have once had were now gone, forever beyond recall. He would never grow up to maybe work for his father in the shop and even, one day, take over the family business. Nor would he ever grow up to be some unambitious, jobless statistic – his time evenly divided between standing in line waiting for his monthly check, and wasting away in a slummy house or apartment; drunk, high, or both. He would never again fall in love (or lust), get some girl pregnant, and have to decide if he was going to marry her or not. Nor would he ever (and this thought really seemed to stick Jacob like a knife right in the pit of his stomach and twist around in the wound) have a chance at redemption. He would never decide that there was more to life than the niche he was so eagerly carving out for himself, that he didn't *have* to grow up and be just another version of his father, he didn't *have* to wear hate like a badge, as a replacement for the love he'd never known. All those choices, all those worries, all those opportunities were now forever beyond his reach because he was currently lying on his back in the middle of Jim's trailer, his ruinous head resting in a puddle of his own blood and brains, his one remaining eye staring calmly and patiently at the ceiling.

Jim was dying, Jared was balled up on the floor, sucking his thumb and crying, staring wide-eyed at everything but seeing nothing at all. But Mike was gone forever, no ambulance or surgeon or psychiatrist could do a single thing to help that boy.

Another wave of nausea, just as powerful as the one that had hit him when he first looked upon Mike's shattered head, washed over Jacob. He doubled over and tried to clutch at his stomach, certain he was about to have another fruitless fit of dry-heaving. He was tempted to stick his fingers down his throat and make it happen. But, as he went to his knees, his eyes fell upon the tarnished cross that dangled out before him, hanging loosely from around his neck. For no reason that he could understand, he grabbed it, squeezing it so tightly in his hands that it actually hurt. He lifted it to his face and pressed it against his cheek, trying almost franticly to take comfort and hope from the small, tarnished piece of metal and what it represented. And finally, his mind flashed back to the brief prayer he'd uttered before setting out, his desperate entreaty to God.

Help me . . . please.

No peaceful, reassuring calm settled around his heart, nor did he feel a sudden surge of energy coursing through his blood. He didn't feel any braver than he had just seconds before. What Jacob did feel, suddenly and unexpectedly, was the return of that sense of urgency that had plagued him since he had first awakened. That, and a flicker of hope. It was too late for Mike; he was dead now and would be dead forever. But it wasn't too late for Jim and Jared, not yet.

Yes, Jim *and* Jared. Jacob had truly believed he hated that boy with a cold and bitter hatred that would never die from the moment Jared had played that cruel prank on him outside Jim's trailer almost a week ago. He couldn't imagine ever feeling anything *but* hate for the boy. But the shock of what he'd seen was now replaced by the reality of it, and a great pity swelled inside Jacob's heart. That woman – that spirit or whatever – had been *inside* of Jared, and the consequence was pretty obvious. Jacob forced himself to remember what he'd seen – the image of Jared's eyes, once so cold and calculating and powerful, now empty and lost, staring vacantly out of an expressionless face as those tears flowed endlessly and his body rocked to and fro and he was *sucking his thumb* . . .

There *was* still hope, no matter how small, for both Jared and Jim. But, as Jim had said, the door had to be closed. And it was up to Jacob, who still felt at least partially responsible for opening it, to do so.

He stood back up, a little unsteadily, and lifted the chain from around his neck. Then, holding the cross out before him like a vampire-hunter from one of those late-night, low-budget horror movies he sometimes watched on TV, Jacob began slowly walking toward the old tree.

The sound of each and every footfall seemed to thump loudly in his ears and, when combined with the throbbing heartbeat that pulsed in his ears and behind his eyes, sounded like some slow, monotonous cadence that he was walking in rhythm with. Maybe the kind that accompanies a horse-drawn hearse moving slowly up an otherwise abandoned street, a gloomy fog rolling along and mixing with a light, misty rain.

As Jacob continued his slow but unfaltering approach of the ancient tree, all of those strange notions he'd had about it came flooding back, taunting and threatening his already tense and uneasy mind. A monument . . . a sentinel . . . a warning. Had he really thought those things, or just dreamed them? He couldn't remember, and knew that it really didn't matter. All that mattered was that each and every one of those words accurately described what he was now looking at. How truly Jim had spoken, when he'd said the place wasn't safe; *really never was*.

And here I am, Jacob thought almost bitterly, *knowing all that stuff, here I am, all alone!*

He finally stopped when he was maybe ten feet from the tree and its gaping, cavernous opening. It still seemed as if darkness was actually spilling out of this opening, and Jacob didn't even try to convince himself that it was just an illusion; a shadow caused by the vague, gray light of the storm and early hour. Nor did he try to convince himself that there wasn't an unpleasant odor in the air, as well. He had noticed it growing with every step, and now it filled the air all around him. It wasn't, however, the same foul reek of death and decay that he'd smelled before, first in his dream and then with David in the Ice House yesterday. This time it was milder – a thick, gassy, almost swampy smell. Like wet, rotting mulch and old leaves, moldy and mildewed, caked around the edges of some scummy, stagnant bog. Jacob leaned forward, straining his eyes and trying to somehow see into the darkness of the cavern without getting any closer, but it was a wasted effort; he was staring into the same impenetrable blackness that had awaited him at the bottom of those stairs in his second dream.

Jacob's heart quailed again; he could not imagine actually standing beside the tree, hands braced against the sides of the trunk that had been torn open by something other than the forces of nature, trying to peer into that darkness. And he certainly couldn't imagine trying to squeeze into that narrow opening when heaven knows what was surely awaiting him, its eyes burning through the pitch black, its teeth bared in a hideous grin of anticipation.

His eyes searched the clearing frantically; looking for nothing in particular, just anything that might help even a little – maybe a big stick he could use to poke around in the opening a little to make sure it was empty (although he already knew full well that it wasn't). They finally came to rest on the half-open door to the Ice House. He remembered his and David's desperate flight from the day before – they had fled in blind terror, leaving the door of the trailer wide open and all of David's treasures scattered on the floor. Suddenly, his heart leapt! The lantern – it was one of the things they'd left behind. He turned and raced to the little clubhouse, flinging the door open wide. Sure enough, the lantern was there, sitting on the table at the back of the trailer. Jacob hesitated. Hadn't he and David left all that stuff scattered on the floor when they'd made their hasty exit? He knew for a fact that they did – but there it was, sitting back on the table. Jacob studied the inside of the Ice House uneasily, but saw nothing to alarm him, other than the fact that someone had come in and cleaned up the mess he and David had left. But who would do that? It took only a few seconds for Jacob to put the pieces together

– Jared. *He must have shown up yesterday after me and David left*, Jacob thought. *That's how She got to him!*

In a flash, the memory of the obscenity he and David had seen came rushing back, and Jacob whirled around, flinching, to look at the pin-up on the wall. There was nothing to flinch about, however, the figure had returned to her natural, beautiful, naked self, once again smiling that seductive smile as if nothing at all was wrong with this place, as if it hadn't been the scene of unspeakable horror. Jacob, however, was taking no chances. He stepped up into the trailer, ripped the picture off the wall, and tore it into shreds. Then, without a second thought, Jacob raced to the back of the trailer and, turning warily to watch the doorway, reached out with his right hand to pick up his prize. Immediately, and with unbelievable speed and force, the door began to swing shut. With a cry, Jacob grabbed the lantern, cleared the length of the trailer in two gigantic strides, and flung himself at the door just as it was about to slam shut. All he managed to get through the vanishing opening was his right arm, which still clung to the lantern, before it closed on him like a vice, pinning him between the edge of the door and the doorframe. Jacob cried out again in fear and pain, and dropped the lantern to the ground. And the door was *still* pushing against him, cutting into his ribs and right shoulder. He could still hear the vague, distant sounds of the storm echoing through the clearing, but mingling with that noise was a new sound – skittering, rattling whispers and laughter, distant at first, but drawing ever closer. Jacob began struggling wildly, squealing like a trapped animal and shouting out words he could barely understand in a high-pitched, fainting voice – *stop, go away, leave me alone!* His words went unheeded as the urgent sounds drew ever closer, soon whatever was making them would seize his arm with icy, dead hands and pull him, screaming, out of the trailer. That, or maybe just continue to push the door with such force that it would sever his arm right off as the door finally slammed shut with a bang (followed by a sharp *snick* as lock slipped into place), leaving him to bleed to death in the lonely dark of the trailer.

Both of these images burned in his terrified mind and suddenly – again acting purely on impulse – he squeezed his left hand out through the narrow opening and brandished the small cross like some sort of oriflamme. He felt some strength returning to his diaphragm, and, his voice, no longer shrill, screamed out, "*GO . . . AWAY!*"

It worked. The whispering voices were suddenly silent, and whatever force that had held the door was suddenly gone. It flew open, and Jacob fell face-first to the muddy ground. He jumped to his feet immediately, still holding the cross before him, and searched the clearing. He didn't see anything, but he did not feel at all alone. Whatever it was that he had heard whispering, that had tried to shut him in the trailer, was still out there, somewhere beyond his mortal sight and only held at bay, Jacob assumed, by the small, time-spanning cross in his hand.

He bent over, picking up the lantern that lay at his feet, and gave it a quick inspection; afraid it had been broken when he dropped it. There was a small crack in the plastic housing around the small bulb, but otherwise it looked okay. He turned the switch, and the bulb began to glow reassuringly. Then, emboldened by both the light and the small cross he carried – something he now felt confident had the power to keep whatever darkness he now faced at bay – Jacob turned with a grim face back to the old oak.

He approached it with both hands held out before him, one holding the light-bearing lantern, the other holding the small, lackluster cross. When he finally reached the cavernous tear in the tree, he took a deep breath and, still holding his two weapons out before him, peered cautiously inside.

At first he saw nothing but the dark, half rotted insides of a hollowed-out tree. There were a few beetles scurrying about, obviously flustered and excited about the sudden, unexpected light that now filled their home. There were also a few slugs and grubs that would also probably be scurrying if they had been able, and a slimy film on the inside walls of the tree; all the things a curious boy could expect to find in a rotted tree or stump. Then, as his eyes adjusted to the heavy darkness, Jacob leaned in closer and looked deeper into bottom of the tree. There, amid the mud and roots and decay, two empty eye-sockets stared back at him.

Jacob gasped loudly and jerked back, again holding the cross before him as a shield, expecting the reanimated body to suddenly spring forth from its disturbed resting place. The empty sockets would burn with that now all-too-familiar fire, and at last she would have him. But none of it happened. Lightning, still thick and bright but somehow unthreatening, forked across the sky above him. Thunder, heavy enough to make the earth tremble but still somehow muffled, rolled across the same sky. That sense of watching and waiting still filled the clearing. And yet nothing happened.

Jacob swallowed hard, held the lantern out, and looked again, this time actually leaning into the opening of the tree. Now he could see the entire body, or what was left of it, anyway. Most of it was caked with mud and dirt, and old roots were intertwined throughout; one seemed to wrap around a leg, another weaved in and out of the ribcage, and one had burrowed into an empty eye-socket. Most skulls seem to wear a perpetual grin, but the jawbone of this one had come unhinged and fallen upon its breast, creating the illusion that it was screaming out in fear and rage. Jacob wondered if this really *was* just an illusion, and he shuddered. He moved the lantern a little closer to get a better view, causing the shadows to glide across both the body and tangled roots. Now it looked as if the body and roots *were* alive, cringing and scrambling against the intruding light as the bugs had done.

A few rags that had probably once been clothing still clung tightly to the bony corpse, and twinkling from beneath one of those folds, Jacob finally saw what he'd been looking for. The chain it hung on was tarnished and rusted, but the small, round trinket sparkled and gleamed like new in the light. Jacob's eyes strained into the gloom, trying to get a better look. It looked like a bright, silvery crystal that, despite where it had now rested for well over half a century, didn't appear to have a single blemish. Engraved in the crystal-like stone was the image of the palm of a hand, a staring, lidless eye at its center, and its entire border was adorned with symbols Jacob had never seen before. In a fascinated, almost trance-like state, Jacob reached out his hand to take it. His fingers got within maybe of foot of the strange amulet before he was reminded of the unnatural power he was facing.

The entire body began to shudder, and the skull tilted toward him, its teeth suddenly clicking together with an angry, creepy sound that reminded Jacob of one of those chattering, wind-up toys. Out of the depths of the ground there appeared the ghostly shapes of two disembodied heads. Their foreheads and jaws were both unusually large and desperately malformed, and their twisted ears stuck out at odd angles. Both shapes were a sickly, pallid color and hairless, with wild eyes set in small, scrunched-up faces that somehow looked both ancient and newborn. The toothless mouths were opened wide, and Jacob could hear the sounds of shrieking moans building up, as if about to explode from the center of the earth. He jerked back with a cry, again holding up the cross like a shield. Immediately, the two ghostly faces dissipated, and the shuck-and-jive boogey of the skeletal corpse stopped without another twitch.

Jacob jumped back from the opening and, still holding the cross up before him, simply stood there, breathing hard and shaking violently. Whatever it was that had just happened had somehow increased both his terror and his faith in the power of the amulet he now bore over the one waiting for him in the darkness of what he now officially thought of as Della Hanes' grave. Again he forced himself to remember the urgency of the situation, and then tried to make himself calm down. His breathing became deep and slow, but the violent trembling still racked his body. Finally, with a set jaw, he took another look around the clearing (just to be safe), and tried again.

This time, he slipped the handle of the lantern over his forearm, freeing up his right hand. Then, making sure the cross in his left hand remained out front, he again approached the opening in the tree. He peered in again, and saw that everything remained unchanged from his first peek; bugs, roots and skeleton were all exactly where they'd been before. Jacob took another deep breath and held it, and this time, bracing his left elbow against the side of the tree, actually stepped into the tree with his right foot. It came to rest on something soft and yielding. He face grew mildly queasy (*it's probably just a root, man, that's all, it's a root and not some nasty, rotted part of Her body*) as he put a little weight on the foot, making sure that whatever he was trying to balance on would hold. He then double-checked his left foot, which was braced on one of the larger, twisted roots outside of the tree. When he felt sure that he would be able to keep his balance, he leaned back into the tree, spent a few seconds screwing up his nerve by counting to three, then, wearing an expression of desperation and revulsion, made a quick grab for the amulet. It felt like ice in his hand, and he had just enough time to think *I got it!* before absolute darkness, blacker than any he'd ever known, completely engulfed him, and he was falling.

Jacob's eyes were wide, but he could see nothing at all. All around him was that complete and total darkness – the black dark of nothingness, emptiness; the black dark of Genesis, of *"In the beginning . . .*" He could no longer feel the weight of the lantern hanging on his arm, but he could still feel both the strange crystal squeezed tightly in his right hand, and the small, faded cross in his left. The former seemed to be freezing into his very bone, while the latter had begun to give off a calm heat. It didn't burn him, but he could feel the warmth coursing through him, holding the icy-cold of the other amulet at bay. Still Jacob fell, and now, to his great terror, he realized that he *could* see something. Those pallid, grotesquely malformed, disembodied heads suddenly began to appear again out of the heavy blackness, swooping and swirling all around him as he continued to fall. There were hundreds of them, thousands of them, *millions* of them. Some were right beside him, others were only specks that bunched together like galaxies in the distance, the rest filled the space in between, but all had wild eyes that stared directly at him; all were shrieking through those gaping, toothless mouths. Jacob squeezed his eyes shut and began to scream himself, and now his ears and mind were filled with nothing but the sounds of those horrible shrieks and his own screams. Underlying it all was the sound of rushing wind that grew and grew until all else was shut out. Then suddenly, all the sounds were gone, and Jacob found himself standing on solid ground in complete silence.

There was no jarring impact, as if after that seemingly endless sensation of falling he had finally landed miraculously on his feet. Instead, he was simply standing, as if the fall had never happened, although there was still a vague sense of dizziness and disorientation. Jacob looked down and opened his eyes. Sure enough, his feet were firmly set on the floor. Not the wet, muddy ground of the clearing or the damp, moldy roots and decay inside the tree, but a floor made of strips of slightly dusty wood. A hazy light seemed to fill the air.

Jacob finally looked up, caught between the relief of being away from those creepy, bizarre floating heads, and the growing panic of not knowing where he had escaped safely to. In a sharp but soundless gasp, he caught his breath and took two steps back. Standing before him was Della Hanes.

There was no mistaking her, although she was now more incredibly beautiful than he could have possibly imagined. Gone was the deadly, cold, hollow mockery of beauty. Her skin, no longer deathly white but a rich mocha color, was flawless, as was her face. As was, in fact, her whole body. She was, without a doubt, the most stunning woman Jacob had ever laid eyes on. And there, hanging from her neck on a silvery chain and glistening in the weak light was the same amulet that he still felt freezing like ice in the palm of his right hand. As he stared at her, dumbfounded, she looked right at him, as if seeing him for the first time. She seemed surprised.

"What are you doing down here?" she asked. Or rather, she *appeared* to ask; Jacob hadn't heard a single word that came out of her mouth. In fact, he realized that he couldn't hear anything, the air was filled with the kind of silence that is so complete that he should have been able to hear his own breathing, even his own heartbeat. But he heard nothing, absolutely *nothing*, a state that multiplied his fear and confusion exponentially.

The young lady took a step toward him, and seemed to repeat herself, "Why are you down here?"

"I don't know," Jacob tried to answer in what he was afraid would be a high-pitched, panicky voice. He was only a little shocked to discover he couldn't hear his own voice, either.

Della took another few steps toward him, and Jacob involuntarily jumped back. As he did so, a chilly wind seemed to blow right through him, and suddenly there was someone else standing between him and the young maid. It took Jacob mere seconds to figure out that she hadn't speaking to him at all; she'd been speaking to whoever this was that now stood before him. Maybe one more second passed before Jacob figured out who that other person was, and maybe a millisecond after that, he finally understood what was happening. He could hardly believe it, even though he was seeing it, seeing it just as clearly as he'd seen Mike, Jared and Jim earlier this morning. Only, if he was right, it was no longer this morning. It was late in the evening of October 31! And the year was 1933!

Jacob's heart turned cold as he realized that he was finally about to discover the answer to the one question he'd been asking almost from the moment he'd had that first, haunting dream – exactly what had happened that night? He somehow had gotten a front-row ticket, and was about to witness whatever had happened firsthand. He backed away a few more steps, stopping beside a crate upon which rested a small lantern, the only source of light in the otherwise dark basement. Then, with his heart beating furiously in his chest, Jacob watched history unfolding before his eyes.

The healthy, well-dressed young boy, who would grow up to be a trailer-dwelling, alcoholic bum, was now speaking to the lady. His face wasn't angry; it was pleading, but it was also set and resolute. It was clear that he wasn't going to back down. He was also very animated, waving his arms and pointing, but not in a threatening way. Like his face, his movements seemed to be imploring, almost begging.

For a few happy moments it appeared as if his words seemed to be reaching their mark. Della's face, which at first had been as resolute as young James's, began to soften. She nodded understandingly a few times, then shook her head a few times. She also interrupted him several times, as if trying to make a case for herself, but it seemed as though the boy had a rebuttal for whatever argument Della made – he had been planning this confrontation, she had pretty much been ambushed.

Finally, the young lady lowered her head and nodded, and James seemed to grow a little excited. It lasted only for a moment.

Suddenly, both of them started, jerking their heads in the direction of the stairs, which were to Jacob's left. There, still two or three steps up, one hand clutching his own lantern, stood James Stockton I. The look of surprise on his face was so complete that it was almost comical, but that illusion lasted only a few seconds. It quickly melted away to complete and utter rage, which seemed to be directed primarily at his son. He barreled his way down the few remaining steps, his face red and quivering, his finger pointing at the young boy, whose resolution had given way to pale, unmasked fear.

Just as he was closing in, the maid suddenly stepped between them, arms upraised, trying to shield the boy while at the same time trying to calm down his raging father. James, Sr. pushed her roughly to one side, then loomed over his son, teeth bared, threatening the terrified boy with words that Jacob, for the first time since arriving at this place, was glad he couldn't hear.

Then Della was back, gripping the older man by the shoulder and forcing him to turn and face her. Eyes that would one day burn like a flame were almost burning now, with hatred and defiance. She pointed one finger almost in his face, and Jacob was sure that if her mouth could have spewed acid instead of words, it would have. Then they were both at it: both pointing, both shouting, both boring into each other with malice-filled eyes. Della finally stopped shouting long enough to let Stockton complete whatever venomous, hate-filled phrase was rampaging from his twisted, sputtering mouth. She took two steps back and, now wearing an expression of cold, smirking irony, announced *I'm pregnant!*

Jacob, who had almost managed to adjust to the complete silence as he watched this fearful drama play out, saw her lips form these words quite clearly. And ironically, although he was the only one there who couldn't actually hear the words, he seemed to be the only one who had understood what she had said.

Father and Son Stockton both just stood there, opened mouthed, staring at the young lady with stricken faces. And she smiled a taunting, mocking smile as she repeated the earth-shattering news – *that's right, you filthy, cold-hearted pig. Pregnant, and it's yours!*

Jacob's eyes went instinctively to those of the younger James. The boy's face had gone pale as he listened to this news, and his eyes now drifted almost listlessly back and forth between his father and the young maid. They finally came to rest on his father, and an incredible change came over his face; rage and hate came bubbling out like a festering boil. He launched himself at the elder James, screaming out words that Jacob could neither hear nor understand. His father, however, was both unphased and unimpressed by the boy's sudden attack. He grabbed his young son by the arm, slapped his face, and pushed him roughly back into a stack of crates. The young boy fell in a heap, knocking over the large, wooden boxes, and came to rest on the floor. Only Jacob seemed to notice that the small lantern that had been set on one of these crates had fallen to the ground and had rolled into a corner, behind some other boxes and crates. He ran over to look and, sure enough, it lay on its side; the small flame of the lantern still flickering as a small puddle of oil began to form at its base. He instinctively reached out to pick it up, but his hand simply passed through it as if it weren't even there. *Wrong again, idiot*, Jacob thought to himself in a crazy, desperate, laughing voice, *Let's get it right, dude. The lantern's here, but* you're *not!* With a shock that almost felt like a blow to the gut, Jacob realized for the first time what it really meant to be here as an observer only. What he was watching had already happened, and there was absolutely nothing he could do to stop it.

Despite this knowledge, he turned desperately to the small group, trying to scream at the top of his lungs; trying to warn the rest of the group of what was going to happen. What had *already* happened. But of course, no sound came, and the group moved on toward a destiny none had expected only ten minutes ago.

Watching the three of them, Jacob wasn't sure they would have noticed him even if they *could* hear him. Della had attacked the older James, her claws raised and extended like a panther, but though her rage and hate gave her a fierceness that the younger James lacked, it was still a wasted effort. Stockton wrestled her to the ground, one hand around her throat, the other slapping at her face, over and over. The younger James tried his luck again, this time hitting his father in the back of the head with a broomstick that had been lying in the corner. Mr. Stockton seemed to be stunned for just a moment, and finally released the young lady. He stood up, grabbed his son by the arm and slapped him again, this time a vicious, backhanded number that sent the boy spinning. Della used this opportunity to get to her knees, grab the elder James by the leg with both hands, and bite his calf hard enough to not just draw blood, but to actually tear a chunk of flesh loose.

The man looked down in shock and seemed to bellow in pain before he hit her again. This time it was no angry, frustrated slap meant to calm her down or teach her a lesson. He hit her full in the face with a tight fist, and she fell back, stunned by the blow. Then he grabbed her by the hair with both hands and slammed her head against the floor. She collapsed completely, and then he was astride her, both hands locked firmly around her throat.

Jacob watched it all with an expression of complete horror. He wanted to turn away, to close his eyes, to hide his face in his hands, but he couldn't seem to even move. And finally, as he saw the blood flowing from her nose and mouth (the blood around her mouth was actually her attacker's, a trophy from the vicious bite she'd given him), as he saw the bruises and lumps that had risen on her face take on a dark, purplish hue, as he saw the fierce defiance in her eyes giving way to unmasked fear as she finally realized what was happening, Jacob felt his own rage and hatred of the man well up inside. He knew that it was a pointless, wasted effort – he was nothing more than an unseen ghost here; a phantom, not even a shadow – but still he charged at the old man. And, just as a part of him knew would happen, he simply passed through both man and woman, and ended up sprawled on the floor, just as the younger James had. He turned to look again, his vision now blurred by the tears of sorrow, rage and impotence filling his eyes.

Della's face had gone slack, and her eyes had a vacant, far-away look to them. Her arms and hands still struggled against the man, but it was a losing battle, a lost battle, and they slowly gave up their grip and fell to the floor. And still Stockton squeezed, his eyes wild and frantic and full of excited hate.

Then, with a suddenness that surprised Jacob and James Stockton alike, the fierce defiance returned to the young woman's eyes. One of the limp hands suddenly went to her chest, grabbing at the charm that hung there and squeezing it tight. She looked directly at the man astride her, a man who had once professed love for her, a man who had taken her, used her over and over to slake his darkest lusts; to do for him the things his wife would never have done. And now, this night, he would take from her again, take the one thing she had sworn he would never have: the lives of both her and her unborn child. She glared at that man with her fierce, defiant eyes and, for the last time, spoke. Jacob was shocked to discover he could actually hear her. And though he didn't understand the meaning of the words that came from her mouth, the power of the words seemed to cut through him like a blade of ice.

I swear my very soul to you; my soul for his

Her lips curled into a bitter, smirking snarl, and her eyes blazed defiantly one last time. Then her eyelids began to flutter, her eyes became lackluster, and finally seemed to roll back in her head until nothing but white was visible. The snarl melted away into a grimace, and the body began to buck, as if she were coughing. Finally, with a last wheeze that looked almost like a relieved sigh, the body grew still.

The elder Stockton finally released her. He held his hands out and stared at them for a moment as if he had never seen them before and had no idea exactly what they were. Then, his red face now dripping with sweat, his chest heaving for breath like a racehorse, he finally stood. For a few seconds the father and son just stared, struck mute by shock, at Della Hanes' lifeless body. Her face was already taking on an unnatural hue; the whites of the eyes were still all that showed beneath the drooping eyelids, and her tongue lolled out through the corner of her mouth over a slack, hanging jaw. Jacob stood unsteadily, devastated by what he'd seen, but somehow almost relieved it was finally over. He quickly found out how wrong he was.

As he stood there, unwillingly remembering the look on Della's face when she'd realized that she was about to die, then seeing again that fierce defiance that had glowed in her face to the last; watching Mr. Stockton and his son James as they both stared unbelievingly at her limp body; and almost casually wondering if the inexorable fire from the overturned lantern had caught yet, the world around him suddenly changed again. It became not so much blurred as smeared, as if it were a painting someone had wiped a damp cloth across. He stood perfectly still, once again fighting a sensation of vertigo, as he watched the scenes around him spin by at an impossible speed. Then, as abruptly as it had started, it stopped. The world came back into focus, but it was now much darker.

Jacob was standing in a clearing in the woods, lit only by a full moon that shone brightly through the opening in the trees above him. He looked around cautiously, realizing that he knew this place, and knew it well – it was the clearing where he'd been standing only moments ago, before setting off on this involuntary, time-traveling, trans-dimensional expedition. Only now it was larger than he remembered it, with patches of tall grass growing where he remembered only dirt. The old refrigerator trailer was no longer in its accustomed spot – or, more accurately, had not yet been placed there – and the ancient oak was sixty-plus years younger, though it was still bigger than your average tree. But there was no mistaking the place.

A twinkling light caught Jacob's attention. He turned to look, and here came both Mr. Stockton and his son. The elder had the lantern he'd brought to the cellar hung over his forearm, the same way Jacob had when he'd peered into the tree earlier. Both of his hands were full; one held a shovel, the other gripped one of Della Hanes' limp wrists. His face was set and grim.

Following behind, each arm locked around one of the dead woman's legs, weeping desperately and shaking like a frail leaf in a high breeze, was his son. He staggered a few times, but never fell. Jacob wasn't sure if that was because of some sort of determination that there be at least a little dignity in this unofficial funeral ceremony, or out of fear of what his father would do if he should fall or drop their lifeless cargo. Both James and his father were soaked with sweat from their toil.

Dignity and poise seemed to be the last thing on the elder Stockton's mind. When he was maybe ten feet from the tree, he simply let go of the arm, and the top half of the body fell rudely to the ground. The younger James had not been expecting this, and he stumbled again, this time falling roughly right on top of the corpse. With a cry, he scrambled away to a distance of ten or twelve feet, then just sat there, his arms wrapped around knees that were drawn up to his chest, still weeping and shaking violently as he rocked back and forth, back and forth. His eyes never left the limp, crumpled body that lay in a heap on the dirty ground.

Mr. Stockton watched all this with an expression of cruel amusement before cutting the boy a withering glance and shooting another withering comment at him. As before, Jacob couldn't hear a single thing, but he didn't have to hear the words to know that they were calculating and cruel – the first of many such words, each and every one of which would stay with the boy throughout his entire life.

The man then turned back toward the tree and, starting maybe three feet from its base, began to dig. He went through no more than fifteen shovel-fulls, working around the larger roots and chopping through the smaller ones. Then he stopped abruptly. He turned and said something to his son. Young James began to shake his head, rocking back and forth even faster, and his crying became a wail. His father's face became twisted in anger; he shouted at the boy, waved one of his arms around wildly, and finally pointed at the boy while making what Jacob assumed was another threat as his cold eyes glared.

James finally got to his feet and, still wailing and trembling, walked obediently to his father, took the shovel, and began to dig. Mr. Stockton took a few steps back and placed his hands on his hips, every once in a while shouting something. He looked like a foreman, supervising the workers at one of his sawmills. Every time he shouted, his son would flinch, but kept right on digging.

Jacob watched with pity and revulsion, thinking, *no wonder he grew up to be what he is. No wonder he grew up thinking it was his fault*. His father had heaped an almost unbearable burden upon the boy's shoulders, a burden that should never have been his. And he had carried it, crawling on his hands and knees, for sixty-six years.

He watched as the man stood there, hands still on hips and barking orders out at his son, as the grave grew ever deeper. Jacob's pity was replaced by anger and hatred, and he found himself willing every bit of it at the elder Stockton. Every ounce of rage he'd ever felt in his twelve years welled up inside, and all of it was now directed at the man standing arrogantly before him. And then a strange thing happened. As the scene before him began to once again melt away, Jacob could swear that the man had suddenly started, then jerked his head around to stare directly at Jacob. He stared hard, squinting his doubtful, guilty eyes as if puzzled for a few moments, then turned back to watch his son. The last impression Jacob had was of young James struggling to drag the corpse toward its final resting place while his father watched, one hand still on his hips and the other pointing as he roughly barked out instructions and the occasionally cruel, accusatory remark. Then, once again, the whole world seemed to be spinning past him in a rush. And once again, it quickly came back into focus, and now Jacob beheld an all too familiar scene.

Before him, the great house was an inferno. It lit up the night sky like a beacon of flame as sparks and embers drifted off, dancing and whirling like fireflies on secret, urgent errands, into the night. Jacob was standing exactly where he'd stood in his dream, directly behind the house at the edge of the woods. But this time he was alone; there was no forlorn, preadolescent Jim Hanes or mysterious, shadowy woman to speak dark phrases and intangible riddles to him. Nor could he feel the heat of the blaze or smell the smoke that filled the air. Just as was the case with the other two tragic episodes, he was here as an observer only. Jacob understood this completely, and yet he suddenly found himself running desperately, bolting with all the speed and energy he could muster toward the place where he knew the elder James Stockton now stood, cursing and threatening his only son, terrorizing the boy into an oath of silence and introducing him to a life of guilt, pain and remorse.

Jacob ran harder than he'd ever run in his life; he was fueled with the image of Mr. Stockton turning to look at him with that puzzled, guilty expression. That, and a frantic hope. It had seemed to Jacob that the older man had somehow *felt* his animosity and outrage; it was as though he'd understood that somehow, someone had seen exactly what he'd done and how he was trying to conceal it. And maybe, Jacob now prayed, if he could reach them in time; if he could somehow pull up all those emotions again, focus them, and direct them at James or his father, he could make them understand that maybe it wasn't too late. Melinda was still inside the burning house, but maybe they could still somehow get her to safety. If he could only hurry, and if he could somehow make them understand . . .

Jacob was brought out of this frantic, trance-like state of determination when he realized that he was no longer approaching his destination. He was being pulled backwards, away from the two people he so desperately needed to reach, away from the burning house, and away from any chance, no matter how small, he might have had to defy destiny and somehow save the life of Jim Hanes' mother. He redoubled his efforts, once again crying out silently in rage and desperation, but still he was pulled away; not into the woods behind the house, but back into the darkness that had first brought him here. And finally the burning house faded completely; there was nothing but that desperate pitch black all around him. He closed his eyes, still crying as he felt himself falling backwards. The rushing sound of wind once again completely filled his ears. Then there was a thick, dull popping sound, as if he'd just had his ears boxed, and Jacob felt himself land roughly on the ground, flat on his back.

The first thing Jacob realized was that he *was* lying on the familiar wet and muddy ground. The next was that he could hear again; the unmistakable sounds of that terrific storm were once again in his ears, although the sounds were still somehow vague and distant. Encouraged, Jacob finally opened his eyes. He was back where he'd started, in the small clearing; a playground and refuge for nearly three generations of young boys that had more history and significance than any of them ever would have guessed. He was lying on his back beside the old oak, staring up into a sky that still rolled with dark thunderheads and flashed with bright, forked lightning. He cautiously got to his feet, still looking around in wide-eyed wonder, as though he was really seeing the place for the first time. In a way, that wasn't too far off the mark. It took him a few moments to realize that the lantern still hung from his right arm. It was apparently quite the sturdy little piece of hardware, he mused; despite having fallen roughly to the ground twice, the small bulb still glowed. Jacob also realized that each of his hands was still tightly gripping his two trophies. He could feel the power of both; the cross still pulsing with that calming, reassuring warmth, the crystal still biting with an icy cold that sought to worm its way through his body and freeze his heart. There was still a battle raging between these two diametric forces, the door still had to be closed, and Jacob realized that if he just stood here and continued to cling to the two amulets, he'd likely end up little more than the human equivalent of a burned-out, ravaged battlefield. The image of what had happened to Mike came rushing back, and Jacob reflexively slung both arms out, open-handed, intent on throwing both talismans as far away as he could. He would watch them duel it out from a safe distance. He then made to inspect the palms of his hand, to see if any marks had been left after holding them so tightly for so long. He was unable to see any such marks, however, because both the crystal and the cross were still nestled firmly in his hands.

Horrified, Jacob began to run in a crazy circle, screaming madly at the top of his lungs and slinging his hands wildly about, but still they wouldn't let go. He tried rubbing them against each other, hoping to use one to dislodge the other. As soon as the two amulets touched, there was a loud, sharp cracking sound, and a plume of glittering, bluish-green sparks erupted from both hands. A jolting shockwave reverberated throughout his entire body, leaving both arms numb right up to his shoulders. Jacob froze, struck motionless by the loss of feeling in his arms and the growing, panicked fear of what would be left of him when this struggle was finally over. The strange numbness, while terrifying, only lasted for a few seconds, and he was relieved when the feeling quickly returned to both arms, accompanied by that peculiar tingling sensation he'd always associated with the unpleasant feeling of bumping his funny bone.

As soon as the feeling was fully restored to his arms, he held up both hands before his eyes, staring at the focal point of the two opposing forces in awe, still feeling the power of both surging through his body. Both amulets looked unchanged; neither seemed to be swelling or glowing or visibly changing in the least. But the power of both was undeniable, and Jacob could feel it growing by the second.

At that moment, a familiar shrieking moan began to pour forth from the opening in the tree. Jacob, who had completely forgotten about those weird, floating, bodiless heads (or maybe he'd subconsciously dismissed them, believing on some level that they were perhaps only guardians of the passage that had led him back to the year 1933, the night when all this had begun), jerked his head toward the tree, then recoiled in desperate, fearful revulsion.

Those grotesquely malformed heads were coming for him, all right. Maybe they were drawn by the amulet he now bore (and considering that said amulet seemed to have grafted itself to his hand, Jacob was certain this was the case and it would therefore be impossible to run or hide from them). Maybe they were simply here to collect the levy that had to be paid for using their passageway to that other side of reality, or wherever it was that Jacob had gone to watch those dreadful scenes that were really only the dark shadows of secret history. Whatever the reason, they – like the spirit of the dead maid – had punched a hole in the wall (a very thin wall, it now seemed to Jacob) of the world, and as he watched with a thrumming heart and feet of lead, they were finally making their way in. Their already ghastly appearance was made all the worse by the fact that they weren't coming out of the opening in the tree; they were coming out of the tree itself, perhaps using its life-force to sustain them. The texture of their skin had become like the rough, gray-brown texture of the tree, stripped with bark and patches of mossy growth; the entire trunk of the tree had become an orgy of bulging, misshapen faces rising and falling, swelling and subsiding. Even the tips of the tree's long branches seemed to have grown a legion of the grotesque shapes; they hung like some kind of repulsive, half-rotted fruit from the ends of every sagging, swaying limb. None seemed capable of actually disengaging from the old oak, but they were all stretching and straining out toward Jacob, as if these malformed heads had finally grown bodies; long, writhing, and serpentine. Or maybe the old oak had grown tentacles armed with those misshapen, deformed heads and the tree itself would take him; it would drag him screaming back into the dark, cavernous tear. Then that tear would close again, sealing Jacob inside, forever beyond the reach of light or hope. And there he would lie, with the rotted, forgotten body of Della Hanes, for the rest of time.

The wretched, heart-stopping shrieks continued to grow; pouring from those yawning, toothless mouths and filling the stormy morning air. Every one of those wild, bulging eyes was fixed on Jacob; every twisted, gaping mouth seemed now to be screaming his name. He finally looked down at his hands one last time, staring hopelessly at the two charms that were fixed to his palms. For the first time, he saw them not as amulets or charms and not just as symbols; he saw them as the actual, physical manifestations of those diametric forces each represented. Good and evil. Love and hate. Reason and madness. And above all, redemption and damnation. In a moment of unexpected calm and resolution, he remembered the jolting power that had surged through him when he'd brought the two together. There was only a moment's hesitation and then, in a final, desperate attempt to end this raging battle, Jacob squeezed his eyes shut and brought his hands and the two talismans together in a forceful clap.

There was a blinding flash of light, so bright it seemed to tattoo the inside of his brain (if the darkness he'd witnessed before was the darkness of *In the beginning*, then surely he was now seeing the blinding white of *Let there be light*). Then Jacob was thrown backwards through the air, landing hard on the muddy ground amid the sounds of an ear-splitting crash of thunder. It seemed to Jacob that this was the sound of a thunderstorm as heard from inside the clouds themselves; this was the sound of the tempest in all its rage and power. Then, to the echoes of desperate wailing, almost identical to that endless, wretched sound he'd heard back at Jim's trailer – only this time so deep, so loud and so *powerful* that he thought that he'd probably hear nothing else for the rest of his life – all of Jacob's thought and mind was lost to darkness.

28

Jacob slowly became aware that the darkness had finally given way to dim light. It wasn't the stormy morning light that he'd last seen before the darkness came; it had a weaker feel about it, a man-made feel. He lazily moved his head to one side, then the other, and was pleased to find that it rested comfortably on a pillow. Then he wiggled his feet a little. This proved to be a little more difficult; the blanket and sheet covering him were tucked snuggly into the mattress he was resting on. He finally opened his eyes, a chore that required a lot more effort than it usually did. When he finally managed the task, he found himself staring not at the ceiling of his bedroom, but another, unfamiliar ceiling patterned with large tiles and spotted with the occasional water-stain. He turned his head a little to the right, and saw that the dim light was coming through the partially opened door of a bathroom in the far corner of the room. He turned his head a little more, and there were his mother and father, squeezed in beside each other on a small couch that sat against the wall, beneath a long window, its thick curtains drawn tightly to shut out the bright sunshine. His mother seemed to be trying to read a magazine by the weak light seeping out of the bathroom, but his father was out cold – head back, mouth open, and breathing heavily. He sounded a little like Darth Vader.

Jacob tried to call out to his mother, but his parched mouth was thick and swollen; his lips and tongue heavy and ponderous. All that came out was a pitiful little sigh that even he could barely hear. He forced himself to swallow, breathed deep, and tried again. This time he managed a croaking sound that came pretty close to the word he was trying for.

"Mom?"

Mrs. Hunter looked up immediately, her face shocked and concerned. That first expression quickly melted away to pure, unabashed relief and joy. She dropped the magazine to the floor and rushed to his side, her loving face simply beaming, and for the first time since he'd set foot in Logtown, Jacob felt completely at peace. For a few moments, mother and child simply looked at each other, smiling and teary—eyed. Then she leaned over, kissing him gently on the forehead.

"Oh, honey, are you alright? Do you hurt anywhere?"

Jacob nodded that he was okay as his father's face appeared over his mother's shoulder. He had been startled out of his sleep when his wife had jumped up and rushed over to Jacob's bedside. He looked every bit as pleased as his wife, but his face did reflect a little more concern. He spoke his usual chipper words without their usual chipper tone.

"Hey, buddy! How ya feelin'?"

Jacob again nodded that he felt okay, although when he tried to turn and face them a little better, it seemed as if every muscle in his body grumbled about it. They were sore and stiff, as if he'd spent the day before hauling enough bricks and cement to build a two-story house.

"You want anything? Some ice or water?"

Jacob nodded a third time and croaked out, "Water." Again, it took some ingenuity to make an actual word out of the sound.

Mr. Hunter stepped out of the picture again, but only for a moment. He returned in a flash, and held out one of those large, lidded cups that are pretty much standard issue in every hospital in the country – light blue in color, with the hospital's name and logo emblazoned on the side. A long, transparent straw jutted up from a hole in the lid.

Jacob tried to reach for it, but his left arm was foiled by a coiling spaghetti of tubes and a brief but sharp stinging in his hand. He looked over and saw an I.V. bag hanging on a tall, narrow stand; a tube extended from the bottom of the bag, wrapped a few times around the bed-rail, and finally plugged into the back of his left wrist below a tightly wrapped hand. He looked to his right and saw that this hand was wrapped up the same way – thick gauze and adhesive tape.

"I'll hold it for you, honey," said his mother. "You just drink."

Careful not to move his left arm even a fraction of an inch (Jacob had never had an I.V. before, and assumed that the needle might easily pop out, despite the huge gob of tape securing it; his blood would then jet out like a gusher, spraying everything and everyone in the room while they screamed and he bled to death), he propped himself up on his right elbow. His mother gently placed the straw in his mouth, and he took a greedy and mighty suck. The water was tepid, had a powerful chlorine aftertaste, and at the moment seemed to be the most wonderful thing he'd ever tasted. He swished it around in his mouth a little, then finally swallowed and took another pull.

"Careful, little man," his father warned. "Don't overdo it and make yourself sick." Jacob ignored him, continuing to drink until his mother finally pulled the cup away.

"That's enough for now," she informed him as she placed it on a small, crowded table that sat beside the bed. "You can have some more in a little bit."

Jacob was disappointed, but nodded as he lay back gently on the pillow. His head was suddenly full of questions, and at first he didn't even know where to start. Then, in a flash, the most urgent came barreling to the front. He sat urgently back up, leaning on both elbows and heedless of the I.V. tube.

"Where's Jim? I mean Mr. Hanes. Is he alright?"

Mr. and Mrs. Hunter looked at each other wordlessly, and Jacob immediately knew the answer to his question before either of them spoke. He lay back on his pillow and closed his eyes. After a few moments of silence, his father finally spoke the words Jacob had already read on both his parent's faces.

"Son, he didn't . . . well, he died last night, Jacob. I'm sorry."

Jacob's eyes blurred and stung with tears, and the back of his throat began to hurt. But worse than that, something inside had begun to hurt.

It was all for nothing.

That one thought seemed to echo soundlessly in his mind. It wasn't a taunt, only complete and utter grief, perhaps tinged with a bitter anger that seemed to bite at him for lack of any other tangible target. *All of it . . . for nothing. Everything I went through, everything he went through for his whole life.* Jacob had learned the word "irony" in school two years ago, but until this very moment, he hadn't understood how bitterly cold that word could be. Now he did; he had his own special definition for that hateful little word.

Once upon a time, a man lived a long, lonely life of guilt and self-loathing because his selfish, heartless jerk of a father convinced him that he had essentially killed two people, one of them his own mother; the only person on earth that he truly loved. After years and years of wallowing in that self-reproach and shame, having been reduced to living in squalor and being treated as if he didn't even exist by everyone in town (unless they were observing what a pitiful excuse for a human being he was; drunk and wasting away in his trash-pile trailer, or maybe throwing rocks at that trailer for kicks – they had called it an initiation, but it was all just for kicks), he finally comes to realize that it wasn't his fault after all. Immediately upon discovering this happy little tidbit, he dies. The End.

Jacob was awakened out of his cynical, mocking revelry by the sounds of his mother crying. He opened his eyes and looked over at her. She was once again sitting on the couch, weeping into her hands. Mr. Hunter sat next to her, one arm wrapped tightly around her shoulders. It took only a second or two for him to realize that she was crying not just for a son that was in the hospital, she was crying for a son that might have been lost. This thought made his heart ache even more.

"Mom," he finally whispered, trying hard not to start bawling himself, "I'm okay. Everything's okay now." He wasn't sure that he believed it, but it seemed like the right thing to say.

When she looked up at him with those wet, swollen eyes, Jacob was completely unable to read her expression. He saw fear there, yes, and maybe a little anger. But he thought that mostly he saw love. When Mrs. Hunter had collected herself, she finally spoke.

"Jacob, how could you do that? What were you thinking? What if . . ." and here she had to pause, making a deliberate effort to keep herself under control. "What if something had happened to you? That boy was crazy; what if he'd shot you, too? What would your father and I have done? My God, Jacob!" The very idea seemed to overwhelm her, and she broke down again. Mr. Hunter squeezed her even tighter, and whispered to her the same words Jacob had; everything was going to be okay; their son wasn't hurt too badly and it was all over now, and everything was going to be alright.

Jacob looked away, suddenly awash with guilt. He had absolutely no idea what to say to either of them. He had thought at the time (and still thought now) that he had done the right thing. He hadn't wanted to do it, but he had. He was grateful beyond his ability to describe that he had somehow survived, and he never wanted to experience anything like it again. In a way, he was kind of proud that he had done it. But now, seeing his mother crying and listening to his father trying to comfort her, he also felt paradoxically ashamed and guilty.

He finally spoke, unsure if he was trying to justify his actions to his parents or himself.

"I had to help him, Mom," he finally said, but it sounded awfully weak.

"Jacob," Mr. Hunter started, then paused a moment as if searching for the right words. This was how his father spoke when discussing subjects that were important or sensitive – like a politician who knew his words would be scrutinized by the press, and wanted to make sure he didn't say anything that could be misconstrued or taken out of context. He had covered the topic of the dangers of drugs and alcohol much the same way.

"Son," he finally continued, "we know you were trying to do the right thing . . . and that does make us proud . . . but it's important to understand that when a situation arises . . . a serious situation, like this was . . . Jacob, you can't just go barreling out there and try to save the world, or whatever you were trying to do. Son, that boy was crazy . . . you were lucky, we're *all* lucky, that there aren't four dead people instead of just three."

Jacob was at a loss for words, wanting desperately to tell them he was sorry while at the same time wanting to justify what he'd done. He was almost to the point that he was considering telling them the whole story; the dreams, the ghostly spirits, his horrible time-travel back to the night of the original tragedy . . . everything. Then something clicked in his head, and he realized what his father had said; three people had died. He looked back over at his father.

"What three people?" he asked. "Did Jared die, too?"

Mr. Hunter shook his head and leaned back on the couch as he answered, "No, but that poor boy will probably end up in an institution for the rest of his life. And no wonder, being drug around by his brother and forced to watch while he did all those things."

Jacob's head was almost bursting with questions now, but he didn't even know where to start. He decided the best thing to do was to find out exactly how much his parents actually knew before telling them about his own role in Friday morning's misadventure. He leaned to his side, facing them, and tried to put on a completely bewildered expression. When he spoke, it was with a tone of innocent confusion.

"What do you mean? What else did he do, besides shoot Jim and . . . himself?"

His parents looked at each other again, then his dad turned to face him. When he began speaking again, it was in that same careful, measured, politician-style tone.

"Jacob, I'm going to tell you what we – and by 'we' I mostly mean the police – have found out about that boy. I'm not telling you this just to frighten you, but it's important for you to know just how serious a situation you put yourself in. The investigators were able to get some of this from Mr. Hanes before he died, and I had a chance to speak with him briefly, too. The rest they just kind of put together based on the scene at Mr. Hanes' trailer, and at the trailer where the boy's younger brother – what did you say his name is, Jared? – lived with his mother."

What Mr. Hunter told Jacob was that, according to the police department, Mike was (to put it gently) a troubled youth. He had a history of getting into trouble at school – including three suspensions, for threatening a teacher and for getting into several fights. Among the things found in his car were a fake I.D. (putting Mike's age at 23 years) and a baggie containing traces of what turned out to be marijuana, and based on those finds and interviews conducted the day before, they concluded that he probably used both the drug and alcohol fairly regularly. Based on what they'd gotten from Jim, the police had also figured out that there was some sort of feud going on between Jacob and Jared. Jim had recounted the story of stumbling upon the fight between Mike and the two younger boys, and told of how, upon being backed down and sent away by Jim, Mike had sworn to kill every one of them.

The police figured that afterward, Mike had gone on a binge of drinking and possibly pot-smoking; they were waiting for the tox-screen results from the autopsy to know for sure. Thursday evening, he had returned to his mother's trailer, and at that point had probably already made his plans. There had apparently been an altercation between him and his mother – about what, they admitted they might never know – and he had strangled her, possibly right in front of his younger brother. The two brothers remained in the house for the rest of the night, although what they did during that time was unknown. Jared was unable to tell them in his current state, and if he were unable to recover, those hours would also be filed under "we may never know". One or two of the neighbors interviewed thought they'd heard Mike's noisy car leaving the trailer park sometime before daybreak. Upon arriving at the trailer, he'd parked it right behind Jim's old car, although by that time the sudden and unexpected thunderstorm was in full force, which was why Jacob and Jim never heard its approach.

According to Jim, Jacob had shown up at the trailer maybe two or three minutes before Mike and Jared, trying to warn Jim that he thought the old man was in danger. "Said he'd had a dream about it, if you can believe that," was what Jim had told the investigators during a short but painful interview amid the wires and tubes and the beeping of monitors (and with a scowling doctor in attendance, ready to dismiss the officials if the interview became too stressful for the old man). "Maybe them two boys had been on his mind a lot, ever since that fight, and that's why he was dreamin' about 'em – who knows? Anyway, he hadn't been there two minutes before them other boys came burstin' in, the older one acting all crazy, waving the gun around and screamin'. The younger boy, his brother, didn't say nuthin', he looked half scared to death from the minute he arrived, like he was already on the verge of losin' it . . ." A pause, a few shallow breaths as if to gather his strength, and another dark scowl from the attending physician. "Well, as you can see, he shot me. Then, all the sudden, he got all scared lookin'. I mean, *really* scared; if he wasn't already crazy before he shot me, he sure was now. Out of nowhere, he suddenly took that gun and just shot hisself, right in the head. His brother really wigged out then – just curled up on the floor and started suckin' his thumb – and that's when the other boy, that Jacob boy, ran to get help, cause I ain't got no phones." That was pretty much all that the detectives were able to get out of Jim, and although they thought his story sounded pretty strange, they had yet to find anything at either trailer to disprove it. Even if they had come across something to poke holes in, the doctor wouldn't have allowed it. He was already angry that a seventy-eight year old gunshot victim was being questioned by the police less than seven hours after surgery, although Jim seemed to be recovering admirably.

Recovering admirably, that was, until the interview was over. It was almost as if he'd been saving all of his strength just to get through that one brief moment. He'd begun going downhill almost immediately upon its conclusion, straining his way through his brief talk with Jacob's father (a talk that had been at Jim's request). Two and a half hours later, he was dead.

It was actually Mr. Hunter who had called the police to Jim's trailer. The storm had knocked out the power and, afraid he'd overslept, he'd gotten up to look at a wall clock hanging in his office. He'd looked in on the boys on his way back to his bedroom and seen only David. At this point he was only mildly concerned, but after a quick walk-through, could find Jacob nowhere in the house. Then he'd come across a strange message scribbled on the refrigerator message-board. He'd run back to Jacob's room, and shaken David awake, asking where Jacob was. David seemed confused and disoriented at first, babbling something about how the dreams were his now and they were feeding on him, sucking his life away. When he'd finally come to his senses, he disclaimed any knowledge of what the scrawled out message meant, but the boy had gone pale when he saw it, and exclaimed that Jacob must have gone to Jim's trailer. Mr. Hunter immediately called 911, then awakened his wife, and the three of them threw on some clothes and headed out the door and into the storm. They'd arrived at the trailer right behind a police cruiser, its strobe lights flashing in a rare moment of excitement in the small town. Two officers got out and instructed Mr. and Mrs. Hunter to wait in their car (which, of course, they didn't). After banging on the door, the policemen crashed inside, guns drawn, while the Hunters and David stood just outside the fence, drenched by the rain and watching with growing terror and desperation. Only seconds later, one of the cops, a short, thick, hairy man, stepped quickly back out the door, speaking urgently into his radio and calling for an ambulance and backup.

Mr. Hunter finally stepped into the yard and demanded to know where his son was. The officer instructed him to wait, they were still trying to sort things out, but Jacob's father was becoming irate and the cop finally relented, allowing him to step inside the trailer long enough to see if he could identify the people inside. When he stepped into the trailer, what Mr. Hunter saw froze his blood. Accompanied by one of the policeman, he quickly walked through Jim's small home, and was only slightly relieved to see that Jacob wasn't anywhere in the trailer. Finally, after he overheard the worried father badgering the officer, Jim had managed to gasp out that Jacob had been there, but had gone for help.

Mr. Hunter went back outside to relay this info to his wife, and they decided that he would wait here at the trailer while she took David back to the house to see if Jacob had maybe gone back there in search of help. At that moment there was what seemed to be a tremendous stroke of lightning. The blinding flash appeared in the woods between Jim's trailer and *The Pines* subdivision, and was followed by a thunderous boom that seemed to shake the ground beneath their feet. Then, as if the enormous crash had been some sort of declaration by the storm that its point had been made – enough was enough and its business here was done – the storm just sort of died away; the rain and wind stopped and everything grew eerily quiet. As one, the Hunters, David, and the policeman looked in the direction where the lightning had struck, and saw a thick plume of smoke curling into the air. David had suddenly screamed out, "He's on the trails; he's at the Ice House!" and away he'd run, skirting the fence, with Mr. Hunter and one of the policemen in tow. That was how they'd found Jacob so quickly.

He was lying on his back on the muddy ground of the clearing, unconscious, with ugly blisters on both hands and what looked like an intense sunburn on his arms and face. The old oak tree had been split right down the middle, and its upper branches were in flames. The police eventually came to the conclusion that Jacob had taken off running down the trails in a state of hysteria, an action that seemed pretty reasonable considering what he'd just witnessed back at Jim's trailer. Because of his panic and the storm, he'd become disoriented, and had ended up at the clearing by accident. They also concluded that his mild injuries were the result of his close proximity to the old tree when it had so obviously been struck by lightning. After examining Jacob at the hospital, a doctor eventually conceded that this was the most likely scenario, although he confided in Mr. and Mrs. Hunter that he'd never seen anything like it. It wasn't until later that afternoon that a policeman informed Mr. Hunter of what two volunteer firemen, making sure the fire in the old oak wouldn't spread, had found in the hollowed-out recesses of the large tree.

Jacob listened to this extraordinary narration quietly, his head resting on the pillow and his eyes sometimes squeezed tightly shut, sometimes staring blankly at the ceiling. And when the story was finally finished, Mr. Hunter did not follow up with the 'We can all learn a valuable lesson from this . . . ' type speech that Jacob usually got at the tail end of a lecture. Instead, he simply leaned back into the small couch and put his arm back around his wife's shoulder, squeezing her tightly once again, and allowing the silence to spin out in the room while his son presumably would reflect on the danger his actions had put him in, how lucky he was to be alive, and how he'd never do anything else this foolish for the rest of his life.

Jacob was already aware of each and every moral that he was expected to glean from his father's narration; he'd been aware of them from the moment he'd set out on that dark errand Friday morning. So instead of pondering these lessons, he instead pondered Jim's story to the police, not only trying to get a feel for the story (in case he was questioned later), but a sense of it as well. Why had Jim told it like that, laying all the blame on Mike? There were two likely answers, both very simple, and they came to Jacob almost immediately.

The most glaringly obvious was this: what alternative did the old man have? Was he likely to tell the police that the gory scene at his trailer had been the work of an evil spirit; not necessarily the ghost of a woman he'd watched his father murder sixty-six years ago (for a second, the image of those malformed, disembodied heads danced before his eyes, their gaping mouths shrieking, and a prickling chill ran down his arms), but a spirit nonetheless? The answer to that was, of course, an emphatic no! Such a story would be dismissed as either the rants of an alcoholic who was likely suffering the ill effects of a gunshot wound, old age, and years of too much cheap booze, or a dismally pathetic attempt to cover up his own involvement in the tragedy.

The second answer was directly tied to the first: if the 1933 murder of Della Hanes was linked for any reason to what had just happened, there could be little doubt that the police would eventually make the connection between Jim Hanes and James Stockton. For whatever reason, Jim had clearly not wanted this to happen. Jacob also supposed that Jim's eagerness to speak with the cops was the result of wanting to get his story on the record, and subsequently to Jacob's ears, as soon as possible. But what reasons could Jim have, now that it was all over, for still wanting no connections made to that other life?

Jacob thought back to the last time he'd looked at Jim before high-tailing it out of the trailer and back into the storm. The old man's eyes had been shining, and his face had almost glowed with peace and serenity. For the first time since he was twelve, he had been able to look, if only for a brief moment, into his mother's eyes. In those eyes he had seen no blame or reproach, only love. Now, after a lifetime of undeserved penance, James Stockton II would finally rest in peace. And not alone: the entire tragic affair would finally die, quietly, along with him. Perhaps that was how it should be, and Jacob finally understood.

His eyes were wet again when he turned back to his parents. He was feeling tired again, more tired than he'd ever felt in his life. But there was one thing more he wanted to know, *had* to know.

"What did Jim – I mean, Mr. Hanes – want to talk to you about, Dad?"

Mr. Hunter leaned forward with his arms on his knees.

"He wanted me to make sure the police found something that's in his trailer. He told me that it won't tell them too much, but it should be all they need to close the matter up. He said he figured he could trust me to do that; that with a kid like you, I must be an okay guy." Mr. Hunter smiled at that last part for a moment, then looked deeply into his son's eyes, holding them as he concluded. "He also told me to tell you thank you for saving him. Whether you understand it now or not, you really did save him. He made me promise to tell you that, and no matter what happens, you should never forget it."

Jacob's tears started again when he heard those words. He turned back away from his parents and closed his eyes tightly, wanting nothing but sleep, the kind of sleep that's deep and dreamless and takes you far away from this place called Planet Earth for at least a little while; the kind of sleep that carries you to a place with no memories.

He knew now that he had been right when he'd looked into the old man's face for the last time and seen that there was no longer any fear. It was gone, all of it: not just the fear of dying, but the fear of living as well. The burden had been lifted, after such a very long time, and all that mattered was that the fear was finally gone. Jacob's exhausted mind lazily remembered thinking, just moments before, about the cruel irony of Jim's dying almost immediately upon finally discovering such a true peace. As he drifted into his own peaceful place, it now seemed to him that he finally understood . . . after all these years, maybe Jim had finally found the ultimate peace. Perhaps this was exactly what he'd wanted all along. This thought gave Jacob comfort, and seemed to help him along as he slipped into a blissful, deep sleep. The dreamless kind, in a place with no memories.

It was almost four o'clock in the afternoon when Jacob was awakened by a nurse taking his temperature and blood pressure. The I.V. had been removed (with absolutely no bloodshed, he was relieved to see), and his mother was standing by with a change of clothes for him. It seemed as though Jacob's first visit to the hospital had been a success: he'd be leaving in better shape than he'd arrived, and with no permanent damage, although the bandages would remain on his hands for another week. As per hospital policy, Jacob was wheeled to the front door, but he actually walked out to the parking lot on his own feet. He and Mrs. Hunter got into the car, and finally, after almost two full days (which felt more like two months), Jacob was home again. It was a place he'd feared several times the day before that he'd never again see, and just walking through the door seemed to make his whole body sigh in contentment. He walked straight back to his room and, despite the bandages on his hands, spent the next hour and a half playing Nintendo.

His father had been nowhere in sight when Jacob left the hospital with his mother and headed for home; he'd accompanied the police back to Jim's trailer to direct them, as instructed by Jim, to a small filing cabinet tucked behind a pile of junk in the bedroom closet. After only a cursory glance at its contents, the cops became very excited, and what they found became the talk of the small town for several weeks. The cabinet was crammed full of twenty-four years worth of statements and summaries, each containing figures that, to anyone who'd known the man, were almost impossible to comprehend. More important, however, was a name and phone number that appeared on each of the statements. Unfortunately, after trying the number, they discovered the necessary call would have to wait until Monday morning.

Even after the call was finally made, everyone came away pretty disappointed. Instead of answers, the police were left only with brief but strict instructions and more questions than ever. These detailed instructions included the purchase of a casket, a pre-purchased plot at a specific cemetery, and the particulars of a no-frills, graveside funeral service. Funds for these expenses had already been set aside, and would be wired by the end of the day. The detective on the phone tried to press for at least a few juicy tidbits, but was informed tersely that, unless he had official business that required this knowledge, he wouldn't be getting it. Because the police department already had a suspect, and it wasn't Jim, they were more or less forced to abandon their quest, unfulfilled.

After hanging up the phone, the attorney who'd been on the other end of the line with the disappointed Logtown police detective looked around his spacious Park Avenue office and smiled. Why not smile? He'd been expecting, almost waiting for this call for nearly ten years. He leaned down and spoke into the intercom, "Rachel, bring me the Hanes Living Trust file." He then sat back into the soft leather of an over-sized chair, sipping his coffee and waiting.

When the file arrived, he spent the next two hours taking notes and making phone calls. With those simples tasks completed, he sat back and reflected on the fact that, in the short span of time it had taken to take those notes and make those calls, he'd become (on paper, at least) a multi-millionaire. And it had required little more than patience on his part.

He could easily recall the one and only time he'd met the man in person, though it had been so long ago that he couldn't even remember what his oldest client (both in terms of actual age and the number of years of service) even looked like. In the spring of 1975, maybe three years after he'd joined the firm, this man had shown up, no appointment, with five million dollars and some very strict directions. The request had been unusual but not unheard of, and the man had been adamant about what he wanted and how he wanted it done. Being a good and responsible lawyer had required of the young attorney that alternative, more lucrative routes be suggested to his new client, but the man wouldn't be deterred. Essentially, he had just inherited a fortune in business and assets, but he'd wanted nothing to do with it, nor, did it seem, did he want anything to do with the name he'd be leaving behind. The businesses and assets had been all but given by him to some relatives (there was no immediate family but several cousins, all of whom had their own little business empires going). All of the real estate he had inherited was included in that deal, with the exception of a small, three-acre tract in some little Podunk town down in south Mississippi. This parcel was carved out of the only piece of real estate sold to those distant relations that had any restrictions attached: none of that tract of land contiguous to the three acre tract could be sold without his approval.

The trust itself had been remarkably uncomplicated, as had the legal changing of the name. He had come into the lawyer's office with approximately five million dollars – the net proceeds from his "sale" of the businesses and assets – and it was all to become the property of the trust, invested in nothing riskier than savings accounts and CDs. A monthly stipend of one thousand dollars was to be paid out of the interest to the beneficiary, whose new name was Jim Hanes. The attorney's annual fees were also to be paid out of the interest; the balance of said interest was then to be reinvested. The attorney, who was of course the trustee, now marveled at the relatively few number of times he'd been unable to resist temptation and had taken a larger fee than he was strictly entitled to. He told himself that each and every one of those incidents was more or less justified, and he'd been able to manipulate the paperwork so that, without intense scrutinizing, most people wouldn't know the difference. If Mr. Hanes *had* ever noticed, he'd never said anything.

Not that it mattered now, anyway. The trust was about to be closed, and the directions on how that was to be done had been set forth from the very beginning. A certain amount had been set aside for funeral expenses. Five million dollars, the amount Mr. Hanes had originally stepped into his office with, was to be split evenly between two designated charities. The balance of what had grown over the past twenty-four years into a healthy figure approaching fifteen million dollars now belonged to the attorney. This stipulation had been carefully structured by Mr. Hanes himself for the explicit purpose of insuring his new lawyer would keep his mouth shut and keep his hands out of the cookie jar. For the most part, it had worked.

The lawyer took another sip of coffee, and then leaned even further back into his expensive chair. His smile grew until it was maybe one notch shy of becoming an idiotic grin. Maybe it was time to start thinking about an early retirement . . .

Rumors flew wildly for almost two full months, but everyone seemed to find it much more gratifying to hypothesize rather than pursue the few clues that had been left behind, as each and every one of them seemed to lead to a dead end. Even after the excitement finally settled down some, the subject remained a favorite topic that was guaranteed to liven up any party or office break-room for many years to come. And whenever people tired of discussing the mysterious Mr. Jim Hanes, they could always turn the conversation to the mysterious body that had been found in the hollowed-out recesses of the old oak tree. The report out of the state pathologist's office, where the remains had been promptly sent, included the facts that the body was that of a female, age estimated at between twenty and thirty years. It was also estimated that the individual had been dead for at least fifty years, but because of the poor condition of the remains, the cause of death was classified unknown.

Ironically, the discovery of the body coming on the heels of the discovery that Mr. Hanes was apparently leading a double life, and further complicated by the double-murder/suicide, seemed to cause an overload in the town's collective psyche. In the rush of the inevitable surprise and excitement, and despite the clues set out in the pathologist's report, even Mr. MacDonald failed to put two and two together – despite having told the entire story, complete with rumors and innuendo, to Jacob, David and Mr. Hunter barely a week before.

Because of the time wasted pursuing the origins of Jim Hanes (a pursuit that ended up leading nowhere and was therefore dismissed as being unrelated to the events of Friday morning), the investigators didn't get around to interviewing the remaining witnesses until Tuesday. This allowed the only two of any significance more than ample time to prepare.

A cursory run of the serial number from Mike's gun through the state's computers showed that it was registered to one Jimmy Ray Jarrell, of Gulfport, Mississippi. Mr. Jarrell had heard about the shooting Friday evening, and had been expecting a call or visit for four days. When the investigating officers finally arrived Tuesday morning, accompanied by a detective from the Gulfport City Police, he was more than eager to cooperate, leading them quite willingly to his bedroom closet, where an empty box rested on the top shelf (it had been placed there Friday evening). He exclaimed shock and disbelief when he opened this box and saw that his gun wasn't there. Yes, he told the police, he knew the boy in question: his son Eric had been good friends with Mike. But he, of course, had never approved of the friendship. And he could see now that he'd been right on the money in his assessment. In fact, he had no doubt now that all the trouble his own boy had gotten into over the past year or so was a direct result of the unhealthy influence Mike had held over Eric.

"That boy wasn't nuthin' but trouble," was what he told the cops. "I knew he was trash from the first time I ever seen him. Told Eric I didn't like the look of him, and he didn't need to hang out with that sort. Little jerk prob'ly snuck in here one day while he was over and stole the gun. Must have been recent, too, 'cause I know I saw it in there no more'n a couple a weeks ago. We can ask Eric, see if he knows anything about it. If he does, I'll get it outta him, I guarantee." He called Eric (who just happened to be at home, waiting nervously in his bedroom for his cue to step onstage), into the room.

"Son, I'm only gonna ask you this one time. You know anything about that boy Mike comin' in here and takin' my gun?"

Eric, who was almost as bad an actor as his father, shook his head with dismayed shock and exclaimed, quite emphatically, "No, sir!" just as he'd been instructed by his father last Friday evening.

"Well," said Mr. Jarrell, as he escorted the policemen back to the front door, "I wish I could've been more help. Sure do hate that all this happened, but take it from me, we're all prob'ly better off. I just wish he hadn't taken all them other folks with him. And using *my* gun to do it? That little S.O.B.!"

The cops fumed all the way back to their car, but by the time they'd made the forty-five minute drive back to Logtown, they had decided to let the Gulfport police handle any pursuit of Mr. Jarrell for supplying Mike with the gun; their primary concern was still the double-murder/suicide that had occurred in their city. There were still four more witnesses to speak with, but the police weren't optimistic – all were just kids, and none but the Hunter boy had been an actual witness to the shooting.

Stevie Varnado, Greg Byrd and David Phillips were each interviewed that afternoon, all with their parents in attendance (Stevie's parents also made sure to have their attorney present). None of these interviews lasted more than thirty minutes, and all of the questions revolved around their personal knowledge of Mike – specifically the fight that had erupted Wednesday afternoon between the older boy and Jacob. Stevie was particularly eager to distance himself from both Mike and Jared, and declared proudly that he'd had nothing to do with either boy since the day of the fight. He was also quick to point out that he had been nowhere near the trailer/clubhouse since that day, although he said nothing about what he'd personally experienced in the clearing on the afternoon of the fight, after all the other boys had left. His mind had gone back to that frightening few moments many times over the past few days, especially when he'd heard about what had happened to Mike and Jared. He had finally reached the conclusion that the strange, almost paranormal incident had been a sign from God; a warning to get his act together and live a cleaner, more wholesome kind of life. And for the next year or so, he actually tried.

Greg and David's testimony was essentially the same – both boys had liked Jared okay, but neither had been particularly fond of Mike (it was pretty clear that Greg had actually *disliked* the older boy, and had always been a little afraid of him as well). Both verified Mike's threat to kill not only Jim Hanes, but also each and every one of the boys in the clearing, with the presumed exception of Jared and Stevie. Neither, however, had expected him to do what he had done.

Like Stevie, David mentioned nothing about ghosts, dreams, or anything supernatural. He had gone to visit Jacob Sunday afternoon, and the boys had huddled in Jacob's room, whispering and talking for almost two hours. David had spent most of that time listening fearfully as Jacob recounted what he'd seen and experienced, and in the end the boys easily agreed upon exactly what each would say when their turn to talk finally arrived.

The parents of each and every one of the boys were shocked and horrified to discover their children had been playing in an old refrigerator trailer, using it as a clubhouse. No one seemed to know exactly how long it had been in that clearing, or exactly how it had gotten there. By the end of the week, the county had hauled it off. Over time, the clearing became overgrown and seldom visited; it was almost like the abandoned, dilapidated old house that you can find in almost any town in America. Rumors that it was haunted; that strange figures could be seen flitting about under a full moon and strange, spine-chilling cries sometimes could be heard on cloudy, windy nights became favorite stories among the younger generations of the Logtown population. Eventually the only kids that would visit the place did so on dares, and always in groups. And although none could truthfully boast of witnessing any of the spectral activity that supposedly surrounded the place, all could easily name at least two or three friends that had seen *something* . . .

Because he had actually been at Jim's trailer during Mike and Jared's raid, and had witnessed the shooting, Jacob's interview lasted longer than any of the other boys. The officers interviewing him (like the other parents, Mr. and Mrs. Hunter sat in on the interview) were quite naturally skeptical of his claim that he had been led to the trailer by a dream that Jim was in danger, especially now that he claimed he was unable to remember any specifics from this dream. He said that he must have been sleepwalking, and when he came out of it, he was standing in the kitchen, in a wild panic because of the dream. He told them that, in the half-asleep state he'd been in when he first set out, he must have thought that whatever he was dreaming was really happening (part of this statement had already been recited to his parents when they'd questioned him about the strange words scribbled on the message-board stuck to the refrigerator). The rest of his narration stuck closely to the account he'd heard from Jim via Mr. Hunter; how Mike had come in, waving the gun and screaming; how shocked and frightened Jared had seemed; and how, after Mike had shot Jim and then himself, Jacob had run off in a wild panic, somehow ending up at the clearing, where they'd found him.

None of the detectives felt particularly comfortable about describing in their report how the witness had been led to the scene of the crime by a dream or precognitive vision. They probably could have browbeat the kid a little, just to see if any of his story became inconsistent or changed, but his parents were present, and such behavior would undoubtedly cause an outburst on their part. Added to that was the fact that the kid's story jived almost perfectly with the old man's, and the fact that the kid was clearly a witness to rather than a participant in the tragedy. There was simply no reason to badger him any more.

And so, when the police department finally released their final report, it basically reflected what they'd initially assumed; Mike was a troubled youth who used both alcohol and marijuana at least some of the time (according to the tox-screen results, he had used both the Thursday before the incident in question; the tests were inconclusive as to whether he was still under the influence at the time he'd strangled his mother and subsequently shot Mr. Hanes and himself). It was believed that the murder of Jim Hanes had been premeditated; the murder of his mother had not.

Jared was never interviewed, so it was never determined whether whatever story he might have told would or would not have supported this theory. One of the investigators actually visited him once, Friday afternoon after he'd been taken to a special cell at the city jail – usually referred to as The Tank – that was reserved for individuals who were being committed to the state mental hospital at Whitfield, or were either under the influence of some serious drugs and/or were coming down from whatever high they'd been riding. On Tuesday, while the other boys were being interviewed, Jared was finally shipped off to Whitfield, at his father's request. He hadn't spoken a single word – had, in fact, hardly made a sound – since being found on the floor of Jim's trailer. Until the move to Whitfield, he'd spent all of his time in The Tank in the same fetal position they'd found him in, his thumb forever corked firmly into his mouth. The only time his thumb left his mouth was when they removed it to feed him. The orderly charged with this responsibility had to hold Jared's arm down the whole time; as soon as it was let go, the thumb would *pop* right back in his mouth. A large plastic bib was hung around his neck at each meal to catch what amounted to about half of every spoonful that was put in his mouth. Jared would chew on command, he just didn't do a very good job at it, and big gooey clumps of each meal (nothing more solid than oatmeal, mashed potatoes or grits) would ooze out of his open mouth and down his chin, finally coming to rest in gelatinous puddles on the clear plastic of the bib. They'd also had to put him in what Jared and his friends used to call "granny diapers" because he no longer seemed to have any control over those particular functions either, and didn't seem to notice after those functions had been activated.

After the transfer, Jared spent four uneventful years at the state mental hospital. Then, on the four-year anniversary of his brother's death, he somehow managed to hang himself with a bed-sheet. His doctors were all shocked when the body was found; he had never shown any signs of being suicidal. In fact, he'd never shown signs of being much of anything; he'd been near comatose during his entire stay. Jared's father wasn't very impressed by the shock professed by the doctors; he proceeded to hire an attorney and sue the state of Mississippi, the hospital, and each of the doctors treating his son, individually. The case could have dragged on for several years and might have yielded a hefty verdict if it ever went to trial. But the man just couldn't bring himself to wait that long and, over the strenuous objections of his lawyer, jumped at the first settlement offer made. In less than a year's time, he'd lost it all at the casinos. After that, most of his time was unevenly divided between his mechanic shop (as little as possible) and favorite bars (as much as possible). Once in a while, on those nights when he couldn't find a woman to share his bed and hadn't consumed quite enough liquor to pass out, he would lie in bed and stare at the ceiling, thinking about the fact that he'd once had a family; a wife and two sons, and trying to remember exactly how and when it was that he'd lost each and every one of them.

Jacob and David remained the best of friends throughout school. Even after graduation, when they were finally split up (Jacob wanted to be a writer like his father, and enrolled at the University of Southern Mississippi; David had decided to fulfill his friend's prediction and become an attorney, and of course that meant the Ole Miss School of Law), they always managed to set aside time together when they were visiting home over the holidays.

It would be foolish to expect that they would never speak about that terrible Friday they had both been a part of ever again; it was after all a small town and, even after several years had passed, there always seemed to be someone who wanted bring it up from time to time. Sometimes they would even bring it up themselves, maybe while reminiscing about good times they'd at the Ice House as kids (David had much more of those memories than did Jacob), or once again pondering the forever-mysterious life of Jim Hanes. But whenever they spoke of that fearful experience, even amongst themselves, it was always the version that Jim had told the police before he died; nothing paranormal or supernatural was ever discussed. The Sunday afternoon after the tragedy was the one and only time Jacob and David ever spoke of their personal experiences leading up to that horrible morning.

There was never a deliberate, spoken decision to avoid the topic, nor was it subconsciously repressed out of some intuitive fear or survival instinct. Both boys simply seemed to understand that, for just a moment, they had seen something of what existed beyond the membrane of the 'real' world. Jacob, in particular, believed he had actually passed through the veil, and although brief, his time there had been long enough to catch a real glimpse of that dark place. That glimpse was enough for now. He was alive and a part of this world, the 'real' world; he would not darken it or test his own place in it by dwelling on the things he'd seen. In time it was almost forgotten, and ultimately all discussions of the late, great Jim Hanes, the Ice House, and the tragic events that had taken place that morning in August, just one week before they started sixth grade, didn't drudge up memories of anything worse than a raving teenager with a gun. That, and a tragic sense of waste and regret that always seemed to linger whenever Jacob thought of the lonely old man.

On the Wednesday following his death; a miserably hot and humid morning without a single cloud in the hazy sky, Jim Hanes was finally laid to rest in the Holy Meadows Cemetery. His casket, suit, and plot had been carefully selected long ago, and all were nice if not extravagant. Jacob was surprised at the number of people besides himself and his parents that had shown up for the short service. He felt an undefined sense of anger and bitterness; understanding that most of these people simply wanted a peek at the man they'd disdained the entire time they'd known him. Now that it turned out they hadn't known him as well as they'd thought, he'd become a sort of side-show; a mystery for them to ponder and resolve now that he was dead. Jacob had originally been relieved that it would be a closed-casket affair; he felt sure he'd break down if he had to look at the man's old, creased face ever again. He wanted to remember it as it had been when he'd last seen it – happy and at peace. Now, upon seeing the curious crowd that had gathered, he also felt a small but strong twinge of perverse pleasure – they'd leave empty-handed, so to speak, denied the opportunity to gawk at his body as they discussed their wild theories.

Jacob almost felt sorry for the pastor conducting the funeral – how does one speak eloquently about a man that, for nearly twenty-five years, everyone assumed was a worthless drunk? The pastor did make a valiant attempt, and managed to speak *almost* eloquently about Mr. Hanes for *almost* ten full minutes. He was aided by the fact that Jim, upon his death, turned out to be something of a mystery, and managed to get in a piece of sermon about how no one but God truly knows our hearts and innermost secrets. Then, after a short prayer entreating God's love and mercy upon the deceased, everybody was dismissed with a reminder to be in church the following Sunday. In the end, though, Jacob's memories of the funeral service would always seemed to revolve around the deep sense of bitterness he felt toward the people who were suddenly so interested in the life of a man who'd spent almost forty years among the residents of Logtown without a single friend.

He came back later that same day, riding his bike under that blazing sun, wearing shorts and a t-shirt as opposed the "church clothes" his mother had dressed him in that morning. By then a mound of dirt stood where the coffin had rested. The curious people, the track-hoe, the small tent and folding chairs were all gone. Graveyards had always struck Jacob as being creepy places, but on this day, even under that merciless sun, it seemed peaceful and . . . well, restful. Even the birds and humming insects seemed somewhat subdued. Maybe it was just the heat of the day that made nature a little quieter than usual, but Jacob knew it really didn't matter. What mattered was that the feel and the mood of the day were now just as he thought they should be. This was the memorial that Jacob would always remember. He stood long, but without speaking a single word, not even "goodbye." Instead, he pondered Jim's long life and sudden death. His long suffering and the peace he'd finally found. That word, that *idea* . . . peace . . . was what kept coming back to Jacob now. Peace . . . peace in the valley; peace like a river; peace that passes understanding. He thought back to when he'd still been in the hospital, remembering now his own acceptance and understanding of the peace that Jim had finally found. His acceptance of that idea – the idea that Jim was now where he'd wanted to be for so long – had helped him break through the bitterness he'd felt at the injustice of it all. Now, all that remained was peace. The peace he'd seen on Jim's face; the peace found in those words, the last words Jim had spoken to him, through Mr. Hunter.

Thank you for saving me. Whether you understand it now or not, you really did save me. No matter what happens, you must never forget that.

Jim had died, but he'd died as a man finally free of those terrible burdens – the guilt, the anger, the hatred of self and life – that he'd carried for so many years. He'd died knowing peace and love, and Jacob remembered thinking maybe *that* was the ultimate peace. He believed with all his heart that it was, and such was the place where Jim now rested. He stood a moment longer, then stuck his hands deep into his pockets and walked to his bike. After one last look, Jacob hopped on and rode home. He never returned.

Even after two visits, Jacob failed to notice the weather-worn inscription on the headstone resting directly behind the head of Jim's grave site. It was on the next row, facing away from the plot that had been carefully selected by an old drunk many, many years before. Time and weather had eaten away at the stone; it was cracking and chipped it in some places, and tarnished with a brownish film of grime and age. But in the full light of day, the words could still be read:

MELINDA BROOKS STOCKTON

MARCH 12, 1900–OCTOBER 31, 1933

BELOVED WIFE AND MOTHER

THE END

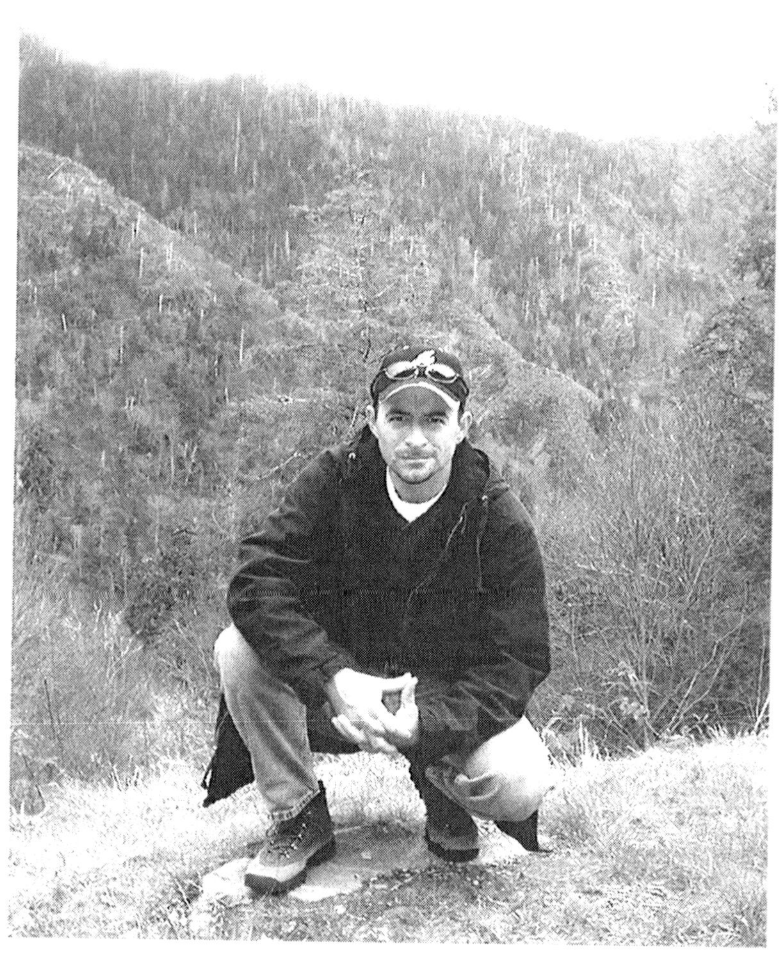

Photo by Matthew Hall

CPSIA information can be obtained at www.ICGtesting.com
Printed in the USA
LVOW060759281011

252499LV00001B/1/P

9 781456 767563